THE
SERPENT
ON THE
CROWN

The Curse of the Pharaohs★

The Love Talker

Summer of the Dragon

Street of the Five Moons

Devil-May-Care

Legend in Green Velvet

Crocodile on the Sandbank★

The Murders of Richard III

Borrower of the Night

The Seventh Sinner

The Night of Four Hundred Rabbits

The Dead Sea Cipher

The Camelot Caper

The Jackal's Head

and

Amelia Peabody's Egypt

★AMELIA PEABODY MYSTERIES

ELIZABETH PETERS

HarperLargePrint
An Imprint of HarperCollins*Publishers*

THE
SERPENT
ON THE
CROWN

THE SERPENT ON THE CROWN. Copyright © 2005 by MPM Manor, Inc. All rights reserved. Printed in the United States of America. No part of this book may be used or reproduced in any manner whatsoever without written permission except in the case of brief quotations embodied in critical articles and reviews. For information address HarperCollins Publishers Inc., 10 East 53rd Street, New York, NY 10022.

HarperCollins books may be purchased for educational, business, or sales promotional use. For information please write: Special Markets Department, HarperCollins Publishers Inc., 10 East 53rd Street, New York, NY 10022.

FIRST HARPER LARGE PRINT EDITION

Printed on acid-free paper

Library of Congress Cataloging-in-Publication Data

Peters, Elizabeth.
    The serpent on the crown / Elizabeth Peters.—1st ed.
        p. cm.
    ISBN 0-06-059178-1 (Hardcover)
    1. Peabody, Amelia (Fictitious character)—Fiction. 2. Valley of the Kings (Egypt)—Fiction. 3. Excavations (Archaeology)—Fiction. 4. Blessing and cursing—Fiction. 5. Women archaeologists—Fiction. 6. British—Egypt—Fiction. 7. Egyptologists—Fiction. 8. Egypt—Fiction. I. Title.

PS3563.747S44 2005
813'.54—dc22
                                                                2004061868

ISBN 0-06-075948-8 (Large Print)

05 06 07 08 09 /RRD 10 9 8 7 6 5 4 3 2 1

**This Large Print Book carries the
Seal of Approval of N.A.V.H.**

TO SALIMA IKRAM

I HAVE ROBBED THEIR
NOSTRILS OF THE BREATH OF
LIFE AND MADE THE DREAD
OF YOU FILL THEIR HEARTS.
MY SERPENT ON YOUR BROW
CONSUMED THEM.

—The Poetical Stela of Thutmose III

ACKNOWLEDGMENTS

I am indebted, as so often before, to my official and unofficial editors—Jennifer Brehl of Morrow, Kristen Whitbread of MPM Manor, Dennis Forbes of KMT, and George B. Johnson. It is impossible for mere mortals, even those as talented as the above-mentioned, to attain perfection; but thanks to them, I believe I've managed to eliminate the most egregious of the little lapses that marked the first draft. Any remaining goofs are my responsibility, not theirs. I can't imagine what I would do without them.

Informed readers will spot various Egyptological jokes. Dennis Forbes is responsible for what I consider the most entertaining of these: the unexpected appearance of a certain golden statuette.

The translation of Thutmose III's Poetical Stela is based on that of Miriam Lichtheim in her indispensable **Ancient Egyptian Literature.**

THE
SERPENT
ON THE
CROWN

ONE

He woke from a feverish sleep to see something bending over him. It was a shape of black ice, a tall featureless outline that exuded freezing cold. He tried to move, to cry out. Every muscle was frozen. Cold air touched his face, sucking out breath, warmth, life.

We had gathered for tea on the veranda. It is a commodious apartment, stretching clear across the front of the house, and the screens covering the wide window apertures and outer door do not interfere with the splendid view. Looking out at the brilliant sunlight and golden sand, with the water of the Nile tinted by the sunset, it was hard to believe that elsewhere in the world snow covered the ground and icy winds blew. My state of mind was as benevolent as the gentle breeze. The delightful but exhausting Christmas festivities were over and a new year had begun—1922, which, I did not doubt, would bring additional success to our excavations and additional laurels to the brow of my distinguished spouse, the greatest Egyptologist of this or any age.

Affectionately I contemplated his impressive form—the sapphire-blue eyes and ebon hair, the admirable musculature of chest and arms, half bared by his casual costume. Our son, Ramses, who had acquired that nickname because he had the coloring of an Egyptian and, in his youth, the dogmatism of a pharaoh, sat comfortably sprawled on the settee, next to his beautiful wife, our adopted daughter, Nefret. Faint cries of protest and distress drifted to our ears from the house the dear little children and their parents occupied; but even Nefret, the most devoted of mothers, paid them no heed. We were well accustomed to the complaints; such sounds always accompanied the efforts of Fatima and her assistants (it took several of them) to wash and change the children. It would be some time before the little dears joined us, and when a carriage drew up in front of the house I could not repress a mild murmur of protest at the disturbance of our peace.

Emerson protested more emphatically. "Damnation! Who the devil is that?"

"Now, Emerson, don't swear," I said, watching a woman descend from the carriage.

Asking Emerson not to use bad language is tantamount to King Canute's ordering the tide not to surge in. His Egyptian sobriquet of "Father of Curses" is well deserved.

"Do you know her?" Emerson demanded.

"No."

"Then tell her to go away."

"She appears to be in some distress," Nefret said. Her physician's gaze had noted the uncertain movements and hesitant steps. "Ramses, perhaps you had better see if she requires assistance."

"Assist her back into her carriage," Emerson said loudly.

Ramses looked from his wife to his father to me, his heavy black eyebrows tilting in inquiry. "Use your own judgment," I said, knowing what the result would be. Ramses was too well brought up (by me) to be rude to a woman, and this one appeared determined to proceed. As soon as he reached her she caught hold of his arm with both hands, swayed, and leaned against him. In a breathy, accented voice she said, "You are Dr. Emerson, I believe? I must see you and your parents at once."

Somewhat taken aback by the title, which he had earned but never used, Ramses looked down at the face she had raised in entreaty. I could not make out her features, since she was heavily veiled. The veils were unrelieved black, as was her frock. It fit (in my opinion) rather too tightly to a voluptuously rounded figure. Short of prying her hands off his arm, Ramses had no choice but to lead her to the veranda.

As soon as she was inside she adjusted the black chiffon veils, exposing a countenance whose semblance of youth owed more to art than to nature. Her eyes were framed with kohl and her full lips were skillfully tinted. Catching my eye, she lifted her chin in a practiced gesture that smoothed out the slight sagging of her throat. "I apologize for the intrusion. The matter is of some urgency. My name is Magda Petherick. I am the widow of Pringle Petherick. My life is threatened and only you can save me."

It was certainly the sort of introduction that captured one's attention. I invited Mrs. Petherick to take a chair and offered her a cup of tea. "Take your time," I said, for she was breathing quickly and her face was flushed. She carried a heavy reticule, which she placed at her feet before she accepted the cup from Ramses.

Leaning against the wall, his arms folded, Emerson studied her interestedly. Like myself, he had recognized the name.

"Your husband was Pringle Petherick, the well-known collector?" he inquired. "I believe he passed away recently."

"November of last year," she said. "A date that is engraved on my heart." She pressed her hand over that region of her person and launched, without further preamble, into the description I have already recorded. "He woke that morning from a feverish sleep . . .

"This is what killed him," she finished. Reaching into the bag, she withdrew a rectangular box painted with crude Egyptian symbols. "He had purchased it only a few weeks earlier, unaware that the curse of the long-dead owner yet clung to it."

A long pause ensued, while we all tried to think of an appropriate response. It had occurred to me, as I feel sure it has occurred to the Reader, that there was a certain literary air about her narrative, but even Emerson was not rude enough to inform a recently bereaved widow that she was either lying or demented.

"If I may ask," Ramses said, after a while, "how is it that you were able to describe his death so—er—in such vivid detail? He was—that is to say—he was dead, wasn't he?"

"He lingered for a while," said Mrs. Pringle Petherick composedly.

"Oh," said Ramses.

Nefret, who had been staring fixedly at Mrs. Petherick, said, "Forgive me, but your face is familiar. Aren't you Magda, Countess von Ormond, the novelist?"

Aha, I thought. That explains the accent. According to her publicity releases, the countess came from a noble Hungarian family. She had fled that country during the upheaval of the world war.

The lady's mouth opened in a wide, pleased smile. "You have read my books? I will be happy to sign the ones you have with you."

"I didn't bring any with me," said Nefret, her expression bland as cream. "I saw you several years ago at a literary luncheon in London. At that time, I believe, you were not married."

"My dear Pringle and I became one only a year before his dreadful death. And now," she continued, "the curse has fallen upon me. Twice I have beheld that grim black figure, and my intuition tells me that the third time will mean my death. Take it. I beg you!"

She thrust the box at Ramses. Eyeing it askance, he stepped back. I took it, and was about to lift the lid when Mrs. Petherick let out a ladylike shriek.

"Don't open it! I never want to see that evil little face again!"

"Am I to understand," I inquired, "that you are passing the—er—curse on to us?"

"But you are experienced in dealing with such things," Mrs. Petherick exclaimed, rolling her black-rimmed eyes. "You can do it safely. You have done it before. I have heard the stories."

The stories to which she referred were lurid newspaper articles, many of them written by our journalist friend Kevin O'Connell. Though in every case the purported curse had been proved false, and the evils attributed to it had been found to be caused by a human criminal, many readers remembered the sensational theories and ignored the rational explanations. If the woman actually believed we could cancel curses and defeat evil spirits, she had to be acquitted of deliberate malice.

The children would soon be joining us, and I did not want their juvenile imaginations stirred up by such nonsense. I was about to suggest to Mrs. Petherick that she tie a stone to the confounded thing and toss it in the Nile, when Emerson cleared his throat. His sapphirine eyes were bright and his handsomely tanned face bore an expression of amiable concern. Curse it, I thought.

"Very well," he said. "You may leave it with us, madam. I will perform—er—I will take care of the matter."

Mrs. Petherick leaned back in her chair, ignoring Emerson's hint. "What are you going to do? Return it to the tomb from which it was stolen?"

"That might prove a trifle difficult," Ramses said, with a critical look at his father. "If, as I assume, it was purchased on the antiquities market, there is little hope of tracing the original thief and finding out where he obtained it."

"Hmph," said Emerson, giving his son an equally critical look. "You know my methods, Ramses. Rest assured, madam, that you need not give the matter another thought. Good day to you."

This dismissal was too direct to ignore. Mrs. Petherick rose to her feet, but made one more attempt to prolong the conversation. "It killed my dog, too," she offered. "My poor little Pug. He choked and twitched, and was gone, just like that."

Fatima, seeing that we had a guest, had managed to detain the children, but I could hear them expostulating in their high-pitched voices. Emerson heard them too; he got Mrs. Petherick to the door of the veranda, but not before she had told us where she was staying and had asked to be informed when the curse had been officially lifted. She added, with an air of complacency quite at variance from her initial distress, "Perhaps I should participate in the ceremony."

"That will not be necessary," said Emerson, shoving the lady into her carriage and motioning the driver to proceed.

"Really, Emerson," I said. "What ceremony? You made no promise, but your failure to deny her suggestion was a tacit—"

"Well, what else could I have done?" Emerson demanded. "The woman was in considerable distress. Her mind will now be at ease."

"Oh, bah," I said. "Are you familiar with the literary (I use the word loosely) works of Countess von Ormond?"

"Good Gad, no," said Emerson.

"I've read some of them," Nefret said. "**The Vampire's Kiss** was her first. All her novels are about vampires and curses and hauntings."

"Quite," I said. "I suspect that the vivacious account of her husband's death was the first paragraph of her next novel. She means to use us and our questionable reputation with the newspapers in order to get publicity. I understand that her sales have been falling off."

"The later books aren't nearly as entertaining as the first four or five," Nefret said critically. "They were really quite good. I had to leave the light on all night while I was reading **Sons of the Werewolf**."

"Good Gad," Emerson exclaimed. "I had no idea you indulged in such trash, Nefret. Peabody, why did you let her—"

"I do not believe in censoring the reading material of adult persons, Emerson."

"In fact it would be a question of the pot and the kettle," said Emerson. "Your penchant for sensational novels like those of Rider Haggard—"

"Which you also read on the sly," I retorted. "Hypocrisy does not become you, Emerson. To return to the point, I do not intend to allow the woman to make use of us. I will return that object to her tomorrow, unopened, with a stiff note."

"Not unopened," said Emerson. "Aren't you even a trifle curious about the accursed object?"

"It is only a crude wooden box, Emerson, not even ancient."

"Ah," said Emerson. "But what is inside the box? Your analysis of the lady's motives may be accurate, my dear, but it overlooks one interesting fact. Petherick was a wealthy, discriminating collector. She may have purchased the box in Cairo, but if the contents came from Petherick's collection, they will be worth looking at."

He took the box from me and was about to lift the lid when I exclaimed, "No, Emerson. Not now. Put it away."

Seeing that our visitor had departed, Fatima opened the door to the house and the juvenile avalanche descended. There were only two of them, and they were only four years old, but they made enough noise for a dozen and moved so rapidly that they gave the impression of having been multiplied. As usual, they dashed at their grandfather, who tried to hide the painted box behind his back. He was not quick enough.

"It is a present!" Carla shouted. Her black eyes, so like those of her father, shone with anticipation. "Is it for me?"

Her brother, David John, who had his mother's fair hair and blue eyes, shook his head. "The assumption is without foundation, Carla. Grandpapa would not have a present for only one of us."

"Quite right," said Emerson. "Er—this is a present for me."

"Did the lady give it to you?" Carla demanded.

"Yes," said Emerson.

"Why?"

"Because—er—because she is a kind person."

"Can we see what is inside?"

David John, whose methods were less direct than those of his sister, had already headed for the tea table, where Fatima had placed a plate of biscuits.

"Don't you want a biscuit?" Emerson asked Carla.

Carla hesitated only for a moment. Insatiable curiosity won over greed. "I want to see what is inside the box."

Emerson tried to look severe. He did not succeed. He dotes on his grandchildren, and they know it. "I told you, Carla, that it is not for you."

"But it might be something I would want," Carla explained coolly.

"It is something you may not have," said Ramses, drawing himself up to his full height of six feet and fixing his small daughter with a stern look. Not one whit intimidated, Carla stared back at him from her full height of three feet and a bit. She was comically like her father, with the same black curls and dark eyes, and downy black brows that were now drawn into a miniature version of his frown.

I said, "David John is eating all the biscuits."

My understanding of juvenile psychology had the effect Ramses's attempt at discipline had not. Carla ran to get her share and Nefret informed her son he had had as many biscuits as he was allowed. A discussion ensued, for David John had inherited his father's Jesuitical skill at debate, and Nefret had to counter several arguments about the needs of growing children for sugarcoated biscuits. While they were thus engaged, I gestured to Emerson.

"Now you have aroused my curiosity," I admitted. "Open the box, Emerson."

The object inside the box was roughly cylindrical in shape and approximately thirty centimeters long. That was all we could make out at first, since it was swathed in silken wrappings tied at intervals with tightly knotted gold cords.

"She was taking no chances, was she?" Ramses

said, while his father picked at the knots and swore under his breath. "It could be an ushebti, it's the right shape."

"Surely nothing so ordinary," I objected. The little servant statues, placed in the tomb to serve the dead man in the afterlife, had been found in the thousands; most were of crude workmanship and cheap materials such as faience.

"Why not?" Ramses inquired. "The notion of a curse is pure superstition; it can be attached to any object, however humble."

"Petherick wouldn't have owned anything humble," said Emerson.

But his wife might have purchased something of the sort to add verisimilitude to her sensational account. I did not voice this sentiment, since Emerson would not have accepted it. Anyhow, I told myself, it would do no harm to have a look.

Since neither Emerson nor Ramses carried even a small penknife (David John was an accomplished pickpocket and particularly interested in sharp objects), Emerson had to go into the house to get a knife with which to cut the cords, the knots being beyond even my skill. By that time, I candidly admit, we were all agog with anticipation. Even Nefret abandoned her maternal duties and came to lean over my shoulder as Emerson removed the wrappings.

Sunset light set the small statue aglow, as if a fire burned within. This was no crude ushebti, of common material; it was the golden figure of a crowned king. His face was youthful, rounded and faintly smiling, his half-bared body gently curved. He wore an elaborately pleated kilt, the lines of which had been rendered with exquisite precision. The small sandaled feet and delicate hands were models of graceful beauty.

Nefret caught her breath and Emerson gave me a triumphant look. Even Ramses's normally enigmatic countenance betrayed astonishment verging on awe.

"How beautiful," I murmured. "There is nothing evil about this face."

"The devil with that," said Emerson, lifting the statuette out of the box. "Where did it come from? Where did he get it? How could such a thing come onto the antiquities market without causing a sensation?"

"Is it genuine?" Nefret asked breathlessly.

Emerson weighed the statuette in his hand. "Forgers don't use this amount of solid gold."

We agreed to postpone further discussion until the children had been sent off to bed. Our friends the Vandergelts were dining with us, and as Emerson and I dressed I inquired, "Are you planning to show it to Cyrus?"

"Hmph," said Emerson.

I had learned over the years how to interpret Emerson's wordless grunts. "You must, Emerson," I said. "We can't keep the statue, you know, it is far too valuable. An ordinary accursed ushebti is one thing, but this—"

"Yes, yes, confound it," said Emerson. "I intend to pay her for it."

"If she had wanted money, she would have asked for it."

"Everybody wants money," said Emerson. He pondered the matter for a moment and then went on, "It is odd, though, that she would hand over something so valuable to complete strangers in order to support a fantastic story which could have been equally well served by a cheap antiquity such as an amulet or ushebti."

"Better served," I admitted. "One of the monster-headed Egyptian gods like Tausert or Sobek would be more likely to appeal to a melodramatic mind like hers. How much is this object worth, do you suppose?"

"You ought to know better than to ask me, Peabody. I never purchase antiquities and I do not follow the vagaries of the market."

"All the more reason to invite Cyrus's opinion.

He too is a collector, as well as a knowledgeable and respected excavator."

"Hmph," said Emerson. This time it was a tacit acknowledgment of the correctness of my statement.

So Emerson took the little box with him when we went to the drawing room. He had adamantly refused to assume proper evening dress, which he hates, but I had managed to persuade him into a tweed coat and a nice sapphire blue tie, selected by me. Given his own way, he would have gone to dinner in the same open-necked shirt and unpressed trousers he wore on the dig—a costume which, I would be the first to admit, becomes his stalwart form to best advantage. However, certain standards must be maintained.

We found Nefret and Ramses waiting for us. Ramses was dressed like his father, but Nefret, who enjoyed pretty clothes and had enough money to buy all she liked, wore a clinging frock of Nile green that set off her golden-red hair. The Great Cat of Re had also condescended to join us. He was the only cat in residence that year, Nefret's unpleasant old pet Horus having passed on to whatever hereafter awaited him (I hoped it was someplace uncomfortable). The Great Cat of Re—who was always referred to by his full name—was more agreeable and a good deal more ornamental than Horus had been: striped gray and white, with a tail as bushy as a Cavalier's plume. He had arranged himself at the feet of Ramses with the expression of a creature who expects to be admired.

Ramses's eagle eye immediately fell on the box his father held.

"So you mean to let Cyrus in on this?" he inquired.

Emerson frowned. "I do not know why you put it in those terms, my boy. Surely you don't meant to imply I would keep this remarkable discovery to myself? Even if I could."

The regret in the last phrase brought a smile to Ramses's tanned face, and Nefret laughed aloud.

"You cannot," I said firmly. "We haven't even begun to discuss the ramifications of this business. I confess that my initial interpretation of Mrs. Petherick's motives has been shaken. An ordinary amulet would have served the purpose if she wished only to—ah, here are the Vandergelts. Prompt as always! Good evening, Cyrus— Katherine—Bertie, dear boy. But where is Jumana?"

Jumana was a member of our dear departed reis Abdullah's family, not a Vandergelt, though Katherine's son Bertie had more than once attempted to persuade her to become one. After completing her training in Egyptology, she had joined our staff but she lived at the Castle, since Cyrus's palatial home near the Valley of the Kings was more commodious than our humble abode.

Bertie's amiable countenance darkened. "She said she had to finish a paper. The girl thinks of nothing but work."

"She bears a heavy burden on those slender shoulders," I said. "As the first Egyptian woman to practice Egyptology, she feels she must outshine all others. An admirable attitude, in my opinion."

Having served our guests with their beverage of choice, Emerson flung himself into a chair and took out his pipe. "We had a most interesting visitor this afternoon," he said. "A Mrs. Pringle Petherick."

Animation lit Cyrus's lined countenance. "Petherick's widow? What's she doing in Egypt? Pringle said she hates the place."

Emerson countered with another question. "Were you a friend of his?"

"As good a friend as one die-hard collector can be with a fellow who is after the same artifacts," Cyrus said. "I saw his collection one time—some of it, anyhow. He frankly admitted he had some pieces he could never display, since he'd got them illegally. He'd do anything, pay anything, to get what he wanted. Say!" He leaned forward, his eyes brightening. "Is his widow putting the collection up for sale? Is that why she called on you, to get your advice? Emerson, old pal, you wouldn't cut me out, would you?"

"That never occurred to me," Ramses said thoughtfully. "It makes better sense than her nonsense about a curse, though it's an extremely roundabout way of capturing your interest, Father."

"Not necessarily," I said. "If she knows anything about your father, she must realize he would reject a request for assistance in marketing the antiquities. Perhaps the statue could be considered a sample. It certainly succeeded in capturing his interest."

"What are you talking about?" Cyrus demanded. "Sample? Statue?"

"And what's this about a curse?" Katherine asked.

I recounted our conversation with Mrs. Petherick. Being in receipt of several grunts and meaningful glances from Emerson, I stopped short of describing the statuette. He wanted to spring it on Cyrus himself.

"How can she believe anything so preposterous?" Katherine exclaimed.

"I don't know why it should surprise you, Mother," Bertie said.

The oblique reference to Katherine's former career as a spiritualist medium brought a frown to that lady's face. After years of happy marriage and complete respectability, she would have preferred to forget that part of her life—which, I should add in justice to her, she had taken on solely as a means of earning a living for herself and her orphaned children. Generous soul that he was, Cyrus regarded Bertie and his sister Anna as his own, and Bertie had repaid his stepfather's kindness by becoming his affectionate and skilled assistant in his excavations.

"It isn't at all surprising," Cyrus said impatiently. "The world is full of people who can't think straight. Come on, Emerson, let's see the thing."

Emerson removed the statuette from the box and held it up.

The effect was all my husband could have desired. Cyrus actually and literally went white. Bertie leaned forward, his eyes wide. Katherine was not so violently affected, since she had not the expertise to understand what it was she saw, but even she exclaimed in admiration.

"I presume this was not one of the objects you saw when you visited Petherick," said Emerson.

Cyrus shook his head. In silence he held out his hand—it trembled perceptibly—and Emerson gave him the statue.

"Mrs. Petherick said he did not acquire it until shortly before his death," I said.

"She . . ." Cyrus cleared his throat. "She gave you this? In exchange for what?"

"My promise that I would take upon myself the wrath of the original owner," said Emerson with a superior smile. "Bad luck, Vandergelt. Had you my reputation for superstitious hokery-pokery, she might have gone to you."

"Don't tease, Emerson," I said.

The drawing-room door opened, and Fatima appeared. "Dinner is—" Before she could finish the sentence, a man pushed past her and entered the room. He was tall and cadaverously thin, the black of his evening suit matching windblown ebony hair, his long face as white as his shirtfront; but I believe no one took much notice of his appearance at that time. Our attention was concentrated on the pistol he held.

"Give it back," he cried, waving the weapon wildly. "Give it to me now, and no one will be hurt."

His hungry eyes were fixed on the statuette. Clutching it still more firmly, Cyrus took a step back. "Now see here, young fellow," he began.

"Don't argue, Vandergelt," said Emerson. "If the statuette is his property, we must certainly return it. Sir, may I suggest you put the gun away? There are ladies present."

The appeal had an effect reason had not. The fellow's high white brow wrinkled. "I beg your pardon," he said.

He took his finger off the trigger and lowered the weapon a trifle; it now pointed at my feet instead of my head. This was something of an improvement, but not entirely reassuring. I smiled graciously, holding his gaze, and Ramses, who had been edging sideways in that noiseless fashion of his, caught hold of the fellow from behind, gripping his right wrist and forcing his arm down. The weapon thumped onto the floor and the intruder let out a cry of pain.

"It was locked on safety," said Ramses coolly.

"Very good," said Emerson, who had, of course, been aware of the maneuver from the start. "You had better keep hold of him."

The intruder stood passive in Ramses's grasp, his head bowed. Cyrus took a handkerchief from his breast pocket and mopped his brow; Katherine sank back in her chair with a long sigh. Fatima had prudently retired to the farthest corner of the room, but had betrayed no signs of alarm, since she took it for granted that we could handle any situation, up to and including armed assault.

"Sitt Hakim," she said somewhat accusingly, "dinner is—"

She got no further with the announcement than

she had before. This time the person who pushed her aside was a woman, smartly dressed in a beaded evening frock and a cloak trimmed with marabou feathers. She let out a piercing scream, flung the cloak aside, and rushed at Ramses. "How dare you! Release him at once!"

She began pounding at Ramses with clenched fists. Ramses raised one arm to protect his face, and Nefret, swearing, went to his assistance. Avoiding the flailing fists, she administered a sharp kick on the ankle. The woman sat down suddenly on the floor.

"Well, really," I said in exasperation. "It appears we are not to dine anytime soon. Young woman, who the devil are you, and what do you mean by this?"

The fall had knocked the breath out of her, and some sense into her. Despite her undignified position, limbs asprawl, long dark hair loosened and skirt crumpled, she maintained an air of self-possession. "I came for my brother," she said. "Adrian, have they hurt you?"

Holding his mute, unresisting captive with one arm, Ramses said, "The only damage inflicted on anyone has been done by your brother and you. Is it his habit to threaten strangers with a pistol?"

She hadn't seen the pistol until then. Her lips tightened and she looked up at Ramses with a stare that held more accusation than apology. For a moment their eyes locked. Then she got slowly to her feet, straightening her skirt. She was tall for a woman, and her bearing was more manly than feminine—feet apart, shoulders squared. Her hair was long and black and lustrous; it had come loose from its combs and hung untidily around her face. Her eyes, of a soft hazel, were her most attractive feature; her nose was prominent and her lips thin. "Apparently I misunderstood the situation," she said coolly. Her gaze turned to me. "Are you the one they call the Sitt Hakim?"

"It is my Egyptian sobriquet, meaning Lady Doctor," I said. "Dating from my early days in this country, when I endeavored in my humble fashion to alleviate the sufferings of the local people. You, however, are not entitled to use that name, since—"

"Peabody!" Emerson said in a loud voice.

"Nor that one," I said. "Only my husband employs my maiden name as a title of affection and—"

"Amelia," said Emerson even more loudly.

I know Emerson is out of temper with me when he employs my given name. I nodded, in acknowledgment of his implicit complaint, and said to the young woman, "You will address me as Mrs. Emerson, and apologize for your rude intrusion.

You and your brother have probably spoiled our dinner. Fatima, will you tell Cook we will be a few minutes longer?"

"He will cry," said Fatima darkly.

Our former cook had burned the food when we were late. This one wept.

"Tell him we will be as quick as we can. Young woman, I will give you ten minutes to explain, apologize, and remove your—er—impetuous brother. You might start by introducing yourself."

"Harriet Petherick. This is my brother, Adrian." Her eyes went back to Ramses. "I beg you will let go of him. He is quite calm now. Aren't you, Adrian?"

"Yes, of course." He gave a brief, embarrassed laugh. "I can't think what came over me. Come along, Harriet, we mustn't keep these people from their dinner any longer."

"Not just yet," said Emerson, removing his pipe from his mouth. "Ramses, let the fellow go. And pick up that damned gun. Excuse me for not rising, Miss Petherick; I do not consider that your behavior warrants your being treated like a lady. Sit down, both of you, and explain yourselves. I take it that you are the children of Pringle Petherick, whose widow called on us this afternoon."

Miss Petherick nodded. She led her brother to a settee and sat down next to him, holding his hand in hers. Ramses scooped up the pistol and examined it.

"German," he said.

"A war souvenir," said Adrian Petherick, smiling.

Bertie let out a soft exclamation and came forward, staring at Petherick. If he had intended to speak, he was not given the chance; Miss Petherick at once launched into the explanation I had requested.

"Mrs. Petherick is our stepmother. We accompanied her to Egypt, at her request, on what she described as a sentimental pilgrimage in memory of her dear departed husband. We had no idea that she had the statue with her, or what she intended to do with it, until she returned to the hotel this evening and informed us she had given you one of the most valuable objects in Father's collection. We are both fond of Mrs. Petherick, and Adrian is quite protective of her. He believed you had taken advantage of a grieving woman who is not, perhaps, as intelligent as she might be. His indignation explains his action, I believe."

"No, it does not," said Emerson. "Your high-handed manner may intimidate some persons, Miss Petherick, but I am not one of them. Does your brother often have attacks of dementia?"

She reacted as if he had struck her, with a loud gasp and a hand raised in protest. Emerson's steady blue gaze did not alter. After a moment she said, "It is not what you think. He has never injured anyone. He would not have injured you."

"Hmph," said Emerson. "We will leave that aside for the moment. Mrs. Petherick told us that the object she gave us was accursed. That it had killed her husband, sucking the breath out of him."

There was no reaction from young Mr. Petherick, who was staring off into space. His sister frowned. "I am not surprised she should say that. But her superstitious fantasy does not alter the facts of the case."

"How did your father die?" I asked.

"Of purely natural causes," said Miss Petherick. "He had a stroke, which left him partially paralyzed. The second finished him."

Emerson took out his watch. "Let me be brief. Maaman will be sobbing into the soup, and I want my dinner. I will of course pay Mrs. Petherick a reasonable price for the artifact, or return it to her, should she prefer that."

"She wants it back," said Miss Petherick. "She sent us to retrieve it."

"Oh, come now," Emerson shouted. He had kept his temper under control until that moment, but hunger always makes him irascible. Brother and sister flinched, and Emerson skewered them with a terrible glare. "You insult my intelligence, young woman. I don't know who the legal owner of this object may be. I intend to hang on to it until I find out. I shan't bother asking you, since I wouldn't trust your word in any case."

Miss Petherick recognized that she had met her match. She scowled.

"Hmph," said Emerson. "Do you know from whom your father purchased the statuette?"

"No."

"Did he ever discuss his purchases with you?"

"No."

"So your only interest in his collection is in its monetary value?"

The young woman flushed angrily. "You have no right to imply that."

"Oh, bah," said Emerson. "Go away."

Miss Petherick rose. "If that is your attitude, Professor Emerson—"

"Ramses," said Emerson. "Hand Miss Petherick her wrap and escort her to her carriage."

When Ramses attempted to put the garment around her shoulders, she snatched it from him. "Come, Adrian," she said. Her brother stood up, smiling vaguely. She took his arm and swept out of the room, followed by Ramses.

"Dinner," said Fatima, in a near shriek, "is served."

• • •

Cyrus had not relaxed his grip on the statuette. He carried it with him into the dining room and was with difficulty persuaded to put it down in order to pick up his napkin.

"What a family," Emerson grumbled. "The stepmother is a hysteric or a liar, the brother a lunatic—"

"And the sister has a fist like a boxer's," said Ramses, whose cheek was beginning to darken.

A wordless grunt from Fatima, who was serving the soup, indicated her opinion of the proceedings. She had been in a happy frame of mind since, for the first time in many years, she did not have to share the cherished chore of serving meals with our butler, Gargery. He was really too old for the strenuous activities that accompany our excavation seasons, but he had agreed to remain in England only because our ward Sennia, whom he adored, had also stayed behind in order to further her education. She was twelve, and bright as a button; the schools of Luxor and Cairo had nothing more to offer her.

"You ought to have given the confounded girl a good hard shove," said Emerson, who would have done nothing of the sort. He swallowed a mouth-

ful of soup and made a face. "Salty. Well, Vandergelt, what do you think?"

"You did the right thing," Cyrus said. "I
remember hearing that Petherick left nothing
except his collection. It's worth a pretty penny,
but I don't know who his legal heirs are. Maybe
the kids are trying to put one over on the widow."

"If she really believes the statue carries a curse,
she won't take it back," I remarked.

"Emerson," said Cyrus piteously, "I'll pay the
lady. Anything she wants. I've got to have that!"

Emerson pushed his soup plate away. "Frankly,
Vandergelt, I don't give a curse who gets it. What I
want to know is where it came from."

"A dealer, one presumes," I said.

"And before that?"

I shrugged. "Another dealer. A tomb robber or
illicit digger. What are you getting at, Emerson?"

"Tell her, Ramses." Emerson picked up the little statue and handed it to his son.

"Yes, sir. We may or may not be able to trace the
object back through its previous owners; but the
statue itself offers certain clues as to where it was
found." Holding the statuette up to the light, he
ran an appreciative finger along the delicately
modeled cheek and down the curves of the body.
"It's one of the Amarna kings."

I nodded agreement. "The style is unmistakable—the soft outlines of the body, the delicate fingers and toes. Since this artistic technique was only employed during the reign of the so-called heretic king Akhenaton and his immediate successors, we can pin it down to a period of—oh, I would say fewer than fifteen years, since it is of the later Amarna style rather than—"

"Amelia," said Emerson forcibly. "We know that."

"Katherine was looking a trifle confused," I explained.

"Thank you," Katherine said with a smile.

"The term Amarna," I continued, before Emerson could stop me, "refers to the site in Middle Egypt where Akhenaton founded a city dedicated to the worship of his sole god, Aton."

"Can it be Akhenaton himself?" Cyrus asked. "There's no name on it, I looked."

Ramses turned the statuette upside down and inspected the soles of the little golden feet. "I think it stood on a pedestal, with perhaps a back column, which would have been inscribed with the name of the king."

"Maybe," Cyrus said doubtfully. "But that doesn't tell us where this came from, does it?"

"There are only a few possibilities," Ramses said. "Amarna itself is the most obvious. Mother and Father excavated there in the 1880s, and there have been archaeologists at work off and on ever since—not to mention local diggers. The site is huge. This might have come from a shrine in a courtier's house, or from a sculptor's workshop like the one the Germans found before the war."

Emerson shook his head. "Unlikely, my boy. Borchardt found plaster models, intrinsically valueless. Everything that could be reused was taken away when the city was abandoned. A statuette of solid gold certainly wouldn't have been overlooked."

"You can't be sure of that," Cyrus objected. "Maybe the owner buried it to keep it safe, and died before he could retrieve it."

"Anything is possible," Emerson retorted. "But don't pack up and head for Amarna just yet, Vandergelt. We know that Akhenaton's successors returned to Thebes. One of them was buried in KV55, the tomb Theodore Davis ripped apart back in '07."

"Unless the mummy in that tomb was Akhenaton himself," Cyrus said. "Weigall believes—"

"Weigall is wrong," Emerson said flatly. "The remains have to be those of Smenkhkare, Akhenaton's son-in-law. That's beside the point. This statue is precisely the sort of thing that might have been part of the tomb furnishings, which, as you recall, were a hodgepodge of objects belonging to different royals. You may also recall that Davis's workmen made off with some of them. And so did another individual. Isn't that right, Amelia?"

All heads turned, all eyes focused on me. Emerson's bright blue orbs were as hard as sapphires.

Bertie, chivalrous chap that he was, broke the silence with an indignant question. "Surely you aren't accusing your wife, Professor?"

"No," I said. "He is accusing his brother."

There was no need to explain which one I meant. Walter, Emerson's younger brother, was a reputable scholar and a man of integrity. Seth, their illegitimate half brother, was . . . not. Even Katherine knew his strange history; before I reformed him, Sethos (to give him his nom de crime) had been the most successful dealer in illegal antiquities ever to operate in Egypt. His keen intelligence, his skill at the art of disguise, and his charismatic personality had placed him at the head of an organization that had wreaked havoc with the Service des Antiquités and caused us no little personal inconvenience. All that was in the past. Sethos had served his country honorably during the war and had sworn to me that he had given up his criminal activities.

However, it was the past to which Emerson referred, and I had to admit that Sethos was the most logical suspect. I knew for a fact that he had looted Davis's tomb.

So did Emerson. I keep nothing from my husband (unless it is unlikely to accomplish anything except to arouse his formidable temper). A violent explosion had, in fact, ensued, when I described my somewhat unusual and (in Emerson's opinion) unnecessarily intimate conversation with Sethos following the excavation of Tomb 55; but once he cooled off he agreed there would have been no point in pursuing the matter. Sethos had calmly admitted taking a number of antiquities from the tomb, but by the time I learned this it was too late to prevent them from being sent out of the country. They were irretrievably lost, and so was Sethos, who could change his appearance as readily as he did his name.

"By the Almighty," Cyrus exclaimed. "Well, but Sethos is now a reformed character and a friend. All we have to do is ask him—"

"Whether he took the statue," Nefret cut in. "A man is innocent until proven guilty, isn't he?"

She had always had a weakness for Sethos. Most women did. Ramses shook his head. He did not have a weakness for his uncle. Most men did not.

"When it comes to Sethos's past history, the reverse is true. He usually **was** guilty. Where is he now?"

"I don't know," I said. "He is still working undercover for the War Office."

"I can't see that it matters," Nefret declared. "Mr. Petherick was the legal owner."

"It does matter, though," Ramses said. "If Sethos denies taking this from KV55—and if we believe him—we must look elsewhere for the origin of the statue."

"Hmph." Emerson tossed his napkin onto the table and stood up. "Let's get to work."

I knew what he meant to do, and understood his reasons, but I felt obliged to protest. "Emerson, it is very late, and we have guests."

"We aren't guests," Cyrus said, rising in his turn. "I reckon we're of the same mind, Emerson. It's a pity David isn't here. He's the best artist in the family."

"We may be able to hang on to the statuette until he arrives next week," Emerson said. "But if we are forced to return it we will at least have a record—photographs, scale drawings, perhaps a plaster cast."

"It will take all night," I protested.

"What does that matter?" Emerson demanded.

It did take most of the night, for Emerson was not satisfied until the object had been photographed from every angle and detailed notes taken. Under close examination, certain minor flaws were apparent in what had seemed a perfect work of art. One of the small fingers had been broken off. The long embroidered sash and the wide collar had once been inlaid with tiny bits of glass or precious stone; almost all of them were missing. There was a hole on the Blue Crown, in the center of the brow. Here the uraeus serpent, the symbol of kingship, had reared its lordly head. It must have been a separate piece, inserted into the crown, and it had fallen out.

"Poor little king," I said whimsically. "Without the guardian serpent on his brow he was helpless to prevent the humiliation of being passed from hand to greedy hand, and exposed to the gaze of the curious."

The only person who responded to this poetic statement was Emerson. "Stop talking nonsense, Peabody."

After the Vandergelts had left and Ramses and Nefret had gone to their house, Emerson dropped off to sleep immediately. I never allow fatigue to keep me from my nightly routine, so I sat before my dressing table giving my hair its customary one hundred strokes. Candles on either side of the mirror lent a ghostly softness to my reflected face, and the soothing effect of the repeated strokes allowed my mind to wander.

The astonishing events of the evening had postponed a serious discussion about our future plans. In previous years Cyrus had shared with us the site of the workmen's village at Deir el Medina; while we excavated in the village itself, Cyrus and Bertie investigated the tombs on the hillside. We were shorthanded this year, and it had become increasingly evident to me, though not to my stubborn and self-centered spouse, that we were on the verge of momentous changes.

Hitherto we had depended on friends and kin to assist us in our archaeological labors. Selim, the son and successor of our dear reis Abdullah, could be depended upon for many more years, and the younger members of his family were filling the positions left vacant by death and retirement. It was a different matter with David, Abdullah's grandson, whom we had freed from his cruel master when he was still a child. He had amply repaid that favor, if it could be called such, with years of loyal and skilled service; but he had built a successful career of his own as a painter and illustrator. He and his wife, Lia, Emerson's niece, now had four children. I need not explain to any mother of four why Lia had given up her career as an archaeological assistant. Her father was a philologist, not an excavator, and he had finally confessed that the arduous life of a field archaeologist had become too much for him. His wife,

Evelyn, preferred her role as grandmother to that of staff artist.

That left us with Nefret and Ramses, neither of whom had uttered a word of complaint; but I foresaw a time when they would want more freedom from the bonds of family and from Emerson's dictatorial control. Nefret was able to employ her medical skills in the clinic she had opened in Luxor, but I suspected she secretly yearned for a more specialized practice, such as the one she would have in Cairo in the women's hospital she had founded some years earlier. Too many "buts"! The children's needs for schooling, Ramses's interests in other areas of Egyptology—everything pointed to the same conclusion. We must let our dear ones go their own ways, and that meant we must hire a new staff. How I was going to convince Emerson of this without a battle of epic proportions, I could not imagine. However, I rather looked forward to the argument. Emerson is at his most imposing when he is in a rage—and I had never yet lost an argument that really mattered.

A breeze swayed the candle flame. I leaned forward, peering more closely at my image. Was that . . .

It was. They seemed to be occurring more frequently these days, the silvery strands in the black of my hair. Well! That was another argument I did not mean to lose. Glancing over my shoulder to make sure Emerson still slept, I took out the little bottle of coloring liquid.

FROM MANUSCRIPT H

The children woke at dawn. Dragged out of heavy slumber by the piercing voices of his dear little offspring, Ramses groaned and pulled the blanket up over his head. He hadn't had more than two hours' sleep. It wasn't entirely his father's fault; there had been an additional distraction, once he and Nefret were alone.

The blanket didn't help. Lowering it, he turned over and looked at his sleeping wife. And, as usual, his bad humor was dispelled by the very sight of her: golden-red hair spread across the pillow, white arms and shoulders bared by the narrow straps of her nightdress. It seemed impossible that they had been married for six years. He had worked longer than that to win her, almost as long as the fourteen years Jacob had served for his beloved Rachel.

He lifted a tangled strand away from her eyes. They opened. After a moment the hazy look of sleep was replaced, not by the appreciation he had come to expect, but by consternation. "Oh dear," she groaned. "It can't be morning already."

"Stay in bed," Ramses said, wishing he could do the same. "I'll tell Father you're a little under the weather."

"No, don't do that. He'll think . . . you know what he'll think."

"Yes." The twins were four years old and his father had taken to dropping not-so-subtle hints about another grandchild. Oddly enough, his mother had not.

"There's no need for you to get up," Ramses insisted. "Today is Friday. The men won't be working anyhow. If I know Father, and I believe I do, he's planning one of two things: tracking Sethos down, or calling on Mrs. Petherick. I've never seen him so fascinated by an artifact."

Nefret sat up, knees raised, arms wrapped round them. "I wouldn't miss that for the world!"

"Which?" Ramses asked, returning her smile.

"Either." She flung the covers back. "Though I can't imagine how he hopes to get on Sethos's trail."

Leaving the children eating—and dropping bits of egg and buttered toast into the waiting jaws of the Great Cat of Re—they made their way along the winding tree-shaded path that led to the main house, where they found the parents at their breakfast. Emerson greeted them with his habitual complaint: "Why didn't you bring the twins?" and his wife countered with her habitual response. "Not until they stop throwing food at each other and the cat." The Great Cat of Re had stayed behind. Ramses was his preferred companion, but Ramses didn't drop as much food on the floor as the twins did.

His mother was looking particularly bright-eyed and alert, her hair the same unrelieved, improbable jet black, her chin protruding. Ramses deduced that they had interrupted a parental argument. These disagreements were not uncommon; his mother and father both enjoyed them, and they were seldom deterred by the presence of their children. As soon as Fatima had served them and returned their greetings, his mother went back on the attack.

"Your proposal to go to Cairo in search of Sethos is perfectly ridiculous, Emerson. He could be anywhere in the Middle East, or in the world. I don't know why you have got this particular bee in your bonnet. Not only must we cope with Mrs. Petherick and her eccentric children, but you cannot abandon your work."

"Who said anything about abandoning Deir el Medina?" Emerson demanded. "I will only be away for two days. The rest of you can carry on quite well without me for that length of time. Which reminds me—where the devil is Jumana?"

Ramses had finished his eggs and toast. Fatima, who thought he was too thin, immediately replenished his plate. He looked up with a smile of thanks. Her round, friendly face, framed by the neat folds of her headcloth, bore an uncharacteristic frown.

His mother had got the bit in her teeth and was going full steam ahead. "You know perfectly well, Emerson, that Jumana goes to the site with the Vandergelts, since she is living with them for the time being. Which reminds me that you never settled her precise duties with Cyrus. He needs her even more than you, since he has only Bertie to supervise his men. I have been meaning to talk with you about this for some time. The fact is that we are shorthanded and—"

"Excuse me, Mother," Ramses said, knowing she could go on like that indefinitely. "Fatima, you look worried. Is something bothering you?"

"Thank you, Ramses, for asking me," said Fatima. "I want to know whether those two will come here again, or others like them. I could not keep them out, they pushed me away. I have told Jamad he must guard the door."

Her outbursts of sarcasm and complaint were so rare that they all quailed before her, even Emerson. "Er," he said. "Sorry, Fatima. But there is no need—"

"There is need, Father of Curses." She folded her arms and gave him a stern look. "In Cairo we had a proper doorkeeper to announce visitors or send them away. On the dahabeeyah we had always a guard at the gangplank. Here it is all open. It is not fitting that strangers can come as they please."

"She's right, you know," Nefret said. "The Pethericks aren't the only ones who have invaded our privacy. Remember that awful woman last week who offered Father ten pounds to show her round the sights of Luxor? Tourism is flourishing and some of these people have no manners."

"There have always been people without manners," said her mother-in-law, frowning. "But what can we do? I refuse to give up the veranda, it is too pleasant, and if we build a wall it will spoil our view."

"We might build a guardhouse or lodge, some distance down the road from the house," Nefret suggested. "And get one of the older men to sit there during the day. Jamad has enough to do."

"Do as you like," said Emerson impatiently. "Thanks to your mother's fussing I have missed the morning train. Just as well, perhaps; Ramses, I want you to come to the Valley with me."

"The Valley of the Kings?" Ramses asked in surprise.

"There is only one Valley in Luxor," said Emerson, emphatically if inaccurately.

"Yes, sir. May I ask why?"

"I promised Carter I would keep an eye on the place." Emerson pushed his plate away, took out his pipe, and made a great business of filling it. "He and Carnarvon are dillydallying about in England and won't be out for several more weeks."

His wife fixed him with a steely stare. Like Ramses, she had recognized the signs. Emerson wasn't exactly lying, but he was concealing something.

"That is unfair," she said. "Howard had a serious operation last month and is still recuperating. Why did you promise him that?"

"It is the least a fellow can do for a friend," said Emerson.

"Bah," said his wife. "No one could possibly carry out an illegal excavation in the Valley, there are too many tourists and guards—even if there were any tombs yet to be found. Howard has been excavating there off and on for years, without success. What are you up to now, Emerson?"

"Are you impugning my motives?" Emerson demanded, with a fair show of righteous indignation. "I resent that, Peabody. Come, Ramses."

"What about Mrs. Petherick?" his wife asked.

Emerson, already halfway to the door, came to a stop. "It is up to her to make the next move."

He didn't sound as decisive as usual, though, and his wife took immediate advantage. "Nonsense. When you accepted that object you had no idea of its value. Your motives **will** be impugned if you don't return it at once, or at least offer to do so."

"Curse it," said Emerson.

"Mrs. Petherick ought to be informed of her stepchildren's bizarre performance last night," his wife went on. "You said you were uncertain as to who the legal owner of the statue may be. Well, isn't she in the best position to answer that question? She may also know the name of the dealer from whom her husband purchased it. That is surely the most practical way of discovering its origins, by tracing it back from one purchaser to the—"

"Yes, yes." Emerson turned to face his wife. "You have made your point, Peabody, you needn't hammer it into my liver. We'll pay the cursed woman a visit. As soon as possible. I want to get it over with."

"I am glad you agree, Emerson. I dispatched a little note to Mrs. Petherick this morning, inviting her to take luncheon with us at the Winter Palace."

"Hmph." Emerson took out his watch. "What time?"

"Two o'clock."

"Then Ramses and I have plenty of time for a visit to the Valley. We will drive the motorcar."

"Not unless it can be driven with only three wheels," his wife said. "I don't believe you and Selim ever got round to putting the fourth one back on."

"Oh." Emerson fingered the cleft in his chin. He had bought the motorcar over his wife's strenuous objections. She had pointed out, correctly, that its use was limited by the lack of good roads, but her chief objection was the way Emerson drove—at full speed, with complete disregard for objects in his way. However, the car spent most of the time in the stable annex, since Emerson and Selim kept taking it apart.

"We will ride the horses, then," Emerson said. "You needn't come, Peabody."

"I wouldn't miss it for the world, Emerson."

Ramses hadn't been in the Valley for months. The firman was held by Lord Carnarvon, whose excavations, under the direction of Howard Carter, had been going on intermittently since 1913. He had found nothing except a few workmen's huts and a cache of calcite jars. It was generally agreed that Carter was wasting his time. There were no more royal tombs in the Valley.

As they walked along the dusty path from the donkey park, where they had left their horses, Ramses was conscious of a certain nostalgia. Excavation wasn't his primary interest, but there was no site on earth more evocative than the burial place of the great pharaohs of the Empire. The family had been allowed to work on the more obscure and uninteresting tombs until 1907, with the grudging consent of the American dilettante Theodore Davis, who then had the sole right to search for new tombs. He'd found a lot of them, too, or rather, his archaeological assistants had. It was Davis's mishandling of the enigmatic burial in KV55 that had driven Emerson into a particularly outrageous explosion, and M. Maspero, then head of the Service des Antiquités, had been forced by Davis to ban them from the Valley altogether.

What a season it had been, though! As they passed the entrance to KV55, now blocked and sealed, Ramses felt a remembered thrill. He would never forget his first sight of the pieces of the great golden shrine lying dismantled and abandoned in the entrance corridor, the shattered but magnificent inlaid coffin, the canopic jars with their exquisitely carved heads. The excavation had been badly botched, no question of that, but if Emerson hadn't insulted Maspero, they might have had a chance of getting the firman when Davis gave it up. Of all the sites in Egypt, it was the one Emerson yearned for most.

But Emerson passed the entrance to KV55 with only a sidelong glance, pushing through the throngs and muttering anathemas against empty-headed tourists. As they went on, past the side branches that led to the most popular of the royal tombs, the crowds decreased. The sun had risen over the enclosing cliffs. Ramses took his mother's arm.

"I'm ready for a rest. How about you?"

The pith helmet shadowed the upper part of her face, but he saw her tight-set lips relax. She was limping a little that morning, or rather, trying not to limp. He had noticed it once or twice before, but she would never admit fatigue or pain. "If you like, my dear."

Emerson came back to ask why they were stopping. His wife, who was wearing her famous belt hung all round with various "useful objects," unhooked her canteen and offered it to the others. Nefret accepted gratefully, and so did Ramses, after his mother had had her turn. Emerson shook his head. He could go without water as long as a camel, and his son had often wondered why he had never collapsed from dehydration.

They went on, exploring one side wadi after another, until they reached a cul-de-sac walled in by jagged cliffs. High above them, in a narrow cleft, was a tomb entrance—that of the great warrior pharaoh, Thutmose III.

"What's Father doing?" Nefret asked.

Her mother-in-law opened her parasol. It was frequently used as an offensive weapon but, as she was fond of pointing out, it served a number of useful purposes, including that of sunshade.

"Looking for signs of unauthorized digging, I think. If anything of that sort has occurred, it would more likely be in this area, away from the main part of the Valley. But don't ask me what he hopes to accomplish by this."

This remote sepulchre had an atmosphere of majesty and mystery the main part of the Valley had lost when the Department of Antiquities smoothed its uneven paths and erected neat, modern retaining walls next to most of the tomb entrances. Here, far away from the hubbub and bustle, it wasn't difficult to imagine the funeral cortege winding along the rocky ravine, the chanting of the white-robed priests and the wailing of the women, the gold-encrusted coffin catching the rays of the sun in a blinding glitter. Like all the other tombs, that of Thutmose III had been robbed millennia ago, but he had been one of

Egypt's richest and most powerful kings, with the wealth of Nubia and Syria in his hands; it boggled the mind to imagine the treasures that must have been buried with him.

Emerson's bellow roused Ramses from his reverie, which was born partly of lack of sleep. He hastened to join his father, who was prowling around the piled-up rock chips and pebbles at the base of the cliff a little distance away. The debris was head-high here, left, if Ramses remembered correctly, from Davis's excavation of the nearby tomb of Siptah.

"Didn't Carter work in this area last year?" Ramses asked.

Emerson didn't answer. Instead he began digging in one of the heaps, ignoring his wife's shout of "Emerson, your gloves! Put on your gloves!" Ramses pitched in too, wondering what the devil he was supposed to be looking for. They found a number of pottery shards and the foot of a faience ushebti—Davis had never bothered to sift his fill. Finally Emerson let out a grunt of satisfaction and pulled out a torn, crumpled sheet of newspaper. "July of last year," he announced.

"A tourist," Ramses said.

"It's in Arabic," said Emerson. "**Al Ahram**. We had better start back now." He folded the paper and tucked it carefully into his pocket.

They retraced their steps. As soon as they were out of sight of the place where they had been digging, Emerson stopped and began making violent gestures at the others. "Go on," he hissed. "Keep talking." He turned and ran back the way they had come, beckoning Ramses to follow.

Their approach was not silent, but Emerson could cover ground quite rapidly when he had to. They arrived on the scene in time to see several men fleeing in all directions. Emerson leaped on one of them and Ramses collared a second. Ramses knew him—Deib ibn Simsah. The nearby village of Gurneh housed many of the most skilled tomb robbers in Egypt. The ibn Simsahs had proudly assumed the sobriquet of an accomplished predecessor in the business; they were second only to the Abd er Rassul family when it came to finding and looting new tombs. After a half-hearted attempt to wriggle free of the grip on his arm, Deib subsided and gave Ramses an ingratiating smile.

"We were doing nothing wrong, Brother of Demons. You know me; you know my brother Aguil."

"I know you only too well," Ramses said, his eyes fixed on the figure of the third man, who was climbing with the agility of a goat. "But who is that?"

Deib shrugged and rolled his eyes. Emerson let out an inventive oath and started scrambling up the cliff face after the fugitive. Ramses caught hold of him. "No, Father! He's got—"

The crack of a pistol shot made it unnecessary for him to finish the sentence.

TWO

Emerson's abrupt volte-face took me by surprise, but only briefly. I hastened after them, with the others following. The sound of a shot lent wings to my heels. Arriving upon the scene, I found Emerson interrogating two of Gurneh's most notorious citizens. He interrupted his shouted accusations and glared at me. "Curse it, Peabody, I told you to go on!"

"Nonsense," I said. "Who fired that shot? And at whom? And why?"

Hands on hips, head thrown back, Ramses was staring up at the top of the cliff. "There was a third man. Father was about to go after him when I noticed the fellow had a weapon."

"Good Gad," I exclaimed. "Emerson, my dear, are you injured?"

"No, no. He wasn't trying to hit anyone, just give himself time to get away. Which," Emerson added in vexation, "he has done. Who was it, Deib? Speak up!"

Deib and his brother had gone pale with terror.

They knew the penalties for injuring a foreigner. Deib wrung his hands and burst into incoherent protestations. They had never seen the man before. They did not know he had a pistol. They were only looking for a scarab one of them had lost the day before. As the Father of Curses knew, they sold such things to tourists, but they had come by this one honestly, purchasing it from a fellow Gurnawi and hoping to make a small profit—

Emerson cut him short. "I don't believe a word of it. You were watching us, and when you saw us digging here you decided to have a look for yourself."

"And what is the harm in that?" Deib asked, contradicting himself without shame. "We would have told you, Father of Curses, if we had found a tomb."

"Oh, bah," said Emerson. "Describe this man whom you never saw before."

It would have been hard to say whether the vagueness of the description was due to Deib's inadequate powers of observation or to calculated caution—or to a sizable bribe. The man was dressed like a howadji (that is to say, he wore European clothing). He was neither tall nor short, thin nor fat. A hat hid his hair, tinted glasses his eyes, and a large beard covered the lower half of his face. They could not describe his voice, since he had not uttered a word, only stood watching.

Finally Emerson dismissed the brothers with a stern warning and they made a hasty departure. He had let them off more easily than they deserved, and his expression had a hint of complacency that made me wonder what he was up to. When I informed him we must return to the house, he went along without complaint—another highly suspicious sign.

We arrived at the Winter Palace in good time. Tourism was back to prewar levels, and the lobby was filled with people returning from their morning tours and waiting for luncheon. We were expected; no less a person than the manager, Mr. Salt, informed us that Mrs. Petherick had asked to be notified of our arrival, whereupon she would join us in the lobby.

Instead of taking the lift, she swept down the stairs, moving slowly. The staircase was a handsome structure, rising in a gentle curve, so that by the time Mrs. Petherick reached the bottom, all eyes were upon her. A mantilla-like scarf of black lace framed a face that irresistibly reminded me of the vampires in which the lady's fiction specialized— eyes heavily outlined in black, lips bloodred against the (powdered) pallor of her face. She offered a black-gloved hand to Emerson. She intended him to kiss it, but, being Emerson, he seized it and shook it vigorously.

"It was good of you to come," she enunciated. "I am in such need of reassurance. I saw him again last night. When, oh, when will you perform the ceremony that sets me free?"

As she intended, this remark was overheard by all those who stood nearby. A little buzz of excitement arose. I would not have given her the satisfaction of asking to whom the pronoun referred, for I knew what she was up to, but Emerson could not resist.

"Him? Who?" he demanded.

Her voice dropped to a thrilling but penetrating whisper. "He has no name. The faceless black shadow I saw drain the life from my darling husband. He has followed me here!"

His hat in his hand and his face studiously controlled, Ramses said, "The third time, was it not? I thought you said the third visit would be the last."

"You misunderstood," said Mrs. Petherick, lying like a veteran. "But he will come again, and the next time—"

I took her firmly by the arm.

"Let us go into the dining salon. Mr. Salt has reserved a table for us."

Emerson was in no mood to be trifled with. As soon as we had ordered, he fixed Mrs. Petherick with a stern stare. "Let us hear no more of illusions, madam. Are you aware that your stepchildren invaded our home last night? That the young man threatened us with a pistol?"

"Poor Adrian," the lady murmured. "He has suffered greatly, and he is deeply attached to me. You were in no danger from **him**."

"But we are in danger from someone else?" I asked.

"Stop that," Emerson said loudly. "You are encouraging her and I won't have it. Mrs. Petherick, when you handed over the—er—object to us, were you aware of its value?"

"Oh, yes." The lady sipped daintily at her soup. "Pringle said it was the most valuable object in his collection."

Emerson removed the box from his capacious pocket and put it on the table. "You are, I assume, the legal owner?"

"Oh, yes." She gazed, as if mesmerized, at the box.

"As you must have known, madam, my principles do not allow me to accept such a gift. I will return it or purchase it from you, whichever you prefer."

Her manicured fingertips brushed the painted surface. With a sudden movement she raised the lid and lifted the statue out.

"I thought you never wanted to look on that evil little face again," Ramses remarked.

"It was my dear Pringle's pride and joy. He loved it so . . ." She held it up, high over her head.

"Damnation," said Emerson. On this occasion I did not reproach him for bad language. I had never seen a more deliberate attempt to attract attention.

"Put it away, madam," Emerson growled.

Mrs. Petherick rolled her eyes at him and showed her teeth. I hadn't noticed before that the canines were longer than normal. A little buzz of interest ran round the room, and people at distant tables stood up in order to see better.

Emerson snatched the statue from her and replaced it in the box. "Well?" he demanded.

"Take it with you, Professor Emerson. I know that you will deal fairly with me. So long as I do not have it in my possession."

She had accomplished her aim of courting public interest. Our questions elicited no information. She did not know the name of the dealer from whom her husband had purchased the statue. Someone in London, she thought . . . Yes, she might consider selling the rest of the collection, in due time. It was in the process of being valued by the court.

"What about the statuette?" Ramses asked. "Isn't it part of the estate?"

Mrs. Petherick's crimsoned lips stretched in a

smile. "I took it away. It was my duty to my dear dead husband, to make certain its malevolent influence was ended."

I looked at Emerson, whose shrug expressed my sentiments exactly. What she had done was probably illegal, but it was not our affair.

Mrs. Petherick made an excellent lunch. She was tucking into a rich strawberry tart, topped with cream, when a lady of a certain age, gray-haired and tightly corseted, sidled up to her. "Countess? I don't want to intrude, but I am such a devoted admirer of your books . . ."

"You do want to intrude," said Emerson loudly. "You have just done so."

Mrs. Petherick—now in the role of Countess Magda—raised a bejeweled hand. "I am always delighted to meet my faithful readers. Would you like me to autograph a book?"

The lady hadn't brought one to Egypt, but she eagerly accepted the countess's signature on a piece of hotel stationery. Emboldened by her example, several other "devoted readers" followed suit. The author made quite a performance of it, scrawling her name in bold script, the gems on her fingers sparkling. I decided they were paste.

The trickle of admirers ended. Mrs. Petherick shoved the last bite of tart into her mouth and rose to go. When Emerson rose in response, she caught hold of his hand and squeezed it. "There will be a ceremony?" she asked. "An exorcism? I must be present."

You and every journalist you can collect, I thought. The idea of the Countess Magda throwing herself about, black veils flapping, and possibly falling into a fit while Emerson stood helplessly by, was too awful to contemplate.

"I cannot permit any such thing," I said firmly.

She paid me no heed. Clinging to Emerson's hand, she demanded, "When?"

"Cursed if I know," said Emerson, his patience at an end. He wrenched his fingers from the lady's grasp. "Let it be clearly understood that I accept this object in the role of a custodian. Good afternoon, madam."

At my suggestion, we took a brisk walk along the corniche so that Emerson could work off some of his temper. He was extremely put out and did not scruple to express his feelings.

"Now you see, Peabody, what comes of your ideas. We played right into the cursed woman's hands. She made a spectacle of herself and of us, and if anyone in Luxor did not know about the statue and the curse, they know now."

"I expect the story was already known," Ramses said, in a vain attempt to pacify his father. "And we did obtain some useful information."

"Oh, bah," snarled Emerson. "You didn't believe the woman, did you? She'll say anything that comes into her head. It is possible that she is unaware of the name of the dealer from whom Petherick purchased the statue; she wouldn't have taken any interest in that sort of thing. But until I learn the terms of his will from an independent source, I won't trust her word."

"How do you propose to do that?" I asked.

"I have my methods," said Emerson. "Hurry up, Peabody, you have wasted half the afternoon."

Ramses and Nefret went straight to their house, for they had a standing appointment with Selim and his family every Friday, and they were already a little late. When Emerson and I reached the veranda, we found that Jumana and Cyrus had dropped in and had been invited by Fatima to stay for tea. She loved feeding people, the more the better. Jumana embraced me and gravely shook hands with Emerson. She was a pretty little person—I almost wrote "unfortunately," for as women learn, being pretty and/or little leads many men to treat them like toys instead of reasoning beings. Slim and fit as a boy, her big dark eyes sparkling, she burst into an emphatic apology. One could almost hear the exclamation points.

"It was very rude of me not to come last night, very rude not to tell you beforehand! I am so sorry! I was working, and I forgot, until Bertie came to fetch me, and I was not clean or dressed." She went on, without drawing breath, "So I am punished because I missed the excitement! Can I see it now? Mr. Vandergelt has talked of nothing else!"

"Oh, very well," said Emerson. He took the box from his pocket and handed it to me. "Do the honors, Peabody, and then return it to my desk. Excuse me. I have a number of things to do before I catch the evening train."

"Where are you going?" Cyrus demanded in surprise.

"Cairo." Emerson threw the word over his shoulder and vanished inside.

Fatima brought out the tea things, assisted by the unfortunate youth who was her latest candidate for the role of footman. I wondered how long this one would last. Fatima's standards were exacting and her criticisms forceful.

Jumana exclaimed over the statuette, and after she had held it for a while, we passed it round. Its effect was increasingly hypnotic. The shimmer of the golden surface and the subtle curves of the body and face made one want to stroke it. Emerson returned, portmanteau in hand, in time to take it from Cyrus and return it to the box. He got a cup of tea for himself and drank it standing.

"So when are you going to talk to Mrs. P.?" Cyrus asked.

"We did so this afternoon," I replied. "It was an extremely exasperating discussion. She still insists on the absurd notion of a curse, but when Emerson said he had no intention of accepting the statue as a gift I noticed a smug little smile on her face."

"She knew she could trust the Professor to deal honorably with her," Jumana said.

"Very smart of the lady," said Cyrus. He added, with a grin, "I don't know that I could have withstood the temptation. Is she willing to sell it, and does she have the right to do so?"

"She was deliberately ambiguous," I said. "But I have the distinct feeling that she would be open to the right offer. As for the second question, she said her husband had left the collection to her."

Emerson drained his cup. "I wouldn't take her word if she swore on a stack of Bibles."

"Aha," said Cyrus. "Is that why you're going to Cairo?"

"One of the reasons," said Emerson.

"Well, while you're there you ought to see Lacau."

Emerson did not reply, but my forthright spouse is not very good at hiding his feelings and I have become expert in reading his countenance.

"Why should he see the director of the Antiquities Service?" I asked suspiciously. "We paid our courtesy call on him when we were in Cairo."

"Well, I guess you didn't get around to mentioning what we talked about at the end of last season," said Cyrus. "We were gonna reconsider our plans, remember? The French Institute has expressed an interest in Deir el Medina. They're prepared to make it a long-term project."

"Hmph," said Emerson, trying to look as if this news came as a surprise to him.

"Why, Emerson," I said in surprise. "Are you thinking of giving up Deir el Medina? You might at least have consulted the rest of us."

"I have every intention of consulting you," said Emerson loftily. "Vandergelt is obviously in favor of the idea. Getting bored with your little private tombs, are you, Cyrus?"

Cyrus did not answer directly, but his reply made his feelings plain. "I was up at Deir el Bahri the other day, where the Metropolitan Museum crew are working. They've found some darned fascinating things. That queen's sarcophagus with the painted scenes inside, as fresh and bright as if they had been finished yesterday . . ." He sighed longingly.

"That's true," Emerson said. "But you haven't

a prayer of getting permission to work in their area, Cyrus."

"No, but there's lots of other places that have possibilities."

"Possibilities of new tombs, you mean," Emerson said. "Is that all you can think of, Vandergelt? Our excavations at Deir el Medina have contributed—"

"Yeah, sure. Be honest, Emerson, you're losing interest too. You're as set on temples as I am on tombs."

"Well, well. As a favor to you, I will discuss the matter with Lacau. Good-bye. Peabody, my dear, I will see you in a few days."

My husband's machinations were clear to me now. Emerson had had no intention of giving up Deir el Medina until a more glittering prize glimmered like a mirage on the horizon. He had his eye on the Valley of the Kings. In my opinion his chances were slim; Lord Carnarvon had held the concession for years, and so far as I knew he had no intention of giving it up.

FROM MANUSCRIPT H

Emerson deigned to have a few words with Ramses before he left for Luxor. He had refused his son's offer to accompany him, which roused what Ramses's mother would have called dire forebodings.

"You mustn't give up your Friday visit with Selim and his family," Emerson said. "The dear children enjoy them so much."

"What am I supposed to tell Selim?" Ramses demanded. "He will expect to start work tomorrow."

"That you will work, of course. But not at the site," he added. "Get him and Daoud here and start going over last year's notes and plans. I want to see a detailed summary of what we accomplished and what remains to be done."

"But, sir—"

"My boy." Emerson put his hand on Ramses's shoulder. It was an unusual gesture, for him; equally unusual was the diffidence in his voice. "I know I am being arbitrary and dictatorial. It is not because I lack confidence in you. It is because I lack confidence in myself."

"You, sir?"

"Well, no." Emerson grinned with all his old assurance. "However, I am wrong now and then. I have an idea so vague and preposterous that I would be embarrassed to mention it. I may be on the wrong track, and I would rather not discuss my theory until after I have pursued several lines of inquiry. I will return on Sunday or Monday, and then we will reassess the situation. Just do me one favor: Try to keep your mother away from the Pethericks until I get back."

"I'll do my best."

"That is all any man can do. Especially with your mother. Run along now, the children will be waiting."

"Aren't you going to say good-bye to them?"

"Er—hmmm—no," mumbled Emerson. "Only be gone for two days."

The truth was, he dreaded Carla's reaction. She enjoyed drama and carried on like a juvenile Niobe when any of them went away. Her parents and grandmother had learned to ignore these demonstrations, but Emerson took them very much to heart, despite the fact that he had been assured the storm soon blew over. Was that why he was leaving several hours before the train departed? More likely he had business in Luxor he didn't care to discuss with his son.

The twins always looked forward to their Friday visits with Selim and his children, who were their favorite playmates. Another attraction was that they were allowed to ride with their parents. Thus far their equestrian activities had been limited to little donkeys, but both of them admired the beautiful Arabians that were the pride of the Emerson stables. After considering the relative sizes of himself and his father's stallion, Risha, David John had announced he would wait a year or two before attempting to mount the animal. Carla, whose temperament was more adventurous, had sneaked into Risha's stall one day and had managed to climb the side of the enclosure far enough to launch herself onto the astonished stallion's back. Risha let out one piercing whinny and then stood like a stone, ignoring the small hands that pulled at his mane and the small heels kicking his sides, until Ramses came running to see what had aroused the placid horse. It was one of the few times Ramses had ever spanked his daughter—not only, as he was careful to explain, because she had disobeyed his orders, but because she had hurt a gentle animal that was too well bred to defend himself.

That reproach had more effect than the spanking. Carla had been apologizing to Risha ever since, bringing him carrots and sugar lumps. Risha, who had probably found the whole performance fairly amusing, had been gracious enough to accept her effusive apologies, and when Ramses took Carla up with him on the stallion, Risha greeted her with a friendly nudge.

Anticipating their visit, several other members of the family had dropped in, including their assistant reis Daoud and his wife, Khadija. Ramses noted with a slight pang that there was more gray in Daoud's beard than there had been the year before, but the big man's hearty embrace could still make your ribs creak. Khadija inspected them with anxious eyes, looking for any sign of illness or injury. She let out a cluck of disapproval.

"Your hands, Ramses. What have you been doing?"

"Digging," Ramses admitted. "Please, Khadija, not the green ointment! There are only a few scratches."

She had already vanished inside the house.

"Digging where?" Selim asked. He at least hadn't changed. Straight and trim, dressed in his best woolen robe to do them honor, he watched with a grin as Khadija smeared the famous ointment on Ramses's hands. It was a traditional recipe in her Nubian family and it had amazingly therapeutic powers, but it left long-lasting stains on skin and clothing.

"The Valley of the Kings," Ramses answered Selim's question. "Near the tomb of Siptah."

Selim's fine dark eyes widened. "Why there?"

"It's a long story."

"Tell it, then," said Daoud. "Tell about the golden statues and the man with the gun."

Damnation, Ramses thought. He ought to have known that Fatima would spread the tale. After all, no one had sworn her to secrecy, and her new "footman," Kareem, was a notorious gossip. He decided it would be better to set the record straight before Daoud, the family's self-appointed chronicler, could embellish it any further. He had intended to discuss the business with Selim anyhow. Selim knew everyone in Luxor, including tomb robbers and dealers. The children were playing some game that involved intermittent screaming and a lot of rushing around, so he suggested to Daoud and Selim that they go for a walk.

There was no chance for a quiet conversation in the village; the narrow twisting paths led past open courtyards where the women were grinding grain and the men working at various chores or just sitting around smoking water pipes and drinking coffee. Everyone had a greeting or an embrace for Ramses, and questions showered them: "When would the Sitt Hakim visit? How were the little ones, God's blessing be on them?"

After leaving the village they turned by unspoken consent toward the village cemetery, and Ramses began his narrative.

"Only one statue?" Daoud asked, visibly cast

down. "I thought there were many, and rich jewelry."

"Kareem is a great liar," Selim declared.

"It isn't so much what Kareem said as how others embellish the basic story," Ramses said. "Do some of the Gurnawis believe we found the statue during our excavations?"

"It is not true?" Daoud asked.

Selim gave him an exasperated look. "You know it is not, Daoud, you heard of the lady giving it to Emerson, and of the son who came to take it back."

"Ah, yes." Daoud stroked his beard. "I had forgotten. But some of the Gurnawis do not believe that story."

"We ran into two of them this morning," Ramses said. "Deib and Aguil. There was a third man, who got away after firing a pistol in our direction."

"He dared to shoot at the Father of Curses?" Daoud rumbled. "Who was it?"

"Deib said he was a howadji. Someone he'd never seen before and couldn't describe."

"Deib is a greater liar than Kareem," Selim said through tight lips. "It must have been the third brother, Farhat. He is a bad egg, Ramses, who has been in trouble with the police. Though how he dared . . ."

"I will see to him," said Daoud.

Selim was almost certainly right, Ramses realized. Only the more gullible of the locals would have believed the statuette had been found in the Valley. Emerson must have known that too and suspected the brothers were lying about the identity of the third man. Yet he hadn't pressed them. Why?

He was still pondering this when Selim said, "Yes, we will see to him. One golden statue is wonder enough. It is genuine? Of what period?"

"Amarna. Yes, it's genuine. We don't know how long ago it was found, or whose hands it passed through before Petherick bought it. You would know, wouldn't you, if such a thing had turned up in Luxor?"

Selim stroked his neatly trimmed beard. "There are always rumors of rich finds. Most are lies. If this happened a long time ago, I might not know. Are you sure the statue came from Thebes?"

Ramses shook his head. "It's only one possibility."

Their steps had led them to the beautiful little tomb David had designed for his grandfather Abdullah. It was the most prominent monument in the cemetery, and the most frequently visited, for Abdullah was now regarded as a saint. Cords strung across the opening supported an unseemly but touching collection of offerings: cheap beads, kerchiefs, crude amulets. The current "servant of the sheikh," the custodian of the tomb, was seated on the floor, his head bent, presumably in prayer or meditation. Rather than disturbing him, they stopped a little distance away and stood in respectful silence.

Ramses thought of the first time he had come to Abdullah's grave, with his mother, before the tomb had been constructed. He had helped her bury a collection of small amulets, images of the ancient gods, over the grave. She had never explained why, and he had never asked; but it seemed to comfort her, and she had needed comfort badly. Over the years the conservative old Egyptian and the Englishwoman whose background and beliefs were so utterly different from his own had developed a close relationship, inexplicable in rational terms. But then, Ramses thought, love wasn't rational, was it?

"Now tell about the man with the gun and his sister," Daoud demanded, hoping for drama after the disappointment of the treasure.

He was disappointed in that too. Ramses made light of the business, as it deserved.

"Wallahi," Selim exclaimed. "What a strange family! Will they trouble you again? Is it because of them you are going to build a wall?"

"Not a wall, only a sort of guard post, to keep out uninvited visitors," Ramses said, thinking he must have a word with the inventive Kareem.

"And what of the curse?" Daoud asked hopefully. "Will the Father of Curses cast the demon out?"

Emerson's exorcisms were extremely popular. Ramses couldn't deny the possibility; for all he knew, his father might have something of the sort in mind. There was definitely a streak of theatricalism in the family, a fondness for disguises and playacting. He was in no position to criticize his father. Like his unregenerate uncle, he had been known for his skill in disguise, and now that that sort of thing was behind him he could admit he had quite enjoyed it.

"The lady invented the curse, Daoud," he said.

Daoud's face fell. "No curse? No threat? Then why are you building the barricade?"

Selim laughed. "I know what my honored father Abdullah would have said. 'There is no harm in protecting yourself from that which does not exist.'"

When Fatima set her mind on something, she went at it with all her energy. She had put a gang to work making bricks for the guardhouse, as she called it; until the structure could be built she had assigned Wasim to sit by the road under a temporary shelter. He was one of the older men, who had gone blind in one eye, and he obviously relished his new assignment. When I went, later that afternoon, to see if there was anything he needed, his beard split in a wide grin, showing the brown broken teeth of his generation.

"No, Sitt, I have everything I want," he said, indicating a water jar, a narghile, and the rug on which he squatted. "You may depend on me. I will not allow any thief to pass."

Lying beside him on the rug was a rifle. I asked, "Who gave you permission to have that gun?"

"What is a guard without a weapon?" Seeing my expression, he added quickly, "It is not loaded, Sitt, it is only for show. Fatima said I should bring it."

"Oh, very well. You understand, Wasim, that you are not to threaten people, only stop them and ask their business. If it is a friend of ours, let him pass. If it is a stranger, ask his name and come and tell me or Fatima."

"Oh, yes, Sitt, I understand. No thief will pass me."

I was halfway back to the house before the import of that word "thief" struck me. He had used it twice. I ought to have known our people would gossip about the "treasure." Nor were they the only ones. To whom had Mrs. Petherick told her preposterous story? How far had the news spread?

When the children and their parents returned from Selim's, the former were in their usual state of grubbiness, overindulgence, and crankiness. Their nursery maid, Elia, was accustomed to dealing with this; she hustled them off to baths and bed. It was a rare pleasure to settle down with only my son and daughter. Compared with my husband and grandchildren, they are restful company. Twilight deepened; the stars began to shine over Luxor; and Ramses served the whiskey.

"Who gave Wasim permission to have that weapon?" Ramses asked somewhat critically. "He'll shoot someone; his eyesight is so bad."

"The gun isn't loaded."

"Is that what he told you?" Ramses took a refreshing sip of whiskey. An afternoon with his children often left him somewhat on edge. "Oh, well, we can only hope for the best. Maybe he'll shoot a journalist."

"How do you know the press has been informed of our so-called treasure trove?"

"If they don't know about it they must be deaf, dumb, and blind. Mrs. Petherick has done her best to spread the word. I wouldn't be surprised to learn she gave interviews to the newspapers before she left England. All the local people have heard of our acquisition and have exaggerated its value as they are inclined to do. Daoud and Selim knew all about it, and about our encounter with the Pethericks."

He glanced at Fatima, who was moving quietly about lighting the lamps. She ducked her head and murmured something about Kareem.

"It's all right, Fatima," Ramses said. "The story is like an amoeba, oozing out in all directions." He glanced out the screened windows toward the little shelter, where the yellow glow of a candle betokened the presence of our guard. "That was a good idea of Fatima's. In fact, I believe I will station another fellow at the back of the house."

"You don't really believe anyone will try to break in, do you?" I asked.

"I don't believe in taking chances, Mother."

FROM MANUSCRIPT H

Ramses couldn't have said why he was so uneasy. His mother was the one who specialized in premonitions, and for once she didn't seem to anticipate trouble. She went calmly off to bed at her usual hour, leaving Fatima to close up the house. Ramses made the rounds with her, checking doors and windows and gates, going through the same procedure with Nefret's and his house. The children's windows were barred, not only to keep his peripatetic offspring in, but to keep others out. They had had an unpleasant experience a few years earlier with someone who had terrorized Carla by whispering at the window. If a thief was after the statuette, there was one sure way of getting it. Emerson wouldn't have bargained with an abductor who held one of the adults, but he would instantly have exchanged the statuette and everything else he owned for either of the twins.

As he did almost every night, Ramses stood in the doorway of their room looking at the small quiet bodies. David John slept flat on his back, arms and legs thrown out, head thrown back. Carla was a restless sleeper, twisting and turning, sometimes ending up with her head at the foot of her bed and her little bottom bared by the twisted folds of her nightgown. Now she lay curled up like a kitten, the covers clear up to her button of a nose. They looked so helpless. Love, and terror at the thought of anything happening to them, stabbed through him like a knife.

Nefret was already in bed, golden hair spread enticingly across the pillow. She opened half-closed eyes when he came in. "You were a long time," she murmured.

"I was watching the children. Carla is almost as active when she sleeps as when she's awake."

"I expect you were too when you were her age." She smiled sleepily. "Are you coming to bed?"

It was a tempting suggestion, but that unconquered restlessness made him shake his head. "Soon. I feel like a walk."

The stars were bright, the moon a sliver of silver. What he really wanted to do was sit under their windows all night, guarding the three who were dearest to him, not trusting anyone else to do it. That was foolish, and he knew it. He was a light sleeper; if anyone came near either window he would hear, especially in his present state of nerves. Daoud's son, Ali Yussuf, was stationed in the courtyard of the main house—almost certainly an unnecessary precaution, since several servants slept in the house, and his mother was an army unto herself.

Pacing restlessly up and down, his eyes on the darkened window of the room where his wife slept and the faint glow of the night-light from that of the twins, he tried to analyze his malaise. Had something happened to alert what his mother poetically called "the sleeping sentry"—part of the unconscious mind that took note of suspicious circumstances? God knew there had been a number of weird happenings in the past two days, and a number of people had expressed interest in their prize, but he couldn't believe any of them would stoop to crime to retrieve it. Except possibly for Adrian Petherick, in one of his fits. But I have his gun, Ramses thought. It would be easy for him to acquire another, but surely his sister will keep an eye on him after what he did. The men of Gurneh were peaceful souls, and the house of the Father of Curses was protected by that gentleman's formidable reputation.

We need a dog, Ramses thought. They'd had several—strays taken in by Nefret along with other abandoned or injured beasts and birds. One of his mother's favored psychologists would probably have said Nefret had been moved by a combination of maternal instinct and frustrated medical talents. The twins and her clinic on the West Bank kept her fully occupied now, but . . .

We'll get a dog, Ramses decided. I'll see about it tomorrow.

He was about to go back inside when a sound made him stiffen and turn. High-pitched, sharp, it might have been the cry of a bird or animal, but he knew it wasn't. He broke into a run, heading for the back of the main house.

The courtyard gate was closed and there was no sign of anyone outside, but he heard his mother's voice, raised over Ali Yussuf's protests.

"You aren't seriously hurt. Stop complaining and tell me what happened!"

Ramses didn't waste time pounding on the gate. He pulled himself to the top of the wall and dropped down inside. His mother, modestly enveloped in yards of dressing gown, had Ali Yussuf's head firmly between her hands. She glanced at Ramses.

"Just a bump on the head," she said, sounding as brisk and alert as if she hadn't just been shocked out of sleep.

Ali Yussuf pulled away from her and groaned theatrically. "I have failed."

"Not if you kept someone from entering the house," Ramses said, patting the disconsolate youth on the back. "Tell us what happened."

Ali Yussuf was not about to admit falling into a doze, but he must have done, since he had been unaware of an intruder until he heard the scrape of falling plaster and saw the figure perched atop the wall.

"Black, all black, like a shadow," Ali Yussuf said. "But I was not afraid, Brother of Demons . . . Not much afraid. When it jumped down from the wall I threw myself at it and caught hold of it. I called out—not in fear, no, in warning, as you told me . . ."

"And then it hit you?" Ramses asked. "The black shadow?"

His mother patted the boy's drooping head. "Don't be rude, Ramses. He did his best. His cry for help—er—of warning wakened me, but by the time I had lit a lamp and got to my window I caught only a glimpse of a form going back over the wall."

"I suppose you had your parasol," Ramses said.

"Naturally. Goodness, you are in a snappish mood tonight. And before you wax sarcastic again, I will admit I saw only a pair of trousered legs, and that for a split second."

"Black?"

"No," said his mother composedly. She bent over, lifted something from the ground and held it up. "You will admit, however, that this is black."

It was a long garment, full sleeved and hooded, like the robe of a medieval monk.

Selim and Daoud turned up next morning as requested. They had, of course, heard about the midnight intruder, and both of them expressed indignation at not being allowed to assist in defending the house. Ramses had to agree to let Selim arrange a rota of guards at front and back, though, as he pointed out, there was no danger to any of the family.

"I don't know what the fellow hoped to accomplish," he added. "He'd have had to search the whole house without waking anyone. It isn't as if Father left the statue lying out on a table in the sitting room. You don't suppose Farhat was having a try?"

"Farhat has broken his leg," said Selim.

"Broken—"

"His leg. Yes. He will not be climbing cliffs or walls for a while."

Ramses looked from Selim to Daoud, whose countenance bore its usual amiable smile. He decided to drop the subject.

"I have thought that we might get a dog. Have you any likely candidates?"

Daoud, whose large soft heart encompassed even animals scorned by his fellow Gurnawis, knew of several that might suit. "I will look at them and bring the best tomorrow. A large fierce dog, that is a good plan."

"Not fierce," Ramses said in alarm. "Not with the twins around. I don't want an animal that would injure anyone, I just want him to bark."

He brought out the statuette, which Daoud and Selim hadn't yet seen, and let them examine it. Selim's eyes brightened at the sight of it; he knew enough to appreciate its rarity and its value. Daoud touched it with reverent fingers. "The snake on the crown is missing," he said. "What happened to it?"

"We think it had been broken off before the thief sold it," Ramses explained. "Petherick certainly wouldn't have been so careless."

"It would be good to find it," Daoud said slowly. "The snake has much power."

Ramses laughed and gave him an affectionate slap on the back. "There's not much chance of that, I'm afraid."

After a leisurely breakfast they all headed for the Castle, so that the Vandergelts could participate in the meeting. Ramses had decided to take his father's orders one step further. If Emerson wanted a master plan, with recommendations for future work, that's what he would get, and Cyrus was entitled to express his views.

Seven of them sat down with Cyrus at the table in what Cyrus was pleased to call his conference room: Ramses, his mother, Nefret, Daoud and Selim, Bertie and Jumana. Jumana was her ebullient self, her tendency to dominate the conversation repressed by her awe of the Sitt Hakim.

Emerson would be pleased at the results of the conference, Ramses thought. Unlike a good many excavators, they had kept meticulous records of their progress—photographs, notes, and Bertie's plans. He was the best surveyor of the group, and his skills had been honed by Emerson's demands. There were actually three separate areas at the site: the village of the workmen, their small tombs on the hillside nearby, and the remains of the temples and shrines in which they had worshiped the gods. The tombs were Cyrus's responsibility, and when Ramses looked through his reports he agreed that Cyrus and his crew had covered the area thoroughly. Almost all the tombs had been robbed in antiquity, their grave goods carried off, their small chapels destroyed. What the ancient thieves had missed, modern looters had found and sold to tourists and dealers.

The meeting held only one surprise: Cyrus's announcement that he was considering hiring a new artist. "He called yesterday to ask if there was a position open. Name's Maillet. Ever heard of him?"

"Didn't he work with Newberry at Beni Hassan?" Ramses asked.

Cyrus shook his head. "Can't be the same fellow. This lad is in his early twenties. I told him I'd like to see his portfolio, and he promised to bring it by one day soon. What do you think, Amelia?"

Hers was always the last word with Cyrus. She pursed her lips and looked thoughtful. "If he suits you, I think you should take him on. We could certainly use more help, and we cannot count on David to come out every year. He has other responsibilities now."

Ramses looked at her in astonishment. David hadn't expressed discontent, not even to him, but he knew how difficult it was for his friend to abandon wife and children for several months a year. How did his mother know?

Because she knew everything. She was the Sitt Hakim, the true head of the family. Everyone acknowledged that, even his father.

They joined Katherine for a late luncheon and then the Vandergelts went with them to where their horses were waiting. Walking with Ramses, Bertie slowed his steps till they were some distance behind the others, and Ramses braced himself. He was Bertie's chosen confidant, a role he would rather have refused, since he could offer the disconsolate lover no encouragement. Bertie had set his sights on the pretty Egyptian girl several years ago, but Ramses wouldn't have given much for his chances. Jumana was an ardent feminist and fiercely dedicated to her career, and Bertie's mother had done her best to discourage her son. Katherine had lost most of her prejudice against "colored races," but marriage with her son was a different matter, the last barrier of bigotry, which few Europeans ever overcame.

"Perhaps you've been too assiduous," he suggested. "Try ignoring her for a while, or pay attention to another girl."

"I did try that," Bertie said morosely. "It didn't have the least effect."

"Try again."

"I guess I could." Bertie tried to sound casual. "Is Maryam coming out this year?"

Ramses bit back a caustic comment. Bertie had an absolute gift for falling in love with women his mother considered totally unacceptable. Sethos's daughter Maryam had even more strikes against her than Jumana; she was illegitimate, of what Katherine would call "mixed blood," and the mother of a three-year-old son. Not to mention her earlier connections with a gang of criminals.

"I don't know," he said. "We haven't heard from her or her father for some time. For God's sake, Bertie, can't you find yourself a nice harmless English or American girl? You don't have to marry her, just—er—amuse her for a few months."

"They're all alike," Bertie complained. "Dull, conventional little dolls."

"How about Miss Petherick? She's not dull."

Bertie stared at him in horror. "You're joking. She's a dreadful woman!"

"Yes, I was joking. Not the sort of family one would care to become intimate with."

The others were already mounted and waiting. Bertie stopped and said softly, "The brother. I thought his name was familiar, and now I've remembered. He was an ambulance driver. His ambulance took a direct hit, the wounded he was transporting were blown to smithereens. He got off without a scratch, but . . ."

"Shell shock?"

Bertie grimaced. "I heard they found him crawling along the road, collecting bloody arms and legs and heads and trying to fit them back together."

"Good God."

"So be easy on him."

"I will. Thanks for telling me."

Bertie's story gave him a new sympathy for Adrian Petherick, but it didn't make him any more eager to establish friendly relations—or relations of any kind. He could only hope he would be able to keep his mother away from the Pethericks.

There was one silver lining to his father's absence. It gave them all some uninterrupted time to get on with their own work. The workmen's village had contained masses of written material, some on the scraps of pottery called ostraca, some on papyrus. He had published one book of translations of the Deir el Medina papyri, and was working on a second. Before he excused himself he asked his mother what she intended to do for the remainder of the day. Her answer was a knowing smile. "With your father out of the way, I can work on that article he was supposed to have finished two months ago. Tea at five, as usual, my dear."

It was an implicit promise that she wouldn't go scooting back to Luxor. His father would be furious when he discovered she had finished his article, but insofar as Ramses was concerned, that was definitely the lesser of two evils.

We were not infrequently annoyed by uninvited visitors, most of them total strangers armed with letters of introduction from people we knew only slightly or did not know at all. Glancing from time to time out of the window of my little study, I saw several carriages and persons on donkey-back stop at the completed guardhouse. The structure lacked architectural merit, being only a square of mud brick pierced by a door and several windows with a roof of woven reeds. It was, in fact, as commodious as many of the village houses, and Fatima assured me Wasim was so pleased with his quarters he intended to sleep there. No one interrupted my work, so I assumed Fatima had decided they were intruders and had told Wasim to send them away. I was about to stop for tea when Fatima entered and informed me that two of our archaeological colleagues had dropped by.

"Ask them to stay for tea," I instructed, rising and stretching stiffened limbs. "I will join them as soon as I have freshened up."

"Yes, Sitt." She handed me a small sheaf of calling cards. "These are the ones I told you were not at home."

"Good heavens, so many?" I went quickly through them. None of the names was familiar— but one was that of a representative of a newspaper. "Confound the cursed woman," I said. "I was right about her; it is publicity she is after. She must have told everyone in Luxor about the curse. It was wise of you, Fatima, to suggest we needed a guard."

"Yes, Sitt." I didn't blame her for looking smug.

My guests were Mr. Barton, one of the Metropolitan Museum crew, and an acquaintance of his, whom he introduced as Heinrich Lidman. Barton always put me in mind of a good-natured scarecrow, with his long gangly limbs and shock of sandy hair. His companion was several inches shorter and somewhat stouter. He peered at me through steel-rimmed eyeglasses and at once burst into speech.

"Mrs. Emerson, I cannot tell you what an honor it is to meet you, of whom I have heard so much and with whose work I am of course well acquainted, particularly the excellent excavations conducted by you and your distinguished husband at el Amarna in the—"

"Shut up, Heinrich," Barton said amiably. "You have to interrupt him once he starts talking, or he never stops," he explained to me.

"It is my failing," Lidman admitted sheepishly—and he did rather resemble a sheep, with his long nose and head of tight fair curls. "Excuse me, Mrs. Emerson, I was carried away by—"

"Do sit down, gentlemen," I said, taking Mr. Barton at his word. "Emerson is away, but I expect Ramses and Nefret will join us shortly."

In fact, it was after five and I was surprised at their tardiness. The dear little children were always on time for tea. When my son and daughter-in-law appeared they were alone, and looking a trifle harried.

"Where are the children?" I asked.

"Sent to bed early," Ramses said shortly.

"They misbehaved?"

Ramses nodded. It was not an unusual occurrence, but this misdemeanor must have been serious, since being deprived of tea with the family was the worst punishment in our power. I did not pursue the subject, since we had guests.

Barton was greeted by Ramses and Nefret as the old friend he was. He introduced Mr. Lidman, who began spouting compliments.

"It is an honor, such an honor, Dr. Emerson."

"I don't use the title," Ramses said. "Pleased to meet you, Mr. Lidman. Nice to see you, George."

Fatima brought the tea tray. I dispensed the genial beverage and she offered a plate of cakes, the sight of which brought a greedy glitter to Mr. Lidman's brown eyes.

"I thought for a few minutes you weren't going to see me," said Barton, laughing. "Wasim didn't recognize me at first, kept waving that antique rifle at me. Never known you folks to set a guard before. What's up? Don't tell me those wild stories are true."

Having learned caution from my encounters with the vultures of the press, I replied with another question. "What wild stories are you referring to, Mr. Barton, and from whom did you hear them?"

Eating and drinking kept Mr. Lidman silent while Barton explained that his workmen had been full of the tale that morning. It was as I feared; the news had spread all over Luxor, and our acquisition had been exaggerated to the point of absurdity: jewels, golden statues, vessels of precious metals—a veritable hoard, in fact. I decided it would be advisable to correct these misapprehensions, so I went and got the statuette and explained how it had come to us.

Barton gasped at the sight of it, and Mr. Lidman began babbling. "It is Akhenaton, no doubt of that, and it must have come from his tomb at Thebes, I have long believed that his funerary equipment, barring the sarcophagus, was brought here from Amarna after the city of the Aton was abandoned, and it must have been found by local tomb robbers who, as you know, have made more important discoveries than archaeologists; for example—"

"There are other possibilities," I said. But this was one none of us had proposed, and I made the fatal mistake of asking a direct question. "Where could such a tomb be located?"

Mr. Lidman proceeded to tell us, talking faster and faster, with scarcely a pause to draw breath. Mr. Barton finally took pity on me, and himself, and uttered the magic words.

"Shut up, Heinrich."

Ramses, who had been studying the visitor intently, said, "The West Valley is a possibility, I suppose; the tombs of Akhenaton's father and one of his immediate successors are there, as you pointed out, Mr. Lidman. You seem very familiar with the Amarna period."

"I worked at the site before the war." For once, Mr. Lidman's loquacity had deserted him. He looked sadly at his empty plate.

"With Borchardt?" Ramses asked.

"Yes. You would not know my name, of course. It has been some years since I published anything, and since the war I have been unable . . ." He looked up; something he saw in our faces encouraged him to go on. "To speak truth, I am looking for another position. I know the language, I have had experience in excavation under one of the best, I speak Arabic and am accustomed to dealing with native workmen . . ."

"Am I to understand that you are applying for a position with us?" I asked, taking pity on the poor man. I did feel sorry for him. The war had interrupted many promising careers, some of them ended forever.

"I will accept any position, however humble, if not with you, perhaps with Mr. Cyrus Vandergelt. I know the influence you have with him . . ."

His imploring eyes were fixed on Ramses, as if his decision were the only one that mattered. Just like a man, I thought.

My son had also been moved by the fellow's

obvious need. Like many who had risked their lives during the conflict, he bore no grudge against former enemies. They had all been victims of the arrogance and stupidity of their leaders.

"My father is the one who makes such decisions," Ramses said. "I will speak to him about you when he returns."

"Thank you. Thank you. I will be forever grateful."

It had been an awkward interlude, and I was thankful when George Barton changed the subject. Holding up the statuette, he said, "If this was bought from a dealer, it could have originated anywhere in Egypt. Right, Mrs. Emerson?"

"Quite right," I said. "The most logical way of tracing its origin is through the dealer from whom it was purchased. Mrs. Petherick claims she does not know his name, and I am inclined to believe her, since she is a silly woman and keeps rambling on about curses."

Realizing I was beginning to sound like Mr. Lidman, I stopped myself and offered the gentlemen another cup of tea.

"Thank you, ma'am, but we must be getting back," Barton said. "Sorry to have missed the Professor, but we'll be seeing him soon, I hope."

"Yes, yes," Mr. Lidman said. "It will be an honor. I trust you have a safe hiding place for this remarkable object. Every thief in Luxor will be after it."

"No one would dare rob the Father of Curses," Barton said with a grin. "That's one of Daoud's sayings, and it's right on the mark. Do let us know, ma'am, if the Professor plans to perform one of his notorious—er—famous exorcisms."

After our visitors had left, I asked Nefret what crime the children had been guilty of. "I presume it was Carla—as usual."

"Carla was the instigator," Nefret said with a sigh. "Honestly, Mother, I sometimes think that temper of hers will be the death of me. She tore up the drawing David John was making as a welcome-home present for Father. He'd been working on it for hours—beautiful little colored hieroglyphs and a picture of a cat."

"Then why did you punish David John?"

"Because he punched her square in the face," said Ramses. He had had time to calm down, and I thought I detected a tone of unwilling amusement. "Her nose started to bleed, and then David John burst into tears. It was quite noisy. Carla howled and David John hugged her and said he was sorry, and she said she was sorry, and they ended up smeared with tears and blood."

"Good heavens," I said weakly.

"It was just a nosebleed," Nefret assured me. "But David John must learn that there is no excuse whatsoever for physical violence, and Carla must learn to leave other people's property alone."

"Quite right," I said. "But they are only four."

Ramses smiled affectionately. "Spoken like a true grandmother. We'll make it up with them after dinner, Mother."

Conversation during that meal returned to the subject of our new acquaintance. "Are you going to recommend him to your father?" I asked Ramses.

"I can think of no reason not to. I believe I recall hearing his name mentioned as a competent excavator. You keep saying we need more staff."

"We do. The difficulty will be getting your father to admit it."

After he and Nefret had said good night I worked on Emerson's article for a time, but found myself yawning. His academic style is not electrifying (most academic style is not) and I had had a disturbed night. Finally I gave it up and sought my lonely couch.

I dreamed, not of Abdullah, but of Emerson. He was strolling through the narrow streets of the Khan el Khalili, dressed in Bedouin robes and holding aloft a golden statue. A rock whistled past his head. Emerson ducked and went on. A shot rang out. It missed him by a scant inch. Emerson went on. I called out to him, but my voice was no louder than a kitten's mew. I **was** a kitten, scrambling at his heels, clawing at the skirts of his robe, in a vain attempt to attract his attention. A woman, scantily clad and veiled, slipped out of a doorway and threw her arms around him. Superbly oblivious, Emerson went on. The perfume shop just ahead of him collapsed with a crash, showering the street with broken glass bottles. I cried out . . .

And woke, perspiring and shaking. The sound had not been a dream. The echoes still reverberated.

I sprang from bed and rushed to the window that overlooked the veranda and the road. A cloud of dust, pale in the moonlight, rose above the ruins of the guardhouse.

I was not the only one to be awakened by the catastrophe. As I reached the front door, hastily fastening the sash of my dressing gown, I saw Ramses running toward me. He carried a torch—something I had not thought to do—and was trying to button his trousers—his only garment—one-handed. "Mother, are you all right?"

"Yes, yes. The guardhouse has collapsed. Hurry."

Mud brick is not the most stable of building materials. Only one wall was standing. The rest of the structure was now a heap of rubble, strewn with the reeds that had formed the roof. And under it somewhere, I feared, was Wasim.

"God Almighty," Ramses breathed. "Here, Mother, take the torch."

He fell to his knees and began tossing bricks aside. I was about to go to his assistance when we were joined by other members of the household. They all pitched in with a will and before long they were rewarded by the sight of a groping hand. The rescuers cheered and had soon cleared the body of the unfortunate watchman. He was lying facedown. Nefret, who had been the last to join us, caught Ramses by the arm as he was about to turn the poor fellow over onto his back. "Don't move him yet. Wasim, can you hear me?"

She ran expert hands over his limbs and body. "Is it you, Sitt Hakim?" said a muffled voice. "Am I dead?"

Obviously he wasn't, but we had some difficulty convincing him. According to Nefret, he had got off easily, with only cuts and bruises. Nevertheless, we removed him carefully to a stretcher and she went with him to the clinic.

Not until that moment, when anxiety was relieved, did I have leisure to think the matter through. How could the building have collapsed? It had not been designed to last forever, but the men had had long experience, and they would not have taken a chance on shoddy construction. Looking about me, I saw that every servant in the house was there. And that meant . . .

"Ramses," I said urgently. "Is anyone on guard?"

"Dammit," said Ramses.

He moved too fast for me in my trailing garment. When I reached Emerson's study, Ramses had found Emerson's keys and was in the act of unlocking one of the desk drawers. With a long sigh of relief, he removed the painted box and lifted the lid.

"It's safe," I exclaimed. "A false alarm."

"No. Someone has been here." He indicated a set of dusty footprints that ran back and forth across the floor. They were those of bare feet.

"Not yours?" I asked.

"Those are mine." He indicated a single line of prints, narrower and longer than the others.

We followed the intruder's prints along the hall. They led into Emerson's and my sleeping chamber.

"He came here first," Ramses muttered. "He looked under the bed and in the drawers of the chest. One of them is still partly open. Unless you—"

"I am never so untidy. It was a quick and somewhat superficial search. He knew he couldn't count on much time. Finding nothing here, he went to your father's study."

"He heard us coming and fled before he had a chance to search thoroughly," Ramses finished. "Which means he didn't know precisely where it was hidden. Let's see which way he went."

The dusty prints faded out in the corridor, but it was not difficult to deduce that the intruder had come in through the courtyard and left the same way.

"Hell and damnation." Ramses ran his fingers through his disheveled hair, dislodging a shower of sandy dust. "He didn't leave a single clue. As Father would say, this is getting monotonous."

FROM MANUSCRIPT H

The children had been awakened by the commotion, and were indignant at Elia for not letting them join in the fun.

"It was not fun," Ramses said sternly. "Wasim might have been badly hurt."

Carla looked ashamed, and David John considered the comment. "We should not be angry with Elia. She did what you told her to do."

"So it's my fault?" Ramses inquired, tucking the blankets around his son.

"You acted for what you believed to be the best," David John conceded. "Was it an unfortunate accident, or an attempt at distraction?"

Silently Ramses cursed his son's precocity. He tried to avoid lying to the children, so he phrased the answer with some care. "We don't know yet. Now go to sleep."

He kissed them both good night and left, knowing full well that his attempt at equivocation would be a failure. They'd hear the whole story, and a number of wild theories, from the servants.

Instead of going to Deir el Medina next day, they conducted another kind of excavation. The rubble had been disturbed by their frantic attempts to free Wasim, but close examination, of the sort Emerson would have approved, confirmed Ramses's suspicion that the sturdily built structure couldn't have been brought down by anything less than a battering ram or an explosive charge. They found a few fragments of a stick of dynamite and, some distance away, traces of the fuse.

Dynamite wasn't hard to come by. (Nothing was, in Egypt, if you knew where to go.) Examination of the blackened, fragmented bricks at what had been the northeast corner indicated that the effect of the blast had been limited to that area. The collapse of the rest of the building had followed, but it might not have been intended.

"It was lucky for Wasim that he was sleeping near the door," said Selim, brushing powder off his hands. "But this is not good, Ramses. We must question the men of Gurneh and find out who has an alibi."

Ramses smiled and clapped him on the shoulder. "You are getting to be quite a detective, Selim, but I doubt that line of investigation will get us anywhere. I photographed the clearest of the footprints this morning, but that is probably a forlorn hope too. The fellow wasn't missing a toe or anything useful of that sort."

"All the same, we will ask," Selim said. "How is Wasim?"

"Enjoying a nice rest and all of Fatima's food he can eat. Nefret treated his bruises and scrapes and told him he could go home, but he says he's too weak to move."

"We must find another guard," Selim declared. "And rebuild the house."

"I'll leave it to you, then. There's no use going to Deir el Medina today."

He went back to his papyri. He felt slightly guilty, though he knew he wasn't needed. From time to time he went to the window and looked out. Selim had a dozen men at work setting up a temporary structure of poles and canvas, and making new bricks. Their aggressive presence was enough to deter the few curiosity seekers whose carriages approached.

When they met for luncheon his mother was sorting through the messages that had arrived. "Nothing from the Pethericks?" Ramses asked.

"No. I am somewhat surprised. Mrs. Petherick must be getting bored."

The communication came that afternoon, in the form of a hand-delivered message. David John, who had learned to read at an alarmingly early age, was poring over a book and Ramses was playing tag with Carla when his mother joined them in the garden. "Where is Nefret?" she asked.

"She has a patient." Ramses took the note from her and eluded his daughter by pulling himself up into a tree. Ignoring Carla's enraged, and justified, shrieks of "Not fair. Not fair!" he read the message.

"You're right, Carla," he said, dropping back to the ground. "I cheated, so I lose. You win. Now run along and clean up for tea. Papa has to go out for a little while."

"Fatima has made a plum cake," his mother added.

"Are you going out too?" Carla demanded.

Her grandmother smoothed the little girl's ruffled black curls. "Yes."

Carla weighed the advantages and disadvantages, her dark eyebrows drawn together in a thoughtful frown. David John had already reached the logical conclusion: With only the indulgent Fatima to supervise their tea, the entire plum cake would be theirs. He closed his book, gave his grandmother a quick hug, and trotted off toward the house, followed by Carla.

Ramses picked up the coat he had tossed on a bench, and his mother said, "I am glad you agree that we must go. Mrs. Petherick sounds on the verge of hysteria. If we don't turn up before dark, heaven knows what she'll do."

Ramses looked again at the note. The ragged handwriting was certainly suggestive of shaken nerves and shaking hands. " 'He will come for me at nightfall. For the love of God, hurry!' "

"I agree that you have determined we must go," he said. "It must have struck you, Mother, that this frantic appeal has the same calculated air as her earlier performances. I was under the impression that you considered the entire business a publicity stunt."

"Life is seldom so simple as that," said his mother sententiously. She took his arm and led him, gently but inexorably, along the path. "People are capable of incredible feats of self-delusion, as we see in cases of hypochondria. Mrs. Petherick may have convinced herself that the menace is real, in order to justify her actions in her own mind, and—"

"Yes, Mother."

She was right, but her complacent smile and the briskness of her stride betrayed her real motive. It had been a forlorn hope that he could keep her from meddling in the Petherick affair.

They paused only long enough to collect Nefret, who had finished with her patients. By the time they reached the riverbank and had selected a boat to take them across, the sun was low in the west. Its slanting rays brightened the splendid columns of the Luxor Temple and, in incongruous juxtaposition, the modern facade of the Winter Palace Hotel. They hurried up the stairs from the quay to the street. As they waited to cross, Ramses referred again to the note.

"She asks us to come directly to her room. She's afraid to open the door, she says!" He took his mother's arm. With the skill of long practice they wound their way through the procession of camels, donkeys, and carriages that filled the street.

"Which room?" Nefret asked, looking up at the long facade of the hotel. The first floor, with the lobby and reception rooms, was reached by a pair of opposed curving stairs; guest rooms were on the second and third floors, with the ground floor reserved for storage and service areas.

"Three fifty-two and -three," Ramses said. "A suite. It's the one at that end."

"The one with the balcony? I'm surprised she didn't . . . Oh, good Lord! What's that?"

There was no mistaking what it was, despite its distance from the ground. Sunset shone with theatrical intensity on the stone balustrade of the balcony and the form leaning over it. Man-high, shrouded, dead black, it seemed to drink the sun's rays. As they stared in disbelief, the shape slowly bent forward and fell, forty feet, toward the terrace below.

Ramses shook off his wife's hand and went up the stairs three at a time. People in the lobby turned to stare as he ran past. He didn't wait for the lift, which was uncertain at best, but headed straight up the staircase. He reached the third floor and ran full tilt along the long corridor, damning the architect of the Winter Palace for wasting so much space on staircases and passageways. Most of the guests were at tea, on the terraces or in the tearoom; only a few soft-footed servants stared as he passed.

Mrs. Petherick's suite was at the end of a right-angle turn in the corridor. As Ramses knew from visits to other friends, her two rooms were reached through a small antechamber which gave greater privacy to the occupant of the suite. In front of the closed door of the antechamber stood Abdul, one of the hotel servants, tricked out in a red fez, a gold-braided jacket, and inauthentic but picturesque baggy trousers. Ramses cut short his cheerful "Salaam aleikhum" and pounded on the door, calling out her name and his own. No answer, no sound at all from within. He turned to the servant. "Is the lady not here?"

"She has not come out, Brother of Demons." Abdul thought for a few seconds and then proudly came up with a conclusion. "So—she must still be there, yes? She gave me much baksheesh and told me to let no one in. No one at all except you or the Sitt Hakim or—"

The door wasn't locked. Thinking she might be cowering in the closet or bathroom, Ramses hammered even harder on one of the inner doors, the one that led to the sitting room. Still no answer.

"What's she playing at?" he demanded. There was no answer from Abdul, who knew the question hadn't been addressed to him. Ramses realized he had no choice but to play along, but he would have a few words to say to the confounded woman when he located her.

The inner door wasn't locked either. The tall French doors to the balcony stood open, the filmy curtains blew in the breeze. A blazing, bloody sunset reddened the sky. The room was in perfect order, and so were the adjoining bedchamber and bath. Mrs. Petherick's garments filled the wardrobe, her toilet articles were laid out on the dressing table, but the lady herself was nowhere to be found.

THREE

It was an empty robe," I said. "There was nothing inside. I realized that at once, naturally, from the way it fluttered down."

Yes." Ramses was pacing up and down Mrs. Petherick's sitting room, picking up objects at random as if hoping to find something he had overlooked. "How many of the damned things does the damned woman own?"

"Several, I expect. She favors black, and it is a popular color for evening cloaks and wraps."

Nefret and I had hastened upstairs as soon as we had made certain we did not have to deal with a mangled body. I spread the garment out across the back of the sofa. It was similar to the one the intruder had abandoned at our house, though not identical; the first had been of corded silk, while this was of a heavier velvet, trimmed across the shoulders with jet beads. In the inconsequential way it does sometimes, my mind wandered off into speculation about what this garment was supposed to suggest. Undefined powers of evil? The notorious Prince of Darkness? It was not Egyptian, ancient or modern. However, those who believe in evil spirits are not prone to logical ratiocination.

We searched the suite again, finding no more than Ramses had. Nothing was missing, so far as we could tell. Before long we were joined by Mr. Salt. The manager of a large hotel is not easily rattled, but Mr. Salt was not a happy man. His guests had informed him that a dead body had been thrown from a third-floor window or balcony. Or, according to one imaginative witness, from an invisible hand in the heavens above the hotel. He requested—his voice only a little tremulous—that we tell him what we knew of the matter.

Our assurance that there was no dead body cheered him quite a lot. "Then the police will not have to be called," he said, wiping his perspiring brow.

"Not yet," I replied.

"Not yet? But Mrs. Emerson, if there is no body—"

"That is the difficulty, you see," I explained. "Mrs. Petherick's living body is not here either. She seems to have disappeared."

"Forgive me, Mother, but that conclusion is a trifle premature," said my son. "There may be a perfectly innocent explanation for her absence.

We must question the other guests, and Mrs. Petherick's son and daughter, and her maidservant."

"She did not bring an attendant with her," Mr. Salt said. "One of the hotel maids waited on her when she required assistance. But I am sure there is, as you say, a perfectly innocent explanation!"

"You have no objection to our conducting an inquiry?" I asked.

"I would be infinitely obliged if you would, Mrs. Emerson."

Mrs. Petherick was not in the dining salon or the other public rooms. The concierge had not seen her, nor had she left her key at the desk. The keys had large, heavy bronze tags attached, so it was unlikely she would take hers with her, even supposing she had suddenly changed her mind and gone out without leaving a message for us. Adrian and Harriet Petherick were not in the hotel. They had left their keys, but no one knew where they had gone. The hotel maid was so unnerved at being questioned she could only dither and deny knowledge of any kind. We decided to postpone further investigation. Questioning all the hotel guests would take hours, and was likely to produce as much imaginative fiction as fact. Had I not known this from my previous acquaintance with criminal investigations, it would have been brought home to me when we attempted to make our way across the lobby. As soon as we emerged from the lift we were surrounded by a curious crowd, all asking questions, some claiming to have vital information. I was forced to employ my parasol in order to pass through, and one importunate fellow, who had announced himself as a journalist, followed us all the way to the dock.

We took our places in the boat. It was a beautiful night, as most nights in Luxor are; moonlight rippled along the water and the stars were bright. I glanced at my watch. "Late again. Fatima will be wroth."

"And Maaman will be weeping into the soup," Nefret said. "Well, Mother, what do you make of this?"

"There are only two possible explanations," I said, settling myself more comfortably on the cushioned bench. "Either Mrs. Petherick left of her own accord or she was carried away against her will."

"How could anyone carry her off without being seen?" Ramses demanded. "Abdul isn't the brightest lad in Egypt, but even he would have noticed a man encumbered with a struggling, screaming woman—or even an unconscious woman, who was, to put it tactfully, a well-rounded armful."

"You noticed that, did you?" Nefret murmured. "Perhaps he lied."

"Not to me. Oh, hell," Ramses said, running his fingers through his windblown hair. "I didn't mean that the way it sounded. If he had been threatened or extravagantly bribed he wouldn't have been able to greet me so unselfconsciously, or look me in the eye. He's terrified of Father. Anyhow, he's an honest man, in his fashion. No, Mother. The lady has pulled another stunt. She had plenty of time to get out and away before I reached her room."

"Leaving everything she owned?"

"Packing a suitcase would have spoiled the effect," Ramses said.

"But then honest Abdul must have lied when he said she had not come out of her room."

"Not necessarily. He wasn't smack in front of her door the whole time; he admitted he'd left his post once or twice or, yes, Brother of Demons, perhaps more often, to sneak a cigarette with one of the other men or answer a call of nature. She could have got past him if she was quick and careful. A kidnapper couldn't have done."

In my opinion he was now jumping to conclusions. Admittedly his was the most obvious interpretation, but clever criminals are capable of ingenious schemes. If the villain had been disguised as a servant and Mrs. Petherick as a rug or bag of laundry . . . I decided not to pursue the subject, since Ramses was in a rare state of exasperation.

"I wonder if we should notify your father of this latest development," I said.

"Why bother? He'll read about it in the Cairo newspapers tomorrow."

"Oh, good Gad. I suppose he will, won't he? He isn't going to like this at all."

"Particularly," said Ramses, "when he reads the comments we made to the press."

"But we didn't say anything," I protested. "Except that those who had information should give it to Mr. Salt."

"That won't prevent the journalists from quoting us," said Ramses.

"I wonder what Abdullah would say about all this," I mused.

"Have you dreamed about him lately?" Ramses's voice was studiously noncommittal. The family was still skeptical about those strange dreams, but they were more than dreams to me, so realistic that they were like seeing my dear departed friend in the flesh. He had given his life for mine, acting as instinctively as a father who throws himself in front of a threatened child. He had loved me as I had learned to love him; but that act of supreme sacrifice had also been his way of taking his fate into his own hands, defying the god who threatened him with the failing strength of old age.

"Not lately," I said.

Nefret smiled affectionately. "At least he won't complain that we have a new corpse on our hands. Remember what he used to say? 'Every year, another dead body!'"

Every year, another dead body!" said Abdullah. He came striding along his usual path, the one from the Valley of the Kings. My route had led me up the steep slope of the cliffs behind Deir el Bahri, and as the sun rose behind me, my shadow rushed forth as if to greet him.

"What do you mean?" I demanded. "We haven't had any dead bodies this year. You might say 'hello' before you start complaining," I added.

He never did, though. I suppose that to him, in this place where there was no time, it was as if we had spoken together only moments before. He smiled sardonically and stroked his beard. It had been pure white the day he died in my arms. In these dreams it was black, and his face was that of a young, hearty man.

"Not yet, Sitt," he said.

"Who?" I demanded. "Not Emerson? Not Ramses? Not—"

"I cannot tell you the future. It is yet to be determined. But is there not always a dead body? Always you look for danger, Sitt."

"If you are referring to Mrs. Petherick and her statue, she came to us, not we to her. And what danger can there be? She is a silly woman who invents foolish stories."

"The statue is not invented."

"Where did it come from, Abdullah?"

He rolled his eyes and smiled. "From the last place you would expect, Sitt."

"I might have known you wouldn't give me a direct answer! Not Amarna, not Tomb 55?"

His teasing smile vanished. He came a step closer and put out his hand, as if to touch my cheek. "Sitt, heed my words. Stop seeking trouble, rest in the shade and be at peace. As it was for me, so it is for you. Do not the days grow shorter, the paths longer, the loads heavier?"

The words fell like stones onto my heart and the sky seemed to darken; but I shook my head and spoke resolutely. "All the more reason to make the most of the shorter days and brace one's strength to bear the heavier loads. I never expected to hear such talk from you, you whose strength and courage never failed."

"Ah," said Abdullah. "I knew you would say that."

A ray of sunlight brightened his smiling face and I said in exasperation, "What I want from you is practical advice—not that I ever get it! If you won't tell me where the statue was found, at least give me a hint."

"I have," said Abdullah, stroking his beard. "And now I will give you another. Once before, not long ago, you asked me a similar question and I answered it. Remember that question and that answer, Sitt."

He turned and walked away. I stamped my foot with annoyance. Over the years I had asked many questions; the answers I had got were, to say the least, enigmatic. I had not the least idea which of those questions he meant.

If I had entertained any expectation of going out next day, I abandoned it as soon as I went to the veranda after breakfast and saw the people who were gathered round the temporary guardhouse. Our new guard, Daoud's son Hassan, stood foursquare in the center of the road, Wasim's antiquated rifle in his hands; and I believe the sight of the weapon (which I devoutly hoped was not loaded) was the only thing that prevented some of the curiosity seekers from skirting the guardhouse and coming at us from one side or the other.

To be honest—which I always endeavor to be—I became increasingly restless as the morning wore on. I was itching to know what was happening in Luxor: whether Mrs. Petherick had turned up, whether any new information had been learned, and what her children thought of it all. After surveying the scene with a particularly stony expression, Ramses had strictly forbidden me to leave the house—or rather, since he knows me well, he had strongly suggested that I follow his advice on the matter. I agreed (while reserving the right to act otherwise should the situation change) and he went off, declaring that he meant to spend the day working on the hieratic papyri we had found in such numbers. The Egyptian language was Ramses's specialty and major interest, and he had fallen behind on his translations.

My thoughts strayed to my conversation with Abdullah. He had been as annoyingly mysterious as usual, and there was nothing new in his lecture about my habit of looking for trouble, as he called it. But this was the first time he had had the temerity to hint that I was getting too old for such adventures! He ought to have known that would only spur me on.

Perhaps that was why the old rascal had done it. Not that I needed any such inspiration. Like Abdullah, I would be the master of my own fate. A swift and honorable death, particularly if it were in the service of a loved one, was preferable to slow decay of mind and body.

What the devil had he meant by that last "hint," as he called it? I tried to recall the many conversations I had had with him. He had often told me that time had no meaning in the afterworld; what had seemed years to me might have been only a few moments to him. We had spoken of many things; try as I might, I could not call to mind any reference to Amarna or Akhenaton.

After Nefret had tended to the patients who had turned up that morning—an infected toe and a case of ophthalmia—she joined me on the veranda, admitting that she was unable to emulate her husband's lack of curiosity.

"Who are all those people?" she asked, accepting a cup of coffee from Fatima. "Don't they have anything better to do?"

"Many people lead lives of crushing boredom," I said. "They are so lacking in imagination and intelligence they don't even realize how bored they are until something like this happens. That flashily dressed lady and gentleman in the carriage, for instance—I think I remember meeting them last year. Idle, uninformed members of the aristocracy."

"Who is that fellow in the shooting jacket and broad-brimmed hat?"

"A journalist," I said with a sniff. "No, I don't know him, but I can spot the villains a mile away. Goodness, I do believe the fellow is offering Hassan a bribe!"

"He is probably not the first to do so. Hassan knows better."

"Wasim knows better too, but I wouldn't be at all surprised to discover he extracted a sizable amount of baksheesh from various people."

"By promising to deliver messages, which you had instructed him to do anyhow? So that's why he is now anxious to return to his duties. One would have supposed that having a house collapse on him would put him off the job."

"Greed is a motive strong enough to overcome cowardice," I remarked. "Curse it, look at all those people. I wish . . ."

"That you could find out what is going on? So do I," Nefret admitted. "But we daren't risk leaving the house. We would be surrounded."

"I had thought of borrowing a robe and headcloth from Fatima and going just as far as the guardhouse."

"Somehow that doesn't surprise me. Please

don't, Mother. I have a feeling that before long we will hear from either Miss Petherick or Cyrus."

It was neither of the above who came first. I was a trifle surprised when I saw Hassan stand back and try to hide the rifle behind his back. Then I recognized the man who came walking up the road—taller than most Egyptians, his white uniform crisp, his close-cropped black beard framing a keen dark face. A wise man does not argue with the chief of the Luxor police, especially this one. Ibrahim Ayyid was still young, but in the past few years he had acquired a reputation for strict discipline and fair dealing.

With an exclamation of pleasure, Nefret went to the door to admit him and offered her hand. He bowed over it and greeted me in military fashion, clicking his heels and inclining his head.

"I apologize for the intrusion," he began.

"Not at all," Nefret replied. "In fact, you have saved our lives, Mr. Ayyid. We were both dying of curiosity."

I asked Fatima to bring fresh coffee and Ayyid eyed us quizzically. "As I understand it, you have been involved in the case from the beginning. You were at the hotel last night. That is the reason for my visit, to request information from you."

"Not until after you have given us the latest

news," I said, smiling to indicate it was just one of my little jokes. "Has Mrs. Petherick returned?"

"No. Mrs. Petherick's children insist that she has been abducted, and the police, as well as the British authorities, have been asked to assist in the search for her."

He took out a notebook and pencil, and opened the former.

"This is an official visit, then?" I inquired.

"Yes, madam."

"You can count on our full cooperation, of course," I declared. "The Professor is in Cairo, but my son is here. Nefret, will you go and tell Ramses he is wanted?"

I noticed that Mr. Ayyid's black eyes followed Nefret's slim form as she left the room. They had a look of wistfulness quite alien to his normal keen gaze. The two had not often met socially, for Mr. Ayyid had consistently if courteously refused our invitations, but he had called upon her on several occasions to assist in identification of remains. Meeting under such circumstances would not seem conducive to the development of tender feelings, but it was obvious to me, for I am sensitive to such things, that he had conceived a great admiration for her. Being a gentleman and devoutly religious, he would never tell her so.

What he needed was a wife. Daoud had a grand-daughter, a pretty girl of seventeen, who had attended Miss Whiteside's school in Luxor . . .

Ayyid shifted position, and I realized I had been staring rudely as my thoughts wandered. "I may as well give you the background," I said. "It will save time in the end. This business began when Mrs. Petherick called upon us two days ago."

I had not got far before Ramses and Nefret came in. Fatima brought more coffee and a plate of buns. She hadn't been asked to do so, but she was looking for an excuse to listen in on the con-versation. I continued my account, up to and including our search of Mrs. Petherick's rooms the previous night, and then invited Mr. Ayyid's comments.

"It is a strange story," he said slowly.

"Not so strange, if one considers Mrs. Pethe-rick's probable motive," said Ramses. "The whole thing is a hoax, designed to bring her publicity and promote the sale of her books."

"Then you are not of the opinion that she was abducted?" Ayyid asked. He looked at Nefret, but it was Ramses who answered.

"I believe she stole out of her room, unseen by Abdul, and in disguise. You know the arrange-ment of her suite, sir. There is an outer door, lead-ing to a small vestibule; with two inner doors, one on the right leading to the bedchamber and the other, opposite the outer door, leading to the sitting room. She may even have waited in the bedchamber until Abdul and I were in the sitting room and then slipped out."

Ayyid made a note. "Several of the guests claim to have seen a tall figure robed in black descending the stairs," he said dryly.

"I am not surprised," said Ramses with equal dryness. "There was no such figure. She threw the empty robe over the balcony."

Nefret leaned forward. "What did Mr. and Miss Petherick have to say? Surely they don't believe their stepmother was carried off by a supernatural demon."

Mr. Ayyid did not point out, as he might have done, that he was supposed to be the one asking the questions. "They claim she was abducted by someone who wanted the statue. How valuable is it?"

"Quite valuable," Ramses said. "But that is an absurd suggestion. Mrs. Petherick didn't have the statuette in her possession; we did."

"Who was aware of that?"

"Everybody in Luxor, I should think," Ramses replied.

"And there have been several attempts to break into your house," Ayyid said sternly. "Why did you not inform the police of these incidents?"

"We prefer to deal with such things ourselves," I said. Mr. Ayyid's expression strongly suggested that he disapproved of this point of view. I was about to elaborate, reminding him of our long experience in criminal matters, when Ramses got in ahead of me.

"There was no harm done, sir, and no danger of harm. Only a fool would believe he could locate a hidden object without a prolonged search and the risk of—"

He broke off abruptly. Ayyid's eyes narrowed.

"But Mr. Adrian Petherick is not a sensible man, is he? And he is obviously obsessed with retrieving the statue."

"He's not such a fool as to risk something like that," Ramses said. "He knows my father intends to return the statue to Mrs. Petherick; he heard him say so."

"She is the legal owner?"

"We assume so."

"But you don't know for certain?"

"We are unacquainted with the terms of Mr. Petherick's will," Ramses said. "If you believe that question is relevant, you are in a better position to determine the answer than we."

"Perhaps." Mr. Ayyid made another note. "Can you describe the first intruder?"

"He had gone by the time Ramses arrived," I

said, since Ramses was looking somewhat put out. "I saw only his legs disappearing over the wall. He wore European trousers. Ali claims he was tall and formidably strong, but I do not believe we can rely on that assessment."

"I would like to question Ali Yussuf."

"Feel free to do so, but you won't get much out of him. It was dark and he was dozing."

"And on the second occasion? You would not say no harm was intended that time."

"It may be that there was no intention of causing serious injury," Ramses said. "The primary purpose was to get us out of the house so that the fellow could conduct another search."

"Hmmm." Ayyid looked skeptical. "No one caught even a glimpse of the criminal?"

Ramses explained about the footprints. "We haven't had a chance to develop the film yet. I will make sure you see them, but I admit there was nothing distinctive about them."

"Bare feet," Ayyid said thoughtfully. "Any man can take off his shoes."

"May I ask why you are putting such emphasis on this affair instead of pursuing the search for Mrs. Petherick?" I inquired.

My critical tone did not disconcert Ayyid. He closed his notebook and rose. "I would do so, Mrs. Emerson, if I had the slightest idea of where to look. However, at this moment we have no evidence that her disappearance can be considered a criminal matter. Should you hear anything, I hope you will forgo your normal habits and communicate with . . . Allahu Akhbar! What is that?"

He had not seen it coming. We had; but we were so thunderstruck and its progress was so rapid we had no time to react—a large tawny beast, moving in great bounds like those of the lion it resembled. Behind it was Daoud, waving his arms and uttering broken ejaculations. Behind Daoud the curiosity seekers scattered in all directions, shrieking and shouting. The beast rose on its hind legs and threw itself at the screened door with a force that made that structure shudder. It began to howl.

I must confess that even I recoiled. All I could think of was the Countess Magda's tales of vampires and werewolves. Then Daoud came charging up. He was too out of breath to speak at first; he grabbed hold of the creature's collar and forced it down. It immediately collapsed at his feet, rolled over, and waved four enormous paws.

Ramses was the first to recover himself. "I said a dog, Daoud, not a lioness! Where on earth did you—"

"It is a dog, Brother of Demons," Daoud panted. "A fine dog, a gentle dog. And you hear how loud it can bark!"

Fatima had fled into the house. Opening the door a crack, she cried, "Daoud, you are a crazy man. We cannot have that creature near the children."

"We'll see," said Nefret. "Bring it in, Daoud."

Daoud raised the creature to its feet and led it in, maintaining a firm grip on its collar. There was a moment of suspense, while the dog looked from one of us to the other, with an expression of intense interest. I could not but suspect it was considering which throat to tear out first, but in this case I was wrong and Nefret, who had advanced to meet it, was right. She had always had a knack with animals of all species. The dog dropped at her feet and repeated its performance of submission, paws flopping, tail thrashing. Nefret scratched the great jaws.

"You see? It's perfectly harmless," she said.

"You could put your hand in its mouth," said Daoud proudly. "It belongs to Mohammed ibn Rashid, from Gurneh. He has eight children, and they pull its ears and ride it like a pony. He is happy to give it to you."

"What is its name?" Nefret asked.

Daoud looked blank. Only domestic pets have names, and pets as such are a luxury in a country where a man must struggle to feed his children. Veterinarian medicine is almost nonexistent, even if the ordinary fellah could afford it. Now that I examined the dog more closely, I saw its ribs were too prominent, and that there were untended sores on various parts of its body. Wriggling with pleasure, the dog sat up and leaned heavily against Nefret's lower limbs, lifting its head to invite additional caresses.

"I shall call her Amira," Nefret said.

"She does not look like a princess," said the voice of Fatima, still behind the door.

"She will, when I've fed her up and tended to her," Nefret said. "And when she gets her full growth."

"You mean she is not full grown?" I exclaimed. "How large is she likely to get?"

Nefret laughed. "Goodness only knows. But she's barely out of the awkward puppy stage. Look at the size of those paws, and at her teeth." Unconcernedly she pried the dog's jaws apart. The teeth certainly looked healthy.

Fatima opened the door a little wider, and out came the Great Cat of Re. He stopped and stared. His huge plumy tail began to switch back and forth. Then he marched up to the dog and smacked it across the nose. The dog lay down and covered its head with its paws. The Great Cat of Re swaggered to the settee, jumped up, and began cleaning his foot.

Nefret led Amira off toward the clinic, and I

said, "Well, Daoud, it seems the creature is as docile as you claimed. But why did she fling herself at the door?"

"She wanted to come in," said Daoud.

Looking a trifle bemused, Mr. Ayyid took his leave and the rest of us sat down for an enjoyable gossip—Daoud's specialty. It was sometimes necessary to winnow the grains of truth from the chaff of rumor, but his report was a good deal more entertaining than the terse comments of Mr. Ayyid. He had got the news of Luxor from his son Sabir, who operated a popular boat service to the East Bank, and the views of the West Bank villagers during his visits to friends early that morning. Contrary to what some might believe, the supposedly enlightened European and American tourists were as given to wild superstition as the fellahin of the West Bank.

"Many ladies in the hotel saw the black afrit last night, walking in the hall or looking in their windows," Daoud explained.

"That's a good name for it." Ramses leaned back, hands folded. He was devoted to Daoud, but sometimes he was unable to resist egging him on. "But, Daoud, why would the afrit hang about the hotel after it had carried Mrs. Petherick off? She didn't even have the statue; she had given it to us."

Daoud considered this. "Once an afrit has been

freed to do evil deeds, it will go on doing them until it has finished the task for which it came."

"That is eminently logical," Ramses said gravely. "However, we can't return the statue to its owner, since we don't know where it came from."

"The Father of Curses can send the afrit away," Daoud said. "The villagers wish to know when he will do that. They all want to come and watch."

"I'll speak to Father," Ramses promised.

"No, you will not," I said. "Daoud, have you and Selim learned anything about where and when the statue was found? He meant to question the dealers and the better-known tomb robbers."

Daoud shook his head. "No one has admitted to finding such a thing. But we will go on asking."

After Daoud had departed, Ramses said, "I doubt Selim will come up with anything useful. We've a better chance of tracing the thing if we start with Petherick and the dealer from whom he purchased it. Father means to pursue that line of inquiry while he's in Cairo."

"That isn't all he means to do. You know what he's up to, don't you?"

"I'm beginning to think I do."

We sat in silence for a time, and then I said, "How are your translations coming along?"

Ramses's face lit up, as it always did when someone had the common courtesy to ask about the work that interested him most. "Very well, Mother. I've been working on a group of ostraca we found near the temple—prayers for forgiveness, one might call them. They cover a long period of time, and since only a few are dated, one must rely on textual evidence and linguistic changes to sort them into a sequence."

"Most interesting, my dear. Er—why do you want to do that?"

Ramses leaned forward, hands clasped and eyes bright. "There is a distinct change over time in the attitudes of the penitent—a greater consciousness of wrongdoing, of personal sin. Professor Breasted has lectured on the development of moral standards, as demonstrated in the Wisdom Texts; I see something of the same sort in these simple prayers. Instead of denying guilt, they admit it and ask for forgiveness from the god, whichever one it may be." He broke off with a self-conscious laugh. "Sorry. I didn't mean to bore you with my far-fetched theories."

"I assure you, dear boy, you did not bore me. It sounds as if you have hit upon a most interesting and productive line of inquiry." I put my hand over his. "I intend to see that you are allowed to pursue it."

Ramses eyed me askance. "What are you up to now, Mother?"

"Your father will be back tomorrow morning. We will discuss it then. Run along and enjoy your translating."

I beguiled the rest of the morning watching the activity around the guard post and making one of my little lists. Ramses was probably right in saying that we stood a better chance of tracing the statuette through its recent purchasers, but I saw no harm in speculating a bit. There was a limited number of places from which the object could have originated. I wrote them down in neat order.

1. The tomb of Akhenaton at Amarna. It had been looted and despoiled thousands of years ago. No such artifact—portable and very valuable—would have been overlooked by the original thieves, or by those who transferred the king's funerary equipment to Thebes, supposing this had been done.

2. A private house at Amarna. This seemed to me most unlikely. Not even the wealthiest of courtiers would honor his king with an object so valuable, and if he had, he would have taken it with him when he left the city.

3. The tomb of Akhenaton at Thebes. No such tomb was known, and it was generally agreed (by everyone except Howard Carter) that the East Valley contained no more royal

tombs. The West Valley had also been investigated, though not so thoroughly. There was a far-out chance that an unknown royal tomb remained to be discovered, but it could not have survived intact. All the royal tombs had been robbed in antiquity. Once again, no such valuable artifact would have been missed by the original thieves.

4. Tomb 55, the mysterious sepulchre located by Mr. Theodore Davis's workers in 1907. In my opinion this was the most likely theory. As Emerson had pointed out, the objects in the tomb were a miscellaneous mixture belonging to various members of the Amarna royal family. Supervision of the excavation had been extremely lax. Fifteen years had elapsed since the discovery of KV55. It takes a while to market such unique objects, and the negotiations are often secret. Had Mr. Petherick not died, the statuette might not have surfaced for another fifteen or twenty years—after "the heat was off," to employ a slang phrase.

Having arrived at this depressing conclusion, which pointed the finger of blame at one for whom I had come to feel a certain esteem, I put my list aside and returned to my contemplation of the scene. Before long the proceedings were enlivened by Ramses, who came into sight around the corner of the house propelling before him an individual in riding kit and an oversized pith helmet, whom I identified as the same journalist who had tried to bribe Hassan. Ramses had him by the collar. Upon reaching the road, he gave the fellow a shove that sent him staggering away, and then came onto the veranda.

"Caught him sneaking round the back of our house," he explained. "Peering in the windows."

"What effrontery!" I exclaimed. "I hope he did not frighten the children."

"Quite the contrary," Ramses said grimly. "He and Carla were having quite a nice chat. She explained, rather indignantly, that she saw no harm in talking with him, since she had not accepted any of the sweets he offered her."

"Thank goodness we seem to have driven that point home. And that the windows are barred."

"Insufficient, I fear. I'm going to turn the dog loose."

"Won't it run away?"

"Not a chance. It keeps trying to sneak into the house. The Great Cat of Re has made it clear that the house is his domain. It's given him a new interest in life. He stands guard at the door."

"What are we going to do about this?" I

demanded, indicating the guardhouse. Most of the tourists had departed as midday approached, but there were still a few people hanging about. "I refuse to be beleaguered in my own house."

"Be patient for another day," Ramses pleaded. "Father will be here tomorrow morning and presumably he will have more information. There's nothing you can do just now except provide copy for the newspapers."

I had to acknowledge the justice of this, but I was relieved and delighted to see a familiar form approaching. Two of them, to be precise—Cyrus Vandergelt mounted on his placid mare.

"I had hoped to see you before this," I said, greeting him at the door.

"We've been besieged," Cyrus explained, as Jamad led the horse to the stables. "The town is full of journalists. Apparently the darned women spread the story of the accursed statue before she left England, and some newspapers sent reporters to Egypt after her."

"You will stay for luncheon, won't you?" I asked.

"I was hoping you'd ask. Cat sends her best; she refused to run the gauntlet. I left Bertie to guard the gates. A couple of the rascals tried to climb over them."

We had a pleasant luncheon of cold meats and

salads, while Cyrus told us the latest news. He had also been visited by Inspector Ayyid.

"Asked me a lot of questions," Cyrus said. "I got to feeling like a suspect."

"He doesn't suspect you," Ramses said slowly. "He's fixed on Adrian Petherick. The questions he asked us today made that clear."

"Good Gad," I exclaimed. "I hadn't thought about it, but I believe you are right. The man who tried to enter the house wore European clothing, and young Mr. Petherick has demonstrated a certain degree of mental instability."

"He's not responsible," Ramses said heatedly. He caught my inquiring eye and went on, less vehemently. "He had a horrible experience during the War. He's never completely recovered."

"Well, that's too bad," said Cyrus. "But it seems to me that's another point against him. Does Ayyid suspect him of abducting his stepmother too?"

"Or of murdering her?" I breathed, remembering Abdullah's "every year another dead body."

Ramses gave me a hard look. "Don't let your imagination run away with you, Mother. There was no blood, no sign of a struggle in her rooms. She arranged her own disappearance, she must have done. She'll turn up in a few days with some cock-and-bull story, and get the headlines she wants—and the statue."

"Emerson didn't take it with him, did he?" Cyrus asked.

"No," I said. "It is here, in the house."

Cyrus looked expectantly at me. I laughed and shook my head. "It is better for you, Cyrus, if you don't know its exact location. I am the only one who does, and I assure you it is well hidden."

"You don't suppose I'd tell anyone, do you?" Cyrus demanded indignantly.

"Not willingly."

Cyrus's jaw dropped. "Come on, now, Amelia, that's a little far-fetched. You don't really think someone is going to capture and torture me, do you?"

"No," said my son, giving me an even harder look. "She's saving that little treat for herself."

FROM MANUSCRIPT H

Ramses wondered how many other people had been informed that his mother was the only one who knew the statuette's hiding place. It would be just like her to put the story about as a means of protecting the rest of them from what could only be one of her melodramatic fantasies. What's more, the story wasn't true. He knew where Emerson had hidden the statuette, and he'd be willing to wager that every servant in the house also knew. All the same, he decided he had better spread a rumor of his own.

After Cyrus had taken his departure and his mother had gone off to her study, he took Nefret aside.

"I'm going out for a while."

"Where?"

"Around and about," Ramses said. "I'll be back in time for tea. Keep an eye on Mother. She mustn't leave the house. Hit her over the head if you have to."

"I can see myself doing that," his wife said wryly. "All right, I'll try. But tell me where you're going."

She didn't add "just in case." She didn't have to. It was a family rule, one learned from painful experience.

"Deir el Bahri," Ramses said. "I want to have a chat with Winlock and Lansing and Barton, see if they know anything we don't."

"Be careful."

"I always am." He gave her a quick kiss, and then a longer one.

He went round the back way to the stables, saddled Risha, and headed across the desert toward the place where the Metropolitan Museum crew were working. After finishing their excavations in the small bay south of Hatshepsut's beautiful temple, they had just moved to the remains of the Eleventh Dynasty temple next to her later monument.

The object of excavation was, in principle, the furtherance of knowledge. However, the brutal truth was that museums wanted objects they could display. Funding for excavation depended to some extent on how many such objects turned up; they were, as a rule, divided between the Cairo Museum and the excavator. As Cyrus had said, the Met concession had been lucky at finding "good stuff"—several queens' tombs, the unrobbed tomb of a high official, and a group of charming little models that preserved for all eternity the workshops and outbuildings of an official's estate.

The great natural amphitheater, enclosed by the tawny cliffs of the high desert, had a natural grandeur of its own when it wasn't infested with tourists and archaeologists. That morning, dust rose from the area where the Metropolitan group was working, and the chanting of the workmen vied with the chatter of tourists and dragomen approaching Hatshepsut's temple.

Ramses was greeted with flattering enthusiasm, first by George Barton, with whom he had shared a somewhat unusual experience a few years earlier, and then by others of the staff. He had a feeling he knew why they were so glad to see him. Barton, a cheerfully ingenuous man, went straight to the point.

"So what's the latest? I hear the lady has disappeared. Hope she didn't take the statuette with her."

His superior, Winlock, shook his head disapprovingly and offered Ramses his hand. "Good to have you folks back. Pay no attention to George, his manners leave a lot to be desired."

"Admit it, the rest of us are just as curious," Lansing said with a grin. "George's description of the statuette made our mouths water. Any idea as to where it came from originally?"

"I was hoping you'd have some theories about that," Ramses said. "We are, as the saying goes, baffled."

"We'll take a break," Winlock decreed. He called out instructions to his reis, and led the way to a patch of shadow under the cliff, where he offered Ramses a camp stool. "Anything we can do to help, of course. Oh—" He glanced over his shoulder at a man who was slowly approaching them. "Do you know Mikhail Katchenovsky? He's offered to translate some of the graffiti we found last year. Mikhail, this is Ramses Emerson."

The Russian's shabby clothes hung loosely on him, and his face was a study in downward curves—a long untrimmed mustache, a hooked nose, and a drooping mouth. The mouth twitched in a tentative smile.

"I am of course familiar with Mr. Emerson's work in the field of linguistics. I am pleased to meet you, sir."

Ramses offered his hand. "Didn't you publish several articles on the demotic ostraca and papyri in the Turin Museum?"

The long, sad face lit up. "I am honored that you remember. It was some years ago. Before the War."

"I was impressed by your translations," Ramses said pleasantly. The poor devil seemed to be in need of encouragement. "Especially the one from the fellow complaining about his neighbor's wife."

"Ah, but my understanding of the verb forms was mistaken," Katchenovsky exclaimed. "Your most recent publication pointed out—"

"Here now," Lansing interrupted with a laugh. "Don't you two go off into demotic. We want to hear about gold and treasure."

They passed an entertaining quarter of an hour discussing theories, most of which the Emersons had already considered. Ramses noticed that the usual noise had diminished considerably; he didn't doubt that every one of the workmen was straining his ears to overhear. He waited until the reis had edged up to them, ostensibly to ask Winlock for further orders, before he remarked, in a carrying voice, "Father has the statuette tucked away in a safe place. I'm the only other one who knows where he hid it. He wouldn't even tell Mother."

The others exchanged meaningful glances and Barton tried not to smile. "I hope he wasn't annoyed with her for showing it to us the other day."

"Not at all. He just doesn't want unauthorized persons seeing it. We had another attempted break-in the other night."

They had learned of it, naturally. "No idea who it might have been?" Lansing asked.

Ramses shook his head, and Winlock glanced at his watch. "Best get back to work. Come and have a look, Ramses. We're clearing the southern half of the courtyard. No tombs yet, but the changes in plan are interesting."

Ramses declined the invitation, explaining that he had promised to be home early. "I'd like to come round another day, after things have settled down. At the moment we're surrounded by journalists and curiosity seekers."

"The Professor will take care of them," Lansing said, looking hopeful. Emerson's rages were a source of entertainment to the whole region.

•   •   •

Ramses had almost arrived at the house when he saw another rider approaching. It took a moment for him to recognize her. She was dressed like a man, in breeches and boots and coat, and she rode like one, straight-backed and at ease in the saddle. Realizing she could cut him off before he reached the stables, he stopped and waited for her.

Her greeting was characteristically unconventional. "What a magnificent horse. Arabian?"

"Yes. I assume this meeting is not fortuitous?"

"I've been watching the stables all afternoon in the hope that one of you would venture forth" was the cool response. "I took it for granted you were no more inclined to confront that pack of vultures in front of the house than I was."

"What do you want?"

She leaned back, the reins loose in her hands, and smiled a little. It was the first time he had seen her expression soften so much; it was unexpectedly attractive. "I see you share your father's directness. I will be just as direct. I need your help."

"We have no new information about your stepmother," Ramses said.

She waved one hand impatiently. "Nor do we. That's not what worries me. It's Adrian. That damned policeman suspects him of breaking into your house. You must clear him."

Ramses raised his eyebrows. "Must?"

"Damn." She bit her lip and bent her head. She wore no hat; her black hair was gathered into a loose knot at the nape of her neck. "I'm sorry. That wasn't a very clever way of gaining your support. Ayyid said—no, not exactly. He **implied** you had recognized Adrian."

"That's a favored technique of interrogation," Ramses said. "None of us recognized the intruder. We told Ayyid as much."

"I see. But you think it was Adrian, don't you?"

"Do you?"

"He was with me that night. We sat up late discussing . . . family matters."

"You would say that in any case."

"Of course." The smile was fleeting this time. "Adrian is incapable of harming anyone," she said earnestly. "He is hypersensitive about violence of any kind. It stems from—"

"I know. I am deeply sorry."

"Ah." She was no more anxious to discuss the subject than he. After a moment she said, "I got off on the wrong foot with you and your family. I regret that, and apologize. Can we start again?"

She held out her hand. It would have been churlish not to take it. Her grip was as firm as a man's, her gaze direct and warm. It was amazing what a difference that smile made.

"We'll help in any way we can," Ramses said.

"Thank you. I won't detain you any longer." She set the horse to a trot and moved away. She did not look back. Ramses sat watching her for a while before he turned Risha toward the stables.

Fatima had served tea before Ramses appeared, wearing riding kit and looking windblown.

"We didn't wait for you," I said. It was an accusation, not an apology, and Ramses recognized it as such.

"I'm sorry to be late," he said, over the shrieks of greeting and inquiry from his children. "No, Carla, Papa did not bring you anything. You must not expect a gift every time I go away for a short while."

"Grandpapa always brings me a present," Carla retorted. "When is he coming home?"

I professed ignorance, knowing she would lie in wait for him if she knew the approximate time, and Carla returned to the table and the biscuits. David John repeated the question that had gone unheard because his sister's peremptory voice had drowned him out. "Have the Metropolitan Museum people found anything of interest at Deir el Bahri, Papa?"

"Not lately." Ramses took a chair and addressed his comments to Nefret and me as well as to his son, who leaned against the arm of his chair listening intently. "They are clearing the front part of the Nebhepetre courtyard."

"Never mind that," I said, filling a cup. "Had they heard anything new about the—er—object? David John, give this to your papa, please."

The little boy did so. "Are you speaking of the statuette, Grandmama? I hope you will not take it amiss if I remark that in my opinion I ought to have been given an opportunity to examine it, particularly in view of the fact that so many other—"

"I take your point, David John," I cut in. Though normally a taciturn child, he could talk interminably about a subject that captured his interest. Egyptology was one of those subjects—a fact that delighted his grandfather and roused the direst of apprehensions in his grandmother. I had had to put up with one juvenile pedant and did not look forward to living with another. I did not bother asking how he had found out about the statuette. Those wide blue eyes and that innocent countenance could winkle information out of the wariest. "But I fail to see what you could contribute."

"One never knows," said David John.

"True. However, you will have to discuss the matter with your grandfather. The statuette is safely hidden away and I prefer not to disclose its location." Observing an all-too-familiar gleam in those cornflower-blue eyes, I added, "I strictly forbid you to go looking for it. That is an order, my dear, and admits of no exceptions."

"Yes, Grandmama," said David John. "What, if I may ask—"

"Have another biscuit," I said.

"I believe Carla has eaten them all, Grandmama."

She hadn't quite. The last few were saved by the appearance at the door of the dog, who rose on her hind legs and peered hopefully in at us. Carla rushed to greet her, and Nefret said sharply, "Down, Amira! Carla, do not let her in."

The dog obeyed. Carla did not. We always kept the door bolted. Carla began tugging at the bolt.

Ramses snatched her up, despite her protests. "You heard your mama. How did the dog get loose? I tied her to a post before I left this afternoon."

She had broken the rope. A frayed end dangled from her collar. Pleased at the attention she was receiving, she opened her mouth and let a long pink tongue loll out. It was quite a disgusting sight.

"Take her away," I said. "Carla, it is time you and David John got ready for supper and bed."

"There's no sense in tying her," Nefret said. "She won't run away. She follows the twins everywhere."

She held out a hand to each child. When they

went out the door, the dog fell in behind them, like a military escort.

"It appears," I remarked, "that your idea of a dog was a good one. Now that the little dears have gone, tell me what happened this afternoon."

"Wait until Nefret comes back."

Fatima emerged from the house and began to clear away the tea things. It was a task she left to no one else, since (at her insistence) we always used my second-best tea set, a pretty Limoges pattern of rosebuds and forget-me-nots. Kareem, who had followed her, stood looking on. "Shall I bring the whiskey?" he asked.

"No," Fatima snapped. "You will drop it. Open the door for me."

"I cannot imagine why she wants a footman," I remarked. "She won't let him do anything."

"Status, no doubt," said Ramses indifferently. "I ran into an interesting fellow today—"

Nefret came back, and he broke off.

"Did Mother show you the latest post?" she asked.

I selected one of the missives that overflowed the post basket. "We have been offered five hundred pounds for an article on Mrs. P.'s disappearance and the curse of the golden statue."

"Not a bad offer," said Ramses judiciously. "Who's it from?"

"Kevin O'Connell, of course. **The Times** only proposed three hundred, and the **Daily Mirror**'s offer was a paltry two hundred and fifty."

Ramses laughed, and Nefret, who had been watching him closely, said, "Anything new?"

"I was just telling Mother about the chap I met today. His name's Mikhail Katchenovsky. His specialties are demotic and hieratic. He published several excellent articles before the War."

"How nice for you," I said. "I expect you had an enjoyable chat. Is he working for Mr. Winlock?"

"I don't believe the arrangement is official. He looked a little down-at-the-heels, to tell the truth."

"Perhaps he would be interested in a position," Nefret said.

"Father wouldn't agree to that," Ramses said, with a certain air of regret. "He would claim, correctly, that we don't need another translator." He finished his tea, and then said, somewhat abruptly, "I ran into Miss Petherick on the way home."

Nefret said nothing. I nodded encouragingly, and Ramses went on. "She apologized for her behavior the other night, expressed her belief in her brother's innocence, and asked for our help in clearing him."

"What did you say?" Nefret inquired.

Ramses shrugged. "I was courteous but non-committal."

"Oh?" Nefret's eyes narrowed. "You feel sorry for him. I can understand why; his experience during the War was enough to break any man's mind. But that doesn't mean he is guiltless. And I imagine Miss Petherick can be quite persuasive when she likes."

"Just what are you accusing me of?" Ramses demanded.

His cheeks were a trifle flushed and so were Nefret's. I knew what was on her mind, and although I deplore jealousy in any form, I had to admit that my son's well-cut features and athletic frame—and a certain additional quality that is potent, though hard to define—have a devastating effect on women, especially strong-minded women.

On this occasion I had misjudged Nefret. She burst out laughing and settled herself on Ramses's lap, winding her arms round his neck. "I'm not accusing you of anything, darling, except being irresistible to women—through no fault of your own."

"Oh," said Ramses. He gave me a self-conscious look, then grinned and put his arm round his wife, who wriggled into a more comfortable position. I smiled benignly at them.

"Never mind the Pethericks, your father will be

back tomorrow and we will be in a better position to deal with them. Should we not meet the train?"

"Not under any circumstances" was Ramses's emphatic reply. "We would be followed to the station by every journalist in Luxor, and there is a faint chance Father may be able to escape their attentions if his arrival is not heralded by us."

"They will find out," I predicted. "Emerson is a conspicuous individual."

Emerson's arrival the following morning was certainly conspicuous. As he told us later, several persons on the train had recognized him, and as he made his way through the streets of Luxor, his entourage grew. When we first beheld him striding up the road he was followed by a crowd of people. They stayed at a respectful distance, since Emerson kept swatting at them and shouting threats. Seeing the rebuilt guardhouse, he stopped and stared at it. We could hear him all the way to the veranda.

"What the devil is this?" he demanded of Wasim, who had returned to his duties. Wasim's reply was inaudible, but Emerson nodded in satisfaction. "If anyone, male or female, attempts to get past you, shoot to kill."

He came on at his usual brisk pace. A thrill of pride and admiration ran through my limbs at the sight of that stalwart form, unbowed by the years, impressive as a Roman god. To be sure, his suit was in a frightful state of wrinkles, his necktie was askew, and his black hair (what the devil had he done with his new hat?) looked as if it had not seen comb or brush for days. A smile spread across his tanned face when he saw me waiting at the door, and he quickened his steps.

A slight diversion was occasioned by the arrival of the twins, who were followed by the dog, who was followed by the Great Cat of Re. Emerson's immediate reaction—quite understandable, I admit—was to push both children behind him and aim a blow at the dog's head. The blow missed, since the beast immediately collapsed at his feet.

"Good Gad," said Emerson, as the children tugged at him, emitting shrill cries of explanation and expostulation. "Who—what—where—"

"It's all right, Father. She's perfectly harmless. Ramses thought we needed a watchdog." Nefret opened the door. Emerson, not entirely convinced, pushed the children in and followed. The dog would have done the same had not the Great Cat of Re stepped in front of it. The dog backed off, the Great Cat of Re walked in, and Amira lay down outside, her face pressed to the screen.

"Well, well," said Emerson. "Not a bad idea." He directed a malignant glare at the crowd gathered round the guardhouse. "If you are sure the creature won't harm the children."

"Amira is a noble beast," said David John.

"She would let us ride her, but Mama says we may not," Carla said. "What did you bring me, Grandpapa?"

With a self-conscious look at me, Emerson removed two small packets from his pocket and handed one to each child. He had visited the suk and bought a silver bracelet for Carla and a box of colored pencils for David John. "Now run along," he said. "And take the dog with you."

Carla gave him a huge hug. "I don't want to leave you, Grandpapa. Fatima has made sugar cakes."

Emerson chuckled and I said, "You may not have any sweets, Carla, it's too close to luncheon. Go to Fatima."

Emerson removed his coat, tie, and waistcoat, tossed them onto a chair, and sat down on them. "Good to be back," he said, beaming. "I have wonderful news, my dears."

"You have learned the name of the dealer who sold the statue to Mr. Petherick?" I asked.

"You have located Sethos?" Nefret inquired.

Emerson waved both questions aside. "Better than that, better than that. But where is Ramses? I want to tell him the great news myself."

Fatima bustled out with a tray of coffee and cakes. She was followed by Ramses. "I was working," he said. "But I heard you coming."

"Most of the West Bank heard him," I remarked. "Very well, Emerson, don't keep us in suspense. What is your great news?"

Emerson gulped down his coffee and held out the cup for a refill. "Ah, just what I needed. Thank you, Fatima. No one makes better—"

"Emerson," I said loudly.

"KV55," said Emerson,

"Davis's tomb? What about it?"

"I have Lacau's permission to reexcavate it!"

His grin faded as he looked from one blank face to the next.

"The dam—— The confounded tomb is empty, Emerson," I said.

"You don't know that," Emerson said. "Davis's excavation was careless in the extreme. Lord only knows what he missed. Good Gad, Peabody, you don't seem to grasp the possibilities."

Ramses cleared his throat. "I believe I grasp some of them, sir."

"That's better," Emerson said approvingly. He took out his pipe. "Well, my boy?"

"You wanted an excuse to work in the Valley. That's why you were so pleased when you found the newspaper fragment—it was evidence that someone had been there recently—and when you caught Deib and Aguil in the act of digging. What I don't understand is what you hope to accomplish. Everyone agrees there are no more royal tombs in the East Valley."

"My dear boy, I have no expectation of being allowed to begin new excavations in the Valley of the Kings," Emerson said. "Carter and Carnarvon hold the firman, and I would never behave in an underhanded manner toward another archaeologist."

"Certainly not, sir," said Ramses, his tilted eyebrows contradicting his words.

"Hmph," said Emerson. "The statuette must have come originally from a royal tomb. An Amarna period tomb, since the artistic style is of that period. We know of three that immediately postdate Akhenaton—KV55 and those of Horemheb, in the East Valley, and Ay, in the West Valley. None of them has been properly investigated. Horemheb's was another of Davis's botched excavations; several objects from the tomb have been floating round the antiquities markets for years."

He paused to light his pipe and I exclaimed, "For pity's sake, Emerson, don't tell me you want to reexcavate that infernal tomb of Horemheb. It's one of the longest in the Valley. Ramses is right, and Cyrus was right; you are tired of Deir el Me-

dina and want an excuse to work, in however limited a manner, in the Valley of the Kings. You
cherish the delusion that once you get a foothold
there it will be difficult to get you out. I am astonished at you. A conscientious excavator, which I
had supposed you to be, does not abandon a project in the middle of the season."

Emerson gestured with the pipe. "Don't lecture me, Peabody. I have it all worked out, you
will see."

"Oh, really? Do you also have the Petherick
matter all worked out? I was under the obviously
erroneous impression that you went to Cairo to
pursue our investigation. Are you aware of what
has happened here since you left?"

"Certainly," said Emerson, blowing out a cloud
of smoke. "The Cairo newspapers were full of the
stories. I am deeply hurt by your criticism,
Peabody. If you insist upon a full report of my
activities—"

"I do not insist, Emerson. I request. Strongly."

"Hmph," said Emerson. "Very well. I called
upon the most reputable of the antiquities dealers
in Cairo. All denied knowledge of the statuette.
Which doesn't mean a curse in itself, but their avid
curiosity was indicative of innocence. I sent cables
to a number of people, including Howard Carter,
who have been known to handle antiquities for

Petherick. I cabled Gargery and told him to go up to London and investigate the status and contents of Petherick's will—"

"Gargery!" I exclaimed. "Why did you entrust such a delicate task to him? The old fool will go blundering around—"

"Sometimes blundering accomplishes more than tact," retorted Emerson, who was certainly in a position to know. "I suspect the old fool is getting bored down in Kent. He always enjoys participating in our little adventures."

"What about Sethos?" Nefret asked.

"What about him?"

"Emerson, don't be so aggravating," I said. "Do you know where he is?"

"Yes. At least I know where he is supposed to be." He looked round the room, as if he expected his brother to materialize out of thin air, and then pointed toward the guardhouse. "Ah."

In the center of a jostling crowd, almost as if he **had** materialized out of thin air, stood a familiar figure. I would have known him anywhere.

FOUR

He looked very much like his brother—a scant inch shorter, not so heavily muscled as Emerson but trim and well built. Only an observer familiar with his true appearance would have noticed the resemblance, however; he now sported a mane of white hair, worn longer than was fashionable, a narrow mustache, and a goatee. His linen suit and the silver-headed stick he brandished bore out the impression of a well-bred if somewhat foppish gentleman. Pushing through the crowd, he advanced toward the house, followed by two perspiring fellows who carried several large suitcases and a hatbox. He stopped outside the door and smiled upon us all with impartial affability.

"Good morning, my dears. How good it is to see you all again."

"Who are you supposed to be this time?" I inquired, opening the door.

"A wealthy connoisseur and philanthropist," said Sethos, running a fingertip along his mustache. "Sir Malcolm Page Henley de Montague, at your service. You may omit the title when addressing me." He dispensed baksheesh to his bearers, who deposited his luggage and departed.

"Aren't you taking something of a chance?" I inquired. "Sir Malcolm has supported several excavations in this area. You may encounter someone who knows him."

"You insult my abilities, my dear, if you suppose I cannot bamboozle such persons" was the airy reply. He gave me a brotherly kiss on the cheek, saluted Nefret on the brow, and shook Ramses's hand.

"Sit down and stop showing off," said Emerson irritably. "What took you so long?"

"It wasn't long at all, considering that my imposing appearance and witty conversation distracted a number of persons who might otherwise have trailed you. Every journalist in Egypt must be here."

Fatima appeared with fresh coffee, her plain but kindly face shining with pleasure. She had obviously been aware of his arrival, though how she had recognized him I could not imagine. Over the years he had appeared at the house in various guises, ostensibly to prevent people from identifying him as Emerson's brother. This would have been embarrassing for us and dangerous for him in his role as an agent of British intelligence. However, Sethos was an actor at heart and enjoyed the game for its own sake.

"Did you come down from Cairo on the same train as Emerson?" I inquired.

"Obviously," said Sethos.

"It is not obvious. You might have been in Luxor all along."

"Or somewhere else in Egypt," Sethos suggested helpfully.

"Mother, you are letting him get you off the track again," said Ramses through his teeth. He found his uncle extremely exasperating—a point of view with which I had some sympathy. "Father, how did you locate—er—Sir Malcolm so quickly, and what have you told him, and why is he here?"

"He knew I was in Cairo," Sethos replied. "Hasn't he told you that we have been in regular communication for the past few years?"

"No," I said—through **my** teeth.

Emerson said, "Hmph," and avoided my eyes.

Sethos hadn't missed my response or Emerson's response to my response, and he appeared highly amused. "Given your propensity for inviting trouble, I deemed it my duty to be readily available in case you needed my help. I was not at all surprised to learn that you're at it again. However, this is an even more preposterous situation than the ones you usually get into."

The pronoun could have been singular or plural, but the look he directed at me made his meaning clear. I was about to respond when Nefret came to my defense.

"Mother is entirely guiltless in this case. It was Father who accepted the statuette and promised the confounded woman he would remove the curse." She leaned forward, blue eyes fixed on his face. "Did you take it from Tomb 55?"

Sethos looked uncomfortable. Nefret was one of the few people who could penetrate his mask of smiling cynicism. He answered with equal bluntness. "No. Most of the objects I removed from the tomb had limited monetary value; my chief interest was in their historical importance."

"No doubt," said Ramses, with a skeptical look. "Could you have overlooked something so valuable?"

"Since I haven't been privileged to see it yet, I can't be certain," said Sethos.

Emerson got up, mumbled something, and went into the house. When he came back he was holding the painted box. Silently he handed it to Sethos, who removed the lid. His lips pursed in a whistle and those strangely colored eyes, which could be brown or green or gray, widened. Consummate actor though he was, I felt sure his astonishment was genuine.

"Good God," he murmured.

"I knew it wasn't you," Nefret said, visibly relieved.

"Your confidence touches me, my dear. I assure you that if I had found it I would have snatched it without a second thought. However, if you want additional indication of my innocence, remember my custom of keeping the most beautiful objects for myself." He ran a reverent finger down the curves of the right arm. "I wouldn't have sold this for any price."

Though Sethos did not look at me, Emerson twitched as if at an insect bite. Sethos had once said something of the sort to me, referring, in that case, to my humble self. He had long since got over this attachment, but it still touched my dear spouse on a tender spot.

"Very well," said that individual. "I accept your word. And your arguments. Nevertheless, I intend to reexcavate Tomb 55."

"I can't have missed anything," Sethos insisted. "I was in the tomb alone, or with my loyal assistant, for several days. I had plenty of time to explore every nook and cranny."

"It may have been taken before you arrived on the scene," Ramses said. "There were dozens of visitors in and out of the place, and the workmen made off with several small pieces of jewelry. They turned up shortly afterward in the antiquities market of Luxor, but an object like this would have been handled in greater secrecy."

"Why?" Nefret asked. "Don't all antiquities, large and small, have to be passed by the Service des Antiquités before they can be taken from Egypt?"

Sethos steepled his hands and gave a little cough. "Allow me to deliver a brief lecture, my dear. I believe I am in a better position than most to know the ins and outs of the illegal antiquities game."

"That," said Emerson emphatically, "is certainly true."

"Quite," said Sethos. "In the old days—the good old days, as some of us might say—the Middle East was an open market. No rules, no supervision. That's how we British acquired the Elgin Marbles, the Khorsobad sculptures, and a number of rare objects from Egypt. When Mariette started the Service des Antiquités, he and his successor, Maspero, established new rules. Foreign excavators had to have permits to dig, and everything they uncovered had to pass inspection. The service decided which pieces they could take and which went to the Cairo Museum.

"Some would say that both Mariette and

Maspero were overly generous. There are certainly objects in foreign museums that would never have been passed by our present director."

"Get to the point," Emerson said impatiently. "The problem isn't only legal excavations."

"Quite true," Sethos agreed. "The locals have been digging for years and in the good old days they were able to sell their discoveries to tourists who had no difficulty in exporting them. After the 1860s, to their great indignation, the local lads were told they couldn't do that sort of thing any longer. The Antiquities Department cracked down hard on tomb robbers. You remember what happened to the Abd er Rassul brothers after it was learned that they had been looting the cache of royal mummies."

"Horrible," I said energetically. "Torture should not be permitted under any circumstances. It is to the credit of Britain that we have put a stop to that sort of thing."

"To make a long story short," Sethos said, with a polite nod at me, "modern tomb robbers have to go about their business in secret. Odds and ends, such as the bits of jewelry taken from KV55, don't bother the authorities that much; they can't possibly keep track of all of them. Major discoveries, however, have to be marketed with care so they can't be traced back to the original perpetrators. Some dealers will sit on important pieces for years, while carrying on secret negotiations with various museums and collectors."

"Carter," Emerson growled.

"He and others. Carter is a go-between, a dealer. He buys for his patron, Lord Carnarvon, and for institutions like the Metropolitan Museum. So you see," Sethos concluded, "the existence of this statuette has probably been known for years. The fact that it escaped my attention causes me, I confess, a certain embarrassment. I can only attribute it to the fact that I have been busy with other matters since 1914."

"Are you suggesting that it wasn't found until after that time?" Ramses asked.

"I'm not suggesting anything of the sort," Sethos said. "Even I have lapses occasionally."

"If it was ever in KV55," said Emerson, "some trace of its presence may yet remain. The missing uraeus serpent, for example, or scraps of a pedestal. Many wooden objects were waterlogged and decaying. Davis would have kicked the scraps aside. We must eliminate KV55 before we consider other possibilities."

I had listened in growing impatience to this discussion, in which, I was sorry to see, Ramses had allowed himself to become interested. "If I may say so," I remarked, "archaeological fever is distracting you from more important matters. Are you aware that Mrs. Petherick has mysteriously disappeared? And that there have been two attempted robberies here?"

"Bah," said Emerson. "The intruder was probably a journalist."

"Who also blew up the guardhouse?"

"Those bastards have no scruples. As for Mrs. Petherick, she'll turn up before long with a harrowing tale of her escape from the afrit." He took out his watch, let out an emphatic swearword, and jumped up. "All this time wasted! Ramses, Nefret, Peabody, get your gear together."

"Where are we going?" Ramses asked. He knew the answer.

"Deir el Medina, of course. I told Wasim to send word to Selim to get the crew together."

I settled myself more comfortably in my chair. "I must see to our guest, Emerson. Unlike you, he will wish to rest and refresh himself after that long dusty train ride. If you will wait an hour or two—"

"Bah," said Emerson. "You will follow when you are damned good and ready, I suppose. You two, come with me."

FROM MANUSCRIPT H

Emerson would have walked out of the house just as he was, had not his wife insisted he change out of his good suit and put on a hat. By the time Ramses and Nefret were ready, he was lying in wait for them. Emerson led the way with long strides, up the cliff behind Deir el Bahri and along the path the ancient workmen had taken, between their homes and the Valley of the Kings where they had excavated and decorated the royal tombs. Though this was the most direct path to the village, it was not as easy as the road that entered the valley from the north, but it was one of Emerson's favorite "strolls." Certain other members of the family did not share this viewpoint.

Sun rays seeped down into the narrow valley. At the north end, amid the ruins of earlier shrines, stood the Ptolemaic temple, the only structure that had survived relatively intact. In the village itself, mud-brick foundations and walls outlined the central street and the small houses on either side. It was not an imposing site. The dull gray-brown of the foundations was the same shade as the valley floor, unrelieved by any touch of green, by traces of paint or the glitter of gold. Unlike an ordinary Egyptian town, this one had been built by the state in the fourteenth century B.C. to house the men who worked on the royal tombs, and their families.

Despite its unpromising appearance, the village had yielded one major archaeological treasure— the reburial of the High Priestesses of Amon, containing their rich coffins and collections of jewelry. Bertie and Jumana had been the ones responsible for finding it, and although Lacau had taken most of the artifacts for the Cairo Museum, he had left enough for Cyrus to satisfy that ardent collector. Insofar as Ramses was concerned, Deir el Medina had produced objects that had greater historical value. The inhabitants were skilled craftsmen, and many of them were literate. They had left written documents of all sorts, inscribed on papyrus or scraps of pottery, in the cursive hieratic script or the later, even more cursive, demotic. Having discovered, to their amazement, that Europeans would pay good money for such rubbish, the local fellahin had dug illegally at the site for years and sold the material to collectors and museums. The small private tombs on the hillside, built by the workmen for themselves, had also provided income for industrious diggers— wall paintings, votive stelae, tomb furnishings.

Ramses couldn't imagine living in such a place; yet the laborers had been well off by ancient

Egyptian standards, and the closely packed houses probably suited the inhabitants' tastes well enough. Three thousand years ago the now silent street had been full of people, bustling about on their daily errands, exchanging greetings—and arguing. Some of the letters that had survived indicated that the inhabitants of Deir el Medina were just as prone to family feuds as any modern village population.

With a certain degree of amusement Ramses realized his father wasn't going to be able to start work immediately. Down below, gathered near the north end of the excavation, were Daoud and Selim and a number of their crew—and in the center of the gesticulating, chattering crowd a tall figure elegantly garbed in white linen. Cyrus Vandergelt hurried to meet them as they descended into the valley. Bertie and Jumana were with him, and Cyrus's first words made it clear he wanted to discuss the latest developments.

"Why didn't you tell us you were back? What did you find out? Who's the fellow who came with you? Did you see Lacau?"

"Just got in," Emerson said. "Busy. Lots to do. Selim, Daoud—"

"Oh, no, you don't," Cyrus said firmly. "We've got a lot to talk about, Emerson. You didn't suppose you could sneak into town without me finding out, did you?"

Emerson glowered at Daoud, who smiled amiably at him. "My son Sabir came at once to tell me, Father of Curses. I told Selim you would wish to begin work at once, and Selim told the others, and—"

"You told Mr. Vandergelt," said Emerson.

"Aywa. Of course," said Daoud, surprised he would even ask.

"So who's the legal owner of the statue?" Cyrus inquired.

Cyrus couldn't be ordered about like the Egyptian workers; with a grimace and a growl, Emerson resigned himself to satisfying his friend's curiosity.

"How the devil should I know? I set inquiries in train. It will take a while to get replies. As for Lacau, he has given me permission to reexcavate Tomb 55. The French Institute will be taking over here eventually."

Cyrus caught hold of his arm as he turned away. "What about me?" he cried in anguish.

There's nothing like archaeological fever, Ramses thought. Cyrus still lusted for the golden statuette, but the fate of his excavations had momentarily overshadowed everything else. Ramses glanced at Selim, who was standing by with folded arms, awaiting orders—and listening as intently as the rest.

"You? Oh," said Emerson, rubbing his prominent chin. "What would you say to the West Valley?"

A slow blossoming of delight reduced the wrinkles on Cyrus's forehead. "You mean it? Isn't it part of Carter and Carnarvon's concession?"

"Lacau is a trifle put out with Carter at the moment," Emerson said with obvious relish. "Some of Carter's shenanigans in antiquities dealing have got back to the old cabbage, and he considers them unbecoming a professional excavator. This is in strictest confidence, you understand," he added, frowning at the listeners.

"Sure, sure," Cyrus said eagerly. Daoud stared off into space, as if deep in thought.

"Carter has no plans for working in the West Valley anytime soon," Emerson went on. "Lacau agreed with me that the area is wide open to illegal excavation. I trust that pleases you? Good. Now perhaps you'll allow me to get to work. I don't want the damned French to have any excuse for criticism."

"Then you do mean to shut down here?" Ramses asked.

His father looked deeply affronted. "How can

you think that of me, my boy? I have never yet abandoned an excavation in midseason and I don't mean to do it now. We can do both."

Ramses's implicit criticism had caused Cyrus to have second thoughts. "I can't," he said bluntly. "But I can't bring myself to turn down the West Valley, either."

"You've investigated most of the known tombs here, haven't you?" Emerson demanded.

"Well, yes, but—"

"Finish clearing the one you're working on now and block the entrances of the others." Having settled that to his satisfaction, off Emerson went, followed by his crew.

Thus reassured, Cyrus beamed and rubbed his hands together. Jumana was bouncing up and down on her toes. She was too much in awe of Emerson to interrupt him, but she was bursting with questions. While Nefret answered them as best she could, Ramses looked out across the narrow valley. Now that they were about to abandon the site, he found himself surprisingly reluctant to do so. He knew as surely as if he had seen them that there were more papyri hidden under that sterile surface—more ostraca, more stelae—new inscriptions, perhaps even the missing fragments of some of the tantalizingly incomplete texts he had translated.

There was nothing in Tomb 55 for him, only a corridor and chamber devoid of decoration. And what about next season? Surely Emerson didn't suppose he could find a reasonable excuse for continuing in the Valley of the Kings.

Thanks to Emerson's meticulous methods (and the frequent interruption of their work by distractions "of a criminous nature," as his mother called them), only half the village had been cleared, along with several of the small shrines and temples at the north end. Emerson drove them all hard that morning, filling in partially excavated areas and completing the clearance of a few others. The debris from these piled up. Sifting it was his mother's job, and Emerson bewailed her absence in poignant tones. Ramses's offer to take on the task was refused.

"Get up there with Cyrus and his lot," Emerson ordered, indicating the tombs scattered over the western slopes. "Good Gad, he's just standing there smirking. I shouldn't have told him about the West Valley."

Bertie and Jumana were doing an efficient job, deciding which of the opened tombs should be permanently closed and which required additional work. Ramses went anyhow. As the sun passed the zenith and perspiration soaked his shirt, he wondered whether Emerson intended to stop for luncheon and rest. Nefret had been in the hot sun all morning, photographing at Emerson's direction. He had no right to push her the way he did . . . Then he saw a trio of horsemen approaching along the road to the north, and was relieved to recognize his mother. He ought to have known she wouldn't neglect their physical comfort, she never did. The man who rode beside her was Sethos; following at a respectful distance was Nasir, carrying a large basket.

Ramses hailed the others. "Time to stop. There's Mother."

"Thank goodness," Cyrus said. He straightened and rubbed his back. "Who's that with her?"

Ramses gave the older man a hand as they descended the steep hillside. "An old friend," he said. "Sir Malcolm . . . uh . . ."

Cyrus gave him an odd look. "An old friend whose name you can't call to mind? Say no more, my boy. I've got a hunch he has another name that's more familiar to both of us."

They made their way to the shelter his mother had erected in the shade of the Ptolemaic temple. Assisted by Nasir, she was laying out the contents of the picnic basket and giving orders to all and sundry.

"Emerson, stop grumbling and sit down. Selim, Daoud, come and join us. Ah, there you are,

Cyrus. Bertie—Jumana—may I present Sir Malcolm Page Henley de Montague, an old friend."

Cyrus looked "Sir Malcolm" over, from his pristine pith helmet to his expensive boots, and held out his hand. "Good to see you again, sir. We met several years ago in London, though I dare not hope you remember me."

"It would be impossible to forget you, Mr. Vandergelt," Sethos said cautiously.

"Especially since I outbid you on that Seventeenth Dynasty crown."

"Ah, yes." Sethos acknowledged the tactful reminder with a nod. "No hard feelings, Mr. Vandergelt. It was a rather ugly object, and quite possibly a forgery."

"You really think so?"

"I came to that conclusion later." Sethos permitted himself a condescending smile. "Sour grapes, you will say. But let us not dwell on the past. How is your work here proceeding?"

Having enjoyed his teasing, Cyrus accepted the change of subject. "Pretty well. We're turning the site over to the French Institute. Emerson's got us permission to work in the Valley of the Kings."

Emerson was not amused by the little charade. He gave them only a few minutes to eat and drink before he got everybody back to work.

"Thank God, David will be here in a few days,"

he grumbled. "No offense, Nefret, you are doing a fine job with the photography, but we could use another pair of hands."

"That is certainly the case," his wife agreed emphatically. "Cyrus, what happened to the young man who applied for the position of artist?"

"Never heard from him again. Odd, now that you mention it."

"We don't need any more people," said Emerson, contradicting himself without shame. "Peabody, back to your rubbish heap. Sir—er—Malcolm, you can give her a hand."

Sethos smoothed the white kidskin gloves which he had removed while he ate. "Nothing I'd like better, old chap. Unfortunately, my physician has warned me against manual labor. I bruise easily."

He spent the rest of the afternoon lounging in the shade while the rest of them sweated.

Sethos had got away with his masquerade so far, though Jumana kept looking at him curiously. She had met him before, on several occasions and under several names, and she was a sharp little thing. I wondered how long it would be before she put two and two together. Like his stepfather,

Bertie knew of Sethos's real relationship to our family, but the dear boy was not the world's quickest thinker. He had followed the exchange between Cyrus and Sethos with a puzzled frown. An hour or two later he edged up to me and hemmed and hawed until I took pity on him and confirmed the identification he had just then arrived at.

"So is it all right if I call him by his real name?" Bertie asked. "That is—he knows that I know, doesn't he?"

"Yes. Just don't use his real name in the presence of those who don't know."

"Oh." Bertie scratched his chin. "Righto, Mrs. E. And may I—that is—would it be appropriate if I asked after Maryam?"

"I see no reason why you should not."

"Oh. Righto."

He repeated his oath of secrecy and went off looking relieved. He was such a nice boy. Hopelessly nice, in fact. I was only surprised that some forceful young woman had not bullied him into marrying her. Apparently the only forceful young woman he fancied was not interested in marrying him.

I got Emerson to stop work by reminding him that he had promised the children we would join them for tea; otherwise he would have gone on until the rest of us dropped. It was an unusually warm day, but Emerson never feels the heat and is genuinely astonished when others suffer from it.

I had never been more appreciative of my nice tin bathtub. While I lay back, enjoying the cool water that stroked my tired limbs, Emerson availed himself of a more primitive arrangement, standing on a stone slab while Nasir poured jars of water over him.

I had ordered the ewer and washbasin in Sethos's room to be filled (and, if Fatima had her way, strewn with rose petals). He had occupied the room once before, and when I showed him into it he looked round with raised eyebrows.

"Good to be home," he said.

"I presume you are attempting to be sarcastic," I retorted. "Considering that the last time you stayed here you were a prisoner, and you ended up having a knife fight in the courtyard. A fight you lost, I might add."

"I would certainly have come to a sticky end if it hadn't been for Ramses."

It was a rare admission of fallibility. "I don't suppose you ever thanked him."

"Good Lord, no. He'd faint dead away with surprise if I did that."

Reflecting on this characteristic conversation, I dressed in haste and went to the veranda, where

Fatima was arranging the tea things and flirting with Sethos—if I may use that word to describe a harmless demonstration of goodwill. She never behaved that way with anyone else, and he responded with his practiced courtly charm. When Emerson appeared, Fatima bustled off, blushing a little.

"At it again, are you?" inquired Emerson, who had seen the blush. "Can't you leave any female alone?"

"What's the harm in pleasing a lady?" Sethos retorted. "I like Fatima. She's a good woman and a superb cook."

"Hmph," said Emerson, abandoning an unproductive argument. "Where are the children?"

He looked out and then let out an indignant complaint. "Hell and damnation! Wasim has let someone get past him. Who the devil . . ."

The answer was, unfortunately, only too obvious. The man was already nearing the house. Sethos, still standing by the door he had held for Fatima, echoed Emerson's expletive. "Hell and damnation!"

The newcomer stopped outside the barred door and looked in. "Good evening. May I venture to ask for a few minutes of your time? I am Sir Malcolm Page Henley de Montague."

• • •

I pride myself on my ability to rise to any occasion, but for a few seconds I could only gape unbecomingly at the genuine Sir Malcolm. A quick glance showed me that the false Sir Malcolm had vanished. Pulling myself together, I opened the door and invited the former in.

"Emerson," I said, "will you do the honors? I must—I must—uh—tell Fatima . . ."

It was not a nice thing to do to Emerson, who appeared as thunderstruck as I felt, but I felt sure he would manage. I dashed in pursuit of my brother-in-law, whom I found in his room rummaging through a small valise.

"What—" I began.

"Hair coloring," grunted Sethos, tossing out wigs, mustaches, and assorted bottles and jars. "Confound it, I seem to have misplaced the black." He straightened and gave me an appraising look. "I don't suppose you . . ."

Well, I ask the Reader: what could I do? The situation was grave, verging on catastrophic. I went and got my little bottle. "I seldom if ever use it," I explained.

"Quite," said Sethos. "Go and warn Fatima, will you? Tell her . . . damned if I know what you can tell her, just keep her from making any false moves. You had better warn Ramses and Nefret as well."

"What are you going to do?"

"Shave," said Sethos.

I have never been certain whether Fatima is as simple as she appears, or cunning enough to appear simple. She accepted my garbled explanation with a nod and went on arranging tea cakes on a pretty flowered plate. I was too late to intercept Nefret and Ramses. When I returned to the veranda they were already there, and so were the children. The dog had its large face pressed to the screen and its long tongue lolling out.

As I later learned, the presence of the little ones (to say nothing of the dog) had relieved the first awkward moments. Sir Malcolm had made the mistake of trying to pat Carla on the head. Ramses had snatched her away before anything unpleasant occurred, but Sir Malcolm kept a wary eye on the little girl until the arrival of the tea cakes distracted her. David John was not distracted. Leaning against his father's knee, he kept his blue eyes fixed on Sir Malcolm.

"I do beg your pardon, Sir Malcolm," I said, taking a chair.

"Not at all, Mrs. Emerson." The gentleman, who had risen when I entered, resumed his seat. "It is for me to apologize for the intrusion. I would have explained my reason for coming had not your husband suggested we wait until you returned."

Now that I had the opportunity to inspect him closely, I saw that Sethos's masquerade had not been exact. Sir Malcolm's chin was longer and his hairline more receding. However, the resemblance was close enough to have deceived Wasim, who must have taken the newcomer for the same man he had seen with us earlier, wearing the same overly fashionable sort of suit and carrying the same silver-headed stick.

"Proceed, if you will, please," I said.

"It is simply told." Sir Malcolm leaned forward, hands clasped tightly round his cane. "I wish to make an offer for the statuette Mrs. Petherick gave you. I will pay any reasonable price."

"Sight unseen?" Ramses inquired, his heavy brows tilting.

Emerson had been slow to recover from Sir Malcolm's unexpected appearance. Now he got his wits together.

"Ah, but he's seen it before," he said. "Haven't you? When and where?"

"That is irrelevant, Professor Emerson."

"No, it isn't," retorted Emerson, now fully himself again. Nothing annoys him so much as well-bred insolence. "I refuse even to discuss the matter until you answer my questions. Was it in Mr. Petherick's collection when you saw it?"

"No." Sir Malcolm looked warily at Carla, who had joined her brother. The intent gaze of blue eyes and black seemed to disconcert him even more than Emerson's bluntness. "I was offered the piece two years ago by a dealer in London. Unfortunately, Petherick got in ahead of me."

"The name of the dealer?"

"Aslanian."

"Ah. Where did he obtain it?"

"I did not ask. There are unwritten rules about such transactions."

"So I have been told," said Emerson, sneering. "So you know nothing more about its origins?"

"No." Sir Malcolm hesitated. "One can, of course, make certain deductions. You, experts that you are, have no doubt made them."

His tone was more conciliatory, but it had no effect on Emerson, who was now anxious to rid himself of the visitor. "We have. As for the statuette, it is not mine to dispose of. The legal owner would appear to be Mrs. Petherick."

"But she gave it to you. And the confounded— er—excuse me, ladies—the woman has taken herself off."

"She left it in my keeping," Emerson corrected.

"I am not the man, sir, to take advantage of a distracted female. When she turns up I will discuss the matter with her. I should warn you, however, that you are not the only one interested in the piece."

"Vandergelt," Sir Malcolm muttered. It had the ring of a swearword. "Do Carter and Carnarvon know of it?"

"Carter is due in Cairo before long," said Emerson, who was beginning to enjoy himself. "I suggest you ask him."

"Will you have another cup of tea, Sir Malcolm?" I asked.

"I haven't had one yet, Mrs. Emerson."

"Oh dear. Nefret, didn't you—"

"I did offer," said Nefret. "I don't believe Sir Malcolm heard me."

"I was distracted by your daughter snapping at my hand." The gentleman bit off the words. "I will not take tea, Mrs. Emerson, thank you."

He stalked to the door. He was in something of a temper—not surprising, considering the provocation—so much so that he had forgotten the dog. It barked hopefully. Sir Malcolm shied back. "Will someone kindly remove this beast?"

"It won't hurt you," Nefret said. (I suspected she was hoping Amira would knock him down and get his nice suit dusty.)

"I am not inclined to take your word, madam."

"Oh, very well." Nefret slipped out and caught hold of Amira's collar. "Come ahead, Sir Malcolm."

The dog paid no attention to Sir Malcolm, being preoccupied with licking Nefret's hands. Before leaving, he turned and hurled a sentence sharp as a spear. "You haven't seen the last of me!"

"Have we?" Emerson inquired of me.

"When I last saw—er—you know who I mean—he was in the process of altering his appearance. Heaven only knows what he'll look like now." I knew he would have black hair, but I saw no reason to mention that.

"I'll go and tell him the coast is clear," Emerson said. "I expect he could do with a whiskey and soda. I certainly could."

Ramses rose, lifting Carla onto his shoulder. "It's time the children got ready for bed. Come along, David John."

"Before you go, I want a word with Carla," I said. "Young lady, did you really try to bite the gentleman?"

"He patted me on my head, Grandmama."

"That is no excuse."

"I haven't bited anyone for a long time," Carla protested. "I don't like that man. He has a mean face."

"Decidedly," said David John. "Though I would prefer the word 'sly.' He is up to no good."

Ramses carried his opinionated children away and Fatima emerged from the house to clear away the tea things and bring the drinks tray. She avoided looking at me, but I couldn't help noticing her secretive little smile. When Emerson and Sethos joined us she didn't bat an eye, though the latter's hair was black—very black—and so was the dashing cavalry style mustache that veiled his mouth. The distinctive clothing of Sir Malcolm had been replaced by an ordinary lounge suit.

"Whiskey?" Emerson asked.

"Excellent idea. That was a close one. I thought the bas—— the fellow was still in London. Where are the kiddies?"

"Gone to bed," I said. "We were fortunate they never got a look at you as Sir Malcolm. They didn't take to him."

"Carla tried to bite him," Nefret said.

"Good girl. I must find a little present for her."

"I won't have such behavior encouraged," I said sternly. "Don't you want to know why Sir Malcolm called on us?"

"He's after the statuette, of course." Sethos took a refreshing sip and relaxed. "All collectors are a trifle insane, but Sir Malcolm is one of the maddest. There are some nasty rumors about how he acquired certain of his artifacts, and they say he doesn't take kindly to losing."

"But he is known as a philanthropist and supporter of worthy causes," I protested.

"That's his public side. He'd have sucked the breath out of Petherick personally if he could have gained possession of the statue that way."

Fatima had lit the lamps. The flames flickered as the lamps swayed gently in the night breeze, and shadows gathered, as if darkness were hungry for the light.

"The statue has that effect," I mused. " 'Obsession' is not too strong a word, at least for some persons."

"Not for me," said Emerson. "I want to know where the confounded thing came from and how it—" He whirled round. Whiskey splashed. "Damnation! Don't sneak up on a fellow like that, Ramses."

"Sorry, sir." Ramses closed the door behind him.

"He doesn't do it on purpose," Nefret said indignantly.

"I know, I know. I apologize, my boy. Help yourself to the whiskey—and you just might give me a touch more.

"Sir Malcolm did give us one bit of useful information," Emerson went on. "Petherick purchased the statue from Aslanian in London. I shall wire

Walter tomorrow and tell him to go round and interrogate Aslanian. The trail goes farther back, of course."

"Don't bother Walter," Sethos said. "I doubt he can get anything out of Aslanian; the man is an old hand at this sort of thing, and Walter doesn't have your forceful personality."

"True." Emerson nodded glumly, and Sethos went on, "I'll get in touch with some of my people."

"Who will break into the shop and look through Aslanian's records?" Ramses suggested. "I thought you'd retired from the—er—profession."

Sethos said, "I could do with another glass, if you would be so good, Ramses."

FROM MANUSCRIPT H

Emerson sent them all to bed immediately after dinner. He wanted to get an early start next morning. "I intend to finish Section twenty-three tomorrow," he announced.

Ramses would have sworn it was impossible, had he not known his father so well. It turned out to be impossible, even for Emerson; late in the day, when they had almost finished clearing the last of the houses in Section 23, the men came across a layer of debris littered with scraps of pottery and papyri. Cursing, Emerson conceded that a proper excavation would take longer than he had planned. It was a weary, grubby crew that dispersed into the gathering darkness. Not surprisingly, Sethos had avoided the dirty job by announcing he had business in Luxor that could not be put off. When they met on the veranda, after ablutions curtailed by weariness, Sethos was waiting, stretched out on the settee with the Great Cat of Re reclining on his chest as he (Sethos) chatted with Fatima.

"Amazing woman," he remarked, shifting the cat and sitting up. "She seems to take my metamorphoses for granted."

"I trust your day was productive?" Ramses inquired.

His uncle ignored the sarcastic tone. "I sent off a few telegrams. There were two for Emerson waiting at the telegraph office. I took the liberty of bringing them along."

He indicated the post basket, which was overflowing again.

After a suspicious examination of the first telegram—it was still sealed—Emerson ripped it open. "Ah! I told you Gargery would come through. He found out the name of Petherick's solicitor and made friends with the clerk. The terms of the will were easy to remember. Everything to the wife. It seems the lady was telling the truth about that."

He opened the next. "From Carter," he announced, and read it aloud. " 'Appreciate supervision. Arriving shortly to resume excavations.' "

"Quite a tactful way of warning you to restrict your activities," Sethos remarked. "Anything else of interest, Amelia?"

"The usual unwanted invitations and impertinent inquiries. Here's one for you, Ramses. Hand delivered."

"It's from Heinrich Lidman," Ramses reported. "Repeating his application for a position."

"What?" Emerson glared. "You haven't gone and hired someone without my permission, have you?"

"If you had listened to what Ramses said you would have realized we did nothing of the sort," his wife replied. "We told him we would consider his offer, but that you would have to approve it."

"Well, I don't. Who is the fellow, anyhow?"

"He was with Borchardt at Amarna before the War," Ramses said. "Experience like that might be useful to us. I met another fellow the other day you may also want to consider. He's a demoticist and—"

"Why the devil would I want another demoticist when I have you?" Emerson demanded. "I don't want anyone else. Once David gets here, my staff will be adequate. I wish the boy would hurry up. I need a skilled photographer when I open KV55."

"He'll be here in a few days," Ramses said. Emerson was being his unreasonable self. He had curtly dismissed both Ramses's suggestions, and airily ignored David's other skills, which far out-shone his talents as a photographer. Nefret and Selim were almost as competent in that specialty. Trying to conquer his annoyance, Ramses said, "If you need David so badly, why don't you wait for him?"

Emerson stroked his chin. "I suppose another day or two won't matter. Give me a chance to have a general look round."

"And," said his wife, "pursue our inquiries into Mrs. Petherick's disappearance."

"Bah," said Emerson. "There's no mystery about that. She'll reappear in a day or two, and regale the newspapers with lurid stories."

In this Emerson was mistaken. Mrs. Petherick did not reappear next day, or the day after. The search for her was sporadic at best, since no one knew where to look, or what to look for—a living woman or a dead body. The newspapers at-tempted to keep the sensation alive with dire hints of foul play and deadly curses, but the official position was that the lady was presumed to be alive unless proven dead, and without a corpus delicti the press had little to work on. They had taken up the term "black afrit," however, and it appeared frequently in their stories, together with an explanation of the meaning of the word "afrit," how it was pronounced, and fictitious reports of its appearances in various localities. This filled in space which was otherwise devoid of interest.

Emerson, of course, ignored the matter. He was unable to get ahead with his work at Deir el Medina as rapidly as he had hoped (an assessment any sensible individual would have made in the beginning). We had to spend an entire day excavating the broken pots and scraps of papyrus. They had apparently been dumped into a hole in the floor, covered over, and stamped down, and it was necessary to examine and record each bit in order to determine their relationship.

A small rebellion occurred that afternoon. With my tacit support (emphatic nods), Nefret declared she and Ramses would stop work early—that is to say, at the same hour most excavators quit for the day. "We promised the children we would take tea with them this afternoon," she announced. "You won't finish with those fragments today anyhow, Father."

"Yes, I will," Emerson declared. "But—er—if you promised the children . . ."

Emerson is the most stubborn man of my acquaintance. Having made that dogmatic claim, he kept us at it until gathering dusk made careful work impossible, and even then only my insistence made him stop. I was quite out of temper with him. We had missed tea and would barely have time enough to bathe and change before dinner.

However, when we dismounted in front of the house, we saw Sethos, Ramses and Nefret, and a fourth individual on the veranda, and Fatima just clearing away the tea things. The stranger, a shabby, undersized individual with gray-white hair, jumped to his feet when we entered. "Good evening, Professor and Mrs. Emerson. Your son was good enough to invite me to stay, but if I intrude—"

"Who the devil are you?" Emerson asked.

Ramses said, with a defiant look at his father, "This is Mikhail Katchenovsky, of whose work in demotic I told you. I took the liberty of asking him to stay for dinner. I told Fatima."

"My dear boy, this is your home," I said. "You are free to invite anyone you choose. Good evening, Mr. Katchenovsky. Have you two been having a jolly time gossiping about demotic?"

"It has been an honor," Katchenovsky

exclaimed. "To see the very working room where the great translations of texts were made, the papyri themselves."

Emerson's expression indicated his opinion of people who would wax ecstatic over crumbling papyri and obscure texts, but since this group included his son he refrained from stating that opinion. My little reminder, that Ramses had a perfect right to invite guests, had had a humbling effect. "Well, well," he said, with forced geniality. "Good to meet you, Karchenovsky. Ramses tells me you have done good work. Not for me to judge. Demotic is more or less Greek to me."

Uncertain as to whether this was a joke, Katchenovsky smiled, sobered, and smiled again. "I am honored that he should be familiar with my work, Professor. I have not published for a good many years, owing to . . . to circumstances over which I had no control."

Another casualty of the War? I wondered. It had ended four years ago, but some of the survivors of that awful conflict had been slow to recover from physical injury and mental anguish. Close inspection indicated that he was younger than his gray hair and lined face had led me to believe. Perhaps he had resisted the Bolsheviks and suffered imprisonment and privation.

Emerson would have said I was letting my imagination run away with me. Imagination, as I always say, is only another word for sympathetic intelligence.

Nefret said, "Dinner will be a little late, Mother. You have time for a whiskey and soda if you like."

"Excellent," I said. "It was thoughtful of you to tell Maaman to put it back."

Nefret chuckled. "I didn't. I think it's his new method of punishing us for being late so often."

"Better than burned food and salty soup," Emerson said.

He pushed emphatically on the lever of the gasogene. Soda spurted. Emerson wiped the table with his sleeve and handed me the glass.

"Any news of Mrs. Petherick?" I asked.

Nefret shook her head. "Not that we've heard. Nor any word from Miss Petherick. I've been expecting her to make another demand for the statue."

"It is a strange story," Katchenovsky said. "What will become of the statue?"

"I will return it to the legal owners, whoever they may be," Emerson replied. "That has yet to be determined."

"You are an honest man, Professor," Katchenovsky exclaimed. "But I would have expected no less of you."

"Hmph," said Emerson. "My sole interest in the statuette is in where it was found. We are still in the dark as to that."

"I wonder if I might see it," Katchenovsky said hesitantly. "I am by no means an authority, but one never knows what a new observer may notice."

"Have we time?" I asked Nefret.

"Yes, I think so. I wouldn't mind having another look myself."

"I'll get it." Emerson put his glass down and went into the house.

He was back almost at once, wild-eyed and fuming. "It's gone! The damn thing is gone!"

FROM MANUSCRIPT H

No one bothered to ask whether he was certain. The statuette had been in a locked drawer in Emerson's desk. A single look would have been enough.

Emerson drew a deep breath and gained command of himself. "Peabody," he said.

"Good Gad, Emerson, are you accusing me?"

"It would be just like you to decide the hiding place wasn't secure enough."

His wife gave him a look that should have raised blisters. "To be honest, I thought your desk was not secure. It is one of the first places a thief would look, and that lock can be easily broken. However, I would never have moved it without telling you. How can you think that of me?"

"Then who did take it?" Emerson shouted.

All eyes went to the unfortunate Russian. Katchenovsky huddled in the chair and burst into passionate denials.

"It can't have been he," Ramses broke in.

"He was in the house, in the storage room next to my study," Emerson said.

"And with me the entire time. I left the room once, to get a book from your study. I was gone less than three minutes, and Mr. Katchenovsky did not accompany me."

"Thank you," Katchenovsky gasped. "Thank you. It is true, I did not—"

"Oh, very well," Emerson said.

The ensuing silence was heavy with suspicion. Ramses tried not to look at his uncle. It wouldn't have surprised him to learn that Sethos had been unable to resist a piece so unique. Yet such a blatant theft was unlike him; he must have known he'd be the first to be suspected. After a long moment Sethos said, "It wasn't me either. Amelia—you believe me, don't you?"

She roused herself from a brown study. "As a matter of fact, I do. Are the children in bed yet?"

"They are supposed to be," Ramses said wryly. "But I wouldn't bank on it."

His mother rose. "Come along with me, all of you. Yes, Mr. Katchenovsky, you too. You have been accused, you have the right to learn the truth."

"What are you suggesting?" Emerson demanded. "Those dear little innocent children—"

"Do not leap to conclusions, Emerson, just come."

They followed the tree-lined curving path between the two houses. The gardener had lit the lamps; pools of light painted the clumps of flowers in the beds along the way, and leaves rustled like the soft murmur of running water. As they neared the house, a dark form leaped at them, baying like an infernal hound. Katchenovsky got behind Ramses.

"Go away, Amira," Ramses said, shoving at the dog.

The children were in bed, but naturally they were not asleep. Ramses heard the maidservant's soft Arabic. She was telling them a bedtime story. Both children were bilingual, having spoken both languages from infancy.

"And when the good mother snake found that her children were gone, taken as pets by the bad little boys of the house, she became very angry and spat her venom into the water jar, so that all who drank of it would surely die."

Ramses put out his arm to stop the others. "Let her finish the story, or they won't ever drink water again."

It was a very moral tale. Luckily for the household of the bad little boys, their father was a saint who knew the resident snake was benevolent, a protector of the house. When he saw his sons playing with the poor little snakes he scolded them. "In the name of the Prophet, release your victims at once!"

As soon as the little snakes, unharmed, returned to their mother, she was ashamed and thought how she could avert the damage she had done. She coiled herself round the water jar and squeezed until it broke into nine and ninety pieces, spilling the poisoned water harmlessly onto the ground.

"So you see," said Ramses, looking in the door, "it is wrong to torment animals."

"Particularly when they are animals that can spit venom," his mother added.

Carla leaped up with a scream of delight. "Have you all come to say good night again? Mr. Katchenovsky too!"

"You have met the gentleman?" Emerson asked, returning Carla's hug.

"I have had that pleasure," Katchenovsky said. "At tea."

"And Carla didn't try to bite you?"

"Why, no. She is a sweet little girl."

Carla giggled.

"Well done, Carla," said her grandmother. "Now, David John. What did you do with the statuette?"

David John's great blue eyes were as calm as a pool of still water. "It is in my toy chest, Grandmama."

She fished around among the stuffed animals and miniature trains and rocks of various sizes and shapes, and drew out the painted box. Handing it to Emerson, who was staring openmouthed at his grandson, she said sternly, "David John, you are guilty of deliberate disobedience. I told you you were not to go looking for it."

"Yes, Grandmama, those were your precise words. I did not have to go looking for it, since I knew where it was."

Ingenious little beggar, isn't he?" said Emerson with a fond chuckle. "To think of getting into the locked drawer by removing the one above it."

" 'Ingenious' is certainly one word for him," said his wife grimly. "However, I believe I have now composed an order that will thwart future attempts."

Ramses certainly hoped so. His mother had carefully avoided looking at him while she lectured her grandson, but he knew she was remembering **his** youthful exercises in ingenuity. Had he really been that devious? One or two examples came to his mind, and they moved him to take his mother's arm and give it a little squeeze as they walked back to the main house. She looked up at him and gave him a knowing smile.

Emerson has a frightful temper, but he is at heart a just and kindly man. As if to make up for his suspicions of Mr. Katchenovsky, he was excessively polite to the Russian during dinner, urging him to take second helpings of everything and even inviting him to talk about his work. Under the spell of his geniality the Russian gradually relaxed. Emerson listened with a glazed but benevolent eye while Ramses and Katchenovsky carried on a conversation of which none of us understood more than two sentences.

"You restore **dmd.n** at the beginning of the column, but there is not sufficient room for the full spelling of the word, and the final sign does not appear to me to be the bookroll, but rather . . ."

That was not one of the sentences I understood.

It did my heart good, however, to see Ramses enjoy himself so much. I determined to have a little talk with Emerson that very night. The dear fellow was getting out of hand. His plan of working at two different sites simultaneously increased the difficulties I had considered earlier. The plain truth of the matter was that we had not enough staff.

I made it up to him afterward.

Emerson said nothing of the alteration in our plans at breakfast. When we reached Deir el Medina, and he had inspected the area where we had worked the previous day, he called the others to him.

"Another two hours will finish here," he announced. "Cyrus, what about you?"

Cyrus stroked his goatee. "We've filled in the entrances to the tombs that don't have protective gates. I was planning to go over to the West Valley later today."

"Very good," said Emerson. "David's boat got in this morning, so he will be here tonight—"

"You can't count on that, my dear," I said. "He may not have disembarked in time to catch the morning train. Boat schedules are erratic, and—"

"Or tomorrow morning," Emerson said loudly.

"At which time I will open KV55. My staff will consist of—"

"Excuse me for a moment, Emerson, while I get pen and notepaper. I know you keep your notes in your head, or claim to, but the rest of us require—"

"Excuse me, Mother," Nefret broke in. "I have writing materials. Please take them."

It sounded like an order, not a suggestion. I accepted and nodded a silent acknowledgment, since Emerson's face was turning red.

"As I was saying," he said, with a pointed glance at me. "My staff will consist of Peabody and myself, Nefret and David, and half a dozen of our fellows. Selim and Daoud will continue here. Ramses, I want you to get on with your translating."

"I beg your pardon?" Ramses's face was a study in astonishment.

"I won't need you," Emerson said, as firmly as if he had arrived at this decision on his own, instead of giving in after a prolonged shouting match. "The tomb is small and cramped, and there's nothing there for you. If we are to conclude our work at Deir el Medina properly, the inscribed materials we found need to be translated and published. That's your job."

"But . . ." Ramses's eyebrows rose even farther. "But then . . . you mean for me to continue working on the papyri indefinitely? It will take weeks, if not months. There's a lot of material."

"I can help," Jumana said eagerly. "I would like very much to gain more experience in translating hieratic and demotic."

"Your first obligation is to Mr. Vandergelt," Emerson said. "He has greater need of you than Ramses does."

"Yes, sir," Jumana said submissively. Bertie, whose face had fallen when she spoke, brightened up. He hadn't ventured to contribute his opinions. He hardly ever did.

"I say!" Emerson exclaimed, as if the idea had just struck him, "what about employing that Russian fellow—Karnovoskovitch?—to give you a hand, Ramses? You said he was well qualified."

"He is," Ramses said.

"Of course, if you'd rather not share the credit . . ."

"That's never been an issue with me, Father," Ramses said reproachfully.

"I know that. You are generous to a fault. Well, that's settled. Unless we encounter some unforeseen difficulty, we should be able to finish in KV55 within a few weeks at most. While we are there, Cyrus and his crew will be working in the West Valley. If you take my advice, Vandergelt, you will begin with the tomb of Ay and the other unoccupied tombs nearby—Numbers 25 and 26. Look for foundation deposits and make sure you sift the damned debris thoroughly."

"Righto," said Cyrus, in a dreadful imitation of a British accent. "Any further orders, old chap?"

His sarcasm—which was accompanied by an amiable grin—was wasted on Emerson. "A fellow came by the other day looking for a position. Claims to be an expert on Amarna, worked at the site before the war. Name of—um—"

"Lidman," Ramses supplied. "Heinrich Lidman."

"That is what I was about to say," remarked Emerson. "I suggest you consider taking him on."

"Fine with me," Cyrus said. "I'll get in touch with him right away. Where is he staying?"

Emerson looked at his son, who said, "The Luxor."

Emerson nodded and went on. "As soon as we finish with KV55, you can have David and Nefret."

"That's darned generous of you," Cyrus exclaimed.

It was darned generous of **me**. As I am sure I need not tell the Reader, these arrangements were my idea and Emerson had not given in easily. I did not claim the credit, since I had learned that in marriage tact is not only good manners but good strategy.

We finished recording and removing the remaining debris before midday, and I persuaded Emerson to return to the house for a hasty luncheon. He barely gave us time to eat before he was on his feet again, urging us to hurry. "I told Vandergelt to meet us at half past one, and it is almost that now."

"I'll be along later," I said.

"So will I," said Sethos, stretching out on the sofa.

FROM MANUSCRIPT H

Ramses's mother never ceased to amaze him. Though she had not admitted it and never would, he knew she was the one responsible for Emerson's altered arrangements. He would have to think of a way of thanking her.

Cyrus was as impatient as Emerson to start the new work. He was waiting for them, astride his fat mare Queenie, at the foot of the road that led up to his house on the hill overlooking the Valley. Jumana looked like a doll perched on the big chestnut she had selected from Cyrus's stable, but, as Ramses knew, she had wrists of steel and a determination few horses would dare challenge. Bertie was there too, and so was none other than Heinrich Lidman. Cyrus hadn't wasted any time.

"You all know each other, I guess," he said. "Herr Lidman was good enough to respond immediately to my message."

"So pleased," Lidman said, bowing at everyone in turn. "An honor. I only hope I can be of—"

"Quite, quite," said Emerson. "Let's go."

Lidman fell modestly to the rear, beside Jumana. He rode well for a fat man, and his normal loquacity seemed to have deserted him. Or maybe he just couldn't get a word in once Jumana started talking.

Cyrus edged the mare close to Ramses.

"Funny thing happened last night," he whispered. "Fellow paid me a call. Fellow name of Montague. But it wasn't . . . er . . ."

"Sethos? No. It was the real article."

"That's what I figured. Better warn him, then."

"He knows. What did Montague want?"

"Bet you can guess. How is . . . er . . . he gonna get out of this one?"

"Your guess is as good as mine," Ramses said wryly. "He's changed his appearance, but I suspect there will be a few awkward incidents to explain."

They left the horses in the donkey park and passed the barrier into the Valley itself.

"I told Abu I'd be hiring tomorrow," Cyrus

said. "It was too late to get a full crew together today. I haven't even had a chance to read up on what's been done there."

"There's not much to read," Emerson replied. "The curse of our profession is the failure to publish. You may as well assume you're starting from scratch. That is what I intend to do. Ah—there's Selim." He raised a hand in greeting.

"Where are the rest of your fellows?" Cyrus asked.

"Don't need them today. I'm going to have a look round, make sure there's been no illegal digging. I promised Carter, you see."

"Sure, I see," Cyrus said with a knowing grin. "Mind if we tag along?"

They made their way to the far end of the Valley and into the side wadi where the tomb of Thutmose III lay high in the cliff. "I thought those bas—— the Simsahs would be back," said Emerson, inspecting the pile of rubble. It looked pretty much the same to Ramses, but his father's eye was infallible. "They didn't find anything, though."

"Is there anything to find?" Cyrus asked hopefully.

"Who knows?" Emerson rubbed his chin and looked pensive. "One would have to clear the area down to bedrock, and there's the devil of a lot of rubble."

The day passed as they tramped along. The sun beat down; there was no shade, and the heat, trapped between narrow stony walls, climbed rapidly. Emerson kept Nefret and Selim busy with the cameras. Cyrus suggested they return to the Castle for tea. Emerson promptly vetoed the idea and was about to lead the way into another side wadi when a familiar voice hailed them.

"It's Mother." Ramses nudged his preoccupied father. "And Nasir, with a tea basket. Good. I'm parched."

"You should have said so, my boy," Emerson exclaimed.

"Who's that with Mrs. Emerson?" Bertie asked, squinting in the sunlight.

"A friend," Ramses said, wishing he could remember Sethos's latest alias.

Cyrus stared and began to cough violently.

They joined the others, in the entrance to a "nice" empty tomb, where his mother introduced "Anthony Bissinghurst."

Jumana studied "Bissinghurst" with a puzzled frown. "Have we met, sir? Your face is familiar."

Sethos smiled. "I would certainly remember having met you, Miss Jumana. I have heard a great many complimentary things about you."

Ramses eyed his uncle with professional interest. He'd learned a lot from Sethos, but he doubted he would ever match his abilities. The physical alterations—the suspiciously black hair and mustache, the tinted glasses that darkened his eyes—were the least of it. Speech patterns, posture, the frequent smiles and expansive gestures were perfectly in character with an Anthony Bissinghurst. Whoever he might be. He hoped that this time Sethos had had the sense to invent an identity instead of assuming one.

"Only an amateur," Sethos explained modestly, in response to a question from Cyrus. "No formal training, you see. But keen, very keen."

They ended the day in front of Tomb 55. It was on the main path, near two royal tombs popular with visitors, most of whom had returned to their hotels by that time. Emerson stopped and looked over the low wall the Davis expedition had built in 1907. The entrance was almost six feet below this surface, and it was partially blocked by piles of fallen stones and modern rubbish ranging from rotting food to dead animals, and worse. Tourists and guards had obviously used the handy pit as a trash receptacle.

"Let's just have a quick look," said Emerson.

"Not I," said his wife decidedly.

Emerson looked pointedly at his brother. Sethos pressed one hand to his chest and coughed loudly. After a look at the mess, Cyrus shook his head. The others were game, though Ramses had a feeling that Lidman would have declined had he been given a choice. One by one they climbed down into the pit. Bertie lowered Jumana into Emerson's raised hands and then followed her.

Emerson was the first to peer over the fallen rubble in the doorway. "Did anybody bring a torch?" he inquired.

Nobody had. At Emerson's request, his wife produced a candle and matches from her handy pockets and handed them down. In its dim light they saw what they had expected to see: a flight of stone steps, littered with fallen stones. As Ramses knew, there were twenty steps, ending in a sloping corridor that led to the burial chamber, but the candlelight reached only as far as the middle of the stairs.

The stench of decaying organic material was overpowering. Lidman pressed a handkerchief to his face and made choking noises.

"You'll have to learn not to be so squeamish if you want to work with us," Emerson said genially. "Give me a hand, Ramses. I think I can squeeze through."

"No, sir," Ramses said firmly. "The fill is too unstable, and you don't know what's down there. Snakes, for example."

"Quite right," his mother called. "That goes for

you too, Ramses. Emerson, do not attempt to persuade him. It is against all your principles of excavation to go blundering in where proper excavators fear—"

"Curse it," Emerson said loudly. But the reminder succeeded where appeals to common sense failed. Grudgingly he turned away from the enticing opening.

It took two of them to hoist Lidman up to the rim of the pit, with Bertie hauling from above. The German collapsed onto the ground, but he summoned a game smile. "Out of condition," he wheezed.

"Soon get you back in shape," said Emerson, who had required no one's assistance. Ramses wondered whether he would be in the same physical condition when he was his father's age. Probably not. Emerson was unique.

"We start tomorrow morning at six," Emerson went on, cleaning his hands by wiping them on his trousers. "You too, Vandergelt. Er—that is, I presume that is your intention?"

The belated courtesy was the result of a sharp jab in the ribs from his wife. Cyrus, who was well accustomed to Emerson's manners, or lack thereof, grinned and nodded. "Soon as I can get my crew together. What's your hurry?"

"I am always in a hurry," said Emerson.

It was true, but Ramses suspected his father had an even stronger motive for pushing ahead. Howard Carter was due in a few weeks. What Emerson meant to do before that was anybody's guess, but Ramses wouldn't have been surprised to learn that it would constitute a violation of the Carnarvon-Carter concession.

They were at the tomb next morning shortly after 6 A.M. No one had spoken to Ramses about getting on with his translations. He'd have come anyhow. He was as curious as the rest of them about what was inside Tomb 55.

At that hour the Valley was "uncontaminated by bloody tourists," to quote Emerson. They had brought a wooden ladder, which made access to the entrance easier. Clearing away the modern trash was a dirty job. After watching for a while, Emerson said, "This is going to take some time. I'll leave it to you, Hassan. Ramses, shall we ride over to the West Valley and see if Cyrus requires assistance?"

Hassan, a fastidious man, pursed his lips and rolled his eyes but said nothing. Nefret said, "I'll come along too, if you don't mind."

It took almost half an hour, on horseback, to reach the West Valley. Cut off from the main valley by towering cliffs, it was a natural amphitheater of austere beauty, "uncontaminated by bloody tourists." There were good reasons why it was ignored by visitors and largely unexplored by Egyptologists. Compared with the plethora of royal tombs in the East Valley, this was barren ground in archaeological terms, and difficult of access. There were no cleared roads, and the closest of the tombs, that of Amenhotep III, Akhenaton's father, was some distance from the entrance to the gorge. Only one other decorated royal tomb had been found, attributed to one of Akhenaton's successors, the Father of the God Ay. It was even more isolated, at the far end of the valley. As they came nearer they saw the cloud of dust that indicated activity, and heard the sounds of voices. Emerson nodded approval.

"He took my advice, I see."

Advice was hardly the word; he had all but ordered Cyrus. Risha stepped daintily around a boulder in the middle of the track, and Ramses said, "So he did. Why the tomb of Ay, Father? There's room in those cliffs for Lord knows how many other tombs, and nobody's ever done a complete survey."

"Process of elimination, my boy. Ay was a high official under Akhenaton before he took the throne for himself, and although he returned to the old religion, he may have had enough affection for his king to retain a memento of him."

"So that's it. You're still fixed on finding the original location of the statue."

"When I set my mind on something I don't give it up," retorted Emerson—an understatement if ever there was one. "Ay's successor, Harmhab, was the first to begin the damnatio memoriae of Akhenaton, and the Ramesside rulers were equally hostile to him. They'd have melted the statuette down."

"Mother will be glad to hear you don't mean to investigate that huge tomb of Harmhab."

Emerson smiled and then scowled. "I like to stir her up now and then. D'you know she finished that article of mine?"

"Did she really?"

"It was overdue," Nefret said sweetly. "Wasn't it?"

"Hmph," said Emerson.

A hail from one of the workmen announced their arrival, and Cyrus came to meet them. "Checking up on me, are you?" he asked.

"Not at all, not at all." Emerson dismounted. "Just dropped by to see if there is anything we can do."

"Nothing to do, nothing to see. We've just begun. How about you?"

"The same," said Emerson. He ran a critical eye

over the scene. Jumana waved and Emerson waved back. "Where's that fellow Lidman?"

"Resting," Cyrus said.

"What? It's not even midday."

"He said he wasn't feeling well."

"Bah," said Emerson.

"Not everyone has your stamina, Father," Nefret said. "I'd better have a look at him."

She headed toward the spot where a lonely figure sat hunched under a sunshade. Ramses followed, leaving his father and Cyrus arguing about foundation deposits.

Lidman certainly looked sickly. He raised a face slick with sweat, round and pale as a winter moon, and started to stand. Nefret put a hand on his shoulder. "Don't get up. Cyrus says you aren't well. What seems to be the trouble?"

"You are a physician?" Lidman asked. "So at least I have heard. It is nothing, Frau Doktor Emerson, it will soon pass. The usual trouble . . ." He hesitated, and then put his hand on his conspicuous stomach.

"A common affliction," Nefret said, with a reassuring smile. She felt his forehead. "I don't think you have a fever, though it's hard to tell, the sun is so hot."

"I am very warm," Lidman said, drooping. "And my heart is pounding."

He extended a limp wrist. Emerson came charging up while she was taking Lidman's pulse. "Nothing wrong with him, is there?" he demanded.

"His pulse is a little fast, but not dangerously so. Just to be on the safe side, I think I had better take him to the house and examine him."

"The Castle's closer," Cyrus said.

"I can do a more complete examination at the clinic," Nefret said, in her physician's firm voice. "Are you able to ride, Mr. Lidman?"

"Yes, oh, yes. It is most kind. I am so sorry, Mr. Vandergelt, to fail you on the very first day, when I had hoped to please you with my—"

"Nothing wrong with his vocal cords, I see," Emerson remarked.

"Not your fault, Lidman," Cyrus assured the man. "You'll be fit again in a day or two. Just take it easy and do what the lady says. She's a first-rate doctor."

"I'll go with them," Ramses said.

"What?" Emerson scowled, and then nodded reluctantly. "Yes, I suppose you had better. In case he falls off the confounded horse. Hurry back."

Ramses tactfully refrained from replying. If the afflicted German's condition was serious, Nefret might need his help.

Lidman kept up well at first, chattering with

forced cheerfulness about the life and times of Akhenaton. Hoping to distract him from his discomfort, Ramses kept up the conversation (when he could get a word in); but the hot sun and the rough terrain eventually took their toll, and by the time they reached the house Lidman was bent almost double over the horse's neck. He slid awkwardly off into Ramses's grasp and had to be helped into the clinic.

"Do you want me to stay?" Ramses asked.

He had addressed his wife, but it was Lidman who replied. Flat on his back, clutching modestly at the neck of his shirt, he gasped, "Please. If it is not too much trouble."

"You needn't be embarrassed," Nefret said, from the sink where she was washing her hands. "I just want to listen to your heart and take your temperature. And I've seen a lot of men with their shirts off. Ramses, would you help him?"

The flabby white torso bared by the removal of Lidman's shirt was not an attractive sight, but he submitted without visible embarrassment to Nefret's quick examination.

"No fever," she announced, shaking down the thermometer. "And there's nothing wrong with your heart."

Lidman groaned and pressed his hands to his

belly. "You can give me medicine? Then I will return to my duties."

"Not today," Nefret said. "I can give you something that will settle your stomach, but I want to be certain it is working properly and that there are no adverse side effects. You had better spend the night. We'll see how you feel in the morning."

"But I must—I must—"

"It's a waste of breath arguing with her," Ramses said pleasantly. "We can fit you out with pajamas and the rest."

He left it to Nefret and Fatima to make the arrangements, and went off to his workroom in a thoughtful frame of mind.

They were all on the veranda waiting for tea, except for his mother, who was upstairs working on her notes, when his father returned. After a word of apology, he headed straight for the bath chamber, leaving a distinct smell of garbage in his wake. Emerson wouldn't ask any man to do a job he shirked.

"Good heavens," said Sethos, wrinkling his nose. "I see I was wise to remain here today."

"I do hope you weren't bored," Ramses said. "How did you pass the time?"

"Playing with us," Carla said. "He knows lots of good stories about tomb robbers."

"I'll just bet he does," Ramses muttered.

"But he cheated at blindman's buff."

She grinned admiringly at Sethos, who grinned back at her. "So did you. How is your patient, Nefret?"

No need to ask how he had found out about Lidman. Fatima, arranging the tea things, was humming quietly.

"It's nothing more than the usual stomach trouble," Nefret said. "But I want to keep him here overnight to be certain."

"There's no time for sickness in this business," said Emerson, erupting from the house in his usual abrupt fashion. "Get the fellow up, Nefret, work is the best medicine—as Peabody has often said."

He held the door for his wife. "Isn't that right, my dear?" he inquired politely.

"Generally speaking, yes." She took a chair and beckoned to Fatima. "However, Nefret is quite right to be cautious. Egypt is full of perils for those who are not acclimated."

"Hmmm, yes," Emerson said. Ramses deduced they had had another argument. They were always excessively polite to each other afterward.

Lidman did not appear for tea or for dinner.

Fatima had taken him a tray. Nefret reported that
he had eaten everything on it and seemed better,
but her mother-in-law couldn't let that statement
stand.

"I will just have a cheerful little chat with him,"
she announced.

"So will I," said Emerson. "Good Gad, can't
have the fellow lying about for days. Where have
you put him, Nefret?"

She had given Lidman one of the guest rooms in
their house. The whole family trailed along, even
Sethos, though Ramses tried to dissuade him.

"If you wake the children, there'll be hell to pay."

"I will be as silent as a little mouse," said his
uncle.

Lidman was wearing one of Emerson's night-
shirts, since Ramses's pajamas wouldn't button
around his waist. Propped on pillows, he looked
up from the book he was reading, his eyes widen-
ing in alarm. Ramses couldn't blame him; the
combined family gave the impression that this was
an inquisitorial delegation rather than a call on a
sick friend.

"Better, are you?" Emerson inquired, in what
he presumably thought was an encouraging tone.

His wife had gone to the bedside. Lidman
shrank back as she felt his forehead. "Nice and

cool," she announced. "Have you taken your medicine, Mr. Lidman?"

"Yes, madam. I am better. Oh, yes, much better. You are very kind."

"Breakfast at six," said Emerson. "Then off to the Valley, eh?"

"That depends," Nefret said. "We're right down the hall, Mr. Lidman. Don't hesitate to call out if you need anything." She added pointedly, "Good night."

Sethos was one of the last to leave. "I believe we met several years ago, in Cairo, Herr Lidman. At the shop of Zaki Gabra, wasn't it?"

"I am sorry," Lidman said. "I do not remember."

That wasn't surprising, Ramses thought, since Sethos had probably been someone else at the time—if the meeting had actually taken place. He said good night and followed his uncle out.

"Was that a test?" he asked softly.

"If it was, he passed. Admitting to an acquaintance that never existed is a sure sign of guilt."

"What do you suspect him of?"

"Like your dear mother, I suspect everyone of everything."

"I'll escort you past Amira," Ramses said, following him along the corridor.

"No need. I spent part of the afternoon getting to know the dog. She adores me."

"That's no compliment. She adores everyone she's ever met."

"Think about that," Sethos said, and went on his way.

It wasn't the dog that wakened Ramses. He was on his feet and out of bed before he realized what had. Emerson's voice was noted for its carrying qualities, and he was employing it freely. Ramses hurried down the hallway toward the children's room. For a wonder they were both sleeping quietly. There was nothing at the window. On the way back he ran into Nefret—literally—caught her round the waist, and reported, "They're all right. Stay here."

He didn't waste time putting on his boots; his feet were as hardened as those of an Egyptian. Most of the lamps along the pathway to the main house had burned out, but as he ran on he saw the dim light of a torch ahead. His mother held it.

"Ah, there you are," she said. "This contraption needs a new battery."

His father was bent over a dark form sprawled on the paving stones. Somehow Ramses wasn't surprised to recognize Lidman's round pale face and portly form.

"Wake up, damn it," Emerson said, shaking the fallen man. "Peabody, stick those smelling salts under his nose."

"I fear I neglected to bring them" was the calm reply; but by the time she finished the sentence, Lidman's eyes were open.

"What happened?" he gasped. "Where has it gone?"

"Where has what gone?" Emerson demanded. Lidman's head rolled back and forth.

"Stop shaking him, Father," Ramses said.

"Oh, yes."

Emerson let go. Lidman's head hit the ground with a thump. "Sorry," Emerson said. "Answer me, Lidman. What are you doing out here in the middle of the night?"

Emerson's methods were brutal but effective. Lidman raised clenched fists, crossing them over his chest. "It was at the window. I was afraid for the children. I went out, and saw it running toward your house. I caught hold of it, and then . . . I remember nothing more."

"Damnation," Emerson said. " 'It'?"

Something protruded from one of Lidman's clenched hands. Ramses pried his fingers apart and removed a tattered scrap of black cloth.

FIVE

FROM MANUSCRIPT H (CONT.)

They found Amira lying beside the path. No one's heart skipped a beat at the sight of the motionless bulk, since they had located her by the volume of her snores. Poking her and yelling in her ear had no effect; presumably she had been given a drug of some sort, and letting her sleep it off seemed the wisest course. Nefret prescribed the same treatment for Lidman, who was trembling and even paler than usual. She led him to his room, and the others went back to the main house.

"Doesn't this family ever get a full night's sleep?" Sethos asked, concealing a yawn behind his hand. Ramses had noticed he was fully dressed.

Emerson, who considered pajamas a newfangled fad, had pulled on a pair of trousers over his nightshirt. Waving this rhetorical question aside, he said, "His story doesn't ring true. Someone tried to get into the house. That was what woke me." He glanced at his wife, whose silence fairly rang with the words she wasn't saying. "Er—well, to be precise, it woke Peabody. For once she had sense enough to rouse me before she dashed out."

"To be precise," she corrected, "it was Sethos who woke first."

All eyes turned to Sethos, who was draped elegantly across the settee. "I wasn't asleep," he said.

"What alerted you?" Ramses asked.

"I was sitting in the courtyard enjoying a quiet smoke and listening to Ali Yussuf snore," Sethos explained. "I wouldn't count on him to warn you, he's a growing lad and needs his sleep. Unfortunately the intruder—I hate the phrase 'man in black,' if you don't mind—came round the front, by way of the veranda. He heard me coming and beat a quick retreat. He'd bolted the door on the outside. I had to go back through the house, and I took the liberty of waking Amelia as I did so."

"How long did that take?" Ramses asked.

"Not long enough for the purported afrit to return to your house, stare in the window, wake Lidman, and dash back in this direction," Sethos said.

"If it was Lidman, why didn't he simply return to his room? He had time for that, didn't he?" Ramses asked.

"He ran the risk of encountering you before he got there, that's why," Emerson said. "It was safer to lie down and make up a wild story."

"And the scrap of black cloth in his hand?"

"Prepared in advance," Emerson said. "In case he was caught."

"What about the dog?" Ramses persisted.

"Lidman had access to Nefret's dispensary for several hours this afternoon, and a hearty dinner," Sethos said. "Roast lamb, wasn't it? I told you the dog wouldn't bark at anyone she had met before. He didn't want her following him, so he slipped her a treat."

"It fits, but it isn't conclusive," Ramses said. "We can't accuse him."

"You are too trusting," Sethos jeered. "Who is the fellow, anyhow? Did anyone take the trouble of investigating his story? Amelia, I am surprised at you."

"Ramses recognized his name. But you are right, we ought to make further inquiries. You will see to it, won't you, Emerson? Yes."

Mr. Lidman came to breakfast with Ramses and Nefret, right on time, and looking no guiltier than anyone else. He assured us he felt quite himself again, and the way he engulfed Fatima's excellent breakfast was testimony to his restored digestion. He couldn't stop talking about his horrible experience with the afrit.

"I assure you, when I caught hold of it I felt nothing except the cloth itself," he said, round-eyed. "It was as if there were nothing inside. I regret I could not apprehend it. I feared, you see, that it meant some harm to the children and—"

"Why should you suppose that?" Emerson asked.

"They are so young, so helpless, so trusting. You watch over them closely, do you not?"

"We do," I assured him, not entirely pleased at his concern for the children. "You will be glad to hear that the dog is fully recovered this morning."

"The dog? Yes, yes, I wondered why it did not bark. What was wrong with it?"

Either he is innocent as a babe in arms or he believes he's got away with it, I thought, watching him as he stuffed his mouth with toast and marmalade. We had agreed not to speak of our suspicions, in order to put him off guard, so no one asked embarrassing questions. Sethos had been right to reproach me for being so gullible, but we would soon know whether Lidman's claim to have worked at Amarna was true.

After a little reminder from me, Emerson

instructed Ramses to remain at the house to get on with his translations. He waved good-bye to us as we rode away, and I thought he looked a trifle wistful at being left behind. He was interested in KV55 too, but I had no doubt that my arrangement was for the best. Sometimes people do not know what is good for them.

FROM MANUSCRIPT H

Ramses knew his feeling of disappointment at watching the others ride off was pure perversity. He had wanted to work on the papyri, and now that he had been given the opportunity, he didn't feel like doing it. After a restless ramble through the house, and a check of the locked drawer in his father's desk, he went to the stable and saddled Risha. He told himself he wasn't exactly disobeying orders. His father had suggested he hire Mikhail Katchenovsky, and the only way of locating the Russian was through the Metropolitan Museum people.

It always lifted his spirits to see Hatshepsut's temple and imagine how it might have looked when the trees from Punt lined the causeway with green ribbons and the newly finished colonnades glowed in the sunlight. Monumental statues of the queen-king had stood everywhere. The remains of them had been found, smashed into bits. The adjoining temple of the Eleventh Dynasty king Nebhepetre had not been as impressive even in its heyday, and there was not much of it left.

Feeling slightly guilty about his dereliction of duty and his interruption of their work, he declined Barton's invitation to dismount.

"I'm looking for Katchenovsky. Is he here?"

"Not yet." Barton slapped at his cheek, which was being explored by a gnat. "He doesn't usually come until afternoon. If you're in a hurry you could look for him. He's staying at one of the West Bank hotels—the one with the bathtub in the courtyard."

"Ah, yes, Hussein Ali's luxurious place. I'm not in that much of a hurry. Just ask him, if you will, to come to the house after he's through here. I have a proposition for him."

Lansing came along in time to hear the last speech. He raised his eyebrows, and Ramses explained that he had no intention of stealing the Russian away from his work with the Met. "I'll only need him for a few hours a day."

"That's okay," Lansing said. "We really don't have much for him to do. Felt sorry for the fellow, actually, he looked as if he needed a job. So you're going ahead with translating the Deir el Medina material?"

Ramses nodded. "I plan to. Unless something else comes up."

"Which it's likely to, with your lot," Lansing said. "You sure you won't stay awhile and catch us up on the news?"

"There's nothing new, except that David is due to arrive today or tomorrow. We'll be having a little dinner party for him one of these days. Mother will let you know."

"I'll settle for an invitation to the exorcism," Barton said. "When is it to be?"

"Where did you hear that?" Ramses asked.

"All the men are talking about it." Barton's voice dropped to a sinister basso. " 'The black afrit walks the streets of Luxor.' "

"Daoud," Ramses said resignedly.

"The Oracle of Luxor," Barton said with a broad grin.

"He's more accurate than most oracles," Ramses admitted. "Father is considering the idea, but he hasn't made up his mind yet. I'll be sure to let you know."

On his way back he stopped at the guardhouse to tell Wasim he was expecting a caller that afternoon. "Let him pass. And no baksheesh," he added sternly.

Wasim fondled the aged rifle. "If you say so, Brother of Demons. But I am a poor man, and there have been fewer visitors."

Katchenovsky turned up several hours later, looking more cadaverous than ever, but he lit up like a lantern when Ramses offered him the position.

"I hoped," he exclaimed. "But I did not dare ask."

He'd done everything short of asking, though, during their conversation at dinner. Had it been that eager timidity that had prompted Ramses's mother to bully her husband into changing his plans? She liked to think of herself as hard-hearted and practical, but everybody in Luxor knew she was the softest of soft touches. Katchenovsky was the sort of pathetic specimen she was fond of rescuing. He must be hard up if he was staying at Hussein Ali's.

He led the Russian to his workroom and explained what he wanted done. "The first priority is to sort and stabilize the material we found yesterday at Deir el Medina. You know how quickly papyrus can deteriorate once it's exposed to the air."

He demonstrated the methods he used. The Russian was quick to catch on. They worked silently and efficiently until Fatima popped her head in and announced that tea would be ready shortly.

"You'll stay, I hope," Ramses said.

"Will your lovely children be there? I am very fond of children."

"Oh, yes, they never miss tea."

They interrupted a violent argument between Carla and David John. Carla was the violent one; her shouts had no effect on her brother, who stood with folded arms, shaking his head. The argument seemed to have something to do with the dog. Ramses deduced that Carla wanted Amira to join them for tea. The dog was peering hopefully through the bars at the door. The Great Cat of Re stared back at her, tail thrashing.

"Shame on you," Ramses said, taking his enraged daughter in a tight embrace. "You know the dog isn't allowed in. Is this any way to behave before a guest?"

Carla's temper was as changeable as a windstorm. Her face was still bright red with fury when she hugged him back and gave Katchenovsky an angelic smile. "Good evening, sir. Can we have tea now, Papa?"

"As soon as the others get here."

"They are here. Grandmama said they wanted to wash first."

She left him to lean against Katchenovsky's chair and tell him about Amira, but she instantly abandoned the Russian when Emerson came out of the house.

"Can we have tea now, Grandpapa?"

"Yes, yes, may as well," said Emerson, pushing his damp hair back from his forehead. "Ah—good evening—er—Kravatsky. Is your work going well, my boy?"

Knowing his father had only asked out of politeness, Ramses said briefly, "Mikhail is being a great help. How did your day go, Father?"

"Well, very well. We have the debris cleared from the entrance and the steps." He paused to light his pipe. "Have to go carefully from here on; there appear to be a number of pieces from the gilded shrine in the rubble in the corridor. You remember it was left there when Davis closed the tomb in '07. Despite my protests," he added, scowling.

"I thought Weigall removed it the following year," Ramses said.

"While my back was turned," Emerson growled.

Well and truly turned, Ramses thought. They had been far out in the Western Desert that year. Emerson's diatribe—"no idea what he did with the damned thing, it never arrived at the museum, probably fell to pieces when he took it out"—was interrupted by the arrival of Nefret and his mother. Sethos was the last to turn up.

"It took a while to dry my hair," he explained unnecessarily.

Fatima brought the tea things and everyone began talking at once, with the shrill voices of the children rising and falling like an obbligato. Ramses smiled apologetically at the Russian. "I'm afraid it's always like this. Pure pandemonium."

Katchenovsky started and came back from whatever internal world he had been occupying. "It is very pleasant. Such a large, loving family."

Emerson continued to hold forth on the iniquities of other archaeologists, particularly those of the Davis excavations. Sensing that he had a new audience, he turned his attention on Katchenovsky.

"Are you familiar with the excavation of KV55?"

"No, sir," the Russian said. True or not, it was the right answer.

"Botched from start to finish," Emerson declared. "It contained the parts of a gold-encrusted shrine made by Akhenaton for his mother, Queen Tiy, and a battered coffin containing the badly decayed remains of an individual Davis insisted was the queen herself. However, examination of the bones proved they were those of a young man—too young, in my opinion, to be Akhenaton. The shrine had been dismantled; the persons who entered the tomb in antiquity were probably government officials who meant to remove it, after cutting out Akhenaton's cartouches on the shrine and other objects. However, they found that the separate pieces were too large to get through the partially blocked corridor. They left one side of it lying atop the rubble in the corridor, and the other parts leaning against the wall of the burial chamber. I won't bore you with the details . . ."

Thank God for that, Ramses thought. Katchenovsky was putting on a good show of interest, though, and when Emerson paused to relight his pipe, he said diffidently, "I did read something about it, Professor. As I recall, the tomb was completely cleared. May I ask why you are reexamining it?"

Emerson told him, in considerable detail. "If Petherick's statuette was there in 1907, there may be some scrap of evidence left. It is imperative that we discover where and when it was found."

"Why is that, sir?" Katchenovsky asked.

"Because," said Emerson, surprised at such ignorance but ready to relieve it, "if it did not originate in KV55, we must look for another source. The thieves who took the statuette may have found equally valuable artifacts."

His wife overheard question and answer. She pursed her lips and shook her head. "Now who is letting his imagination run away with him? We are reexcavating the tomb, Mr. Katchenovsky, because it was not done properly the first time. That is sufficient reason. Enough about that. Ramses, my dear, have you heard anything more from the Pethericks?"

"No, Mother. I have to inform you, though, that Daoud has told everyone on the West Bank that an exorcism is planned. Barton and the rest of the Met crew want to be invited."

"Oh dear," his mother murmured. "Emerson, you must deny the story and give Daoud a talking-to."

"What, no exorcism?" Nefret asked. "I was looking forward to it."

"Hmmm," said Emerson.

At breakfast next morning Emerson announced that they would spend a few hours in the West Valley, "helping" Cyrus. He took it for granted that Ramses would come along. His wife opened her mouth to object, but Ramses said quickly, "That's quite all right. I've arranged with Mikhail to work on the papyri during the afternoon, so I can certainly spare Father a few hours in the morning."

"Oh," said Emerson. "Yes. Thank you, my boy."

Cyrus's crew was hard at work when they reached the site, carrying out baskets of rubble from the stairs and corridor. "Have you been inside?" Emerson asked, peering into the open rectangle of the door.

"Had a quick look yesterday," Cyrus admitted. "It's not as bad as some I've seen; no collapsed walls or ceilings, a fairly thin layer of debris. The paintings in the burial chamber are in poor condition. They need to be copied and photographed. When can I have David?"

"After I've finished with him," Emerson said ominously. He stopped one of the men and examined the contents of his basket. "Rain debris. Washed down. You are sifting it thoroughly, of course."

"Of course," Cyrus said. "Want to go in?"

Ramses had never been in the tomb before, though it had gaped open since the early nineteenth century. He gave his mother a hand during the descent of the rock-cut stairs, which were crumbling and uneven. A sloping passageway led down to a second, longer flight of stairs and to a second corridor, also sloping down. Dust rose from under their feet and dimmed the light of their torches. The air was close and hot.

A chamber, its walls bare like those of the corridors, opened directly into the presumed burial chamber, and the figures painted on the walls seemed to leap out at them: a row of sacred baboons, which had given the West Valley its Arabic name—the Valley of the Monkeys; scenes of sacrifice and worship; a long hieroglyphic inscription from the Book of the Dead; and a badly battered scene which appeared to represent the tomb owner on a skiff in the marshes, hunting birds.

"Unusual to find that theme in a royal tomb," Ramses said, indicating the hunting scene.

This unthinking remark prompted a lecture from Emerson on the design and decoration of royal tombs. The trouble with Father, Ramses thought—one of the troubles—was that he really did know a lot about Egyptology, and he talked about the subject with passion and authority. If only he would chose a nice airy lecture hall instead of the depths of a tomb! After approximately twenty minutes his wife mopped her face for the second time and said, "That was very interesting, Emerson, and I am sure we all enjoyed it. Now let us go."

"Debris is thicker down here," Emerson said obliviously. "Is that a pelvic bone?"

"Cyrus will excavate this room in due course and with all proper care," his wife said firmly. "Out, Emerson."

They retraced their steps, "emerging from the underworld," like reanimated Egyptians.

"Someone really hated the old fellow, didn't they?" Nefret said. "His name and his figures deliberately hacked out, along with those of his wife. How do they know it's his tomb?"

That got Emerson started again. "The desecrators missed one image, which was that of the king's ka figure, identified, not by the usual cartouches but by an unusual spelling of his Horus name. They were working from a list, which didn't include that variant. By the way, Vandergelt, I saw something sticking out of the dried mud in the burial chamber that could be a sarcophagus lid. Will you—"

"I will, I will," Cyrus said with a grin. "What about a drink?"

Even Emerson drank thirstily of the cold tea Cyrus provided. Keeping an eagle eye on the workmen, he said suddenly, "Where's that fellow Lidman?"

"He didn't turn up this morning."

"What?" Emerson scowled blackly.

"I told him to be at the Castle at five-thirty. We waited until six."

"He may be ill again," Ramses suggested.

"Then he ought to have sent word," Emerson grumbled. "You shouldn't have taken him on, Vandergelt."

"You recommended him," Cyrus said mildly. "If we don't hear from him today I'll send someone over to the hotel to inquire."

"Hmph," said Emerson. "You'll let me hear what you find out. Ramses, we had better be getting back."

They did hear from Cyrus later that afternoon. Lidman's body had been found washed up on the bank half a mile north of Luxor.

"It's a miracle he didn't drown," Nefret exclaimed.

"It was a near thing," I replied. "The police consider it an unfortunate accident. According to the barman at the Winter Palace, he had been drinking rather heavily."

I had, of course, felt obliged to go at once to Luxor after we received Cyrus's message. I located the fellahin who had found Lidman and pumped the water out of him—thereby saving his life, as they repeatedly pointed out—and rewarded them appropriately. They had taken him to the office of Dr. Westin, so I turned my steps thitherward.

Westin was not the man our dear departed Dr. Willoughby had been. He bore a certain resentment against us, possibly because Nefret's rate of cures exceeded his. (A most unprofessional attitude, as I had often told him.) A tall, stout man who had compensated for the loss of hair on his head by encouraging an excessive amount of beard, he was at first reluctant to let me see his patient. Naturally I prevailed.

"The poor fellow did not seem to know me at first," I explained to my listeners. "He had suffered injuries to his head as well as his limbs. How severe they were I was unable to ascertain, since Westin had swathed him in bandages."

"Perhaps he charges by the yard," Nefret suggested.

Cyrus, who had dropped in to hear my report, let out a whoop of laughter, and then sobered. "I feel responsible for the fellow, since he was technically in my employ. I'll tell Westin to send his bill to me. Guess I can pay for a few miles of bandages. What did he say was wrong with Lidman?"

"Severe bruises and contusions," I replied. "And a possible concussion, resulting in temporary loss of memory."

"So he doesn't remember what happened?" Cyrus asked.

I glanced over my shoulder at the tea table, where both children were busy with the plum cake and caught the inquiring eye of David John. Ramses can, as Daoud's saying has it, "hear a whisper across the Nile," and I feared his son was following in the paternal footsteps. I lowered my voice.

"He had gone for a walk, a long walk, along the

river toward Karnak. He remembers seeing a shadowy form approach him."

"A shadowy form?" Sethos echoed. "Oh, please, don't tell me . . ."

"I fear I must, since that is what he said. He even employed the term . . . You know the one."

"'The black afrit'?" Cyrus exclaimed.

"Keep your voice down," I said sharply. "David John, I believe you are eavesdropping. When I wish to include you in the conversation I will invite you to join us."

"Yes, Grandmama," said David John. No cherub could have looked more innocent.

"The newspapers are going to be all over this," said Sethos.

"I made it very clear to Mr. Lidman that he was not to repeat the—er—phrase in question to anyone else, including Dr. Westin. I took the liberty of intimating that he stood the risk of losing his position with you, Cyrus, if he were indiscreet."

"Well, that's all right," Cyrus said. "What do you make of his story, Amelia?"

I helped myself to a second cup of tea and sipped it reflectively. I knew everyone was hanging on my words, so I chose them with care. "This event has forced me to revise my tentative theory. There are only three possible explanations for his seeming accident. One, it **was** an accident. He wandered off the road while intoxicated and fell off the bank, hitting his head and losing consciousness. However, there are only a few places along the route that offer the necessary combination of deep water and a rocky shore. Two, he faked an attack in an effort to turn suspicion away from himself. Risking death seems an extravagant expedient, though."

"It might have been a trick that went wrong," Sethos suggested. "He jumped in the river and accidentally hit his head."

"No such risk would have been necessary," I retorted. "All he had to do was give himself a bump on the head and arrange himself in a picturesque position of collapse. No, I fear we must admit the third possibility. He was telling the truth. He did encounter the—er—you know—the other night, and the same person pushed him into the river. And that means—"

"We know what it means," Emerson said. "Or what you think it means. Confound it, Peabody, I weary of meaningless speculation. Is anyone going to Luxor to meet the train?"

We had received a telegram from David explaining he would arrive that evening.

"Nefret and I are," Ramses said.

"Quite proper," I said. "We cannot have dear

David arrive in Luxor without a welcoming committee. Perhaps I should come along too."

The reaction to this was unanimously negative, though the nature of the objections varied. Emerson said he refused to let me on the loose in Luxor with Lidman and the Pethericks. The other remarks were more tactfully phrased and I finally agreed with Nefret's suggestion that I make sure everything was in readiness for David.

Shortly after midnight the welcoming committee, which included Emerson, returned with our long-awaited guest. David's room was in order (including the rose petals in the wash water), but though he looked a little tired he declared he could not sleep until he had heard all about our activities.

"I told you about them," said Emerson, settling down with his pipe and glass.

"About your archaeological activities," David corrected. "At the risk of incurring your scorn, sir, I want to hear about the black afrit and the statue and the strange disappearance of Mrs. Petherick."

He was sitting next to me on the settee, my hand in his. I gave his a squeeze and returned his fond smile. He and Ramses were almost of a height, with the same black hair and well-shaped frames, but David's amiable countenance expressed emotion more openly than that of his friend, and his soft brown eyes were warm with affection.

"I read the Cairo newspapers," David went on. "A good deal of the story is exaggerated, I presume. What's the true story, Aunt Amelia? What are you up to now?"

It was almost two in the morning before we had finished bringing him up-to-date, and he had been shown the statuette. His artist's soul responded to its beauty, and his trained mind to the mystery of its origin.

"At least the journalists did not exaggerate this," he declared, his long fingers gently caressing the golden curves. "You think it may have been taken from KV55?"

Sethos had said very little. Slumped in his chair, legs stretched out and eyes half closed, he appeared to be dozing. He wasn't asleep, though. "I didn't do it," he murmured.

Fatima was hovering, pressing various kinds of food on him and David, so out of consideration for her I proposed that we all retire.

"Breakfast at five A.M.," said Emerson.

"Nonsense," I replied. "David needs a good night's rest."

"Oh, very well," said Emerson. "Six A.M."

• • •

In fact we did not set off for the Valley until mid-morning. The children had not had an opportunity to greet David, who was a great favorite of theirs. He was also kin to half the village of Gurneh through his grandfather Abdullah. His uncle Selim and his cousin Daoud came by to welcome him, and then he had to be introduced to the dog.

"An excellent idea," David said, scratching the great jaw. "But he—she?—doesn't strike me as much of a watchdog."

"She hasn't sounded the alarm as yet," Ramses admitted.

"Evildoers have heard of her presence," said Daoud. "They do not come near."

"I expect you are right, Daoud," I said. I didn't really believe it, for anyone who spent five seconds with Amira knew she was harmless, but Daoud was very proud of his contribution. "Things have been rather quiet of late."

"Except for the near drowning of that fellow Lidman," David said.

"It was an accident," I declared, for we had decided that was to be our official story.

"Only God knows," said Daoud. "His breath left his body, did it not?"

"Is that what they are saying in Luxor?" Sethos inquired.

"Some of them. They want the Father of Curses to perform an exorcism."

"An excellent idea," Sethos said seriously. "What about it, Emerson?"

"I may have to," said Emerson, trying to pretend the idea was not enticing, "if our fellows get it into their heads that the black afrit is still on the loose."

Selim, who did not believe in afrits or curses, smiled and caressed his splendid beard. "It can do no harm, Emerson. They say that the black afrit was seen last night in Luxor, walking by the river."

"Who says?" Ramses asked.

"The usual 'they,'" Emerson retorted. "Someone heard it from his cousin, who had heard it from his friend, who was drunk or under the influence of hashish. Ah well, I will give the matter some thought. Who knows, it might lure Mrs. Petherick out of hiding."

FROM MANUSCRIPT H

In his own way, Daoud was invaluable. It was he who brought them the news next morning that Lidman had been declared out of danger by Dr.

Westin and that Cyrus had invited him to the Castle to convalesce.

"That was sweet of Cyrus," Nefret said.

Not so much sweet as precautionary, Ramses thought. Cyrus hadn't been convinced of Lidman's innocence. His palatial house near the Valley of the Kings was as secure as any prison. High walls surrounded the estate, and the gates were always locked and guarded. Lidman couldn't creep out without being seen, and if another "event" involving the black afrit occurred while he was there, he would have a cast-iron alibi.

"Sweet, bah," said Emerson. "Vandergelt wants to keep an eye on the fellow. Excellent idea. Peabody, I sent word this morning to Winlock and his staff inviting them to dinner this evening. I told Fatima."

"You didn't tell me, Emerson."

"I just did, Peabody. Now let's get to work."

Sethos had condescended to join them that morning, now that the dirtiest part of the clearance had been completed and there were prospects of new finds. He was dressed appropriately for the role of a dedicated archaeological amateur, in worn tweeds and a pith helmet that had seen hard usage. Ramses hadn't been able to stay away either. After all, he told himself—and his mother—

Katchenovsky was only putting in half a day, which included an invitation to stay for tea.

As Emerson had predicted, they found several scraps of the gold-encrusted shrine in the rubble of the corridor. Most of the gold foil had fallen off; there was not enough to reconstitute even part of the scene that had covered the side. It was depressing, but not surprising; Ramses had seen the flakes falling like golden sleet, shaken loose by the entrance of air into the sealed space, and by Davis and his crew and his innumerable visitors crawling along the plank that provided a precarious pathway over the shrine and into the burial chamber. If his father had been in charge, the shrine section would have been copied, photographed, stabilized, and carefully removed before anyone went farther into the tomb, but Davis hadn't been able to wait to see what was down there.

Even Emerson admitted there was no point in marking the location of each scrap of foil. They were so light and so small they had fluttered randomly down. As they collected the bits, squatting uncomfortably, Ramses caught David's eye and returned his smile. In 1907 David had made a copy of the scene, which showed the queen facing the empty space that had originally depicted her son, his image destroyed by the traditionalists who despised his religious beliefs. It couldn't be published, though, since that would admit they had been in the tomb without Davis's knowledge or permission.

He found the whole business more depressing than he had expected—so much lost that could have been saved!—and he wasn't sorry when midday approached and he got ready to return to the house. He was about to head for the donkey park when his father sidled up to him. Seeing Emerson sidle was a sight in itself; he wasn't very good at being unobtrusive.

"A word with you, Ramses," he said in a hoarse whisper.

It was more than one word. "Does Mother know about this?" Ramses asked.

"It's to be a surprise," said Emerson. "Can I count on you, my boy?"

"Sir, I don't think—"

"I'll ask David, if you would really rather not."

He looked so disappointed Ramses hadn't the heart to hold out—or the cruelty of forcing David into a role he would detest.

"All right, Father. Whatever you say."

"And not a word to your mother!"

I knew what Emerson was up to, of course. I always do. There was no way of stopping him, so I ordered work to be halted earlier than usual in order to give myself time to prepare for guests, and for the worst.

It was as well I had done so, since the first of the guests arrived only a few minutes after I had finished bathing and dressing. I had asked Mr. Katchenovsky to stay for dinner, and in deference to him (and Emerson) I assumed a simple frock of blue voile (with a handkerchief hem, elbow sleeves, and a draped bodice) instead of formal evening dress. I was just in time to greet the Vandergelts, whom Emerson had not mentioned, but whom I was not surprised to see. Katherine, attired in green satin that darkened her eyes to emerald, embraced me affectionately and thanked me for inviting them.

Despite my duties as hostess, I observed that Jumana, wearing pale yellow that set off her hair and complexion, had immediately abandoned Bertie and settled herself on a hassock next to Sethos. He did make rather a dashing figure. Like his brother he had always looked younger than he really was, and the black hair and mustache took several more years off his actual age. His smile dazzled. So did Jumana's, and her long lashes fluttered like fans. That would be a nice complication! I thought. If Jumana should take a fancy to

Sethos, and Bertie to Sethos's daughter, she might end up as his mother-in-law.

That idea was a wild stretch of imagination even for me! Nevertheless, I took Jumana away to join the group that included young Mr. Barton.

We were twenty for dinner, including Daoud and Selim. Mr. Winlock was in Cairo, but the remainder of the Metropolitan Museum crew had accepted Emerson's invitation with pleasure. Fatima was in her element; she loved large parties. She even went so far as to allow Kareem to serve some of the dishes. It was a superb meal, from the tomato and leek soup to the huge saffron cake with David's name and "Welcom (sic) to Luxor!" in red icing. Everyone did justice to it, but I sensed anticipation rising, and when Emerson and Ramses excused themselves during the after-dinner coffee service, not an eyebrow was raised.

I turned to Selim, who always had the seat of honor on my right. "Well? What happens now?"

Selim proudly inspected his new wristwatch, which had been a present from us. "In ten minutes, Sitt Hakim, you will lead the way to the veranda."

"So it's to take place in front of the house?"

"We had meant to have it in the courtyard, but too many people wanted to come."

There certainly were too many people for the courtyard. Half the West Bank seemed to be there—men, women, children, and babes in arms, forming a dark and squirming mass approximately twenty feet from the door of the veranda. In front of them and a little to one side was a smaller group, taking the choicer position with the arrogance of their class—tourists, "white" residents of Luxor and a few of the inevitable journalists, pens poised. I recognized some of the faces, but not the one I had rather hoped to see.

The lamps on the veranda had not been lighted. As I took the seat of honor (the settee, moved to a position facing the crowd), curiosity had overcome my vexation. I had seen a number of Emerson's exorcisms, the most memorable being the one in which he had seemingly produced the cat Bastet from an ancient feline mummy case. The cat Bastet had not liked it at all, but the effect had been very fine. I hoped Emerson had no designs on the Great Cat of Re.

A tongue of flame shot up from the wood piled before the door. It rose to a column of shimmering fire that dazzled the eyes—and conveniently left the audience just outside the radius of the light. A voice beside me said, "Shift over a bit, will you, Peabody?"

To the audience outside, it must have seemed

that he emerged from the fire. The flames licking at the tail of his robe added to the illusion and indicated, to his wife, that he had gone a little too close to the fire. Cursing under his breath, Emerson beat the flames out. I think his costume was intended to be that of an ancient sem priest—long white skirts and full sleeves, and an imitation leopard skin draped over one shoulder. He stood still, his arms raised. In the awed silence that followed I heard a snicker from Mr. Lansing.

Having got everyone's attention, Emerson began to speak. He has no trouble at all making himself heard at a distance and the audience hung on his every word.

The black afrit had had the audacity to challenge him, the Father of Curses. Now the time had come to make an end of the wretched being. "No one defeats the Father of Curses!" Emerson bellowed, and a roar of agreement rose from the crowd. Emerson's voice rose to an even louder pitch. "Come forth, evil one, and face your master!"

"Excuse me, Mother," said Ramses. He was almost invisible in the darkness, enveloped in a long black robe. While Emerson, pointing and gesticulating, directed the audience's attention toward the area behind it, Ramses slipped out the door and made his entrance, letting out a piercing shriek. The crowd screamed in unison, including the babies. Emerson whirled. He flung himself at Ramses, who fell to the ground, kicking and struggling. They rolled back and forth, edging ever closer to the shadows at the edge of the firelight. Since I was one of the few people watching for it, I saw an occasional black-clad leg (Ramses's best evening trousers, I supposed, since he had no others of that shade) and glimpses of a black face with grotesquely flattened features (one of Nefret's black silk stockings?).

With a mighty effort Emerson flung his opponent into outer darkness and staggered back into the light carrying the limp black garment over his arms. He moved so fast no one could have got a good look at the object before he hurled it into the heart of the flames.

Shrieks of delight and approval arose from the crowd. I saw a slim black form slither snakelike farther into the darkness. All other eyes were fixed on the mighty form of Emerson. (I was sorry to see he was smoldering again.)

"And now in conclusion," Emerson shouted, "I return the object of the curse to the fires of Gehenna!" From the breast of his robe he drew out a shape that glowed gold-red in the firelight, and pitched it into the flames.

Sethos was laughing uncontrollably. "In conclusion!" he sputtered. Cyrus sprang to his feet with a cry of anguish, and would have rushed out the door had I not got in his way.

"No, Cyrus. Stop and think before you act."

The performance ended rather abruptly when Emerson extinguished the fire with a conveniently placed bucket of water. A column of smoke replaced the flames. Coughing, the crowd retreated, and Emerson came to the door.

"Not so bad, eh?" he inquired. "Curse it, I can't see a thing. Light the lamps, someone."

He entered, tossing off his robe (one of my best sheets).

"How many garments did you destroy?" I inquired, having recognized the "leopard skin" as the remnants of a woolen jumper.

"Was that, by chance, one of my evening cloaks?" Nefret asked in a carefully controlled voice.

"I'll get you another," Emerson said. "Good gad, is that all you can think about? I expected commendation, if not riotous applause."

The applause broke out, mingled with laughter and comments. Emerson was pouring the whiskey when Ramses came in through the house. They **were** his best trousers. Or had been.

"Here you are, my boy," said Emerson, handing him a glass. "And well deserved. I hope I didn't bruise you too badly."

"No, sir. Thank you." Ramses flattened his tumbled hair. "How did it go, do you think?"

"It wasn't bad," Sethos said judiciously. "Not bad at all. Though if you had let me take a hand—"

I gave him a little kick on the shin to remind him that Anthony Bissinghurst was a harmless archaeological amateur, not a Master of Disguise.

"We saw it from behind the scenes, so to speak," Lansing said. He was still chuckling. "From the point of view of the spectators, it must have been extremely effective. Winlock will be sick at having missed it."

"The audience was not uncritical," I pointed out. "How many of them were actually convinced is difficult to say."

"It does not matter," said Selim. "What matters is that they enjoyed it."

"Just tell me," Cyrus pleaded, "that you didn't throw the statue into the fire."

"Don't be an idiot," Emerson said rudely. "It would require a hotter flame than that to melt solid gold. What went into the fire was made from the mold we cast the other night. Plaster of paris. I spent an hour painting it gold."

After our guests had left, Emerson went off to bathe, for he was quite smutty. I was brushing my hair when he returned, a little singed around the calves, but extremely pleased with himself.

"That should settle the black afrit," he declared, embracing me. "What about a reward for the magician, eh?"

I put down the brush and gave him his reward. "It was well done," I said, between kisses. "But I had hoped Mrs. Petherick would be unable to resist attending. I didn't see her in the audience."

"Neither did I. Ah well, she'll turn up eventually."

She did turn up, early the following morning. She had not been as lucky as Heinrich Lidman.

We were officially informed of the discovery by Inspector Ayyid. We were finishing breakfast when he was announced. Looking round at our grave faces, Ayyid said, "I see you have heard the news. I suppose it was Daoud who told you. Perhaps he would consider working for me; he seems to get information before my men do."

"Our informants are assiduous but not always accurate," I said, waving him to a chair. "We would appreciate hearing the facts. You will join us for breakfast, I hope?"

"Coffee, if you will be so good." Ayyid's eyes

fixed on Sethos. "I do not believe I have met this gentleman."

Napkin in hand, Sethos rose and made an elegant bow. "Anthony Bissinghurst, at your service. I am honored to meet an individual of whom I have heard so much."

His excessive courtesy made no impression on Ayyid. "I regret that I have not had the pleasure of meeting you before this, sir. Have you just arrived in Luxor?"

I could tell by the glint in Sethos's eyes that he was tempted to spin the inspector a preposterous story; knowing I would instantly contradict it, he restrained himself. "I arrived day before yesterday with Professor Emerson. I trust that constitutes a sufficient alibi?"

"Don't be a tease," I said, giving my brother-in-law a sharp look.

"You had no connection with the dead lady?" Ayyid inquired.

"None whatsoever," I said. "Where was she found and how did she die?"

The body had been found early that morning by one of the workmen who tended the flower beds in the Winter Palace's famous gardens. It had been laid out neatly and reverently, the hands folded across the breast, under a flowering shrub. So much we had already heard from Daoud, who had hurried to inform us as soon as he got the news from his network of informants in Luxor. He had added a poetic touch: the petals of the flowers lay scattered like snowflakes upon the poor lady's quiet form.

Inspector Ayyid did not mention the petals. "We do not yet know how she died. There were no marks of violence upon the body. An autopsy will be necessary." He added, with a flash of quickly controlled temper, "I am awaiting permission from the British authorities."

Like most Egyptians, Ayyid fiercely resented the refusal of Britain to give Egypt complete independence. That it must come no one except the extreme imperialists in the British government doubted, but the latter group was stridently opposed to seeing Britain yield authority. Even the moderates, led by Allenby, envisaged British troops remaining in Egypt, and England retaining control over Egypt's "national security." As the partisans of independence pointed out, so long as foreign troops remain in a country, it cannot be said to be fully sovereign.

"Would they be more likely to agree if I were to perform the autopsy?" Nefret asked.

It was a bitter pill for Ayyid to swallow; only his

respectful admiration for Nefret enabled him to do so. "I do not like to ask a lady to take on such a disagreeable task, madam."

"I've done it before," Nefret said, smiling at him.

Ayyid nodded. "I took the liberty of mentioning that possibility to the high commissioner, subject, of course, to your decision. If the lady's children agree—"

"I don't see why their permission is required in a case of suspected murder," I said. "But if it proves necessary, I will speak to them. I have no doubt my arguments will prevail. You have no suspects at the present time?"

Ayyid rose. He was obviously unwilling to discuss the progress of the case—or the lack of progress. "Until the cause of death is determined, we have no reason to search for suspects. She may have died of natural causes."

"Nonsense," I said. "After vanishing for a week she returned to the hotel, lay down under a bougainvillea or rosebush, folded her hands, and passed away?"

Ayyid could think of no reply to this—nor could anyone have done so. He bowed himself out, after telling Nefret he would let her know whether her services would be required.

Emerson fixed me with a terrible look. "If you say 'I told you so,' Peabody—"

"As you know, Emerson, I deplore the use of that phrase, especially between married persons."

"Ha," said Emerson. "I have lost count of the number of times you—"

"An unjust and unjustified accusation, Emerson. Anyhow, I did not contradict your—as it has proved—incorrect assumption in so many words. I only—"

"Looked contradictory," Emerson shouted.

"Now, now," said Sethos, trying to control the quiver of his lips. "Do not allow disharmony to mar the spectacle of marital accord, I beg. You wouldn't want to set me a bad example."

"Are you and Margaret about to be married at long last, then?" I asked interestedly. I had thoroughly disliked Margaret Minton when I first met her, in her role as a determined lady journalist, but I had learned to admire her talents and her strong character. She and Sethos had been . . . well acquainted . . . for some years, but she had refused his offers of marriage—for good reason, I should say. Passionate devotion to a man should not blind a woman to his flaws, and Sethos had a good many of them, including his hazardous occupation as a secret service agent and his checkered past.

"We can't seem to come to an agreement," Sethos said. "But we are edging closer, I think. Perhaps you can help, Amelia. You are well known for your success in assisting romantic affairs. I expect Margaret will turn up before long, this story is becoming irresistible."

"Oh, wonderful," snarled Emerson. "That's all we need, Margaret and perhaps her old rival Kevin O'Connell badgering us. I refuse to be distracted by this twaddle. Ramses, Peabody, Nefret, David, get your gear together."

"Where are we going?" Nefret asked.

"Deir el Medina first. Selim said he'd run across something he wants to show me. Then the Valley of the Kings."

Nefret and Ramses rose obediently. I reached for another piece of toast. It was rather leathery, but I spread marmalade on it anyhow.

Emerson began muttering. He hadn't done that for a long time. "Expected this . . . hopeless cause . . . confounded female . . ."

"I presume," I remarked, "that the final phrase applies not to me but to poor Mrs. Petherick. Such sentiments are unworthy of you, Emerson. I cannot so callously ignore the horrible murder of a fellow human being. That takes precedence over all other activities. However, if you are determined to—"

"You don't know that it was murder," Emerson said. "And if it was . . . Damnation! What are you going to do?"

"Examine the scene of the crime. Question witnesses. Offer my condolences to Miss and Mr. Petherick." I took a bite of toast, chewed it thoroughly, and swallowed. "After that, we shall see."

Emerson threw up his hands, literally and figuratively. "What about you, Sethos?"

"Why, I share Amelia's humanitarian views, of course" was the smooth reply. "Anyhow, her activities ought to be much more entertaining than yours."

As Sethos and I walked down the road toward the river, we were amused to observe several Egyptians industriously digging in the ashes of the fire, looking for the remains of the statuette. I didn't doubt that some of the tourists would have been doing the same if Wasim had let them by. With the aid of my parasol and Sethos's stick we made our way through the hangers-on near the guardhouse. There were not so many of them that morning; some had abandoned the unproductive siege and others, I surmised, had been drawn to the scene of the crime. I hoped Ayyid had been able to keep it relatively uncontaminated, but I did not count on it.

It was a fine, clear morning, as are most mornings in Luxor. Sunlight sparkled on the water and the white sails of feluccas dipped and swung. I had sent word to Daoud's son Sabir; when we reached the riverbank, his boat was waiting. The gang-plank, which served as a makeshift oar when nec-essary, was at a challenging angle and quite narrow, but I disdained the hands stretched out to assist me. Long before it became acceptable for ladies to do so, I had given up cumbersome skirts in favor of trousers. Thus attired, I ascended quite nimbly, the various useful items attached to my belt of tools jingling.

"You seem to be carrying more odds and ends than ever," said Sethos, settling himself onto the bench next to me. "Canteen, knife, flask of brandy, coil of rope, candle and matches—what's in this box?"

"Medical supplies. Bandages, sticking plaster, and so on."

"I shudder to think what 'and so on' might con-sist of."

He was being frivolous, so I did not deign to reply. In fact I had fewer "odds and ends" on my belt than usual, since the numerous pockets in my coat and trousers provided an alternative. Emer-son had always complained, not so much about the accoutrements as about the noise they made when I moved. Admittedly this made it more difficult for me to creep up on a suspect unheard, so I had made a few adjustments.

I always enjoy the trip across the river; it is like watching a motion picture unreel, as the structures on the East Bank seem to move ever nearer and clearer. On this occasion, however, impatience tempered pleasure. As soon as we docked I disembarked, instructing Sabir to wait for us.

The gardens behind the Winter Palace are normally a scene of peace and beauty. Paths wind through close-clipped greensward and beds of bright blossom in the shade of exotic trees. Such was not the case that morning. It was as I had feared. Ayyid had left two constables on guard, but they had been bribed or intimidated into turning a blind eye to the depredations of ghoulish sightseers. Cameras clicked and one lady was sawing at a flowery spray with a pair of nail scissors.

My loud but ladylike expostulations dispersed most of the ghouls. The others simply backed off and began photographing ME. I took my own little Kodak from the pocket of my coat, wishing I had insisted on Nefret accompanying me. I have always had a bit of trouble with cameras.

The spot where Mrs. Petherick's body had rested was not under a rosebush or bougainvillea, though both grew nearby. At the base of a splendid specimen of dom palm lay a mass of twining vines which had enveloped the lower four feet of the trunk and climbed farther up it. The plant, I believe, was not indigenous to Egypt, but it flourished here, forming a tapestry of green and vivid pink, the flowers being small but profuse. Part of the plant had been rudely torn away. The broken boughs were already withering. The area they had once covered was bare ground, without so much as an indentation or outline to show the location of the body. The only visible marks were those of shod feet—the ghouls', I presumed. Kneeling, I focused my camera and took several photographs of the spot, hoping the lens would bring out more detail than was visible to the naked eye. I was photographing the wider area when a hail from one of the constables caused me to turn. Coming toward me was Inspector Ayyid.

"You need not bother taking photographs, Mrs. Emerson," he said. "I did so this morning before and after the body was moved."

"Was there any sign of a struggle?" I added, in some vexation, "The area has been so disturbed that even I cannot tell what damage was done by whom, and when."

"It was necessary to cut away the vines before we could examine the body."

"Yes, of course," I said, making a mental note of the fact that he had not really answered my question. "What is the name of this pretty pink vine?"

Ayyid looked blank. "I do not know, Mrs. Emerson."

"No matter. Were you looking for me, Mr. Ayyid, or is this a fortuitous meeting?"

"One of my men told me you were here. I expected you would be."

There was the hint of a smile on his stern face. I smiled back at him. "How is the investigation proceeding?"

"The authorities have been persuaded that the circumstances are unusual enough to justify a postmortem. We await only the agreement of Mrs. Petherick's heirs. They are . . . not pleased at the idea."

"Many people find the idea repugnant," I said—though I would not have supposed the Pethericks to be so sentimental about their step-mother. "I will have a little chat with them. I had intended to do so in any case. I would also like to question the gardener who found the body."

"That can be arranged."

In fact there was no way he could have prevented it. I had observed a man in an earth-stained galabeeyah hovering nearby.

I thanked him, nonetheless, and went on, "Will you be good enough to tell Miss and Mr. Petherick that I will call upon them shortly?"

Recognizing this as a courteous dismissal, Ayyid nodded and walked away. I turned to Sethos, who had not—for a wonder—uttered a word.

"Did you observe any clues?" I asked.

"No more than you, I fancy."

"Hmmm." I beckoned to the gardener, who came limping to me, hopeful of baksheesh. He was a lean little man, probably in his late thirties, though he looked older. I deduced that his limp was caused by rheumaticky knees, probably a result of kneeling long hours on the hard ground.

"You were the one who found the lady?" I asked in Arabic.

"Yes, Sitt!" His right hand quivered. "It was a terrible thing, I do not know whether I will be able to work again in this accursed place."

"The curse will be lifted. My word on that. Now tell me how you found her."

Nothing loath, the fellow launched into his tale. (I omit the expressions of woe and distress.)

He was the head gardener, in charge of the crew, so he made it a point to arrive early. The sun was barely up when he came to the gardens. As he strolled along the paths, smoking and enjoying the solitude and fresh morning scents (and so on, and so on) and appraising the places that needed attention, he saw an ugly intrusion among the pink-flowered vines. At first he thought it was a dead animal or bird. Closer examination disclosed the fact that it was a shoe, with a foot in it.

"I pushed the vines aside, Sitt, and saw her. I fell down in a faint and cried out. Then I ran away—to get help. When the police came they tore away the vines—my beautiful coral vine," he added, with what appeared to be genuine emotion.

"So the vines were in place until the police came? You didn't look to see whether she was dead?"

The slightest tightening of his lips betrayed his reaction to that naive question. "It was not for me to touch the lady, Sitt."

"No," I agreed. "Describe exactly what you saw—her expression, her clothing, everything you can remember."

"I did not see her face, Sitt, it was too dark under the vines. She wore a gown of that color"—he indicated the crimson scarf knotted around my throat—"and shoes like the English ladies wear, with sharp heels and diamond buckles."

"Evening dress," I said to Sethos. "And not her usual black. Interesting."

"The only part that showed was one foot," Sethos said. He had not required me to translate; his Arabic was as good as mine. "So she must have crawled—"

"Or been pushed."

"—or been pushed under the mass of vines, with enough care to avoid disturbing it unduly. In the hope of delaying the discovery of the body?"

"It couldn't have been delayed for long," I replied, reminded of an unpalatable but pertinent fact. "Nor can her burial be long delayed, not in this climate. I must speak with the Pethericks. But first . . ."

I asked the gardener whether he had looked for suspicious signs elsewhere in the gardens. He shook his head.

"I was too saddened, Sitt, and too afraid of the afrit."

"It was not an afrit that killed her," I said. "Come with me now."

We walked slowly along the winding paths, looking from side to side. Several constables were making halfhearted attempts to search, but I did not credit them with keen powers of observation. In fact it was Sethos—I always endeavor to give credit where it is due—who saw sunlight wink off a scattering of crystal beads. There were only a few of them, almost hidden in the loam, but I felt certain they had come from Mrs. Petherick's evening frock.

"She was killed here," I said, retrieving the beads. "It is one of the most secluded spots in the gardens, far enough from the hotel so that an outcry would go unheard."

Sethos looked skeptical. "You have an innocent mind, Amelia. Any lady might have lost a few beads off her frock if she were . . . Shall we say, clasped in a firm but nonlethal hold in a discreetly secluded spot?"

"I appreciate the delicacy of your description. That is of course a possibility; I expect that such encounters are not infrequent."

"Quite," said Sethos, in the tone of a man who speaks from personal experience.

"I consider my theory to be more likely," I went on. "And it will be easy to confirm it, as soon as I compare these beads with the ones on her gown."

The gardener was unable to identify the beads. They might be the same as those on the lady's dress; they might not. He conceded, when I pressed him, that the earth appeared to have been disturbed and then hastily smoothed, not by the rakes employed by the gardeners, but by hand. I wrapped the beads in a handkerchief and tucked them into one of my pockets.

I rewarded the observant gardener according to his merits, adding a few extra coins to console him for his mutilated vine. "I can give you some ointment for your knees," I said in a kindly manner. "Have you had these pains in the joints long?"

"No, Sitt Hakim, only since yesterday. A donkey kicked me."

We made our way into the hotel. When I asked for Miss Petherick, I was told she expected me. She and her brother had rooms on the third floor, on the opposite side of the hotel from their step-mother's suite. My knock on Miss Petherick's door was answered without delay.

I had not expected the lady to show signs of distress. Only her furrowed brow and slight pallor betrayed concern, and that, I thought, was for her brother, who sat huddled in an armchair with his hands covering his face. Miss Petherick was as well groomed as if she had spent hours at her toilet, high-piled hair held by tortoiseshell combs, shirtwaist and skirt without a crease. I introduced Sethos by his most recent name, explaining that he was a close friend and confidant.

"And anxious to serve you, ma'am, in any way," said Sethos, bowing.

Miss Petherick acknowledged this courtesy with a slight nod, and gestured us to come in. The room was large enough to contain not only a bed and wardrobe but a small sitting area, with a table and several chairs in front of the fireplace.

"What, Mrs. Emerson, no floral offering?" inquired Miss Petherick, indicating several vases on the mantel and table. "We have already received them from the manager and a few dear friends whose names I did not recognize."

"I hope I can offer more practical forms of sympathy," I replied, taking the chair she indicated. "You must realize that the poor lady's burial should not, cannot be long delayed. Before she is laid to rest we must know the cause of death."

Adrian Petherick, who had not up till then moved a fingertip, lowered his hands and gave me a wild-eyed look. "I will not have her carved like a piece of beef," he muttered. "They were all carved and torn, bloody, dismembered . . ."

I was too shocked and distressed to respond. Not Sethos. He placed a firm hand on the young man's shoulder and said, in his most syrupy voice, "They are now among the blessed in the mansions of Paradise. As is she."

"The mansions of Paradise," Adrian echoed. "Are you—are you a clergyman, sir?"

"Only a humble believer," said Sethos.

He had not specified **what** he believed in, but the sheer force of the personality he could exhibit when he chose had a comforting effect. Adrian smiled faintly. Taking advantage of his softened mood, I said, "Would it help you to accept the idea of a postmortem if my daughter-in-law were to perform it? You have met her. You know she would act with due reverence and respect."

"Good heavens," said Miss Petherick. "That delicate young woman?"

"She is a qualified surgeon," I retorted. "And has assisted the local police on several occasions."

"She has small, pretty hands," Adrian murmured. "Harriet, what do you think?"

"As I told you, it is in our own interests to cooperate fully with the authorities." She looked at me. "It was Adrian who objected. If his mind is now at ease, we will proceed as you suggested."

She accompanied us to the door, where I paused long enough to discuss, out of Adrian's hearing, certain even more practical arrangements. Miss Petherick accepted my offer to arrange for the burial, which, if matters went as I expected, would take place the following day, but shook her head when I said I would ask the pastor of the local Anglican church to call on her.

"Mrs. Petherick was a Roman Catholic, I have asked Mr. Salt to speak to the priest of that church here." She glanced over her shoulder at the motionless form of her brother. "Perhaps he will be able to offer further consolation."

She added a few appropriate words of thanks to both of us. The sanctimonious expression on Sethos's face was almost too much for me.

FROM MANUSCRIPT H

For once Ramses was in full agreement with his mother. Like it or not, they had become involved with the Petherick affair, and the sooner it was settled, the better for them. It was too coincidental that Mrs. Petherick could have died a natural death under such bizarre circumstances. Either she had committed suicide—an extreme and unsatisfactory method of substantiating her wild story—or she had been murdered. And they were still in possession of the statuette that had started the whole business.

They took the horses that morning, approaching the site from the north, instead of going on foot along the mountain path. It was a long walk from Deir el Medina back to the Valley of the Kings. Selim was on the lookout for them. A fine horseman himself, he greeted their mounts with almost as much courtesy as he greeted them. With the head of Nefret's mare Moonlight resting heavily and affectionately on his shoulder, he said, "Emerson, I think I know what is wrong with the motorcar. If we take off the other back wheel—"

"No time for that now," Emerson said with a sigh. "Everything going all right here?"

"Yes, Emerson. I have followed your instructions to the letter. Daoud has been sifting the fill."

"He doesn't miss much," Emerson agreed. "You said you had found something."

"It is there." Selim led them to an area west of the Ptolemaic temple. They had excavated part of it several years earlier, but it was a complex site, with the foundations of earlier temples intermingled and overlapping. An untrained eye would have seen only tumbled stones and hollows and hillocks.

"Here," Selim said, pointing. "Someone has been digging."

"Damnation." Emerson leaned over the hole. "When?"

"Last night. It was not there yesterday."

"Bastards," said Emerson.

"If you are referring to our friends the local looters, they've been prying around this site for years," Ramses said.

"Why now?" Emerson demanded.

"I wondered too," said Selim, arms folded. "But I think the fools believe our possession of a golden statue has something to do with our work here."

"Bloody idiots," Emerson grunted. "Haven't they heard the true story?"

"They have heard it but they do not believe it. Some people believe what they want to believe."

"It's understandable," David said. "Didn't the original rumors report an entire hoard of gold and jewels? The poor devils are under the impression that you've found a cache, or even a tomb. You can talk yourself blue in the face but you won't convince them they're wrong."

"Try to convince them," Emerson said to Selim. "You and Daoud. Otherwise the whole area will be torn to pieces."

"We will do our best, Emerson, but David is in the right. Shall I have one of the men stay here at night?"

"Hmmm." Emerson stroked his chin. "Yes. And fill in this hole."

He spent an hour going over the notes Selim had taken, while the latter watched him nervously. His nod of approval and curt word of commendation brought a relieved smile to Selim's face.

"I have taken photographs at every stage, Emerson," he said.

"Good," Emerson repeated. "I'll send Bertie over tomorrow or next day to make plans."

Leaving Selim to get on with the job, they started back along the long road to the Valley. It struck Ramses that his father had seemed a trifle subdued that morning—he hadn't even cursed the vandals as eloquently as usual. "Is something bothering you, Father?" he asked.

Emerson gave him a blank look. "I thought you were going back to the house to get on with your translations."

"Mikhail isn't coming until after midday. I thought, since Mother isn't with you today—"

"Oh. Good of you, my boy. I neglected to thank you for your sterling performance at the exorcism."

"I enjoyed it," Ramses admitted. "Didn't you?"

"Yes. Er . . . yes—curse it!" Emerson burst out. "It was a joke, you know. Never meant anyone to take it seriously. Now the poor woman is dead, and I feel . . . well, I feel as if I had made a mockery of her and her fears."

"No one else thinks that, Father."

"I am not concerned about the opinions of others." It was a characteristic response, but Ramses knew he didn't mean it the way it sounded. His father left the lectures on morality to his wife, but he had his own standards and he tried harder than most men to live up to them.

"I'll catch the bastard who killed her," Emerson muttered. "Er—don't repeat what I said to your mother. She'll think me a sentimental fool."

Ramses ventured to put a hand on his father's shoulder. "She thinks you're a great man. So do I."

Emerson cleared his throat noisily. "I want to get that grid in the burial chamber today. See to it, my boy, will you?"

As the morning went on, more and more tourists arrived, and the majority of them stopped to watch, blocking the path and getting in everyone's way. The news of Mrs. Petherick's death had spread; several journalists were among the watchers, shouting questions and leaning over the parapet to point their cameras whenever anyone emerged from the tomb. Finally the inevitable happened; one of them leaned too far and toppled over the wall.

Emerson came running, took one look at the prostrate form, and began to swear. "Nefret!" he bellowed.

Ramses recognized the man as the same photographer who had been talking to Carla. He had fallen on his back, and his camera, by a strange piece of luck, appeared to be undamaged. Ramses stood by watching while Nefret examined the fellow.

"Nothing seems to be broken," she announced. "Try to sit up, Mr.———?"

"Anderson. **The Daily Yell.** Professor, would you care to give me your theory—"

Emerson interrupted with a roar of fury. "One of Kevin O'Connell's henchmen! I might have known. Is there no limit to what you people will do to get an interview?"

"Don't you think I'm entitled to one?" Anderson remained recumbent. His smug smile reminded Ramses of O'Connell's. "Your exorcism didn't do the trick, did it? The black afrit has claimed another victim."

For a moment Ramses was afraid he would have to restrain his father by main force. Emerson was only too accustomed to journalistic tricks, though. With an effort that left him shaking, he said, "No comment. Get up that ladder and make yourself scarce."

Anderson lived up to the honored traditions of the profession; they had to pull him to his feet and shove him up the ladder into the grip of Hassan. His final shot was worthy of O'Connell himself. "I won't sue, Professor, if you'll give me ten minutes of your—ouch!"

"This is too bloody much," Emerson declared. "From now on we work from six to nine in the morning and again in the late afternoon. Hassan, I want this pit roofed over. Now."

"Are we going back to the house?" Nefret asked.

"May as well," Emerson grumbled. "We'll be followed by the horde if we go anywhere else. Ahmet, hop on over to the West Valley and tell Vandergelt Effendi I want to see him immediately."

"Tell him we'd be delighted to have him come to the house for luncheon," Nefret corrected.

"Oh. Yes," said Emerson, rubbing his chin. "David, bring along that tray of odds and ends we found this morning. You can photograph and sketch them at the house."

So far they hadn't found much in the debris of the burial chamber, only a few beads and rotten scraps of wood, and a broken seal. A few of the spectators trailed them as far as the donkey park, but abandoned the chase when they mounted and urged the horses to a canter.

It was not long before Cyrus and his staff turned up. Emerson had been pacing up and down the veranda, hands behind his back, pausing every now and then to look out. He didn't say so, but Ramses knew he was watching for his wife. The Petherick affair had touched his conscience and aroused his detectival instincts. He had been sincere when he swore he would find Mrs. Petherick's killer.

"We met Ahmet at the entrance to the Valley," Cyrus explained. "I was just about to send one of our fellows with a note. Seems there's been a change in our plans."

"Not at all," said Emerson, accepting a cup of coffee from Fatima. "Er—somewhat. Too damned many people in the East Valley. A cursed journalist fell over the wall this morning."

"Was he hurt?" Bertie asked.

"It was a stunt," Emerson said disgustedly. "If he had really fallen he'd have landed on his head, not his backside. I can't concentrate on work under those conditions."

"It isn't easy to concentrate with all these rumors flying around," Cyrus said. "Is it true that the poor woman is dead?"

"That much at least is not rumor," Emerson admitted. "How she died is as yet unknown. Peabody is in Luxor, harassing the police."

"I figured she would be," Cyrus said, suppressing a smile which would have been out of place. "There'll have to be an autopsy, I suppose."

"I have offered to perform it, if the authorities agree," Nefret said.

Bertie let out a little murmur of protest.

"It's my job, Bertie," Nefret said. "Honestly, it doesn't bother me."

"No," Jumana declared. "You do your job as a man would do it. Like me."

"Go and do it, then," said Emerson. He stood up and began pacing.

"You couldn't move me with a block and tackle," Cyrus said, leaning back in his chair. "I want to hear what Amelia has to say. Don't try and tell me you aren't as distracted as we are."

"Bah," said Emerson. He stared out along the road. "What the devil is keeping her?"

Knowing his mother, Ramses expected it would take her some time to finish "harassing" all and sundry. The sun had passed the zenith and Fatima was setting out a cold luncheon when she and Sethos arrived.

"Let's have it, Amelia," Cyrus demanded. "What's the latest?"

"Let me see. Where to begin?"

"With the matter of greatest urgency, perhaps?" Nefret suggested. "The postmortem."

Her mother-in-law patted her hand. "Of course, my dear. The Pethericks have agreed to it. After persuading them I stopped at the station and informed Inspector Ayyid. He would like you to do it this afternoon, so that she can be buried tomorrow."

Nefret nodded and selected a cheese sandwich. Ramses swallowed and averted his eyes. He was accustomed to corpses, ancient and modern, but he would never get used to the idea of his beautiful elegant wife up to her wrists in blood and even more unpleasant fluids.

His mother had gone on to describe the arrangements for the burial, which would be in the foreign cemetery of Luxor.

"One might have supposed she would wish to be buried in England, beside her husband," Ramses said.

"Miss Petherick felt it was unnecessary and impractical," said his mother. Which it was; but

Ramses knew his mother wouldn't give a curse about practicality in a comparable situation. His mind winced away from the idea. He'd deal with it when he had to, if he had to, but he didn't want to think about it.

"Ayyid agrees with me that the circumstances are suspicious," his mother continued. She repeated the gardener's account of his discovery of the body. Her audience listened with morbid fascination.

"I took a number of photographs," she concluded. "Though I don't suppose they will tell us much. The ground had been too trampled. Nefret, perhaps you and David can develop the photographs for me."

Nefret rose and brushed the crumbs off her skirt. "Not today, Mother. I must get my instruments ready."

Ramses had no intention of allowing his wife to go to Luxor alone. He couldn't do anything except be there, but that at least he owed her. He explained the situation to Katchenovsky, who had arrived precisely on schedule, and apologized for leaving him alone.

"Not at all. I am so very sorry," the Russian murmured. "Do you want me to continue cataloging the remaining scraps?"

"I've had a look at most of them. I'd rather you tried your hand at copying and translating the fragment I've laid out for you. It appears to be a list of supplies."

Ramses had known his mother wouldn't miss the autopsy, and where she went, Emerson followed. She refused Cyrus's invitation to dine.

"I don't know how long we will be," she explained. "Come round tomorrow, if you like."

David and Sethos joined the group, and they went straight to the zabtiyeh, where they found not only Ayyid but two other officials waiting. One was an Egyptian, the district commandant of police from Sohag; the other was the British district adviser, a red-faced, stern-looking man named Rayburn. Ayyid's tight lips indicated what he thought of their interference, but it was standard procedure, and there wasn't anything he could do about it. To their obvious relief, Nefret told them there was no need for them to be present while she operated. She was, however, unable to keep her mother-in-law from accompanying her and Ayyid.

Ramses's mother was gone less than ten minutes. "What?" demanded Emerson. "Don't tell me Nefret wouldn't let you help carve the poor woman?"

"Don't be disgusting, Emerson. I only wanted to have a look at her clothes before they were removed."

"Hadn't they removed them?" Ramses asked.

"I asked Ayyid not to do so. Anyhow, given the delicate circumstances, he preferred to have a woman take care of that."

"Quite proper," muttered Rayburn.

"Quite," Emerson agreed. "Well, Peabody?"

His wife gave him a tolerant smile. "I will spare you the details, my dear, since fashion means nothing to you. Suffice it to say that she was wearing evening dress—quite an expensive model, to judge by the designer's label—of crimson satin, pleated across the bosom and caught on the shoulders with diamond clips—fake diamonds—"

"I thought you were going to spare us the details," Emerson objected.

"Though costly, the dress was last year's model," his wife continued, unperturbed. "As I suspected, the beads we found in the garden were identical with others trimming her sleeves and bodice. Her jewelry had been taken."

"How do you know she was wearing jewelry if there wasn't any?" Emerson demanded.

"No woman would have assumed an elaborate evening costume without the appropriate jewels."

"So the motive was robbery!" Rayburn exclaimed in unconcealed relief. "Confound it, Ayyid, you ought to have searched the hotel servants and their quarters."

"I did," Ayyid said tightly.

"They—he—had ample time to conceal the jewelry elsewhere," Rayburn insisted. "Isn't that so, Mrs. Emerson?"

"Robbery was not the motive, Captain Rayburn."

"But, Mrs. Emerson—"

"No thief would have taken the trouble to arrange the body so respectfully. Her eyes were closed and her hands folded on her breast. Pray allow me to continue. Underneath her gown she was wearing—"

"I don't want to hear about it," said Emerson in some confusion. "Get to the point."

"I fear that you are missing the point, Emerson. According to the guests at the hotel, Mrs. Petherick wore only black, in keeping with her role as a grieving widow. Why was she attired that night in crimson? And where had she come from? She had been missing for almost a week. Was she about to stage a dramatic reappearance, but was prevented by the murderer?"

Observing the skeptical expressions of the others, she said impatiently, "Someone was with her when she died, that much is undeniable. Someone who arranged the body, someone who had enough regard for the proprieties to treat it with respect. All her garments were intact, with no tears, cuts or bloodstains."

"Then how did she die?" Emerson demanded.

He repeated the question to Nefret when she returned, looking as calm and fresh as if she had been engaged in arranging flowers.

"Congestive heart failure" was the reply.

"Then—no murder," said Emerson, with a telltale look at his wife.

"Oh, it was murder," Nefret said. "Her heart was damaged, but what caused it to stop was suffocation. I believe she was unconscious when the cloth was pressed to her face, since there were no bruises on her arms and no traces of skin or blood under her nails."

"You're sure?" Rayburn asked.

"Yes. There were threads caught in her teeth. If you would like a second opinion—"

"That won't be necessary." Rayburn sighed heavily. A murder investigation, with the victim a British subject, was a complication he did not appreciate.

"So her breath was sucked out," said Sethos, with unseemly relish. "Just wait till the newspapers hear about this."

SIX

I felt it my duty to be the one to inform the Pethericks of the results of the postmortem. Emerson did not object; in fact, he said he would go with me. I knew why, of course. His detectival instincts were temporarily in the ascendance, and having been proved wrong (by me) on several essential points, he was hoping to win a few points of his own. I did not mind, since I always play fair in our little competitions in crime, but I sent Nefret home with Ramses. Coolly professional she might be, but she was also a tender-hearted individual, and she had been acquainted with her subject. David went with them; as he pointed out, he did not know the Pethericks and it would be inappropriate for him to meet them under such delicate circumstances.

Miss and Mr. Petherick were dining in her room. As soon as we were shown in, Miss Petherick rang for the waiter to remove the table. I observed that one of them had only picked at the food, while the other had made a good dinner. It was not difficult to guess which was which. Adrian Petherick seemed to have shrunk in the past hours; his clothing hung loosely on his body and his face was pasty-pale. Was it guilt or grief?

I broke the news with merciful bluntness. Adrian let out a cry and covered his face with his hands. His sister's expression did not change. "We anticipated this. I presume you want to question us?"

"Not tonight," said Sethos soothingly. He had gone to the table and was examining the floral displays. There were several more, including a vase of lovely white roses. "Allow sleep to knit up the raveled sleeve of care. And think of the dear lady at rest in the arms of Jesus."

"Yes," Adrian murmured. "Yes. Thank you."

Emerson choked. He must have swallowed the wrong way.

"I have a question," said Harriet Petherick. "What about the statue?"

"What about it?" Emerson inquired gruffly.

"There can now be no doubt as to its legal ownership. I would think you would wish to get it off your hands."

"I would not suppose you would want it in **your** hands," said Emerson. "No, no, Miss Petherick, I will not have it on my conscience that I gave such a deadly object to innocents like you and your brother."

"You would prefer to bring the curse on your own family?" She added, with what I could only view as deliberate malice, "We were told of your remarkable performance the other night. It wasn't particularly effective, was it?"

Emerson refused to be provoked. "You and I know such—performances, did you say?—affect only the superstitious. The curse of such objects is the violence they provoke in unprincipled persons. I am capable of protecting my family in more practical ways, and I intend to do the same for you and your brother."

The logic of this silenced the lady. I confirmed the arrangements I had made for the service on the following morning, and she had enough courtesy to thank me. Adrian said nothing. He had taken one of the white roses from the vase and was removing the petals, one by one, and arranging them in a pile on the table.

Curious glances and whispers followed us as we passed through the lobby, but my parasol and Emerson's scowls kept even the journalists back.

"Good Gad," said Emerson to his brother. "I have never heard such hypocritical blather in my life, not even from you. The arms of Jesus, indeed!"

"It made the boy feel better," Sethos said.

"Nor have I known pity to motivate your

actions," grumbled Emerson. "Taking advantage of his weak-mindedness is a contemptible method of winning his confidence."

Sethos grinned, and I said severely, "Speaking of blather, did I hear you nobly promising to protect Harriet and her brother? From what and in what manner, may I ask?"

Emerson stopped short in the middle of the street. I shoved him out of the way of a horse-drawn calèche, and Emerson said, "Do not impugn my motives, Peabody, if you please. We need to settle this distraction so that I can get on with my work."

"And bring a murderer to justice."

"That, too."

Sabir had returned for us after taking Ramses and Nefret across. Emerson helped me up the gangplank and went on, frowning, "Though at the present moment I haven't the faintest notion who it might be. Don't tell me you do, Peabody, or I will regret my candor."

"The Pethericks, brother and sister, are certainly the most obvious suspects," I replied, settling myself onto the bench.

"They are the only suspects," Emerson retorted.

"Which is a strong indication of their innocence, my dear. It is true they had a motive. We know that Petherick's collection was left to his wife. Were they aware of that? Did they suppose the valuables would go to them if she died?"

"That isn't a motive, it is a string of conjectures," Emerson exclaimed. "Curse it, Peabody, make up your mind. First you say they are probably innocent—though your reasoning is as feeble as any I have ever heard—and then you invent reasons for believing in their guilt."

He had a certain logic on his side, so of course I immediately went on the offensive. "It just goes to show that you were foolish to entrust Gargery with the delicate matter of Petherick's will. We need to know the precise terms—whether his wife was to inherit unconditionally, or whether his children were secondary legatees."

" 'Everything to the wife' certainly implies the former," said Sethos. "Her husband predeceased her. Did she have a will? And if she did not, who would inherit? Are stepchildren considered next of kin?"

"More damned conjectures," Emerson shouted. "You don't know, and I don't know, and neither does Peabody, though she will probably claim she does."

"Not at all, my dear. The investigation is in its early stages. For all we know there may be a dozen people who wanted Mrs. Petherick dead. The murderer must have been someone she knew and trusted, or she would not have gone alone to meet him in the garden. She would have had no reason to fear either of her stepchildren. They must have some claim to her property, through her husband's will or hers, or they would have had no reason to dispose of her."

"Confound it, Peabody, you are arguing in circles again," Emerson exclaimed.

The boat bumped gently into the bank and Sabir ran out the gangplank. In a spirit of amity I accepted the hand Emerson offered. "Shall we have one of our little competitions?" I asked.

"What sort of competition is that?" Sethos tried to take my other hand but was foiled by the parasol.

"We each write down the name of the person we believe to be the villain and seal it in an envelope until after the case is solved," I explained.

"What a charming idea," said Sethos. "Is there a prize for the winner? May I play too?"

"I am not yet ready to commit myself," Emerson said, ignoring this provocative remark.

"Nor am I," I said. "As you pointed out, Emerson, we have not enough suspects."

The silvery moonlight of Egypt lit our path, but with Sethos beside us making frivolous suggestions I was not tempted to linger along the way.

Emerson was of the same mind. "Hurry up," he grumbled. "We have missed tea and will probably be late for dinner."

Thanks to Maaman's new schedule, we were not late for dinner. There was even time for a quick whiskey and soda with Ramses and Nefret, who were anxious to learn how the Pethericks had taken the news. Nefret looked grave when I described Adrian's reaction.

"I wish dear Dr. Willoughby were still with us. He had some skill in treating nervous disorders. His successor is a pompous fool."

"Adrian Petherick requires something more than the skill of an amateur," Sethos said. "However, I believe I was of some assistance in calming his mind."

"Safe in the arms of Jesus," Emerson growled. "Good Gad!"

At my insistence the entire family (excepting the children, of course) attended Mrs. Petherick's funeral next morning. I had assumed there would be a scanty number of mourners, since she knew few people in Luxor, but I had underestimated the morbid curiosity of the public and the persistence of the press. A line of constables, impressive in their white jackets and red fezzes, kept the crowd at bay, and as we walked toward the newly dug grave I couldn't help thinking that Mrs. Petherick would have taken the display as only what was due a famous author.

The efforts of the Ladies' Committee for the Beautification of the Resting Place of Our Lost Loved Ones (founded by me, though I must make it clear I am not responsible for the name) had improved the looks of the once desolate cemetery. Flowering shrubs struggled bravely for survival and the feral dogs had been frustrated by an enclosing fence. Fences are no impediments to cats, however, and several families of felines had taken up residence. Tabby-striped and black, gray and orange and calico, they slunk along the fence or guarded huddles of varicolored kittens. In my opinion they added a rather pleasant touch, a testimonial to life in the place of the dead. A good number of the ladies did not share this opinion, but even a fence was insufficient to keep the cats out.

I had been acquainted with a number of those who were interred there—friends from Luxor, victims of the various criminals I had brought to justice, and one or two of the criminals themselves. In a remote corner of the cemetery, under a stone I had caused to be raised, lay the remains of one of my deadliest adversaries—Bertha,

Sethos's former lover and the mother of Maryam. Sethos avoided looking in that direction. He had refused to come at first, fearing I would insist on his paying his respects to the woman who was, after all, the mother of his child. To be sure, she had tried several times to kill him (and me), but the beautiful precepts of our faith tell us to forgive even the worst of sinners. My lecture on this subject had had no discernible effect on my brother-in-law, so I did not persist.

Emerson had not wanted to come either. Stamping along at my side, he said loudly, "Who are all these overdressed people? I thought you said no one would attend."

"I had forgotten Mrs. Petherick's literary reputation," I admitted. "Some of the ladies may be Devoted Readers."

Emerson glared at a youngish man who was holding a camera. "There's that confounded journalist again. If you point that camera at me, sir, I will knock it out of your hand."

We were among the few who were allowed to pass the constables and join the Pethericks and Father Benedict at the grave site. Harriet Petherick thanked us rather perfunctorily for coming and then addressed the priest. "We may as well get on with it, Father."

I kept a close eye on Adrian as the service proceeded. He appeared to be in one of his stuporous states, standing close to his sister and staring dreamily at the cloudless blue sky overhead. I could have wished that some of the spectators behaved as well. Several of the ladies wept loudly throughout, and when Father Benedict had finished, one of them—the stout, heavily corseted woman who had been the first to ask Mrs. Petherick for her autograph—fainted onto a constable, knocking him flat. The photographer whom Emerson had threatened earlier got an excellent picture of her and the constable inadvertently entwined.

"Disgusting," said Emerson loudly. "Let's get out of this."

I resisted his attempt to pull me away. The spectacle held a certain unholy fascination. I had not supposed that Dedicated Readers were capable of such vulgar behavior. The flowers they flung toward the grave fell short, pelting priest and onlookers. Someone started to sing a hymn and other wavering voices joined in. It was an inappropriate melody, given Mrs. Petherick's religious affiliation; most of the singers could not carry a tune and some did not know the words. I caught only a few—something about being deep-dyed in sin. Harriet Petherick's composure finally broke. Tight-lipped and pale, she looked about as if seeking assistance. I was not the only one to observe her distress, and a thrill of maternal pride ran through me when Ramses approached her and offered his arm. She clung tightly to it as he led her past the constables.

Nefret and David had taken charge of Adrian, who went with them unresisting and oblivious. I hastened to precede the group, with exclamations of "Shame! Shame!" I was forced to swat the more importunate Readers away with my parasol, and Emerson knocked down two journalists. When we had got the Pethericks into their waiting carriage, Emerson, in a much better humor, actually remembered to take off his hat when he addressed Harriet Petherick.

"Confounded ghouls! Er—that is to say, Miss Petherick, I regret you should have been exposed to this unpleasantness."

"Thank you. I am grateful to all of you. Would you join us at the hotel for a little refreshment? I believe that is customary after a funeral."

I assumed the invitation included me, though she had looked only at Emerson and Ramses. "We will be along shortly," I said. "I think we ought to rescue Father Benedict."

However, the good father did not want to be rescued. He was a jolly, sociable man who seldom found himself the center of such interested attention. We left him posing for photographs and comforting afflicted Dedicated Readers.

I instructed the driver of our hired carriage not to whip up the horses. We do not permit cruelty to animals. Besides, rapid motion raises a cloud of dust and I was wearing my second-best hat.

Emerson leaned back and took out his pipe. "I presume, Peabody, that this is not so much a visit of condolence as an inquisition."

"That is not a nice way of putting it, Emerson."

"It is an accurate way of putting it, I hope," said Sethos. "Or I would not attend."

"I thought you were concerned about Adrian," I said critically.

"You do me too much credit, dear Amelia." He was silent for a moment. Then he said, "The boy held up well today."

"He is in a state of shock." Nefret's smooth brow furrowed. "I am afraid that the reaction may be sudden and violent. I wish I knew how to help him."

"Your specialty is surgery, not psychology," I said. "Your good heart does you credit, my dear, but you must learn not to take on unnecessary burdens."

"Like you?" Emerson inquired.

We had outstripped the reporters and the sensation seekers; the hotel guests who did not fall into the latter category had gone off to see the sights, so the lobby was relatively deserted. When I asked the clerk at the desk to inform the Pethericks we had arrived, he said we were to go straight up. "The lady is now in the rooms formerly occupied by Madam Petherick."

Adrian answered the door. He had transferred his fickle affection from Sethos to Nefret; with scarcely a glance at the former, he took Nefret's hands and spoke with febrile vivacity.

"So good! So kind of you to come. Please take a chair. Harriet! The Emersons are here."

We were not the only callers. I had observed Sir Malcolm at the cemetery, looking on with a sneer and twirling his silver-headed cane. He must have left before the service was over in order to arrive before us.

"I was not aware that you were acquainted with Mrs. Petherick, Sir Malcolm," I said, acknowledging his bow.

"I was well acquainted with her husband, Mrs. Emerson. I felt obliged to pay my respects."

Harriet came out of the neighboring bedchamber with a hatbox in her hand. Tossing it onto the floor, she said, "Your hypocrisy will not deceive the Emersons any more than it did me, Sir Malcolm. They know quite well why you are here."

"How much did you offer?" Emerson inquired bluntly.

"I hardly think, Professor, that that need concern you."

"Five thousand pounds," said Harriet Petherick. "Will you take tea or coffee, Mrs. Emerson?"

She indicated several trays of light refreshments on the table.

David let out a stifled exclamation. The lady did not miss much. Looking at him, she inquired, "Too little, you think? How would you know?"

"I beg your pardon," I said. "I believe you have not met Mr. David Todros, our nephew by marriage. He is a well-known sculptor and painter, and an authority on Egyptian art."

Harriet's critical expression changed to one of interest. "I am familiar with your work, Mr. Todros. At what price would you value the statue?"

"The worth of such objects depends on the market," David said cautiously. "But that price strikes me offhand as extremely low."

"It is also irrelevant," Emerson said. "Miss Petherick has not the right to sell the statuette."

"Then who does?" Sir Malcolm demanded. "Mrs. Petherick is no more. She had no children. Her property passes to her husband's children. I am offering—"

"You, sir, are no gentleman," I interrupted.

Sir Malcolm's pale face turned pink. "I beg your pardon, madam!"

"The poor lady is barely cold in her grave," I went on with mounting indignation. "Is your greed so uncontrolled that you could not wait a decent interval before intruding on the grief of her kin?"

"And hoping to cheat them," Emerson added. "The statuette is worth four or five times that amount, possibly more. Trying to steal a march on Vandergelt and Carnarvon, are you?"

Sir Malcolm gathered the shreds of his dignity around him and rose. "I see no reason to listen to your insults, Professor. Should you change your mind, Miss Petherick, I am staying here at the Winter Palace."

Emerson called after him. "Don't hold your breath, Sir Malcolm. The ownership of the statuette has yet to be determined—as you are well aware."

The door slammed. Emerson chuckled; then, remembering the solemnity of the occasion, he set his face in sober lines.

"I beg your pardon, Miss Petherick."

"Why should you beg my pardon? It was Sir Malcolm whose behavior was unseemly."

"We won't stay," I assured her. "We only came by to see if we can be of assistance."

Miss Petherick glanced at the hatbox. "I am packing my stepmother's clothing and trinkets. Perhaps you know of a charity here in Luxor that would like to have them."

Needless to say, I leaped at the opportunity to be of service. "I can hardly say until I have seen them. Pray allow me to assist you in what must be a painful task."

Emerson gave me a baleful look. "At least have the courtesy to chat for a while, Peabody, before you rummage around in other people's belongings."

"I appreciate Mrs. Emerson's offer and accept it," said Miss Petherick. "But please, Mrs. Emerson, finish your coffee first and have a cucumber sandwich."

"Are you leaving Luxor soon, then?" Nefret asked, as I bit into the sandwich.

Miss Petherick's lips curved in a sardonic smile. "I have been informed by Captain Rayburn, the British adviser, that we may not leave Egypt until Mrs. Petherick's murder has been solved."

Adrian leaned forward, his hands tightly clasped and his eyes unnaturally bright. "We owe it to Magda and our father to remain, Harriet. He loved her."

"He enjoyed being married to a celebrity," said Miss Petherick.

"She made him happy," Adrian said heatedly. "How could we depart without seeing her killer brought to justice?"

"A very proper attitude," Sethos said. "Had she enemies?"

"Literary rivals, perhaps?" Miss Petherick's smile bared a number of teeth. "Or a Devoted Reader who disliked her last book? We have already informed the police that we know of no one who had a motive to harm her."

"Money, revenge, fear," said Emerson. "Those are the usual motives for murder. You had not known her long. How can you be sure she was not a threat to someone's reputation or that she had not done someone a deadly injury in the past?"

"I said we know of no one," replied Miss Petherick.

She was a worthy adversary, and Emerson's expressive countenance showed a certain admiration. He much prefers women of character to those who "fall weeping onto their beds," as he had once put it. She looked almost handsome in her elegant black coat and skirt, her thick black hair coiled into a heavy knot, and color brightening her cheeks. The hand that held her teacup betrayed not a tremor.

"Come now, Professor," she went on. "Postulating unknown enemies is like chasing will-o'-the

wisps when you have a solid, tangible motive staring you in the face. Mrs. Petherick was my father's
sole heir. His collection is worth a great deal of
money."

"Who are her heirs?" Emerson asked.

"I don't know that either. If she made a will, it
would, I presume, be in the hands of her solici-
tors. I can assure you of one thing, Professor. She
didn't leave her estate to Adrian or me."

"You told me, on the first occasion we met, that
you were both fond of her," Emerson shot back.

"I didn't say she was fond of us," Miss Petherick said, cool and unshaken. "She and I were on
civil terms. If there was little affection between
us, there was no animosity, and Adrian's attachment to her was genuine. Have you any more
questions, Professor?"

"Not at the present time," Emerson admitted.

"Mrs. Emerson?"

'If you are asking for my opinion, Miss Petherick, I think we should get your task over and
done with."

Miss Petherick's doubtful expression indicated
that she had had second thoughts about accepting
my offer of assistance, but of course I proceeded
as I had planned. The others left; I rolled up my
sleeves and went into the bedchamber, followed by
Miss Petherick.

The room was in a frightful state of confusion. Instead of proceeding methodically, she had emptied the wardrobe, flinging the garments haphazardly across chairs and tables and turned drawers upside down onto the bed. I considered this highly significant, though to be honest I wasn't sure what her hasty, untidy methods signified. Had she cared more for her stepmother than she admitted, and found the sight of her belongings painful? Had she detested her so thoroughly that she wanted to remove every reminder as soon as was humanly possible? I confined my comments to a mild "Dear me, this will never do," and began folding sable dresses and silken undergarments into neat piles. Stockings, shoes, handkerchiefs, and scarves went into one of the drawers. All of them, even the handkerchiefs, were heavily scented with some musky perfume. Miss Petherick stood watching me, her arms hanging limp at her sides.

"I know several ladies of limited means who might be glad of the gowns," I said finally. "Mourning, alas, is always useful. The underclothes are worn and a trifle—er—youthful."

"Daring, you mean?" Miss Petherick folded her arms.

"I suppose I do. Ah well, I suggest we simply bundle everything up—hats, gloves and all. I will have them brought to me and I will send them on to the proper persons. There is nothing you would like to keep?"

"No."

"Not even her jewelry?" The contents of her jewelry box had also been tossed onto the bed in a glittering, shimmering tangle.

"The gems are all paste and the gold false."

An examination, which I proceeded to make, proved she was right. I was a trifle surprised that a successful authoress, the wife of a man of means, should not have a few important jewels. I wondered whether Miss Petherick had already taken them.

It was none of my business if she had, but my expression must have been somewhat critical, for she volunteered a statement. "I took a few trinkets that had belonged to my mother. Their only value is sentimental, but if you would like to see them—"

"I assure you, that is not necessary."

"I insist. I don't want you to have any doubts about my honesty."

She pulled open the drawer of the night table.

It took only a single glance to survey the contents. Unlike the tangle on the bed, these ornaments had been carefully laid out on the bottom of the drawer: several small brooches, set with seed pearls and chips of turquoise, two rings of equally modest value, and a garnet parure, consisting of bracelets, hair combs, and a necklace. They were of a style popular fifty years earlier, a mosaic of small gems set in silver. One of the combs had lost two of its teeth.

"She never wore them," said Miss Petherick. Her tone left no doubt as to which "she" she meant. "They were too old-fashioned and restrained."

I was unexpectedly touched by the little mementos and their careful disposal, nor did I blame Miss Petherick for taking them. By rights they ought to have gone to her instead of being handed over to her mother's successor. I said as much, and saw the young lady's stern face soften.

"My mother was a gentle, unassuming woman, Mrs. Emerson. She never asked for much, and she got even less."

I am somewhat ashamed to admit my true reason for offering to take charge of Mrs. Petherick's clothes. Miss Petherick had thanked me for my kindness, but as my more astute Readers no doubt realize, my motive was not so benevolent. I had not had the opportunity to examine the garments closely, turning out pockets and cuffs and looking for stains. All is fair in love, war, and detection, and one never knows when a clue may turn up.

In fact, several new clues had turned up. Most interesting was the young lady's feelings about her stepmother. Civil she may have been, but it was obvious that she harbored a long-standing, deep-seated resentment of the woman who had taken her mother's place, not to mention her mother's poor little ornaments. She might not stand to gain monetarily from Mrs. Petherick's death, but, as Emerson had cogently pointed out, an equally strong motive is the desire for revenge.

Almost as interesting was the fact that the wardrobe I had seen was not as extensive as it ought to have been. Ladies of fashion travel with a wide variety of clothing and accoutrements. There had only been a few changes of undercloth-ing, and they were patched and darned. She had brought at least one flamboyant garment with her—the crimson gown in which she had been buried. And surely she had owned more jewelry than the contents of that single rosewood casket.

Pondering these matters, I made my way along the corridor, exchanging absentminded compli-ments with the suffragis and waiters I encoun-tered. I stopped at the desk to give instructions to the clerk about Mrs. Petherick's things, and then said casually, "Who is the lady in room 354?"

If the fellow had said, "What lady?" my theory would have collapsed on the spot. Instead he replied readily, "A Mrs. Johnson, madam. She arrived a week ago."

"Ah," I said. "I think I may know her. Is she of middle age and medium height, with black hair and eyes?"

The young man was sorry to disappoint me. "The age and size are correct, Mrs. Emerson, but Mrs. Johnson has yellow hair. Bright yellow hair. Very bright."

I was sorely tempted to take the final step that would prove my theory, but the spirit of fair play demanded that I admit Emerson to my confidence first. So I thanked the young man and turned away. My brisk stride (and my raised parasol) got me through the lobby and out of the hotel without being accosted, though the confounded journalist and his camera made an abortive attempt to stop me. "Mrs. Emerson!" he called. "My friend Kevin O'Connell—"

He was mistaken if he believed that name would gain him favor. Kevin was a friend but he was also a journalist, and at times, such as the present, the two were incompatible. I brushed the fellow aside and went on.

They were all waiting for me on the veranda, including the Vandergelts and Jumana. Katherine had decided they should not attend the obsequies, since they had not been acquainted with Mrs. Petherick, so they were understandably curious about what had gone on.

"You were wise to stay away," I said, giving Katherine a kiss. "It was a disgusting spectacle."

"So I have been told" was her reply. "And I gather that the brother and sister have been ordered not to leave Egypt. I cannot understand that, Amelia. There is no evidence against them, is there?"

"So far there is no evidence against anyone," Emerson grunted. "Unless Peabody discovered something while she was examining the lady's belongings?"

All eyes returned to me. Emerson's sapphire blue orbs were narrowed.

"My dear, how can you impugn my motives?" I inquired, with a merry little laugh.

Lounging at ease, legs crossed, Sethos shook his head. "Don't annoy him, Amelia. He is already in a vile humor."

Emerson opened his mouth, closed it, drew a deep breath, and spoke in a soft, controlled voice. "I asked Cyrus and Bertie—and Jumana—to meet with us in order to determine our plans for excavation, not to gossip about matters that do not concern us."

"So you are not interested in what I learned after you left?"

Emerson could not admit he was dying to hear. He said grumpily, "The sooner you get it out, the sooner we can dismiss the subject."

I didn't want to increase his aggravation for fear he would go back on his promise to hire additional staff and give the children more freedom to get on with their own work. So I explained my deductions about Mrs. Petherick's wardrobe and jewelry, ignoring Emerson's muttered comments ("Typical female . . . clothes . . . balderdash . . ."), and went on to describe my conversation with the desk clerk. At that point Emerson gave over muttering in favor of profanity.

"Hell and damnation! Why didn't I think of that?"

"Ramses came close to figuring it out," I said, with a kindly smile at my son. "He suggested she slipped out of her bedchamber while he and Abdul were in the sitting room, but she then had to make her way down a longish corridor before she was out of their sight. The simplest explanation was that she simply went into the room next door. She had taken it under another name, her appearance altered by the simple addition of a wig and a more conspicuous frock."

"So she was there the entire time," Ramses

murmured. "That assumption does answer many of the questions we had."

"It will be easy to prove," I said. "We must have Mr. Salt's permission to enter the room. I thought it best to leave that to you, my dear." I nodded at Emerson.

"Hmph," said Emerson, his rancor assuaged by this concession. "Very well. I will attend to it. Now as to the Valley of—"

"One more little thing, Emerson. I offered to dispose of Mrs. Petherick's belongings. One of the hotel servants will bring them here. I didn't have the chance to examine them closely, you see. It would have looked suspicious."

"Curse it," said Emerson. "Well, don't expect me to help."

"It is a woman's job, my dear. Perhaps Katherine will lend me her advice."

She accepted with expressions of pleasure. There were times when Katherine felt left out of our activities, and this was a way of making her feel useful—which in fact she would be.

We were finishing luncheon when the hotel attendant arrived with Mrs. Petherick's possessions. Katherine and I left the others discussing arrangements, except for Nefret, who expressed an interest in assisting us. Jumana did not express interest. She loved listening to Emerson expound on Egyptology, and since Emerson loved to expound, they complemented each other nicely.

I had the bundles taken to my study, since I knew Emerson would object to the scent of stale perfume in our bedchamber. Nefret, who is sensitive to odors, wrinkled her nose. "The sooner we get these out of the house the better. I don't like handling garments whose owner will never wear them again."

A strange sentiment, some would have said, considering the aplomb with which she had handled the owner herself. However, scents are particularly evocative.

Katherine had begun examining the frocks. The pockets produced a typical motley array: several handkerchiefs, a withered sprig of greenery, two hairpins, and a considerable amount of lint. A good lady's maid would have emptied them before hanging the garments in the wardrobe. I understood now why Mrs. Petherick had not brought an attendant with her. She had planned her dramatic disappearance before she left England, and privacy was essential for the scheme.

I will spare the Reader the details of our search, in the event that he is of the masculine gender. Suffice it to say that we found no suspicious stains, no objects sewn into hem or seam, and, in short, nothing suspicious whatsoever. Except for the underclothing, the garments were relatively new and relatively cheap. People do not anticipate wearing mourning for long. In fact, few modern ladies wore unrelieved black, unless it happened to become them. It did become the Countess Magda and she had not been unwilling to make a show of her grief.

We left the repackaging of the clothes to Fatima, who had participated in the last stages of the search. She had nothing to add to our conclusions. I could see that she and Katherine were disappointed—they had hoped to discover a vital clue—so I said consolingly, "I didn't really expect we would find anything of interest, but the task was necessary. Fatima, will you have these sent to Miss Buchanan, at the school? I will write her a little note explaining the situation. I am sure she can find someone who can make use of them."

Emerson was on the veranda listening (a word which is seldom applicable to Emerson) to the conversation between Ramses and Mr. Katchenovsky. It was heavy with complex verb forms in ancient Egyptian. My husband leaped to his feet when we came in, and offered to escort Katherine home, Cyrus and the others having gone ahead.

"That isn't necessary," she assured him.

"I insist," said Emerson, with heartfelt sincerity. "Don't wait tea for me, Peabody, I won't be long."

"Before you go, Katherine," I said, "tell me how Mr. Lidman is getting on. I neglected to ask after him; my excuse must be that I had a number of more compelling duties."

"He arrived this morning, while you were at the funeral." Katherine's brow furrowed. "I would appreciate it, Nefret, if you could find time to have a look at him. He could scarcely walk—two of the suffragis from the hotel had to help him along—and he refused food."

"That is a bad sign. We will come round later this evening," I promised.

Nefret went off to help get the children ready for tea, and I invited Mr. Katchenovsky to go on with what he had been saying.

"I would not wish to bore you," the Russian said politely. "I fear our discussion became somewhat technical."

"Verb forms are wasted on me," I said, laughing. "But I am sure you are finding some interesting texts."

"That depends on what one considers interesting," Ramses said with a smile.

"Letters," I said promptly. "Prayers, like the ones you spoke of the other day."

Ramses's eyebrows tilted in surprise. "You remembered."

"Certainly. I remember everything you say, my dear. Unlike some persons."

Ramses grinned. "Well, so far we have been chiefly concerned with preserving the scraps of papyrus we found the other day. It's a tedious process, and I'm afraid I've left most of it to Mikhail. The scraps have to be softened and then flattened and covered with blotting paper and pressed down until they are completely dry."

"I am familiar with the process," I said.

"Of course, Mother."

"So when do you expect you will be able to start reading them?"

"They'll have to be sorted and arranged in proper order first. That's where Mikhail is so useful," Ramses added, with a polite nod at the silent Russian. "It's like piecing together a jigsaw puzzle when half the pieces are missing. One must be familiar with the language and with the varieties of handwriting."

"Excellent," I said vaguely, my attention having been distracted by merry childish cries.

"Here they come," said Ramses. "Brace yourself, Mikhail. By the way, Mother, I take it you didn't find anything of interest in the old clothes?"

"How did you arrive at that conclusion?"

"You wouldn't have been able to keep it to yourself this long."

As I had promised Katherine, Nefret and I went to the Castle after dinner. Emerson offered to drive us in the motorcar, but he had forgotten the confounded thing was still in pieces, so I was able to decline. Cyrus was good enough to send his carriage.

The doorman was on the watch for us. The great gates swung open as the carriage approached and closed with a metallic clang after we passed through. Torches made the courtyard bright as day.

Katherine's concern about her patient was evident by her failure to offer us coffee. She led us directly to the elegant guest chamber where Lidman reposed.

"I am sorry to hear you are not feeling well, Mr. Lidman," I said, approaching the bed while Nefret unpacked her stethoscope. "Without wishing to denigrate a fellow practitioner of the medical art, I must say that Dr. Westin's methods are not always for the best. I would like to examine your injuries, if I may. Your lower limb, is it?"

I whisked the covers back. The leg was heavily

bandaged, from ankle to knee. So were his left arm, his head, and his ribs.

"Well," I said, after unwinding yards of bandage. "It appears to me that certain of your injuries would be all the better for being left exposed to the air. This abrasion on your left limb, for example. What do you think, Nefret?"

She had listened to his heart and taken his temperature.

"I don't find any broken bones," she said, running experienced hands over his arms and legs. "You were fortunate, Mr. Lidman, to escape with only bruises."

Lidman raised a feeble hand to the bandage on his brow. "My memory . . ." he muttered. "I can't remember . . ."

"Short-term loss of memory often follows a blow on the head," Nefret said. "Don't try to force it; it will probably return in due course. I recommend bed rest and a nourishing diet. You are in the best possible hands here."

"One of the servants will sit outside your door tonight, in case you want anything," Katherine added.

"It is very good of you. So kind . . ."

"I'll leave these with you, Katherine," Nefret said, after we had bade him good night. "These for pain, these to help him sleep if he needs them.

One cannot trust a patient who is somewhat confused to take them himself."

"Quite right," I said approvingly. "What is your
assessment, Nefret?"

"The injuries are genuine," Nefret said. "And
they are consistent with a hard fall and being
swept about by the current."

"Could he have throttled Mrs. Petherick?" I
asked.

Katherine started. "Amelia, for heaven's sake!
Why would he?"

"I can't think of a motive, Katherine, but as we
criminal investigators know, motive is a secondary consideration. I am only endeavoring to
ascertain whether he was physically capable of
doing the job."

"You know I can't answer that, Mother," Nefret
said indignantly. "Offhand I would say no, but people are capable of extraordinary effort if the need is
strong enough. What makes you suspect the man?"

"I suspect everyone of everything," I said.

I was comfortably tucked up in bed reading when
Emerson entered.

"An early night, eh?" he said pleasantly. "Excellent, my dear. You have been a busy little bee of
late."

"Mmmm," I said, and turned a page.

"What are you reading that you find so absorbing?" Emerson demanded. He began to undress, tossing his clothes in various directions.

"Hang your trousers over the chair, Emerson. This is one of Countess Magda's novels—**The Vampire's Daughter**. I borrowed it from Marjorie Fisher."

"Why are you wasting your time on that rubbish?" Emerson asked. I got the notion he had some other time-wasting activity in mind.

"I was curious. It really is a dreadful piece of trash, but this is interesting." I held up a piece of paper. "It is Magda's biography. Marjorie must have clipped it from a newspaper."

"Oh?"

" 'Our beloved authoress was born in her ancestral home, Castle Ormondstein, the only child of her adoring parents, who, recognizing her genius when she was but a tot, spared neither time nor expense in cultivating it, supplying her with tutors in various subjects and nurturing—' "

"Does that sentence ever end?" Emerson inquired.

"Not for another paragraph. It is typical of journalistic adulation, my dear." I cleared my throat and continued. " 'Her idyllic existence came to a cruel end when the Great War brought tragedy and . . . ' Oh, very well, Emerson, I will synopsize. Her father, Count von Ormond, enlisted in the Austrian army—"

"I thought she was Hungarian," Emerson said, throwing the covers back and getting into bed.

"Austro-Hungarian. He was an officer of the emperor, of course, a cavalryman. When he died valiantly at the Battle of Leningrad—"

"That can't be right," said Emerson.

"Newspapers always get facts wrong. If you continue interrupting me I will never get through this, Emerson."

"Hurry it up, then."

"Her mother died of grief," I continued. "Alone in the world, with the hordes of the bestial Germans advancing . . . Yes, Emerson, I know, that can't be right either. Anyhow, the valiant young girl, whose brilliant novels had already won her worldwide acclaim, fled with two of her faithful servants, and after horrors that cannot be described for fear of rending the hearts of her readers, she made her way to England with only the clothes on her back."

"No papers, no servants, no cherished cross that had belonged to her mother, now an angel in heaven?" inquired Emerson, flat on his back with his hands under his head.

"Very good, Emerson," I said, laughing. "She had lost everything, including the servants, one of whom perished after saving her from a ravisher."

"Not both of them?"

"The other died of a fever, after nursing Magda, giving her beloved young mistress all her food and water."

"Good Gad."

"That's about all there is," I concluded. "Her publishers and her public welcomed her with open arms and she continued to soar in the esteem of critics and readers."

"Turn out the light, Peabody."

"Yes, my dear."

Emerson agreed to accompany me to the hotel the following morning. He grumbled a bit about taking the time from his work, but I could see he was as curious as I—and that he was half hoping I would be proved wrong about the questionable Mrs. Johnson. Sethos went with us, despite Emerson's attempts to dissuade him.

I had not expected Emerson would have any difficulty in persuading Mr. Salt to violate a visitor's privacy. We found the manager more than eager to oblige. The chambermaid had reported that the lady's bed had not been slept in, nor the towels in the bath chamber used. Mr. Salt was in a slightly nervous condition anyhow. A second mysterious disappearance would have a bad effect on the Winter Palace's reputation, especially if it were followed, like the first, by murder.

"I do hope," he said pathetically, "that nothing else has occurred. Perhaps Mrs. Johnson has just gone away for a few days."

"Without mentioning it to you or the desk clerk?" I asked.

Mr. Salt groaned.

The room had the musty smell of a chamber which has not been occupied for some time. Also palpable to the olfactory sense was the scent of stale perfume. The bedcovers had been turned down and a nightgown spread carefully out across them, as was the custom. I went immediately to the wardrobe, where I found what I had expected— several elegant gowns, of the size that would fit Mrs. Petherick. An even stronger scent wafted from the top drawer of the dresser when I opened it.

"It is the same scent she used," I said, sniffing.

"Hmph," said Emerson. "That's not proof, Peabody."

"What about this, then?" I held up a linen underbodice and indicated the name written inside the seam in the indelible ink used by laundries.

"Hmph," said Emerson, in a different tone.

"Oh, come, Emerson, be generous," Sethos said. "She was right on the mark. Acknowledge it."

"I did," grunted Emerson.

We had to explain the situation to poor bewildered Mr. Salt. He kept shaking his head and muttering about the press. "They will have to be told, I suppose?"

"Not by us," I replied. "But the police will certainly have to be notified, and I don't doubt the news will get out."

We made a thorough search of the room. I turned the dresses inside out and felt along the seams while Sethos unfolded the linens, shook them out, and refolded them. Emerson, who would as soon have spied on a naked lady as handle her personal undergarments, watched his brother's long, deft hands with unconcealed disapproval. We found nothing of importance except another jewelry box. The ornaments were few, but of a much more valuable nature than the trinkets I had found earlier. As I had observed, the Countess Magda liked sparkling gems, the shinier the better. Two pairs of diamond earrings, a bracelet encircled by emeralds and diamonds, a tastelessly large diamond brooch, and a string of pearls made up the contents of the box. I handed it immediately to Mr. Salt and asked him to put it in the hotel safe.

"Tell your employees that under no circumstances are they to enter the room until after the police have been here," I instructed.

"Locking the barn door?" Sethos inquired, raising his eyebrows. "They have had ample opportunity to go in and out as they pleased already. Which of them has keys?"

Mr. Salt started. "Oh dear," he murmured. "Oh dear. Keys? Oh. Let me think. The chambermaid, the laundryman, the suffragi on duty, the assistant manager . . ."

"The door might as well have been left open," Emerson said. "Well, well, it's too late to remedy that. Shouldn't we tell the Pethericks what we've found?"

"They went out early this morning," Mr. Salt said.

"Where?" Emerson asked.

"They asked me to recommend a reliable dragoman, so I presume they intended to visit some of the sites. I do not spy on my guests, Professor."

"That's a job for the police," Emerson agreed. He gave the manager a consoling clap on the back. Salt staggered. "Here, now, Salt, buck up. This will all blow over in a few days."

FROM MANUSCRIPT H

Emerson was reverting to his old habits. He sent them all off to the Valley of the Kings before he and his wife left for Luxor, with instructions to continue clearing the tomb, keeping copious notes and taking photographs of every stage. Ramses went without protest. His father's new schedule meant he would have from midmorning until late afternoon for his own work, which was fair enough. His mother didn't protest either; she was suffering from a severe case of detective fever and couldn't concentrate on anything else.

There was only room for a few people to work inside the burial chamber, and dirty work it was. The floor was covered with a layer of hardened mud, some of which had to be removed with dental picks. So far the results had been meager: scraps of broken pottery and stone vessels, bits of gold foil, and a few seals. Examining one of these, Ramses said in disgust, "Unreadable. This looks like a neb sign, but that's all I can make out."

"What part of the tomb did the seal come from, do you suppose?" David asked.

"Your guess is as good as mine. The outer entrance was closed and the seals of the necropolis applied to the stones, but the tomb was entered at least once after the burial. Davis's lot demolished the blocking they found and apparently destroyed or lost any remaining seals."

"Do you think the Professor will want a photograph?" David asked, eyeing the unintelligible scrap.

"Doesn't he always? Take it upstairs with the rest of this rubbish." Ramses put the seal carefully into a tray with the few other objects that had come from the square on which they were working.

A short time later Hassan came down. "There are many, many tourists," he announced. "Two of them ask to see you."

"Tell them to go to blazes." Ramses got stiffly to his feet.

"They say they are the son and daughter of the lady who died."

"The Pethericks?"

Nefret, who had been diligently scraping away at the brick-hard mud, straightened.

"You had better talk to them, Ramses."

"Oh, hell, I suppose I had. We may as well leave off work for now, Hassan. Find anything, Nefret?"

She held out her hand. Cupped in her dusty, scratched palm were several small golden beads. She tipped them into the box Hassan held out and Ramses took advantage of the young man's departure to kiss her scraped fingers. "Not much to show for all that effort."

She smiled and stroked his cheek. "But, darling, it's such a romantic ambience. Here alone, with you . . ."

She sneezed. Ramses laughed and helped her up the three-foot drop between the corridor and the burial chamber. "Here you go, darling. We'll find more romantic surroundings later."

Tourist cameras clicked as they emerged into daylight. "One of the most discouraging aspects of this job," said Nefret resignedly, "is that my dusty, dirty, crumpled image will appear in thousands of photo albums all over the world."

"It will be the most beautiful image in the album," her husband said gallantly. "Damn it, Hassan, get those idiots back from the edge."

Nefret scrambled nimbly up the ladder. Ramses followed, after ordering Hassan to remove the ladder, and joined Nefret, who was talking to Adrian and Harriet. "I'm sorry we have to be so strict about visitors," Nefret was saying. "It isn't only tourists we have to worry about; some of the local people refuse to believe we aren't looking for gold."

"Have you found anything?" Adrian asked eagerly. One wouldn't have known there was anything wrong with him, Ramses thought; he was smiling and at ease, his hat in his hand as he addressed Nefret.

She smiled back at him and indicated one of the boxes of scraps. "As you see."

Harriet Petherick offered her hand. Ramses shook his head and spread his own filthy hands out for her inspection. "It's dirty work, Miss Petherick."

"And unproductive," she said. "What are you hoping to find?"

He couldn't think of any reason for refusing to answer. "Some evidence that the statue came originally from this tomb. In Father's opinion this is the most likely place, so we are looking here first."

"That's a rather negative approach, isn't it? Your failure to find evidence doesn't mean the statue wasn't there."

"Right," Ramses said. She was as quick as she was forceful, and she was looking almost feminine that morning, her thick hair rolled back under the broad-brimmed hat which was tied under her chin with a jaunty bow. He went on, "However, it's the only approach open to us at this time. We've learned the name of the dealer from whom your father bought the statue—"

"How?" The word was as sharp as a shout.

"From Montague. He came to us first, trying to purchase the statue."

"That won't do him any good, will it, so long as your father sticks to his promise."

"You may rest assured that my father will do precisely that."

"I didn't mean to offend you." She put a propitiatory hand on his arm. It was a strong, capable-looking hand, with a broad palm and long fingers. "Professor Emerson's reputation is of the highest. I understand why Mrs. Petherick went to him."

"Thank you." The sun was hot and he wanted to get home and wash. He was about to make his excuses when Nefret addressed him.

"Adrian would like to see the tomb."

Ramses scowled at his beloved wife. "I don't think—"

"We can spare a few more minutes," Nefret said. "Can't we?"

"I'd really appreciate it," Adrian said. "This is my first trip to Egypt, you see, and I am trying to understand why my father was so keen on the country and its antiquities." His eyes fell. "I wish I had taken a greater interest while he lived. It would have pleased him so much."

Ramses looked to Harriet Petherick for help but got only a shrug and a cynical half-smile. It would have been heartless to reject that appeal, even though Adrian's interest was born of guilt, and Pringle Petherick probably wouldn't have given a damn whether his children shared his interests.

"All right," he said. "Just for a few minutes.

Hassan, will you please lower the ladder? I'll go down first."

Adrian had no difficulty negotiating the ladder. Harriet swung herself neatly onto the topmost rung and descended as easily as her brother had.

"Adrian, watch where you step," Ramses said. "Miss Petherick, take my hand, please."

Dust motes swam in the ray of sunlight that angled off one of the mirrors used for lighting. They had lost a good deal of their effectiveness, as the sun had moved since they were last adjusted. Ramses switched on his torch.

"Aren't these mirrors rather an old-fashioned method of illumination?" Harriet Petherick asked.

She'd caught on to the idea immediately. Showing off her intelligence? Ramses wondered. Or admitting to a greater knowledge than her expressed disinterest in Egyptology had implied? If it was an admission, it was deliberate. This was not a woman who made careless mistakes.

Adrian had to have the method explained. "Jolly clever," he exclaimed. "But why not torches or electricity?"

"Torches burn out too quickly and don't give an even light," Ramses explained. "It's hard to get permission to run an electric line. This works well enough."

He stopped them on the edge of the three-foot

drop into the burial chamber. "This is as far as we go. There's not much to see, really."

"Not like some of the other tombs we saw this morning." Adrian sounded disappointed. "Why aren't you digging in places like that?"

Ramses patiently explained again why they were here. Adrian lost interest; he preceded them up the sloping passageway.

"Look here, Miss Petherick," Ramses said softly but urgently. "If you know anything about the statue that you haven't told us, I strongly advise you to do so. Holding back information will only damage you and your brother."

A pebble slipped under her feet; she caught more tightly at his hand. "Can I trust you?"

"To do my best for you and Adrian, yes. I believe in his innocence."

"A carefully equivocal statement," she said mockingly. "So you wouldn't lie for us?"

"No. But I hope I won't have to. He's not entirely responsible for his actions. Though he seems much more cheerful today."

"He has his moods." She stopped and turned to face him. "I admit I haven't confided fully in you and your parents. I doubt I can tell you anything that will throw light on my stepmother's death, but perhaps I haven't the right to hold anything back. May I speak to you in private, without anyone knowing? I will leave it to your discretion to decide what to tell the others."

"Yes, of course. When?"

"Not today. Adrian is determined to see every tomb in the Valley of the Kings. I will send you a message."

His parents returned from Luxor shortly after Nefret and he reached the house. Emerson immediately demanded a report on the morning's work. Ramses was able to condense it into two sentences. "We've finished the burial chamber except for the far corner and the niche. Nothing."

"Hmmm," said Emerson. "Starting tomorrow—"

Perched on the arm of his chair, Nefret interrupted with a laugh and a playful hand across his lips. "Never mind about tomorrow; I want to know what you discovered this morning. To judge by your expression, Mother, you were right about the mysterious Mrs. Johnson."

"It was not a difficult deduction," his mother said. The words were modest, but her expression could only be described as smug. "Mrs. Petherick's name was inscribed on certain of the linens, and the gowns—none of them black—were obviously hers. There was also a jewel case, with several valuable pieces of jewelry."

"Did you find a wig?" Ramses asked.

His mother's smile widened. "Well done, Ramses. No, we did not. She must have been wearing it the night she was murdered, which means the killer took it away with him. One can only speculate about his reasons for doing so, but—"

"Don't speculate," Emerson ordered.

"If you say so, my dear. We intended to inform the Pethericks of our discovery, and ask them to look over the contents of the room to see if anything is missing, but we were unable to locate them."

"They were in the Valley of the Kings," Nefret said. "Behaving like ordinary tourists."

"Except," Ramses added, "that they asked to see KV55."

"You let them in?" Emerson demanded.

"Not into the burial chamber, obviously."

"Oh. All right, then. Now, as I was saying . . ."

Ramses had become accustomed to his father's abrupt changes of plan, but this one caught all the others by surprise—even his mother.

"Join Cyrus in the West Valley?" she exclaimed. "Why, for pity's sake? I thought you wanted to finish in KV55."

"I do. I will," said Emerson, fumbling with his

pipe. "I am only postponing it. Too bloody many tourists."

There would be just as many tourists in a week's time, or in two weeks'. Ramses was beginning to get an inkling of what his father was up to. He had a foothold in the Valley of the Kings, and he intended to hang on to it. The only question was why?

After luncheon, Emerson sent David to Deir el Medina to take photographs and confer with Selim. The rest of them headed for the West Valley, leaving Ramses with his papyri and Mikhail Katchenovsky. Ramses was becoming attached to the quiet Russian; he was so anxious to please and so efficient, and so good with the children. The twins gravitated to him at once when they all met for tea, and as he watched them Ramses wondered if the Russian had had children of his own. It would have been inappropriate to ask, of course; the man's personal life was his own affair, and the subject might be a tender one.

Wasim came up to the house with the post while Katchenovsky was telling a story about an evil werewolf and a princess and the brave peasant boy who had rescued her. Ramses sorted through the messages as he listened.

"And there was this," Wasim said, handing over a much-folded paper. "Delivered by hand for you."

One glance told Ramses it was not the message from Harriet Petherick he had hoped to receive. The dirty paper was addressed in awkward Arabic writing to "The Brother of Demons." After he had read it he folded it again and put it in his pocket.

"Who gave you this?" he asked.

"I do not know, Brother of Demons. I found it with the other letters. There were many people here today."

He had ample time to think about what he should do. Nobody asked him what he had accomplished that day; Emerson was too busy interrogating David about Deir el Medina and describing Cyrus's work in the West Valley. Ramses was still weighing the pros and cons when, after an early dinner, his mother sent everyone to bed. They had put in a hard day and Emerson had decreed they would be out again at dawn. Having made up his mind, Ramses managed to intercept David.

"Oh, no," the latter groaned, after he had read the message. "Not another anonymous letter inviting you to a secret rendezvous in the middle of the night."

"We haven't had one like that for quite a while."

David had had his share of midnight rendezvous during the War. He fixed Ramses with a formidable stare.

"You aren't thinking of accepting, I hope."

"He says . . ." Ramses took the letter back. " 'How did the lady die? I know. Come alone. I will tell you.' His Arabic isn't very good, is it?"

"Not a native speaker."

"Or he's semiliterate. Could be one of the suffragis at the hotel. They are understandably cautious of the police."

"You're going," David said resignedly.

"There's a chance the fellow may really know something," Ramses argued. "A chance worth taking."

"I'm going with you."

"I thought you'd say that. I'm not fool enough to go alone, and you're the only one with enough experience to stay in concealment. Nefret would raise hell if I told her, and Father would raise a different variety of hell, and Mother . . ."

"Would come charging after you waving her parasol. I see your point. What about Sethos?"

Ramses was silent. "You don't trust him?" David asked.

"No. Yes. Damned if I know what to think. He turned up most conveniently and coincidentally just after we got hold of one of the most valuable antiquities even he has ever seen."

"The truth is, you don't like him," David said.

"Yes. No."

"I feel the same way. Well." David leaned back and folded his arms. "I'm with you, of course. It'll be like old times."

"Do you miss them?" Ramses asked curiously.

"If I had no responsibilities and no hostages to fortune, I'd be up to my neck in the nationalist movement. And probably in prison," David added with a wry smile.

"I know. Maybe a murder investigation will take some of the edge off. I hate to ask you, but—"

"I'd have been deeply hurt if you hadn't. How are we going to go about this?"

They met behind the stable, an hour before the appointed time. The rendezvous point was in the hills south of Deir el Bahri, only a short walk, but this would give them time to scout the area and find a place of concealment for David before the informant arrived—if he did arrive. They were both wearing dark galabeeyahs and headcloths, and Ramses noted, with some misgivings, that David appeared to be in a cheerful frame of mind.

"Don't do anything stupid," he said sternly.

"Such as jumping the fellow when he draws a knife on you?"

"Nothing like that is likely to occur."

He hoped he was right. He had told Nefret he meant to work late. She'd have his scalp for a trophy if she found out he had lied to her.

"Are you armed?" he asked.

"Two of them." David waved his arms. If Ramses hadn't known his abstemious friend so well, he would have suspected David had been drinking. It must be the possibility of action that had got his adrenaline flowing.

They walked briskly along the uneven path. It was as familiar to both of them as the passageways of the house, and the moon was bright. No one else was abroad. The villagers went to bed early to save lamp fuel, and would-be tomb robbers had apparently taken the night off—or were busy elsewhere.

When they reached the steep slopes of detritus that edged the foot of the gebel, Ramses said softly, "It's somewhere near here."

The letter writer had been vague about the precise location, possibly because his Arabic vocabulary was limited. Ramses planned to stand full in the moonlight, a safe distance from the cliff face, and wait for the man to come to him. David was no longer smiling; his lean face was set in lines Ramses remembered well from their war days. He nodded without speaking and slipped away, fading into the shadows. He hadn't lost his touch.

There was no one in sight. No sound, no movement. Ramses went back the way they had come, waited for a while, and then retraced his steps. It lacked only ten minutes till the designated time. He came to a stop not far from the cleft into which David had vanished, and removed his turban.

The ten minutes passed, and so did another ten. He moved a little farther away from the cliff face, into full moonlight. He had just about decided his informant wasn't coming when he heard the sound of someone approaching, slowly and cautiously. In the dead silence the crunch of stone under shod feet was as loud as a rockfall.

The footsteps stopped. He was close by now, watching. Ramses didn't move. A few minutes passed with agonizing slowness; then a dark form took shape against the deeper darkness and came toward him.

It was a woman. She was completely covered with the black tob and face veil worn by old-fashioned Egyptian females, but Ramses got the impression of feeble old age from the way she moved, slowly and bent over.

The uneven steps stopped a few feet away, just out of reach and the veiled head tilted as if in inquiry.

"Don't be afraid," Ramses whispered in Arabic. "You know me. You know I won't hurt you."

He took a step forward, his hand outstretched. The veiled form stumbled back.

"It is well," Ramses said quickly. "I will come no closer. What did you want to tell me?"

She flung out a black-clad arm, pointing, and let out a high-pitched cawing sound, like that of a bird. Ramses whirled round, staring in the direction she had indicated.

And that was the last thing he remembered.

SEVEN

FROM MANUSCRIPT H
(CONT.)

Wake up, dammit! Say something!"

He knew the voice. The name escaped him for the moment, buried like other memories under a thick layer of pain, but something told him he owed the speaker acknowledgment.

"What happened?" he croaked. "Who are you?"

"Don't do this to me, Ramses. Open your eyes, will you?"

"I'd rather not." The name came back to him. "David."

"Drink this." An object was jammed against his mouth. One sip of the liquid brought him to a sitting position, choking and sputtering.

"That's better," David said with a long sigh of relief. "I took a leaf from Aunt Amelia's handbook of convenient accoutrements. There's nothing like brandy, she says."

Finding that his eyes were now open, Ramses surveyed his surroundings. The scenery hadn't changed. He was in the same place, but he was sitting instead of standing. Moonlight flooded the ground and shone darkly on a pool of liquid near where his head had rested.

"Blood," he said, pleased at being able to identify it. "Mine?"

"You got a hard knock on the head." David sat back on his heels. "She had a club of some sort hidden in that damned full sleeve. Swung it before I could move."

"She's gone?"

"Damn right she's gone. I fired at her as she was raising her handy club a second time. Missed."

Ramses got out a croak of protest, and David said, "Knowing your dislike of firearms, I didn't tell you I had brought a pistol. I'm glad I did. I didn't mean to hit her, only stop her before she could deliver another blow. She scuttled off. I didn't chase after her, I was afraid you were . . ."

His voice failed. Ramses discovered he was now capable of uttering more than three words at a time. "Have some of that brandy."

"Excellent idea."

"And then give me another nip. God, my head feels as if it's about to fall off."

"Your head ought to be used to that sort of

thing by now. You must have inherited the Professor's thick skull."

David handed him the flask. The blessed stuff ran through his veins like liquid fire. Cautiously he got to his feet.

"Steady." David took hold of his arm. "Maybe you shouldn't try to walk. I can go back to the house and get—"

"No, I'm all right," Ramses said, as they started back along the path. "I don't suppose there's a hope of keeping Nefret in the dark about this."

"What do you think?"

"Not a hope. Dammit, she's going to be furious."

Moonlight made walking tricky, hiding obstacles in shadow. He was grateful for the support of David's arm. By the time they reached home he felt all right except for an aching head; but his spirits plummeted when he saw the main house was brightly lighted.

Nefret was waiting for them, and she was definitely furious. When he had failed to come to bed she had gone looking for him; discovering he was not in the workroom, she had searched the house and, in the process, raised the whole household. They all trailed along when she dragged him off to the clinic and unwound the turban David had used as a bandage. It was like being attended by a flock of magpies, Ramses thought; they all settled down on various pieces of furniture and peppered him with comments and questions while Nefret bathed and bandaged his head. He let David do most of the talking. Nefret had already told David what she thought of him for collaborating in such a crazy scheme, and he was on the defensive.

"We took all possible precautions," he protested. "It was seeing what I assumed was a woman that lowered my guard for a vital second."

"Me too," Ramses said.

"Keep quiet," Nefret barked.

"It wasn't a woman?" Emerson asked.

"If it was, she could run like a gazelle and swing like a batsman," David said. "But that damned—excuse me, ladies—that all-enveloping tob, and the way she—he—moved, like a feeble old woman, took both of us in at first."

"All right, are you, my boy?" Emerson asked anxiously.

"He'll live." Nefret pinned the bandage neatly in place. "If I don't kill him. And David."

"He saved my life," Ramses said. "Again."

"You think she meant to kill you?" his mother asked. Bright-eyed and alert, every hair in place, she sat perched on a stool with the voluminous folds of her dressing gown flowing around her. "Why?"

"That's a good question," David said. "We talked about it all the way back. Ramses claims he doesn't know why."

"People seldom murder other people without some sort of reason," remarked Sethos. He was leaning against the wall, his arms folded. "Logical or otherwise. Ramses, have you been spreading alarm and dissension?"

"No," Ramses snapped. "Well . . ."

"Well?" Sethos echoed.

"It can't be relevant," Ramses insisted. "I did spread the word that I was the only one, except Father, who knew where the statue was hidden. Mother had started a similar rumor, about herself, and I thought it wise to—er—"

"Take the danger upon yourself?" his mother inquired coolly. "That was thoughtful of you, my dear. But I agree that it does not seem relevant. If one wishes to learn a secret, one does not silence the holder of that secret."

"Expressed in your usual pedantic manner," said Emerson, now reassured as to his son's condition. "Perhaps she—he—didn't intend murder, but abduction and interrogation?"

"Man or woman, it would take more than one person to accomplish that," said his wife.

"Thank you," Ramses said. "Now can I go to bed?"

"Definitely," Nefret said. "And if you say one word about breakfast at six, Father . . ."

Emerson looked at her in alarm. He wasn't at all intimidated by his wife—their loud arguments were relished by both of them—but when Nefret spoke in that tone of voice they all knuckled under.

"No, no, wouldn't dream of it. Sleep as long as you like, my boy. Er—eight o'clock?"

Nefret led him off in triumph, her chin set.

Their house was quiet and dark, except for the night-light in the children's room. The dog was stretched out across the threshold. Ramses didn't see her until he stumbled over her. Amira let out a moan of protest, Ramses swore at her, and Nefret told them both to keep quiet.

"Lucky the children didn't wake," Ramses said in an attempt at casual conversation.

"Lucky for you."

She closed the door of their room and turned into his arms. "I hate it when you do this sort of thing," she whispered.

"I know. I'm sorry."

"I'm sorry too. For scolding you. It was only because—"

"Show me you're sorry, then."

The attack on Ramses was somewhat disturbing. My medical experience, confirmed by Nefret, had assured me he was not badly hurt, but if David had not been with him the consequences might have been serious. When we met for breakfast (at eight o'clock) he looked quite normal except for the bandage around his head. Fatima gave him an extralarge helping of porridge and four eggs.

"I have been thinking," I began.

"Rrrrrr," said Emerson. "She thought at me for two hours last night. Bloody nonsense. Not a sensible idea in the lot."

"I can only conclude," I continued, unperturbed by the interruption, "that Ramses knows something the rest of us do not. A fact, perhaps unnoticed by him, that makes him dangerous to our unknown enemy. Something to do with Mrs. Petherick."

"Or the statuette," said Emerson, forgetting he had dismissed my conjectures as nonsense.

"I can't think what it might be," Ramses said. "I had no conversations with the lady when others were not present. As for the statue, I know no more than the rest of you."

"Let's have another look at it," Sethos suggested. The gleam in his eyes might have been interpreted as greed. Emerson interpreted it that way.

"Later," he said, with a hard look at his brother.

"Have you seen the newspaper this morning?" David asked.

"Never read the cursed thing," Emerson said loftily.

Normally I didn't either. The news was always at least a day late, and little of it was of immediate interest to us. Since the "mystery of the black afrit" I had of course perused the Cairo papers, but I hadn't had a chance to see them that morning.

"What do they say about Mrs. Petherick?" I asked.

"Nothing new, Aunt Amelia. There's a rehash of her literary career and her romantic biography, by some gushing female admirer, and a lurid story about Egyptian mummies."

David did not mention the political news, though the major headline read "New Riots in the Delta." He was the only one who followed the political situation closely. It did not make for encouraging reading; the country was still in a state of unrest, anticipating that the forthcoming declaration of Egyptian independence would not answer all the demands of the "radicals," as the British government termed them.

"Howard Carter arrived in Cairo day before yesterday," David added.

"What?" Emerson bounded up. "How do you know that?"

"It's in the social column," David said, smiling. He knew that was one part of the newspaper Emerson would never consider reading. "He's not planning to leave for Luxor for another week."

Emerson sat down. "Ah. Making the rounds of the antiquities dealers, I expect. Hmph. A week, eh? Let's be off. That is . . . Ramses, are you sure you are fit for this?"

"Fit for translating hieratic?" I inquired. "I should think so. Now, Emerson, no objection, if you please. We agreed, did we not, that that was to be his primary task? Yes. Is it advisable for a person who has taken a head injury to work in the dust and heat? No." I patted Ramses's hand. "Have a nice quiet day, my dear. We will be back for tea."

I have never been a skilled horsewoman, but the smooth gait of our Arabians was a pleasure. It was certainly more pleasurable than the steep climb over the hills, which was the only other way of reaching the Valley.

Needless to say, Reader, my thoughts did not dwell entirely on Egyptology. The welfare of my loved ones would always take precedence over scholarship, and there was good reason to assume that danger still threatened some, if not all. Emerson had scoffed at my conjectures, but that did not prevent me from pursuing them mentally.

Mr. Lidman's misadventure had been a blow—to Lidman himself, naturally, but also to me, since I had reached the conclusion that he had been responsible for the attempts to break into the house. However, he had the best of all possible alibis for the attack on Ramses, having been incapacitated and guarded at the time. Were there two villains? Three, four? A gang? The statuette was prize enough to inspire the lust of several persons, but as I had cogently pointed out, Ramses's attacker could not have hoped to gain possession of it by that method.

I was baffled. But only for the moment. Something was bound to turn up.

Emerson sent the others down into the burial chamber and set me to work sifting debris. It was not an onerous task, since there was not much, and our people had already picked out the largest objects, such as they were, so I had ample opportunity to look about me. An hour or so later Emerson pulled himself out of the pit and addressed me.

"How are you, my dear?"

"Hot. Bored. Where are you off to?"

"A little stroll," Emerson said.

"May I join you, Emerson?"

"Need you ask, Peabody?"

Emerson seldom strolls. On this occasion he

actually sauntered, hands in his pockets, whistling off-key and looking interestedly from side to side like an ordinary tourist. From time to time he stopped and stared at nothing in particular that I could see. As I believe I have explained elsewhere, but will repeat for the sake of forgetful Readers, the East Valley is shaped like a maple or oak leaf, with lobes reaching out in all directions. They are not interconnected except at their base; each ends in rugged cliffs, so it is necessary to retrace one's steps after one has explored each. Tomb entrances are everywhere, some blocked with steel gates, some open to visitors. We must have seen a dozen of them during that stroll: Ramses IX, Ramses VI, Amenmose, and others. Instead of entering them, Emerson spent an inordinate amount of time staring at their surroundings. At one point his well-shaped lips parted, and I waited breathlessly for a statement that would explain his actions.

"Workmen's huts," he said.

"So?" I asked, when it was apparent he had nothing to add.

"Interesting," said Emerson.

"Not very."

"Now, now, Peabody, keep an open mind. Everything is of interest to a trained excavator."

The last area we visited was the side wadi in

which the tomb of Thutmose III was located. Remembering our encounter with the ibn Sim-sahs, I moved closer to Emerson, but not a sight or sound disturbed the quiet of the place until Emerson spoke again.

"Might bear investigating," he muttered, contemplating the pile of rubble in which he had dug.

"It won't be investigated by you," I replied somewhat tartly, for his enigmatic comments were beginning to get on my nerves, and I was extremely warm. "Lord Carnarvon holds the concession."

"You need not remind me of that, Peabody. Well, shall we start back?"

The usual crowd of sightseers had gathered round KV55. Among them I saw Sir Malcolm's head, crowned by a fashionable pith helmet. He stood a little distance away from the jostling crowd, eyeing them disdainfully. Seeing Emerson, he moved to intercept us and bade us good morning.

"What are you doing here?" Emerson demanded in his customary forthright manner.

"I believe the Valley of the Kings is open to all visitors, Professor." Sir Malcolm snapped his fingers. A worried-looking dragoman hastened up and opened a sunshade over his head. "Observing an excavation in progress here is a rare treat."

"Weren't you present when Howard Carter was working across the way?" I asked.

"Yes. The fellow is competent enough," Sir Malcolm conceded. "But all he turned up were some wretched workmen's huts. Professor Emerson is in a class by himself. I would consider it a privilege to observe his procedures."

The compliment mollified Emerson somewhat, but like myself he entertained doubts as to Sir Malcolm's motives. "My procedures, sir, are surely known to an aficionado like yourself. This tomb contains nothing of interest."

Hassan's turbaned head appeared. "Emerson," he called. "Will you come? We have found something."

FROM MANUSCRIPT H

"A scrap of wood with a half-obliterated cartouche," Emerson said disgustedly. He laid it on the table in front of Ramses. "But Hassan's announcement got the whole mob in a twitter and there was a considerable amount of pushing and shoving. And that bastard Montague—"

"Now, now," his wife said soothingly. "His interest was understandable. And he was very polite."

"He's changed his tactics," Emerson declared.

"But he's still after the statuette. Can you make out anything, my boy?"

Holding the scrap delicately by one side, Ramses turned it to catch the fading light. "Most of the original paint is gone. The impression at the top of the cartouche could be a sun sign, and this curve part of the kheper beetle."

"Smenkhkare," Emerson said triumphantly. "He was buried there, I knew it."

"Not necessarily," Ramses said. "A number of royal names have those signs, including Amenhotep the Second and Tutankhamon. What do you make of it, Mikhail?"

He handed the piece to the Russian, who received it on the palm of his hand. "It is as you have said, Ramses. Only those two signs are certain. They were usually more deeply carved than others."

"I'll have another look at it in the morning, when the light is stronger," Ramses said. "Though I doubt if it is significant. KV55 was a cache, after all, with objects from various royals."

He replaced the scrap in the box lined with fabric and moved it aside in time to avoid the reaching hand of his daughter. "How many times must I tell you not to touch antiquities without permission?" he asked sternly.

"It is only a dirty piece of wood," said Carla.

"Any object may have historical value," said her brother, blue eyes accusatory. "May I have a look, Papa?"

"Another time," Ramses said. He didn't want to discourage his son, who had already shown an interest in Egyptology, but he knew that if David John were permitted to examine the scrap, Carla would insist on her turn. "Here, Fatima, will you be good enough to take this to Father's study?"

Katchenovsky distracted Carla by producing a piece of string and initiating her into the art of cat's cradle. He really did have a knack with children.

Unfortunately his mother got at the post basket first. Fortunately Harriet Petherick did not indulge in dainty scented notepaper. His mother handed over the plain white envelope without comment. The handwriting was as large and emphatic as that of a man. There were several other letters for him; he read them first, and then opened Harriet's.

It left him in what his mother would have called a moral dilemma. Harriet reiterated her request that he tell no one—and what a depressingly familiar sound that had! In this case, he told himself, there couldn't be any danger in going alone. She'd asked him to come to her room at the hotel. He could imagine what his mother would suspect: poison in the tea, a passionate embrace that would end with a knife in his ribs, a posse of thugs hiding in the bath chamber . . . Plots worthy of the Countess Magda.

He laughed, and his mother looked up from the letter she was reading.

"Something amusing in your correspondence, my dear?"

"No, not very."

The situation wasn't at all amusing. He found himself between the devil and the deep blue sea: breaking his word to Harriet Petherick or deceiving his wife—again.

He could lie with a straight face when he had to, but the trouble with his affectionate, closely knit, inquisitive, helpful family was that the lie had to be clever enough to get them off the track. In the end, he told part of the truth.

"I'm going over to Luxor for a while. I'll be back in time for dinner."

He hadn't expected to get off that easily, nor did he. In the end he had to pretend to lose his temper. "For God's sake, I don't need a bodyguard every time I leave the house! I'm going straight to the Winter Palace and I'll come straight back. I only want to have a chat with Abdul and one or two of the other suffragis."

"You've remembered something?" his mother asked keenly.

"Just an amorphous idea. They're more likely to talk to me if I'm alone. Now, please, Mama, may I have your permission to go?"

"May I beg a ride?" Katchenovsky asked. "I have some business in Luxor."

The children set up a clamor of protest. The Russian smiled and held out his hands to them. "Little ones, I must not take advantage of your family's kindness. I will see you tomorrow."

Feluccas and gaily painted boats crowded the river, as belated tourists returned to their hotels. The sun was setting when they reached the East Bank. Katchenovsky, who had spoken very little during the trip, said good night and left Ramses outside the Winter Palace.

Ramses hadn't spoken much either. He had been remembering Nefret's caresses and loving words. If he had to break his promise to some-one—and he obviously did—that someone ought not be his wife. And yet, mingled with his feelings of guilt was that ungovernable curiosity. Damn it, he told himself, this was an opening not to be missed. His mother would have jumped at it and lied through her teeth if she had to.

He had overlooked one little problem. Several of the suffragis greeted him with knowing grins as he walked along the corridor toward Harriet Pethe-rick's room. They would spread the word, Nefret would find out where he had been, and she would know he had deceived her.

Harriet was some time responding to his knock. When she opened the door he stood frozen for a moment.

He wouldn't have believed she had such a garment in her wardrobe. It was more like the sort of thing her stepmother would have worn, flowing and feathery, ruffled and beribboned. And pink.

Involuntarily he looked over his shoulder. There, only a few feet behind him, was Abdul, grinning and bowing.

"Thank you for coming." Harriet threw the door wide, giving Abdul an excellent view of her dishabille.

Ramses indulged himself in a curt, explosive suggestion to Abdul, stiffened his spine, and went in. He was in no mood to be polite. The fat was in the fire, and he intended to make sure she would sizzle too. He gave her a long, insolent survey, from head to foot and back. Color brightened her cheeks. He doubted it was embarrassment. Rage, more likely.

"Is there anything you won't do for him?" he asked.

She didn't pretend to misunderstand. "What

makes you suppose I wouldn't do this for myself?"

She came closer and put her hands on his shoulders, tilting her head back to look directly into his eyes. The line of her throat was long and smooth, the tanned skin fading into cream between her breasts. Her full sleeves had fallen back, displaying rounded arms. Ramses knew he ought to turn and walk out, but the damage was already done and there was still a chance she had something sensible to say. He took her hands and led her to a chair. "All right, you've made the effort. Why?"

"I told you—"

"Forget that. What's he done that you feel obliged to go to such lengths to protect him?"

She leaned her head back and closed her eyes. Her hands tightened on the arms of the chair. Then they relaxed, and she looked up at him.

"You were attacked last night."

"By Adrian?"

"No! I said I wanted to talk to you, and I do. I will. Please stop looming over me like that. Would you like a drink?"

"No. Thank you."

"Then will you be good enough to get one for me? Brandy."

No poison in the drinks, Ramses thought, as he

went to the table. He didn't take one for himself. At least he would go home without liquor on his breath. Moved by an embarrassing but irresistible impulse, he opened the door of the bath chamber and looked in after he had handed her the glass.

When he came back she was herself again, bolt upright in her chair, the ruffles drawn closer over her breast. She raised her glass in a sardonic salute.

"First round to you," she said coolly. "What were you looking for? A journalist with a camera?"

He hadn't thought of that. Beads of perspiration formed on his forehead.

"Have you anything pertinent to say, or shall I go?" he asked.

"I have a good deal to say. First, it could not have been Adrian who waylaid you last night. Oh, yes, I know all about it. The hotel servants gossip incessantly, especially with the help of a little baksheesh. They saw Adrian go to his room before midnight and will swear he did not leave the hotel."

"I'm afraid their testimony won't carry much weight."

"Baksheesh."

"And our European prejudices. However, there are points in his favor. I can't see him forging a note in Arabic and laying such an elaborate trap.

The fellow had some knowledge of the terrain. Adrian doesn't."

"You'll tell that to the police?"

"If it comes to that, yes." Ramses sat down facing her. "But I can't imagine that it will. There's no firm evidence against Adrian."

"That policeman thinks there is."

"Ayyid? What makes you think so?"

"He's been round again, asking questions. Adrian . . ." She hesitated. "Adrian became agitated. It made a bad impression."

"One can't arrest a man because he became agitated," Ramses said.

"He was so much better before we came here! I had found a new doctor; Adrian was improving. This business has set him back. I want to take him home, but the police won't let us leave."

"They can't hold Adrian indefinitely, they'll have to accuse him or let him go. Was that the reason you asked to talk to me?"

"I wanted to give you some background. I don't know whether it will help clear Adrian, but perhaps knowing more about the persons involved will give you a clue. My father . . ." She paused to take a sip of brandy. "Pringle Petherick was a cold, uncaring father and a thoroughly selfish human being. His wealth and his interests were devoted solely to his collection. He married my mother for her money and spent it buying antiquities. She never had a penny for herself. She died, I have always believed, of indifference."

Brutal as her assessment was, Ramses preferred this Harriet to the seductress. "He doesn't sound like the sort of man who would fall in love with a woman like Countess Magda."

"Love?" She pondered this for a moment, her eyes as cold as stone. "I don't know what the word means, especially in this case. He was dazzled, intrigued, and for perhaps the first time in his life, manipulated. The real question is why she married him. He was not a bad-looking man, and in the eyes of the world a wealthy man. But she can't have been after his money; she was one of the most successful authors of the time and she flaunted her diamonds and expensive gowns.

"Adrian was dazzled too. At first she made a great show of maternal affection. It was rather sickening, really, all that cooing and caressing and flattery, but he was too young to remember our mother and too much in need of love to be critical. His affection for her was genuine."

She stopped speaking and drained her glass.

"Is that all?" Ramses asked.

"Does it help?" She leaned forward, hands tightly clasped. "There must be other suspects besides Adrian. Your mother has quite a reputation as a detective . . ."

"My mother. Yes."

"Sooner or later they will find the person who killed her. It wasn't Adrian. He loved her."

A line of poetry slid into his mind. "For each man kills the thing he loves . . ." He didn't repeat it aloud. It was only poetry, after all.

"I appreciate your confidence." He got to his feet. "I had better be going."

She went with him to the door, ruffles trailing. "Are you going to tell your wife you came here?"

"She'll hear it anyhow," Ramses said sourly. "My only hope is to confess before someone else tells her."

"I've got you in trouble with her, haven't I?"

"Probably."

She was leaning against the door; he couldn't reach for the handle without touching her. "If it's any consolation," she said, "you've had your revenge."

"What do you mean?"

"You refused me, flatly and without hesitation. Do you have any idea what a devastating blow that is to a woman who is prepared to make the ultimate sacrifice?"

"I expect you'll survive the blow."

"It wouldn't have been a sacrifice."

"So you were good enough to say." He reached past her for the doorknob. "Good night."

He went straight out of the hotel without stopping and then stood by the door letting the night air dry the perspiration on his face. Harriet Petherick had enjoyed every moment of that awkward interview.

The terrace was full of tourists enjoying a late-night drink under the twinkling lights. One of them stood up and came toward him.

"How did it go?" inquired Anthony Bissinghurst, alias his uncle.

Ramses was glad to have a subject onto which he could focus his anger. "You followed me!"

Still in character, Sethos leaned languidly against the wall and folded his arms. "I've decided it's time I took an active hand in this affair. You don't seem to have sense enough to take care of yourself."

"There wasn't any danger."

"Of another attack, perhaps not, but it will be all over Luxor by morning that you had a romantic tête-à-tête with the Petherick woman. A photograph of you and the lady together would cook your goose with Nefret and destroy your credibility as an impartial witness."

"There was no photographer either." He started down the stairs. "She isn't as calculating as you."

"Defending the lady, are we? How chivalrous. She was calculating enough to swathe herself in filmy robes and make sure Abdul and the other suffragis saw her." Sethos hurried to catch him up. "Did she try to seduce you?"

"None of your damned business."

"Observe that I said 'try.' If I were married to a woman like Nefret I wouldn't be susceptible either."

Ramses swung round and caught his uncle by the collar. "Why do you keep provoking me?"

"I can't help it," Sethos said plaintively. Without apparent effort he detached Ramses's grip. "Old habits are hard to break. Look here, Ramses, let's declare a truce. Someone was lying in wait for you tonight—lurking, as the saying goes. When he saw me join you he left."

"Did you see who it was?"

"I think it was your friend Katchenovsky."

"Oh, for God's sake! Mikhail is totally harmless. If it was he, he probably only wanted to talk to me, or beg a ride back across the river. You scared him off. He's a timid soul."

"Better safe than sorry."

"You sound like Mother."

"I take it that isn't meant as a compliment."

Ramses didn't reply. They went on down the steps. The area around the hotel and the corniche was brightly lighted, and so was the dock. There were no shadows in which an assassin could lurk. Sethos had probably invented the lurker.

"That could be the man I saw," Sethos said suddenly. He pointed.

The man was Adrian Petherick. He gave the impression of having been out for an innocent evening stroll; there was no guilty start when he saw them, no change in his bright smile.

"Good evening," he said. "A beautiful night, is it not?"

"Yes, it is," Ramses said. "Does your sister know you are out?"

Adrian chuckled. "Dear Harriet. I can't have her trailing me all the time, you know. She had an appointment this evening. Was it with you, by any chance?"

"As a matter of fact, it was."

"What did she tell you?"

His smiling face was without guile, but there was something in his tone that set off alarm bells in Ramses's mind.

"She's concerned about you," he said bluntly. "You oughtn't to go off without telling her. There is still an unknown killer at large."

"Unless it's me," Adrian said cheerfully. "Is there any new information?"

"No."

Adrian shook his head. "The police aren't very clever, are they? That fellow, for instance—" He turned. "He's been following me for two days. Plainclothes, you could say—he's dressed like all the other Egyptians, in that flapping robe and turban. But I spotted him right away."

"Well done," Ramses said. Ayyid's plainclothes detachment needed training. The turbaned head peering out from behind a tree was as conspicuous as a camel.

"I'm going in now," Adrian announced. "Do give my regards to your beautiful wife and the rest of the family."

"He doesn't look anything like Mikhail," Ramses said, watching Adrian ascend the stairs two at a time.

"They are approximately the same height, when Katchenovsky isn't being Uriah Heep, and both are slightly built. I didn't see his face. Standard clothing, pith helmet, dark trousers and coat."

When they reached the dock, Sabir was lying in wait. "You let another boatman bring you across," he said accusingly.

"But you found out," Ramses said.

"Aywa, of course. So I waited to take you back."

"I cannot imagine how a criminal remains undiscovered for long here," Sethos remarked, as they took their seats. "Or is it only your activities that merit such close attention?"

"The latter, I think."

"You don't want to talk about it?"

"About what?"

"Young Petherick. You feel sorry for him because of his wartime experiences, but he is either mad as a hatter or extremely cunning. In either case he is a prime candidate for the role of murderer."

"But why?" Ramses demanded, goaded into argument. "What motive could he have? According to his sister, he was devoted to his stepmother."

"Motive, as all criminologists know, is not evidence. People kill people for the damnedest reasons. Some murderers hear voices. Others have such monumental egos that they appoint themselves judge as well as executioner. Then there are the simple souls who let small grievances pile up, month after month and year after year, until an equally small grievance pushes them over the edge. To say nothing of the—"

"You've made your point," Ramses interrupted.

"No, I haven't. I was working up to the fact that as yet we know almost nothing about any of these people. We need more background. I may have to go to Cairo for a few days."

The boat bumped gently against the bank.

Ramses jumped out, leaving his uncle to fend for himself. His concern for Adrian had been submerged in a more immediate worry.

Ramses was late. I had expected that, but I had not expected he would be accompanied by Sethos. The latter looked particularly bland.

"We've had to put dinner back," Nefret said accusingly. "Even further back."

"Sorry," Ramses said.

Sethos went to the table and poured two glasses of whiskey. He handed one to Ramses and settled himself comfortably in a chair with the other glass in his hand.

"Hmmm," I said. "That bad, was it?"

Ramses took a long swallow and a deep breath. "No, not at all. That is—uh—not in the conventional sense. I've just had an interview with Harriet Petherick."

"I suspected as much," I said.

"I didn't," said Nefret. "I believed you."

Ramses's eyes fell under her accusing stare. "I gave her my word I wouldn't tell anyone beforehand."

"You gave me your word you'd never go off again without telling me."

"I did tell . . . Goddammit!" Ramses slammed his empty glass down on the table. "Do you want to hear what happened, or don't you?"

"Oh, yes, I certainly do," Nefret said gently.

Without further ado, Ramses plunged into his narrative. His description of Harriet Petherick's attire, though vague as one might have expected from a male observer, raised a number of eyebrows. Having completed what was obviously for him the most dodgy part of the story, he paused for breath and for another glass of whiskey.

"Pink," I said thoughtfully. "Veeery interesting. She must have taken the garment from her stepmother's wardrobe. That implies premeditation. What happened after you refused her advances, Ramses? Was that her only reason for inviting you?"

"She claimed she wanted to give me certain background information," Ramses said, more at ease now that the worst was over. "She was extremely critical of her father, who was, in her own words, selfish and cold to his first wife and to his children. The second Mrs. Petherick was quite unlike his first wife, worldly and wealthy, famous and—er—feminine. Harriet couldn't understand why Magda was attracted to Petherick, but she was determined to marry him, and she succeeded."

"There are attractions a daughter might not

understand," I said. "And Petherick was rich, wasn't he?"

"So was Magda," Ramses said. "Flaunting her jewels and expensive gowns, to quote Harriet."

"That is no indication of wealth," I remarked. "Rather the reverse, in some cases. I don't know what her income may have been, but she spent it lavishly. As for her success in—er—trapping Mr. Petherick, men of a certain age are particularly vulnerable to such advances. She caught him at a susceptible moment."

Emerson cleared his throat noisily, and I amended my analysis. "Some men."

"Not I," said Sethos. "I have always been susceptible."

"Is that all?" Nefret inquired of her husband.

"She said that the lady had made a concerted effort to win Adrian over, at least at the beginning, and insists that he was genuinely attached to her. In retrospect," Ramses said slowly, "I believe she was, and is, primarily concerned with gaining our help for her brother. She claims the police have fixed on him as the killer. She wants to take him home for medical treatment."

"He is in need of it," Nefret said.

Sethos uncrossed his legs. "I'm not so sure, Nefret. We encountered the young man on our way to the dock, and his manner and conversation were those of a completely normal, very alert person. He even made a few little jokes about being under suspicion. A clever man can feign dementia, and it's a legitimate legal defense."

"I don't believe it," Nefret said stubbornly. "That is—I suppose you are right, but I don't believe it applies to Adrian."

Fatima poked her head out the door. "Dinner is served. Maaman says he cannot put it back any longer."

"Is he crying?" Emerson demanded.

"Yes, Father of Curses."

"Damnation. We're coming, Fatima."

While the others were taking their places, I had a quiet word with Nefret. "Ramses told you the truth, Nefret. Nothing of—er—nothing happened."

"I know." She put her arm round my waist; her blue eyes were clear and bright. "I just like to stir him up now and then. He's absolutely irresistible when he loses his temper."

She laughed and gave me a little squeeze.

"That's all right, then," I said, relieved. "I remember once when Emerson—"

"Peabody!" Emerson said loudly. "What are you gossiping about? Sit down, if you please."

Over dinner I requested that Ramses and Sethos go into more detail about their conversa-

tions with the Pethericks. There was certainly
food for thought in several of the statements that
had been made.

"So Ayyid is having Adrian followed," I said.
"That is extremely—"

"Interesting," growled Emerson. (The soup was
quite salty.) "What you mean, Peabody, is that you
are vexed because Ayyid hasn't consulted you."

"No, but I am a trifle surprised that Miss Petherick has not applied to ME for assistance." Nefret
gave Ramses a certain look, and realizing I had
revived a delicate subject, I hurried on. "Or to a
solicitor. British justice is British justice, and
Adrian cannot be detained indefinitely."

"I told her that," Ramses said. He put his soup-
spoon down.

"Is it not good?" Fatima asked anxiously.

"It's fine. I'm not hungry for lentil soup, that's
all."

"Ayyid is only after one thing," Sethos said. "Or
rather, two things that are interrelated. He wants
to be the one to catch the perpetrator—it would
be quite a feather in his fez—and he wants to
make sure one of his own people isn't made the
scapegoat."

"That's nonsense," David said. "No Egyptian
would dare kill a foreigner. The penalties are too
severe."

"You know that and I know that, and Ayyid knows that," Sethos retorted. "He also knows that accusing an Egyptian would be the easiest way out of the mess for the British. We've had a number of chats on the subject."

"What?" I cried. "You and the inspector? When?"

"On several occasions," Sethos said with an infuriating smile. "He thinks I'm an agent of British intelligence."

"You are," David said blankly. He jumped. Someone must have kicked him in the ankle. I would have done so had I been closer to him.

"Not the one he thinks I am," Sethos said.

"Who," I demanded, "is Anthony Bissinghurst?"

"He's me," Sethos said. "Or rather, I am he."

"One of your numerous personae?"

"It's one I use when I require official support," Sethos explained. " 'Tony' is a bona fide member of the Interior Department, well known to the authorities."

"Good Gad," Emerson muttered. "So what has Ayyid told you?"

"He's set his sights on Adrian, right enough. I understand why. There isn't anybody else."

"What about Harriet?" I inquired.

"Come now, Peabody," Emerson exclaimed. "It can't have been she."

"Why not? Because she is a woman? I am surprised you should still suffer from prejudice against my gender, Emerson, in view of the fact that we have encountered more than one female antagonist. Harriet is, in my opinion, a much more likely suspect than her brother. Unlike him, she detested her stepmother, and she is tall enough and strong enough to pass for a man."

"I wondered if you would think of that," Sethos murmured.

"You did, of course."

"Certainly. You cannot accuse me, Amelia dear, of harboring prejudices against the female sex."

Before retiring that night, I made one of my little lists.

I waited until Emerson had had his coffee next morning before I produced my list. "In my opinion," I said, "we have been negligent in failing to follow up certain of the inquiries we launched some time ago and in exploring other avenues."

Emerson snatched the paper from my hand. "Good Gad, Peabody, you've outdone yourself this time. I see that under 'Suspects' you have listed Sir Malcolm, Lidman, Karnovsky, Harriet, Adrian, and Mr. Salt, the manager of the Winter Palace! Why not Cyrus, or Winlock?"

"Because we are well acquainted with them, of course. The others are new to Luxor. Mr. Salt took over the management only a few months ago. How do we know he is not a homicidal maniac who was, perhaps, cheated by Mr. or Mrs. Petherick?"

"Anybody can be a homicidal maniac," Emerson said with more passion than accuracy. "There are times when I feel myself leaning in that direction. Really, Peabody!"

"If you will look at the second column of my list, you will see that I have suggested several practical lines of investigation."

"Hmph," said Emerson, scanning the paper again. "We can't check on the backgrounds of all these people; for all we know, any guest in the hotel could harbor a grudge against Mrs. Petherick." He started to close his fist on my list, caught my eye, and handed it back to me. "I haven't time for this nonsense. Let us go."

"Where?" I inquired acerbically. "KV55, Deir el Medina, or the West Valley? You can't seem to make up your mind."

"I know precisely what I am doing," Emerson retorted. "Come, if you are coming."

When Emerson and I are having one of our friendly discussions we are seldom interrupted. Now David ventured to speak.

"Do you want me to bring the cameras, Professor?"

"Certainly. Be quick, if you please."

He strode out, followed by Nefret, David, and, after a moment, by Ramses.

"I may as well go along," I said to Sethos. "What about you?"

Sethos smiled at Fatima, who was trying to refill his cup. "No, thank you, Fatima. Your coffee tempts me to remain, but duty calls. The Professor has questioned my abilities and impugned my talents."

"What on earth are you talking about?" I asked. Fatima, who had even less idea than I, nodded and beamed.

"He thinks I missed something while I was loot—— er—investigating that tomb," Sethos said. "I want to be on hand when he admits I didn't."

We joined the others in the stable. Ramses very kindly offered me Risha, but I declined in favor of one of the stallion's granddaughters, a pretty little mare called Amber. As Sethos had guessed, Emerson led the procession to the East Valley and Tomb 55.

I hadn't been there for several days, and I was impressed at the progress the men had made. Most of the burial chamber had been cleared. Only one corner, and the niche that had contained the beautiful canopic jars, remained to be examined.

The morning's work was as unproductive as our earlier excavations. The far corner contained the same sort of miscellany we had already found: pottery fragments, one of them bearing a red-and-black floral design, an unshaped lump of yellow quartzite, and a few faience beads. The last of these having been recorded and removed, Emerson stood with hands on hips surveying the now empty chamber.

"No hidden rooms," said Sethos in a studiously neutral voice.

"I didn't expect there would be," said Emerson.

"Not even a hole in the wall."

Emerson shot him a hateful look. "There's still the canopic niche."

"Shall we start on it?" Ramses asked.

"Er—not today." Emerson took out his watch. "Good Gad, it is later than I thought. Don't you want to get back to your bits of papyrus, my boy?"

"Whatever you say, Father."

"I'm off to Luxor," Sethos announced.

Emerson muttered something that might have been "Good riddance," and headed back toward the entrance, leaving David and Nefret to pack up the cameras. My brother-in-law gallantly offered me an arm.

"It's odd, you know," he said.

"What is?"

"Emerson's behavior. He's been digging in that wretched hole for the stated purpose of finding some evidence that the statuette was once there, yet he doesn't seem bothered by his lack of success. One would expect a few curses at the very least, wouldn't one?"

"We haven't quite finished yet."

"Hmmm," said Sethos.

"Why are you going to Luxor?" I asked.

"I intend to follow some of the leads you so cleverly suggested. May I borrow that excellent little list of yours? I believe I saw you put it in your pocket."

I handed it over. "You will, of course, inform me of the results of your investigations."

"How could you suppose otherwise, my dear?"

He and Ramses went off toward the donkey park—not exactly together, for although they walked side by side they did not speak or look at each other. As we pushed through the tourists I saw Sir Malcolm, dapper as ever, under a very large umbrella held by his dragoman.

"What luck?" he called.

"None," Emerson bellowed, without stopping.

It was only midmorning, so I took it for granted that Emerson had no intention of returning to the house just yet. "The West Valley?" I inquired hopefully. Cyrus always brought an ample supply of food and water. Emerson hadn't given me time to pack a luncheon basket.

"May as well," said Emerson.

"You are behaving most erratically," I informed him.

"No, I am not," said Emerson.

Nefret and David caught us up soon after we turned into the road to the West Valley. I prefer to set a deliberate pace over rough ground, for the sake of the dear horses.

Cyrus hailed us with delight. "I was hoping you'd come. Seems I'm in need of a photographer."

"Happy to oblige," said Emerson. "David—"

"Let the boy have a glass of tea first," Cyrus said. "You all look pretty hot and dusty."

"The ride is hot and dusty," I replied. "Is that Mr. Lidman?"

Cyrus glanced round. Like myself, he always erected a temporary shelter when there was no convenient empty tomb at hand. My question had been unnecessary; seated under the canvas canopy, beside a large basket, was the unmistakable form of Mr. Lidman.

"He insisted on coming out today," Cyrus replied. "He still isn't fit for much, but he wanted to resume his duties."

Lidman rose and removed his hat when we

approached. In my opinion he had been unwise to leave his bed. Sunburn patched his pale, puffy face, and his attempt at a smile was rather pitiful.

"I have taken on the duties of a houseman, you see," he said. "Alas, I am unable to do more."

Nefret studied him with sympathetic concern. "You ought not tax your strength so soon, Mr. Lidman. Take it slowly."

Emerson had very little patience with weakness and even less with Mr. Lidman. "Quite," he said, having drained his glass. "Now then, Vandergelt, let's see how you are getting on. David and Nefret, unpack the cameras. Peabody, there is a nice high heap of debris that requires sifting. You can help Jumana."

"What, don't I get Hassan and the other fellows too?" Cyrus inquired with a grin.

"They'll be along later," said Emerson, oblivious to sarcasm. "I left them closing up KV55."

"You finished there already?" Cyrus asked.

"Not quite. No, not quite. However, there is more to be done here. Always give a friend a helping hand, eh? Ah, Bertie. What were you doing over there with Jumana? You ought to be working on your plan of the tomb."

"I thought I'd wait until we finished the clearance," Bertie said meekly. "The debris is piling up, and Jumana—"

"Mrs. Emerson will give her a hand. Come along."

Nefret gave Bertie a consoling pat on the arm.

Though Cyrus yielded to Emerson in most cases, he was adamant about stopping work by mid-afternoon. "I've been out here since six A.M.," he announced, "and I'm tired and hot and ready for a long cool bath. I sent Lidman home already, he was looking sickly."

"The man is absolutely useless," Emerson grumbled.

"I can't fire a fellow because he's been taken sick," Cyrus said. "That wouldn't be right. I'll see you folks later."

By the time we reached our house I too was ready for a long, cool bath. Ramses and Katchenovsky were working and Sethos had not yet returned from Luxor, so I was able to take my time. Splashing merrily about in my tin tub, I eventually attracted the attention of Emerson, and we had a nice little interlude. My attempts to persuade him to confess what he was up to failed, however, and I must admit I did not persist in them long.

Emerson's cheerful frame of mind dissipated when he saw Mr. Katchenovsky on the veranda playing with the children. The game seemed to involve feeding one another pieces of biscuit. "I'm tired of having that fellow hanging about," he complained. "Why is he here every day?"

"Not so loud," I protested. "He will hear you. Taking tea with us is part of his agreement with Ramses, as you know perfectly well. Good afternoon, Mr. Katchenovsky. I trust you had a productive day?"

Katchenovsky was unable to reply, since Carla had shoved an entire biscuit into his mouth. Ramses answered for him. "Very productive. We've got most of the fragments flattened and dried, and have begun a preliminary catalog. Several look particularly interesting."

"Ramses has a remarkable memory," said Katchenovsky, after a strenuous swallow. "I believe he could recite a full list of the fragments."

"It's a matter of practice," Ramses said modestly.

"It's a matter of a peculiar mental quirk," Nefret said with a smile. "At one time he could take one look at a room and recall every object in it. Carla, don't keep pushing food into poor Mr. Katchenovsky's mouth, you will choke him."

"He winned," Carla explained. "We do the paper, stone, knife, with our fingers, and the one who wins gets the biscuit."

"Won," I said absently. "Not 'winned.'"

"Are you going to pour the tea, Peabody?" Emerson demanded. "What are you waiting for?"

"Fatima hasn't brought the teapot yet, that is why. I expect she is waiting for your—for Seth—for Anthony."

"He came in a while ago," Ramses said. "And went to bathe and change."

Fatima emerged with the teapot. "He comes," she announced dramatically.

She had even trained Kareem to fling open the door so that Sethos could make his entrance without breaking stride.

"I hope I haven't held you up," he said, with a royal nod at Kareem.

"Pour the tea," said Emerson, to me.

"So what is the news?" I said, to Sethos.

His gesture indicated the children, who had gathered round him and were simultaneously explaining the new game. "Ah," said Sethos. "I believe I will have to consider my strategy before I enter into contention. Practice on Mr. Katchenovsky awhile longer, eh?"

"Something is wrong," I said softly.

"There has been a new development," Sethos said in equally subdued tones. "The Pethericks have left Luxor. They caught the late-night train to Cairo."

"Good Gad," Emerson exclaimed.

"I cannot say I am surprised," I said, pouring tea.

"You wouldn't, would you," Emerson growled. "Come now, Peabody, not even you could have anticipated this."

"I did not say I had anticipated it. I said I was not surprised, not after hearing Ramses's account of his interview with Harriet."

"I said nothing to bring this on," Ramses protested. "Quite the contrary. I did my best to reassure her."

"She was beyond reassurance, I believe," I said. "What a foolish act! The police will take flight for a sign of guilt. How did Adrian and Harriet elude them? Surely Mr. Salt had been told to inform Ayyid if they checked out of their rooms."

"They didn't. They simply walked out of the hotel and went straight to the train station. They had each a single small suitcase. It's taken me all day to find this out," Sethos added petulantly. "And for Ayyid to get permission to alert the police in Cairo. The train isn't due until this evening."

"They won't be on it," Ramses said. He was sitting quite still, his cup in his hand.

"Why do you say that?" Nefret asked.

"Because Harriet Petherick knows the police will be on her trail and that they can't possibly leave Egypt without being intercepted. God knows what she has in mind, but I don't like this development. Adrian isn't . . . dependable."

"You surely don't believe he is capable of harming her?" I exclaimed.

"I'm afraid he might be," Nefret said in a stifled voice. She looked down at her clasped hands. "I've been thinking about what Ramses said last night. Adrian's actions are consistent with a condition called manic-depressive disease—alternating states of energy and lethargy. I was taught that mental illnesses are always a result of damage to the brain, caused by purely physical agents, but that view is changing and the evidence is persuasive. Severe emotional trauma can also trigger such attacks."

"I too am familiar with modern psychiatric theory," I said. "In his manic state he could be dangerous."

"He has been dangerous," Nefret said wretchedly. "Bursting into someone's house and threatening people with a gun can't be considered harmless. If Ramses hadn't taken the pistol from him I don't know what he would have done."

"That isn't the only indication," Ramses said. "I didn't tell you because . . . well, because it seemed a violation of her privacy. There were bruises on her arms. I saw them when her sleeves fell back. Fresh bruises."

EIGHT

I've got to find them," Ramses said.

Not until the next morning did we receive confirmation of our suspicions and fears. The train had been met and the passengers questioned. The Pethericks had not been among them. One of Sethos's colleagues had, at his request, taken part in the inspection, and Sethos assured us he could not have been deceived by a disguise, however ingenious. It was clear that he took the matter as seriously as Ramses.

"Why you?" Nefret's blue eyes were hard. "It isn't your responsibility."

The statement was true in the narrowest sense; but as she knew only too well, Ramses had that rare quality—a burden, some might call it—of feeling responsibility for the weak and defenseless. Harriet Petherick was a woman who had appealed to him for help. He would have done the same for any man, woman, or child. He had got this quality from me, so I did not attempt to argue with him.

Emerson did. "Nefret is right, you know. What

can you do that the police cannot? The girl has lost her head—"

"As women are inclined to do," I murmured.

"Oh, do be quiet, Peabody! Some women are, and some men, too. She doesn't know her way around Egypt and it won't take the police long to locate her and her brother."

"No doubt that is true," Ramses said. He had pushed his plate aside and was pacing up and down the dining room. "I am concerned about what may happen before the police find them."

"'For each man kills the thing he loves,'" Sethos intoned.

Ramses shot him a quick look, and Emerson said in disgust, "Poetry!"

"Poetry often expresses universal truths," I said. "To put it in psychological terms, people may feel ambivalent about those they love, particularly if they are suffering from mental excitability."

"Psychology!" Emerson exclaimed. "I have asked you not to talk psychology at me, Peabody. It is worse than poetry."

"Whether you like it or not, Father, there is some truth in what Mother says," Nefret admitted reluctantly. "Harriet is overprotective of her brother—for good reason, admittedly, but it would not be surprising if he unconsciously resented her."

Emerson clapped his hand to his brow. "Please, Nefret. Not the unconscious. I don't believe in it."

Urged by Fatima, Ramses returned to his chair and picked up his fork. "I'm sure the authorities would agree with you, Father. They will be looking for a pair of fugitives, not for a woman who may be in danger from the person who is closest to her. They got off the train somewhere between here and Cairo. I'm going to try to trace them."

His tone of quiet determination silenced even Emerson.

"There is a local train at eleven," Ramses went on. "I mean to be on it."

"And I," David said, in the same tone.

"Curse it," Emerson said.

"Nefret and Selim can handle the photography as well as I," David said.

"Hmph." Emerson fingered the cleft in his chin. Let me do the dear man credit; consideration for his son overruled even his preoccupation with his excavations. He did not really believe Harriet Petherick was in danger, but he was familiar with Ramses's reckless habits. David was a restraining influence as well as a loyal friend.

"What about your friend Karnovsky?" he asked.

"Katchenovsky," Ramses corrected. "I suppose I am possessive about those scraps. He's competent and reliable, but I'd rather be here while he's working on them."

"And I would rather he were not working here alone," I said. "It is for his own protection, really; he won't be under suspicion if anything untoward occurs."

"Something untoward such as attempted murder or theft?" Sethos hadn't spoken for some time. Unlike Ramses, he was making an excellent breakfast.

"Something along those lines," I agreed. "What are your plans?"

Sethos patted his mouth delicately with his napkin. "In my opinion I can be of more use here. If David is with him, Ramses will be amply protected."

"I'm going to pack a few things," Ramses said, pushing his chair back. "Nefret, will you help me?"

Silently, lips tight, she went with him. Sethos chuckled. "He takes my little jokes too much to heart. A pity he can't get over his dislike of me."

"You go out of your way to annoy him, that is why," I said.

"Ambivalence," Sethos explained. "Unconsciously I am really very fond of the boy."

That was too much for Emerson. He jumped up

and threw his napkin on the table. "Then you can take his place on the dig."

"What dig?" I inquired. "KV55 or the West Valley or Deir el Medina?"

"The West Valley, of course."

There was no "of course" about it. I had a glimmer of an idea of what Emerson was up to. If he had had the courtesy to tell me and ask for my assistance, I would have lent it. As it was, I simply sniffed meaningfully.

"I can't help you there," Sethos said. "I'm no excavator."

"You excavated the best objects out of KV55," Emerson retorted. An evil smile spread across his face. "You can help Peabody sift the fill."

We saw the boys off for Luxor an hour later. (I would never give over thinking of them as boys, despite the fact that I had to stand on tiptoe to kiss them good-bye.) Nefret had herself under close control; only her responsibilities as a mother prevented her from insisting upon accompanying them, but her lined brow and anxious eyes betrayed her concern for her husband.

"Remember," she said, when they were about to leave, "to approach him carefully. Anything that can be interpreted as a threat may set him off. And don't count on her to stop him, she will—"

"I know. You told me." He smiled reassuringly

and gave her a quick kiss. "Don't worry. It's all right, you know."

We watched them set off along the road, side by side as they had so often been, close as brothers and closely resembling each other in the length of their strides and the athletic grace of their tall frames. And their waving black hair.

"Put on your hats," I shouted.

FROM MANUSCRIPT H

"You think I've gone off half-cocked, don't you?" Ramses asked.

"I don't understand all that talk about ambivalence and manic depression," David admitted.

"You understand it, all right. You mean you don't accept it. Like Father. One needn't resort to psychological jargon to acknowledge a not uncommon human trait. Children love their parents, but they also resent their authority. In a way, Adrian is Harriet's child. He's all she's got left. She'd fight for him like a mother tigress."

They arrived early for the train, as Ramses had planned, in order to give them time to fahddle with the porters and clerks. Gossip, in other words. That leisurely, casual sort of exchange, at which they were both experienced, was more likely to yield information than interrogation, particularly by a police officer. Egyptians had a well-founded reluctance to confide in the police.

One of the porters remembered the Pethericks. He had told the police that, but he went on to add information he hadn't bothered to give them. "They had only two small pieces of luggage. The gentleman did not speak. She did all the talking and held him always by his arm and pushed him into the carriage. What way is that for a woman to behave? She had the money. A woman in control of money is like a camel without a driver."

"Perhaps he is an invalid," said one more charitable listener. "God be merciful to him."

By handing out additional baksheesh they got a carriage to themselves, but it was a long, tedious journey. "Quaint" mud-brick villages and humble minarets, groves of palm trees, and water buffalo splashing in the shallows had long since ceased to hold any novelty for them. The trip was enlivened only by their questioning of the porters at various stops. No one had seen the brother and sister at Qena, Akhmim, or Assiut. At Minya a peddler of fruit said he had sold oranges to a lady with dark hair and a voice as deep as a man's. He endorsed the first porter's assessment of women who held the purse strings. "Aywa, there was a gentleman with her, but he did not come to the window, he let her do the bargaining and hand over the money."

"They didn't leave the train, though?" David asked.

"No. Ah, blessings be upon you for your generosity, effendi!"

The train started up again. "That's the last stop before Cairo," David said, closing the window to keep the dust out. It already formed a thin layer on every flat surface. "The train does stop at other stations on demand. They might have got off at any number of places."

"Not in the middle of the night." Ramses lit another cigarette. He was smoking more than usual, an admission of worry he didn't bother concealing from David. "And there are no acceptable hotels in the smaller cities. She'd probably be aware of that."

"Not that I'm complaining, but this is beginning to look like a wild-goose chase. They must have got by the police in Cairo somehow."

"There's one more stop," Ramses said.

"Damn, that's right. Bedrashein. It's so close to Cairo one doesn't think of it as a separate place. You think that's it?"

"They'd have arrived around midday, and tourists get off there to visit Sakkara and Memphis."

"Safety in numbers," David said, looking cha-grined.

"And several alternate routes. They could hire a carriage to take them to Cairo or to the Mena House, from which one can catch the tram."

"Wake me when we get there," David said, and rested his head against the back of the seat.

Ramses had brought a book; in his family it was considered as much a travel necessity as shaving gear and a change of socks. He was unable to con-centrate, though. Harriet Petherick's face kept intruding between his eyes and the printed page. Not the face of the unpracticed seductress, but that of the girl who had met his eyes without flinching and whose features softened when she smiled.

He kept seeing the bruises, too—on her fore-arms, where hands might have gripped her. An exaggerated sense of delicacy had prevented him from mentioning them until he realized it was more likely they had been made by her brother than by a passionate lover. Harriet wasn't the sort of woman who entertained men in her room.

The train didn't reach Bedrashein until after midnight. He and David were among the few who got off at that hour, and they were able to hire a carriage without difficulty. The drivers were responsive but not helpful. Many persons had got off the midday train the day before. All foreigners looked alike, after all.

"Where to?" David asked, as they got into their carriage.

"The Mena House, I suppose. We may as well stay there tonight. I hope we can get a room. It's the height of the season."

The famous hotel, at the base of the pyramid plateau, was full, but Ramses and his family were well known there. They were given a suite kept reserved for distinguished guests, with a broad terrace overlooking the pyramids and a bath chamber big as a drawing room, with ornate gold fittings. When they inquired after their friends, who had arrived the day before, the clerk assured them that no one named Petherick had registered, and that he could recall no lady of Harriet's description. Adrian's description might have fit any of a number of men.

"They must have taken a carriage to Cairo from Bedrashein," David said, yawning widely as he took out his pajamas. "It won't be easy finding them, there are dozens of hotels."

"Are you suggesting we give up?"

"Not at all. I'm perfectly happy to wallow in luxury for as long as it takes."

They took the tram to Cairo next morning.

None of the attendants remembered seeing the Pethericks.

Emerson had been quite serious about enlisting his brother's assistance on the dig, though to be accurate it was more a matter of conscription than enlistment.

"I could stay here and supervise Katchenovsky," Sethos offered, in a last-ditch effort. "And entertain the kiddies."

"You do too much of the latter," Emerson retorted. "David John gave me a lecture the other day on the best methods of forging ushebtis. As for Karnovsky, you know perfectly well he won't be coming. Ramses sent a letter to the hotel for him explaining the change of plan. Now get ready to go."

"I'll help Fatima pack a luncheon basket," said Sethos, and vanished before Emerson could object.

Cyrus greeted Anthony Bissinghurst cordially. "I can sure use you," he declared. "Lidman's walked out on me."

"Good Gad," I exclaimed. "How did he elude you?"

"Walked out, as I said. Right after breakfast this morning, while we were getting our gear together. The gateman had no reason to stop him, not in broad daylight when he wasn't doing anything wrong."

"But without even a word to you . . ." I began.

"Oh, he left me a letter. Apologies, excuses, and so on. He said he couldn't handle the work, didn't want to take advantage of my kindness, needed time to recover."

"Did he say where he was going?" I persisted.

"Nope. None of my business, was it?"

"Hmmm," said Emerson, stroking his chin.

"I rather think it is our business," Sethos said. "We can't let our suspects go scampering off in all directions, now can we? I'll get on his trail."

It might have been only an excuse to get out of sifting the fill—the most tedious and onerous of duties—but I didn't think so. Neither did Emerson. He nodded. "Question the boatmen first. If Lidman has nothing to hide he will have returned to his hotel."

"Thank you for the advice," Sethos said. "I might not have thought of that."

Emerson ground his teeth. Sethos gave us a cheery wave and rode off.

After a cursory glance into the tomb, where the

men were still clearing the corridor, Emerson said, "May I borrow Bertie this morning?"

"I guess so," Cyrus said. "What for?"

"I want to have a look at the other tomb in this area. Number 25."

"What for?" Cyrus repeated.

"For the sake of thoroughness," said Emerson loftily and unhelpfully.

Bertie asked the same question and got a slightly more informative answer. "One of the tombs—number 25—is probably late Eighteenth Dynasty. Some people believe it was meant to be Akhenaton's, but it was never finished because he moved to Amarna and constructed his official tomb there."

"Isn't Tomb 25 the one Belzoni found in 1817?" Bertie asked.

Emerson looked at him in surprise, and then clapped him on the back. "Well done, my boy. You've been reading up on the area."

Bertie directed a longing glance at Jumana, hard at work on the fill, and accepted his fate. "I heard it from Lidman, as a matter of fact. He spouted facts and figures by the yard to anybody who'd listen to him. What do you want me to do, sir?"

"I want an accurate plan. The entrance was blocked by a stone wall when Belzoni found it,"

Emerson explained, as we walked on. "As was the bastard's habit, he used a battering ram to destroy the wall, then left the place wide open. There were four coffined mummies inside—"

"Probably later intrusions," I interrupted.

"Thank you, Peabody," said Emerson with excessive courtesy. "I am willing to accept your familiarity with the literature."

"Belzoni was an entertaining writer, even if his methods were questionable," I said. "He didn't bother removing the coffins. I doubt there will be much left of them."

"There may be enough remaining to prove the mummies were not Eighteenth Dynasty," Emerson retorted. "And that the tomb was never finished or occupied at that period."

"Which will eliminate it as a possible source of the statue," I concluded.

"I see," said Bertie, who didn't look as if he did.

The unfinished tomb was only a short distance away. The entrance had been cut through the hard-packed gravel at the foot of the cliff—a dark opening that led down into deeper darkness. Bertie was the only one of us who had had sense enough to bring a torch. (I would have done if Emerson had bothered to mention what he had in mind before we left the house.) Its light showed the topmost steps of a flight of stairs, though they were so littered with hardened mud and bits of gravel that they looked more like a steep ramp.

"Let me go first," Bertie said, with an anxious look at me.

"No, no, my boy." Emerson took the torch from him and began picking his way down. "Wouldn't want you to fall. Just follow my steps."

We got down without incident, though Bertie's attempts to hold me by the arm were distracting. The dear boy meant well, so I did not object. At the bottom of the stairs a square-cut doorway, typical of tombs of the period, debouched into a narrow room half filled with rubble.

"This is all there is," said Emerson, waving the torch. "It was meant to be a passageway, I believe, with a burial chamber beyond, but they never got that far along."

Belzoni had said there were eight coffins, neatly arranged in two rows. The industrious modern thieves had been there since his time, looking for ornaments buried with the dead; only fragments of cartonnage from the coffins and bits of mummy remained.

"Twenty-second Dynasty," said Emerson, shining his torch on one of the fragments. It was only six inches long by three wide and most of the paint had flaked off, but neither of us questioned Emerson's analysis.

"If you will permit me to say so," I said, "this little expedition was a waste of time. Clearing the tomb out will take days, and for what purpose? It is the most unlikely place to find something like . . . hmmm."

"Hmmm what?" Emerson inquired.

"Nothing." I had remembered Abdullah's cryptic statement: "The last place you would think of," he had said.

But Emerson had thought of it, and my assessment stood. Several other archaeologists had inspected this tomb. It had undoubtedly been ransacked by modern looters, but an Amarna work of art would not have been owned by a commoner who lived several centuries after that period.

We made our way back to the entrance. "I'm afraid, sir," Bertie said diffidently, "that I can't do a proper plan until the place is cleared out. Unless you would like me to—"

"No, no." Emerson winked at him. "I wanted to give you an excuse to get away from the cursed fill. Boring job."

"Thank you, sir."

Emerson strode off with the cocksure pose of a man who has just done a good deed. I took the arm

Bertie offered. "How are you and Jumana getting on?" I asked.

"The same. I've asked her to marry me six times."

"Then stop asking her."

"Ramses said essentially the same thing," Bertie admitted with a sheepish smile. "He suggested I find another girl. As if all I had to do was spin round and point at the first one I saw."

"Spin round and look, at any rate. Keep an open mind. And leave off pressing Jumana. That often has a negative effect, especially with a strong-minded young person like her."

"Was that how the Professor wooed you?"

He gave me a sidelong look, as if he feared he had gone too far. I laughed and squeezed his arm. "My dear, the Professor will tell you I did the wooing. One of his little jokes, of course, but until the moment when he asked me to be his he had done nothing but criticize me and shout at me."

"I could try that, I suppose."

I studied his friendly, ingenuous face and tried to picture him shouting at Jumana. "I doubt you could be convincing. Just ignore her. Let her sift her own rubble."

Bertie followed my advice, and I went to help Jumana. She was bored with the job and told me so. "I have had no chance to practice excavation," she complained. "Or even look for other tombs in the West Valley. Why didn't the Professor let me go with him instead of Bertie?"

I assured her she hadn't missed much, but agreed that her abilities were being wasted. Like many of the youngsters of Gurneh, she had spent her childhood scrambling around the cliffs looking for lost tombs. The Gurnawis had a knack—inherited, some might say, from their ancient ancestors—for locating them.

I kept watching for Sethos, but the day wore on without a sign of him. What could he be doing all this time? Our suspicions of Lidman were based on very slight evidence, after all. One couldn't really say that he had fled; he had left the Castle openly, as he had every right to do.

Thanks to Cyrus's habit of closing down at a reasonable hour, we got home earlier than was the case when Emerson was in charge. I took advantage of the opportunity to have a leisurely bath and to wash my hair. By the time I had concluded this somewhat delicate operation (the coloring had a tendency to run when wet), Emerson and Nefret were on the veranda waiting for tea. Just outside the door, rolling in the dust, were the children, the dog, and my brother-in-law.

"Come in here at once," I ordered. "No, not you, Amira. David John and Carla, you will have to wash your hands again. Go to Fatima."

"It's only sand," Sethos said, dusting off his hands. "Not a germ in the lot."

"There are plenty of germs on the dog."

"Oh, very well."

He was back almost at once. "What took you so long?" I asked. "What did you find out?"

"Not a great deal. None of the boatmen recalled having taken Lidman across the river, but I went to Luxor anyhow. He didn't go back to the Luxor Hotel or to any of the others, nor has he been seen at the railway station. The steamboat offices also denied any knowledge of him. The trouble is," Sethos added, rising to hold the door for Fatima and the tea tray, "Lidman isn't a very memorable individual. Medium height; undistinguished features; a tendency toward embonpoint, but that characteristic is shared by most of the male tourists. He may still be on the West Bank, but I'll be confounded if I can think where."

Fatima looked up at him. "Is it Mr. Lidman, the gentleman who was sick, of whom you speak? He was here this morning."

"Here?" Emerson shouted. "When?"

"This morning." Fatima knew from his tone

that something was amiss; she began twisting her hands together. "He was looking for you. He waited for a while and then went away."

"Hell and damnation!" Emerson jumped to his feet.

"Have I done something wrong?" Fatima asked anxiously. "He had been here before, he works for Mr. Vandergelt—"

"It's all right, Fatima," Sethos said.

Emerson had disappeared into the house. We all dashed after him, followed by the children, who had reappeared looking very pink and scrubbed. One look was enough to disclose the ugly truth. The bottom drawer of Emerson's desk had been broken open. The painted box and the statuette were gone.

"Watch your language, Emerson," I implored. "The children!"

David John shook his head. "If you will forgive me for saying so, Grandpapa, I told you that was not a secure hiding place."

FROM MANUSCRIPT H

Ramses enjoyed the relative peace and quiet of Luxor, but there was something about Cairo . . .

Not a breath of fresh air, since it was far from fresh, but a sense of bustle and excitement. They walked along the river, past the museum. There were plenty of tourists and the usual foreign officials and a number of motorcars, but these intrusive modern elements were submerged by the teeming masses and the cacophonous sounds of the real Cairo—men in turbans and galabeeyahs, veiled women, camels moaning, donkeys braying, dogs barking.

"Would you rather be here than in Luxor?" Ramses asked.

"I'd rather be at home with Lia and the children. But there's something about Cairo . . ."

Their progress was slowed by encounters with old acquaintances. "Beggars and revolutionaries and policemen," Ramses remarked, after they had detached themselves from one of the latter. "Don't we have any respectable friends?"

"Not unless you consider Egyptologists respectable."

The Pethericks were not known at the Semiramis Hotel. In order to save time they took a cab back into the center of town where most of the other leading hotels were located. They drew a blank at the Savoy, the Hotel d'Angleterre, the Continental, and the Eden Palace. Midday came and went. David finally ventured to suggest that they stop and take stock, and perhaps a little nourishment.

"You can't go on like this all day, Ramses. We've only covered a few of the larger hotels. Are you planning to stop over in Cairo tonight?"

Ramses ducked under a tray of bread carried at shoulder height by a baker making a delivery. "I plan to keep looking until we find them. But if you're hungry—"

"I'm ravenous. So should you be."

"Shepheard's, then."

It was one place where they could always be sure of getting a table. Emerson had, from the earliest days, made a profound impression, and the whole family profited by the terror in which he was held by the management. David set a deliberately leisurely pace as they skirted the Ezbekieh Gardens; it was his way of telling Ramses to slow down. Ramses knew he was right. Unless they were lucky, their search was going to take some time. David didn't share his sense of urgency. He would have had a hard time explaining it without referring to premonitions, or to the working of the unconscious mind, neither of which David really believed in.

"We may be in Cairo for a few days," he said.

"Do you want to look up any of your political acquaintances?"

"Getting involved with politics is the last thing I need. The situation is, as they say, volatile."

"Once the Declaration of Independence is published, things ought to settle down."

David made a rude noise. "The contents of that precious document have already been leaked. It isn't independence if Britain reserves the right to protect her own interests—nice ambiguous phrase, isn't it?—and leaves the question of the Sudan unsettled."

"Sorry I brought it up."

David lowered his voice to its normal pitch. "Sorry I got so worked up. You know how I feel. But I promised Lia I'd stay out of politics, and Lord knows we've enough to worry about without that."

They got not only a table on the terrace but a room for the night. According to the desk clerk, there was no reservation in the name of Petherick. "We have been booked solid for months," he explained. "It is only because of our long acquaintance with your family that we are able to accommodate you. Er—you will mention that favor to Professor Emerson?"

Their table was one of the best, near the balustrade, with a good view of the gardens and the busy street below. After they had ordered—and enjoyed some general gossip with the waiters—Ramses scanned the other diners.

"The usual lot," David said. "Tourists and local gentry. You aren't hoping to run across the Pethericks, are you?"

"One never knows. Damn, there's Sylvia Bennett. The worst gossip in Cairo. I refuse to have her prying into our affairs."

"Pretend you don't see her."

"It would take more than that to put Sylvia off."

He ignored her coy, beckoning finger, but as he had predicted, she came to them. Sylvia always kept up with the latest fashions; her hair was bobbed, her lips brightly painted, her skirts short. She doesn't have the legs for it, Ramses thought uncharitably, as he rose to greet her.

After the usual gushing queries about Nefret and the other members of the family—"those dear, sweet, adorable little children"—Sylvia plunged into the subject that really interested her. She wanted to know all about the Pethericks, the Countess Magda, the black afrit, and the statuette. Ramses fended the questions off as best he could; he was damned if he would give Sylvia the satisfaction of being better informed than her equally inquisitive friends.

"We're here on business," he said. "Nothing to do with the death of Mrs. Petherick. It's in the hands of the police. I'm afraid that's all I can tell you, Sylvia. Give my regards to your husband."

Pouting, Sylvia took herself off. She had acknowledged David with the barest of nods.

"What a dreadful woman," David said, resuming his seat. "At least she doesn't seem to have heard of the Pethericks' leaving Luxor. I didn't realize she had met them while they were in Cairo."

"Sylvia knows everyone."

"Except 'natives' like me," David said.

Ramses called Sylvia a rude name. David laughed. "The opinions of people like that don't worry me, Ramses."

"Let's go before we are accosted by another dear old friend intent on gossip."

"You won't be able to avoid all of them," David predicted. "By evening everyone in Cairo will know we're here."

The Bristol, the National, the Metropole . . . Hotel after hotel denied any knowledge of Harriet and Adrian Petherick. "It's unaccountable," Ramses muttered. "We've covered most of the first- and second-class hotels. I can't believe Harriet would settle for anything less. We've missed something, but I can't think what."

"What if they've changed their appearances?" David asked.

"Then we're sunk, since we've no idea **how** they may have disguised themselves. All we can do is proceed on the assumption that they look the same."

"So we stay over tonight?"

"Yes, dammit. Let's clean up and then have dinner at Bassam's in the Khan. He knows everything that goes on in Cairo."

They paused on the corner of the Shari Kasr el Aini and the Shari el Munira, waiting for a chance to cross the former. The traffic was horrendous; nobody yielded the right of way to carriages or carts or pedestrians. People pushed and shoved along the pavement and into the street. It was a wonder there weren't more accidents, Ramses thought, as a camel lumbered past, cutting off a cab whose driver shrieked curses at the camel and its rider. A motorcar, driven at reckless speed, wove in and out among the slower vehicles.

It was almost even with them when a hard shove sent Ramses staggering forward. The driver couldn't have stopped if he had wanted to.

Fatima would not be consoled. "It is my fault. I should not have left him alone. I should have watched him."

Sethos offered her an impeccable handkerchief. "If it's anyone's fault, Fatima, it is mine. I didn't think to warn you."

"None of us thought to warn you." I added my words of consolation. "In fact, to do all of us justice, there was no reason why we should have done."

"Yes, there was," Emerson muttered. "Here now, Fatima, nobody blames you. Please don't cry. You've set the twins off too."

"You do not blame me, Father of Curses?" She mopped her wet face and gave him an appealing look.

"Good Gad, no. David John—Carla—I am not angry with Fatima. Do you hear me?"

They were clinging to her skirts and sobbing in sympathy. The noise level was quite high.

"That will be quite enough from you two," I said. "Have a biscuit."

Their infantile distress reminded Fatima of the need to recover herself. She gave a final swipe to her face and used the handkerchief to wipe their faces and noses. "It is all right, do you see? I am not unhappy. The Father of Curses is not angry. Come, have a biscuit. Have two!"

"He's had five hours or more to make his get-away," I said. "At what time did you interrogate the boatmen?"

Sethos knew what I was getting at. "I left instructions, along with promises of extravagant baksheesh, that they were to report immediately if he turned up."

"We can't just sit here and let the bastard get away with it," Emerson groaned. "She trusted me to take care of the bloody thing. I'm going back to the landing."

"Language, my dear, language," I said gently, touched by his self-reproach.

"Waste of time," said Sethos, holding out his cup. "I suggest we consult Selim. And notify the police."

"The police?" Emerson's eyes widened in surprise. "I didn't think of that."

"You never do," said his brother. "If Lidman is still in Luxor, East or West Bank, we'll catch up with him eventually, but we will be in trouble if he succeeds in getting out of town. We need guards at the railway station. Dependable guards."

"I wouldn't trust any of Ayyid's fellows," I said. "Not that I doubt their loyalty, but none of them know Lidman. They can't ask for identification from every passenger, that would take too long and some pompous idiot would be bound to register a complaint."

"Obviously I am the right man for the job," Sethos said with a martyred sigh.

"Then what do we need the police for?" Emerson demanded.

"Because," said Sethos, slowly and patiently, "I do not have the authority to detain Lidman. I can identify him but only the police can hold him for questioning."

"Hmph," said Emerson. He shifted uneasily in his chair. "Er—do we have to tell them he's stolen a statuette worth a hundred thousand pounds? Good Gad, if that news gets out he'll have a pack of vigilantes on his trail, baying for his blood."

"You are mixing your metaphors, Emerson," I said. "They won't be after his blood, they will be after the statue, and not for the purpose of restoring it to its proper owner. However, I doubt they would be averse to spilling his blood if they had to. Supposing he is innocent after all? He could come to serious harm."

"He is guilty as Cain," Emerson growled. "And personally I wouldn't care if he were torn limb from limb so long as I were the one doing it."

He didn't really mean it. Emerson is the mildest of men, unless provoked—though I must admit it is not difficult to provoke him. His honor and his pride had been sorely damaged, and he held himself personally responsible for the loss. A hundred thousand pounds would make quite a dent in our investments.

"I have it," I cried. "We will accuse Mr. Lidman of making off with some of Ramses's bits of papyrus. The police know we care about such things, but no one else does."

"Well done, Peabody," said Emerson. "Do you think Ayyid will take that loss seriously enough to stay on the hunt?"

"My dear," I said, returning his smile, "I feel certain that if he is not inclined to do so, you can convince him."

"Let's go, then," Emerson said. "You and I, eh, Peabody?"

"And I," said Sethos.

Nefret wanted to come too, but I persuaded her to stay with the children, who had set up an outcry at the prospect of losing both grandparents and a particularly entertaining guest. "Console yourself with one cheering thought, my dear," I told her. "If Lidman is our villain, which seems more than likely, Adrian Petherick is innocent. Ramses and David are in no danger."

FROM MANUSCRIPT H

"Another pair of trousers ruined," Ramses said, inspecting the stained, ripped knees of that article of clothing.

"They can be mended." David's face was pale and his voice unsteady. "I'll tell Aunt Amelia it was my fault."

"It was your fault I didn't fall flat on the road under the motorcar."

He got to his feet. The onlookers who had gathered to offer assistance and advice dispersed. It was a common enough occurrence, and one that often ended more dramatically.

"Somebody shoved me," Ramses said.

"I thought so. You aren't that clumsy. You didn't see who it was?"

"I was too busy trying to stay on my feet. And you—"

"I was too busy trying to keep you from falling forward."

"People were jostling one another. It might have been an accident." Ramses brushed grit and scraps of cabbage leaves off his palms. He had landed on hands and knees after David swung him back onto the pavement.

"Another accident?" David raised his eyebrows. "It looks as if you were right about

Adrian Petherick and I was wrong. We know he's in Cairo—"

"We don't, not for certain."

"How many people are there in the city who have it in for you?"

"Quite a few, I should think."

"You did cut rather a wide swath during the War," David admitted.

"So did you."

"That was a long time ago. Most of them have got over their grudges by now. No, my brother, it looks more and more like Adrian."

Ramses's disheveled appearance raised a few eyebrows as they crossed Shepheard's terrace, and one stylishly dressed woman was heard to say, "I'm surprised they allow riffraff like that in the hotel. And isn't the other man . . ."

When they asked for their keys, the clerk handed them several messages. Ramses looked through them as the lift took them up to the second floor.

"Fancy that," he said. "This is from M. Lacau, summoning us rather peremptorily to his office tomorrow morning. I hope he hasn't changed his mind about allowing Father in the Valley."

"The Professor will ignore him anyhow," David said with a grin. "Who's that one from?"

"Sylvia. The woman couldn't take a hint if you

hit her over the head with it. And this one is from Annabelle, Sylvia's chief rival in the gossip game."

He crumpled the letters and shoved them in his pocket. "One of your former lady friends, wasn't she?" David asked.

"Good God, no. I spent hours hiding behind various objects in order to avoid her."

The suffragi on duty in the corridor hissed in surprise at the sight of Ramses. "What happened to you, Brother of Demons?"

"I fell." Ramses inserted his key in the door. "Was anyone looking for me while I was out, Ahmed?"

"No, Brother of Demons. Shall I take your clothes to be cleaned and mended?"

A look in the shaving mirror told Ramses the man's concern and the criticism of the people on the terrace had been justified. There was a rip at the shoulder of his coat, where the sleeve had been pulled loose by David's desperate grip, and since he had been in too much of a hurry to shave that morning, his beard darkened his cheeks. He took the letters from his pocket and realized there was one he hadn't read.

"Carter," he said, after perusing it. "You were right. Our presence is known. Here, hand these clothes out the door to Ahmed, will you?"

A quick bath and a shave and the only other suit he had brought with him restored him to respectability. When David was ready they walked down the stairs, between the statues of the voluptuous Nubian maidens that were among the famed sights of Shepheard's. The maidens had been photographed, fondled, and even carried off by visitors.

"What did Carter have to say?" David asked.

"Wants to see us. Anytime. Didn't say why."

"He must want to see you very badly," David said. Sitting in the lobby, a cigarette in his mouth and his nose in a book, was Howard Carter.

"They told me you'd come in a short time ago," he explained, after shaking hands with both of them. "I didn't want to intrude."

Ramses had known Carter since his early days, when he was working as an artist and draftsman, and later, when he was appointed inspector for Upper Egypt, and later than that, after he had lost the post and had been reduced to dealing in antiquities and selling his paintings to tourists. Now that Lord Carnarvon was his patron, he looked more prosperous. His face was fuller and his mustache less exuberant. There were new lines around his mouth, though. Carnarvon was said to be a generous employer and amiable man, but having one's livelihood depend on the whim of a dilettante must not be conducive to peace of mind. Carter had no private means and not much formal education. Many of his peers considered him brash and ill-mannered. Emerson despised him for continuing to deal in antiquities, but Ramses couldn't blame the man for hanging on to a sure source of income.

"We're on our way to the Khan and Bassam's," he explained. "Care to join us?"

" 'Fraid I can't this evening. I have an engagement with Lord and Lady Dinwhistle. I've time for a drink or two, if that would suit you."

They made their way to the Long Bar. Since the War the rules about admitting women had been relaxed—Nefret had been one of the first to ignore them—and the tables were all taken. They found a relatively quiet corner where they could stand and talk. Ramses waited for Carter to start the conversation. He thought he knew where it would end.

"We've been hearing some tall tales about you people," Carter began. "Murder, robbery, assault—"

"Same old thing," David said.

Carter gave a bark of laughter. "Quite. Quite. Any discoveries in KV55?"

"Not so far. We didn't expect anything, really. It was good of you to allow us to excavate the place."

Carter inserted a cigarette into an ornate holder. "I couldn't refuse Professor Emerson such a small favor, I owe him too much. Good to me—very—your parents—in past years. Not that I was really worried about illegal excavations in the Valley," he added.

In other words, Ramses thought to himself, your father can get away with more than most people, so long as he doesn't push me too far. The young man who had been so humbly grateful for encouragement and support from those he considered his social superiors had gained confidence.

And he was after something—a return favor. It didn't take him long to get round to it.

"So what about the famous statue?" he asked. "The Professor wired me asking if I knew anything about it. Had to tell him I didn't."

"And you would have known if it had been on the market before last year?" Ramses kept his voice neutral. He wasn't criticizing, he was only asking for information.

"Obviously I didn't," Carter said somewhat defensively. "I—er—assist many of the major museums, you know, in addition to private collectors like Lord Carnarvon. If I'd known of anything so remarkable I'd have—er—entered into negotiations."

"Such negotiations are often conducted in secret, though," Ramses said.

"That's the devil of it," Carter said, finishing his whiskey and beckoning the waiter. "I believe I may claim I am noted for my discretion, but"—another bark of laughter—"so are some of my competitors. Describe it for me, will you? The newspaper accounts can't be trusted."

Ramses glanced at David, who shrugged. There was no reason why they shouldn't be candid with Carter, since so many other people had seen the object. He described the statuette in detail and watched Carter's eyes take on a hard glitter.

"It's absolutely unique," Ramses finished. "And in superb condition."

"I suppose you've already had offers for it," Carter said, trying to sound casual. "I know Cyrus Vandergelt is a friend of yours."

"It isn't ours to dispose of," Ramses said.

"I thought Mrs. Petherick had—"

"Given it to Father? He wouldn't accept a gift so valuable, even if he had the right to do so. We don't know who the legal owner is, now that Mrs. Petherick is dead."

"I see. You're sure . . . But you couldn't be mistaken about its authenticity. You'd be willing to testify to that?"

"Father would probably give his expert opinion if he were asked."

"I see," Carter repeated. "Well, I must go now. Don't want to keep his lordship waiting. I expect I'll be seeing you all shortly—and the statue."

"When are you coming to Luxor?" David asked.

"Oh . . ." Carter gestured with his cigarette holder. "Shortly. Another week or so, I expect. Give my regards to the family."

"He'll be busy for another week 'negotiating' with dealers," David said, after Carter had gone. "Would you care to wager a small sum that Lord Dinwhistle is not in the market for unique antiquities?"

"Not twopence. One can't blame Carter."

"You never blame anyone for anything short of mayhem. I wonder if the Professor realizes that he got permission to work in the Valley because Carter thinks it will soften him up. He wants the statuette for Carnarvon."

Ramses called the waiter and paid for their whiskeys. "Father is even more duplicitous than Carter. He'll take full advantage and admit no obligation."

The sun was setting in a dusty haze. Across the way the lights of the Ezbekieh twinkled in the twilight.

"Why don't we dine here, or at the Savoy?" David suggested.

"Because the food isn't as good as Bassam's, and I am not going to behave like a timid tourist. No," he said, as David raised his hand to hail a cab. "We'll walk."

"Down the dark streets and narrow alleyways. You're hoping he'll try again, aren't you?"

"If he does, we'll be ready for him. We haven't had much luck tracing him."

It wasn't the first time they had strolled the byways of the old city keeping a wary eye out for attack. The ambience was certainly conducive to justifiable paranoia. There were few lights and the balconies of the tall houses overhung the streets, casting shadows even in the daytime.

"Ah, the fond memories," David said, as they crossed a small plaza with a central fountain. "Isn't this where you ended up after you escaped from the lady dressed like Hathor?"

"No, that's farther on. This is where Mother whacked Selim over the head when she mistook him for a spy."

Bassam had heard they were in Cairo and was expecting them. "But where else would you dine?" he demanded. "I have prepared for you bamiyeh and lamb cooked with spices and fresh cucumbers and tomatoes in oil."

"So I see," said David, glancing at Bassam's apron. Bassam had grown stout on his own cooking, but he was still capable of throwing a rowdy patron out the door.

He joined them for coffee and asked what brought them to Cairo. "Has the black afrit come here?"

"You know about that, do you?" Ramses said.

"Yes, to be sure. It seems," said Bassam, "that the Father of Curses did not cast it off after all."

Emerson's reputation was obviously in jeopardy. Suppressing a smile, Ramses said, "That was only a—er—preliminary attempt. Sometimes, with a spirit so powerful, even the Father of Curses has to try more than once."

"Hmmm." Bassam scratched his beard. "That is so. He will perform another ceremony, then."

Ramses let that statement stand. He didn't bother to ask about the Pethericks; this was not the sort of place they would visit. The talk soon turned to politics. Bassam knew they were in sympathy with the cause of independence, so he spoke freely and passionately. His comments gave Ramses a new insight into the situation. If Bassam, a peaceable man and a successful merchant, felt so strongly about the subject, the mobs of Cairo could easily be incited to violence. There would be unrest in Egypt for years to come.

By the time they left the restaurant, the street outside was deserted except for a slow-moving donkey and its rider. Ramses stopped long enough to inform the fellow, in his most courtly Arabic, that beating a tired beast violated the laws of the Prophet and that he was about to discover whether beating a driver made him move faster.

"I did not see you, Brother of Demons," the driver faltered. "I hear and obey."

Beyond the lights from the restaurant the familiar street, hardly wider than a path, was dark as pitch. David fell back a step or two.

The attack did not come from behind. Ramses was the first to hear the sound—not the regular pad of bare feet, but a faint, surreptitious rustle as of cloth rubbing against a harder surface. He broke into a run. The shot whistled past his side and David cried out. Cursing, Ramses whirled round, ran full tilt into David, and caught hold of his sagging body.

"Where are you hit?"

"Not hit. My damned leg gave way when I started to run. Don't worry about me, go after him. Be careful!"

Ramses followed his advice, staying close to the walls on his right. The pursuit was almost certainly futile. He had caught a glimpse of a dark figure disappearing around a sharp curve in the street before he turned back. No hero, that one. Ramses's rapid advance had caught him by surprise and spoiled his aim.

And if he hadn't run away he might have picked both of them off with a second and third shot.

He could hear David hobbling behind him and quickened his pace. Rounding the curve, he saw ahead the lights of the Place de Bab el-Louk. The plaza was deserted except for two cabs hoping for passengers. No fleeing fugitive, no lurking shadows.

He waited for David to catch him up, keeping an eye on the arcade across the plaza for signs of movement.

"No sign of him," he said. He did not inquire about David's leg. The grisly wound David had received during the War would slow him for the rest of his life, but he didn't acknowledge weakness or appreciate solicitude.

"He's not very gung ho," David said. "If he'd gone on shooting he stood a good chance of hitting one of us."

"Well, I was coming at him at a good pace," Ramses said fairly. "If he had waited to fire again, and missed again, I might have caught him."

"Did you get a look at him?"

"I'll give you three guesses what I saw."

"A shadowy figure robed in black," David recited in a singsong voice. "That disguise is rather wasted on us."

"But it's totally concealing and easily obtained. Almost half the women in this country still wear the tob or the habara."

One of the cabdrivers looked hopefully in their direction. Ramses waved him to them and looked the other way while David climbed in. The carriage was an open victoria and the horse was setting a good pace. Ramses leaned back with a sigh.

"Another missed opportunity."

"We learned one thing," David said. "He has a gun."

"Must you always look on the bright side? I took Adrian's away from him, you know."

"He could easily get another. If one looks respectable and has the money, shopkeepers don't ask for identification. Not even a visiting card."

"Visiting card . . . Oh, good God!" He smacked his forehead with the flat of his hand.

"Don't hit yourself on the head, it damages the brain." David recited one of his mother's admonitions.

"I've done it too often, I guess. Why didn't I think of that before?"

"Think of what?" David asked patiently. The cab circled the Ezbekieh and pulled up in front of Shepheard's. It was still early; the terrace was filled, and flower- and souvenir-sellers milled around at the foot of the stairs, vying with one another to see who could yell loudest.

"They wouldn't have to register under their own names," Ramses said. "They wouldn't need passports, not the lordly English."

David was silent for a moment while this sank in. "Oh, hell. Does that mean we have to start all over again? You don't know what they look like or what name they might have used."

"I think I do, though." Ramses tossed the driver a coin and jumped out of the cab. David was slow to follow. He was still favoring his bad leg. Ramses said, "We'll wait till morning. I'm too tired to go on tonight."

Sethos went across to Luxor with us and then announced his intention of returning to the railway station instead of accompanying us to the zabtiyeh.

"There's been only one train since midday and it's a local, with no first-class carriages," he explained. "He'd have stood out like a sore thumb if he had caught that one. I'll wait for the evening trains."

"You'll miss dinner," I said.

Sethos made a face. "I'll have time for a bite at the Station Hotel. A single bite is about all I'll be able to stomach, but my beloved Fatima will leave something in the larder for me. Good luck."

Inspector Ayyid was not at the zabtiyeh. He had gone home for dinner, his assistant informed us. Goodness knows he had every right to do so, but I shared Emerson's sense of urgency, which led him to swear and ask for Ayyid's address.

Torn between his orders from his superior and the looming presence of Emerson, the assistant did not hesitate long. "I am not supposed to do that, Father of Curses, but I know he will not object if it is you who ask."

The inspector had a flat in a new group of buildings behind Luxor Temple. The door was answered by an elderly lady wearing black, who screeched and retreated at the sight of Emerson.

"What did I do?" Emerson demanded in a hurt voice. "I was just about to address her respectfully."

"Your mere presence is enough to frighten the timid, my dear," I replied. "Ah, Inspector Ayyid. Our profound apologies for disturbing you and the lady . . . your mother? Yes. I assure you we would not have intruded had not the matter been urgent. Please go on with your dinner."

"I was not eating," said Ayyid, as courtesy demanded. "Come in."

The small sitting room was neat enough to meet even Fatima's standards, and comfortably furnished with a mixture of European and Egyptian furniture. At Ayyid's insistence we seated ourselves in a pair of matching armchairs upholstered in purple plush and accepted his offer of tea. It would have been rude not to do so—even ruder than our uninvited visit. Ayyid's mother had got over the first shock of Emerson and kept peeping round the door at him.

"We will not keep you long," I promised, and launched into the reason for our visit.

"Papyrus?" Ayyid's eyebrows lifted. "You want me to arrest a man who stole scraps of papyrus?"

"They are valuable antiquities," Emerson began. "Er—that is—oh, what the devil. We may as well tell him the truth, eh, Peabody?"

It was a clever move on Emerson's part, I must say. Ayyid was clearly flattered at being taken into our confidence, and he was in complete agreement with our reasons for not wishing the truth to be more widely known.

"The temptation would be too great, even for some of my own men," he admitted.

"For most men," said Emerson, who was really in top form that evening. "So, you will give the necessary orders?"

"Yes. He is to be held for questioning—at your request, Professor."

Emerson grinned. "That's right. Why should you take the responsibility?"

I had remembered another responsibility—the one we owed Cyrus, who was almost as deeply involved in the business as we. Rather than keeping Nefret waiting for news (or irritating the cook), we went straight back to the house and sent Jamad off to the Castle with a message inviting the Vandergelts to an after-dinner conference. We were just finishing the meal when they all turned up.

"What has happened?" Katherine demanded. "Your message only said the matter was urgent. Has someone been hurt?"

I reassured her on that point and suggested we retire to the parlor for coffee. "I thought it best not to go into detail in a letter," I explained. "But the situation is serious enough. Mr. Lidman came here this morning, and after he left, without seeing us, we discovered that the statue was gone."

"And you're just getting round to telling us now?" Bertie cried. "Good Lord, this is terrible. What can we do?"

In my usual well-organized fashion I described the steps we had taken.

"Well, I guess you've been busy," Cyrus admitted. "It's terrible news, all right, but see here, folks, the son of—the fellow can't get away with this. So long as he doesn't leave town—and it sounds as if you've got that covered—we'll catch up with him sooner or later. You put Selim and Daoud on the job and with their contacts they'll track him down. You just let us know what you want us to do."

Sethos did not return to the house until after midnight. Ayyid himself had been on hand at the train station. Lidman had not.

Where the devil can he have got to?" Emerson demanded, between bites of egg and bacon. Daoud sniffed appreciatively at the latter comestible but of course did not eat any of it. He and Selim had come by to report and to enjoy Fatima's cooking, which included a variety of other dishes besides the forbidden bacon.

"It is a mystery," said Daoud.

"You are sure he has not been seen on the West Bank?" I inquired of Selim.

"Not yet, Sitt Hakim. But before long he will need food and water and shelter. The villages here are small, not like Luxor. He cannot approach any of them without being noticed."

"Perhaps the Father of Curses should use his magical powers to find the man," Daoud suggested.

Emerson, who was still smarting over the failure of his exorcism, looked suspiciously at Daoud, and then concluded, correctly, that his large friend had not meant to be sarcastic.

"The devil with magical powers," said Emerson, jumping up. "I'm going to look for him."

"Please, Emerson, do not go riding off in all directions," I implored. "Wait until I—"

"Make one of your little lists? Peabody, my dear, I have the highest respect for your lists, but—"

"Selim has raised an important consideration, Emerson. How many places on the West Bank are there where a man like Lidman could remain concealed for more than a few hours?"

"Hmph." Emerson sat down again. "He could not take shelter with one of the villagers. They would turn him in, to us if not to the police."

"He wouldn't take the chance," I said. "Not when he has the—ouch!"

"I beg your pardon, Peabody," said Emerson, giving me a terrible look. "My foot slipped."

"The statue, you mean," said Selim. Fatima refilled his cup. He thanked her, and I said, rubbing my shin, "Fatima, did you—"

"No, Sitt," Selim said. "Fatima said nothing. I deduced it, myself. A valuable object and a missing man whom you want to find—it is, as Ramses would say, too much of a coincidence."

He was so proud of himself I hadn't the heart to deny the truth. "We were naive to suppose that the connection would not be made," I admitted. "Though not everyone is as clever a detective as you, Selim. To return to the previous subject: Can we assume Lidman would not openly approach any of the villagers? Yes. He would be just as noticeable if he took a room at one of the West Bank hotels. So that leaves only a hiding place in the cliffs of the high plateau. There are dozens of empty tomb shafts and caves there."

"A somewhat sweeping generalization, Peabody," said Emerson, rubbing his chin. "But I think you are on the right track."

Up he got again. "It is an extensive area," I pointed out. "Why not leave the search to Selim and our other fellows?"

"I can't sit still and do nothing," Emerson said forcibly.

"Wait," said Selim the detective, raising a finger just as Sherlock Holmes might have done. "I have thought of something. It would help if we had a photograph of the man."

"That is a very good thought, Selim," Nefret

said. "I can't recall seeing a likeness of him in any of the films we have printed so far, but a number of the plates we took in the West Valley haven't yet been developed."

It was agreed that she and Selim should get at the job immediately, while the rest of us started the search. It was, in my opinion, a comparatively futile enterprise, but my dear Emerson was too perturbed to sit still. Obviously I could not let him go dashing off without me to protect him. I made sure I had all my accoutrements, including my parasol and my little pistol.

We were about to leave when Cyrus, Jumana, and Bertie rode up. "Where are you off to?" Cyrus asked. "Not planning to work today, are you?"

"No," said Emerson.

"Me neither," Cyrus admitted. "We were talking last night, after we left you folks, and Jumana came up with a real bright idea. Where could this fella go, she asked, that he wouldn't be spotted right away? Assuming he stayed on this side of the river, that is."

"We asked ourselves the same question," I said. "I presume you reached the same conclusion—that he is likely to have found a hiding place in the cliffs? We were about to begin searching there."

"It's a large stretch of territory," Cyrus said.

"Suppose we take one section and you another. What about Selim and Daoud? And—er—"

"Anthony," I said. I couldn't blame Cyrus for forgetting the name; Sethos had so many of them. "He's gone back to the railway station. We sent Daoud to Gurneh; his web of informants are on the lookout and will report to him if they discover anything. Selim is helping Nefret develop some photographs, in the hope that they may contain an image of Mr. Lidman."

"It would sure help to have a picture of him," Cyrus agreed. "So how shall we go about this? We need a plan."

I had, of course, already given some thought to this. It was agreed that Emerson and I would begin at Deir el Bahri and work our way south toward Deir el Medina, while the other three covered the area of the Asasif and the long stretch of cliffs of Drah Abu'l Naga that ended at the road to the Valley of the Kings. Ours was the longest and most difficult path, but we were the more experienced.

I had observed Jumana's disappointment when I anticipated her deductions, so as we rode side by side toward Deir el Bahri I took the opportunity for a cheering chat. "I am counting on you, Jumana, to guide the others. You know the area better than they."

"Yes, Sitt Hakim!" Her face lit up. "You can count on me! I will miss nothing!"

I had a word with Bertie, too. "Don't allow her to bully you, Bertie. Disagree with her. Sneer, if you like."

"Oh, no, ma'am, I couldn't do that. She's so much more intelligent than I am."

Ah, well, I thought, I have done my best. Some persons cannot be helped.

As usual the road to Deir el Bahri was encumbered with carriages and donkeys carrying tourists to that popular site. Emerson and I left our horses with Jamad, who had accompanied us and who was to ride with them to Deir el Medina, where we would eventually meet him. We were further delayed by the Metropolitan Museum people, who were working at the Eleventh Dynasty temple south of Hatshepsut's monument, and who wanted us to stop and chat. Their men had informed them of Lidman's flight.

"We heard he stole some of the papyri from Deir el Medina," Mr. Winlock remarked. "The men don't believe that story, you know."

Emerson fingered the cleft in his chin. I laughed merrily. "Naturally they wouldn't. You, however, know that those scraps are valuable to the scholarly world."

"Sure," Winlock said. "We'll keep an eye out for the fellow."

"Funny, his taking something like that," said George Barton. "I mean, the guy isn't a philologist, is he?"

"One never knows what strange quirks may affect the human brain," I explained. "Well, gentlemen, we must be off. I hope to see you all again soon."

"I wouldn't want to miss another exorcism," Winlock said with a smile.

"Hmph," said Emerson. "Come along, Peabody, we have wasted enough time."

The distance between Deir el Bahri and the workmen's village is only a mile as the crow flies. On foot, over rough terrain, it seemed more like twenty. We followed the line of the cliffs, scrambling over heaps of fallen stone and exploring the innumerable small wadis that pierced the rocky ramparts. As we went on, under a baking sun, the futility of our search became more apparent—to me, at any rate. We could not possibly penetrate into every crevice and hole; all we could hope for was a sign that someone had recently passed that way. There was ample evidence of human and animal presence, from scraps of cloth to gnawed bones, but nothing one could specifically connect with a fleeing German.

By the time we reached Deir el Medina I was hot, dusty, and thirsty, and Emerson was out of sorts. The sight of Jamad, patiently waiting with the horses and the water bottles, was as welcome as a green oasis in the desert. Emerson was all for mounting and riding back immediately, but by feigning exhaustion (which was not entirely feigned) I made him agree to rest and refresh himself, while I did the same.

After a single sip of water he was on his feet again, prowling round the ruins of the ancient temples. "The anonymous digger has not been back," he reported.

"And no sign of Mr. Lidman," I added. "Do sit down, Emerson. I doubt he would have come this far."

I had informed Nefret and Selim of the change in our strategy (or is it tactics?). We were all to meet at the Castle, so Emerson and I went directly there. I apologized to Katherine for our untidiness; she was gracious enough to reply that the search for Lidman took precedence, and showed me to one of the guest chambers, where I was able to freshen up before we enjoyed a late luncheon.

Cyrus's group had had no more luck than we. Jumana was unusually silent; she was taking her failure too much to heart, which I pointed out to her.

"You cannot find something that isn't there, Jumana. I am beginning to believe that Mr. Lidman managed to cross the river without being observed. It is much easier to hide among hordes of people than in a wilderness."

"At least we now have a photograph," Katherine said, trying to look on the bright side.

"Not a very good one," Nefret murmured. "It shows him in profile, with his hat shading his face. But it was the best we could come up with."

"Surely that is another suspicious thing," Selim said. "That he would avoid having his picture taken."

"You mean he's been planning this ever since he came to work for me?" Cyrus demanded. "Maybe so, Selim, but we were photographing the tomb, not people. So what do we do now?"

I was unable to repress a sigh. Emerson focused on me, for the first time in an hour, and frowned. "Tired, are you, my dear? I am afraid I wore you out this morning."

"Not at all," I said briskly. "But I confess I am at a loss as to how to proceed. Perhaps we should wait to hear from Daoud and Seth—Anthony. Tomorrow may bring fresh inspiration."

I declined Katherine's invitation to return to dine, for to be truthful I was a trifle weary. After promising we would inform them immediately of any new information, we returned to the house and I managed time for a nice long soak in my tin bath before facing tea with the children. The little dears were even more boisterous than usual, sensing, as children do, the distraction of their elders. Even the advent of Sethos, looking as disgruntled as Emerson, did not keep Carla from demanding when Papa and Uncle David would come home.

"No messages as yet," I reported, after sorting through the post basket. "I had rather hoped to hear something from them by now."

"I would settle for hearing anything from anybody," said my brother-in-law. "We seem to have drawn a blank everywhere. I went the rounds of the Luxor hotels again, between trains. Not a sign of him."

"Something is sure to turn up," I replied, repressing a yawn. "You can try again tomorrow, now that we have a photograph."

"What a wonderful thought. I know every knothole and every splinter in that station platform, and every desk clerk in Luxor."

However, troubles never come singly, as the saying goes. Bertie arrived next morning before breakfast, on a horse he had ridden hard. Jumana was gone.

NINE

FROM MANUSCRIPT H

The desk clerk at the Mena House remembered the lady very well. "Magda von Ormond, yes. She is a very—er—forceful lady. We had no rooms available but she—er—prevailed upon me to make an exception."

Ramses wondered how much it had cost Harriet in baksheesh, and how much money she had, and where she had got it. Not from her father, if her description of him had been accurate.

"She and the gentleman have been here for several days," the clerk went on. "Her—er—secretary, she said he was."

He rolled his eyes and smirked.

Either he didn't read the newspapers or he had not connected the murdered Mrs. Petherick with her nom de plume. "Are they in their rooms?" Ramses asked.

"They went out early this morning for a ride around the pyramids. It is a favorite ride, as you know, out into the desert to the point from which one can see all nine of the—"

"Yes, I know. Who went with them?"

The answer was reassuring. Ahmed Ali was one of the most reliable and persistent dragomen at Giza. They wouldn't have been able to elude him even if they had wanted to.

"Shall we hire horses and go after them?" David asked as they turned away from the desk.

Ramses thought for a moment and then shook his head. "Nefret said we must avoid doing anything that might agitate him. If he spots us heading directly for them he may interpret it as a threat. They'll be back for luncheon. We will casually encounter them in the dining salon."

"Oh, we get to eat?" David inquired with a grin. "Things are looking up."

It wasn't difficult to pass the time at Giza, where they had once excavated. They spent the morning wandering round the cemeteries of private tombs and examining the six minor pyramids. The three large pyramids were the chief attraction for tourists, and the interior passageways were usually too crowded for comfort.

"Reisner's crew isn't working," David said, as they approached the site where the Boston Museum–Harvard University crew were excavating.

Ramses consulted his watch. "Stopped for lunch, I expect. We'd best go back to the hotel. Perhaps Father's prestige can get us a table."

Fame had its penalties as well as its privileges. They were intercepted by the desk clerk, who proudly announced that he had told Madame von Ormond and her—er—secretary a member of the distinguished Emerson family was looking for them.

Ramses and David stared at each other in consternation. "I suppose they have gone out again," the former said, trying to keep his voice down.

"But surely they will return soon. They have not lunched, nor even changed their clothing." A well-manicured brown hand lifted. Ramses handed over the expected baksheesh. It wasn't the clerk's fault. He hadn't been told to keep their arrival secret.

"God damn it," said David, who seldom used bad language.

"The fat is well and truly in the fire," Ramses agreed. "Let's find Ahmed Ali. There's no hope of a casual encounter now."

For years the normal methods of travel around the pyramid plateau had been by camel, donkey, or the so-called desert carriage, a diabolical conveyance that jolted the occupants' insides to a jelly. Camels were selected by many tourists—

what would a trip to Egypt be without a photograph of the traveler on that picturesque beast?—but they weren't the carefully bred riding animals owned by aficionados of the breed. There was an old saying: "Everyone should ride a camel . . . once."

Ahmed Ali had only recently introduced horses. He and his brother ran the operation, which had proved to be highly successful. They found him sitting in the shade of the shed he had erected, fahddling with some of the other dragomen and enjoying his lunch of bread, cheese, and onions. After the obligatory exchange of courtesies, which took some time, Ramses asked about his friends.

"Strange people," Ahmed Ali said, shaking his head. As befitted a successful merchant, his turban was very large and very intricately wound. "Very strange. No sooner had they returned than they were back again, demanding fresh horses. They wanted to go alone, but I could not permit that, so I sent Ibrahim Mohammed with them."

"Where did they go?" David asked.

"They said to Abu Roash. Now why would they want to go there, where there is nothing to see except El-Ka'ah, the most ruinous of all the pyramids hereabout? Even if I had not feared for my beautiful horses I could not have let ignorant foreigners go so far without a guide."

They bargained for horses, which Ahmed Ali let go at a "price that will ruin me, but only because I trust you to be careful with them." He didn't insult them by offering a guide.

"He should have asked the Pethericks for payment in advance," Ramses said, as they turned their horses' heads north.

"You don't think they've bolted, do you?" David demanded. "Where the devil would they go, on horseback and without luggage?"

Far out into the desert, where a fatal accident could be arranged. Or to the ruined pyramid of Abu Roash, whose superstructure had almost entirely disappeared, but which provided a handy pit and a dangerously steep slope down into the subterranean burial chamber. Few tourists went there; as Ahmed Ali had said, it wasn't much of a pyramid compared with the giants of Giza, and there wasn't even a rest house. Ibrahim Mohammed would have to be disposed of first; a substantial bribe might accomplish that. If it failed, there were other ways.

Ramses didn't reply to David. He would have been the first to admit his fears were based on slight evidence, but there was a possible motive. If Adrian had murdered his stepmother, his sister must know he was guilty. She was the only person who could testify against him. Ramses didn't believe she would, but a killer prefers not to take chances, and Adrian had already shown resentment of her care.

Their route took them through the desert, along the edge of the cultivated land, and then eastward, to the village of Kerdaseh, attractively situated in groves of palm trees. Up to that point they couldn't be certain they were on the right track, but Ramses didn't think the Pethericks would stray from the path they had announced while the dragoman was with them. In Kerdaseh they received the first news of the fugitives. Ibrahim Mohammed had tried to persuade them to stop at the local market, but to the annoyance of the merchants, and presumably that of Ibrahim Mohammed, who received a percentage of all sales, they had pressed on after purchasing only a basket of fruit.

"They do seem to be heading for Abu Roash," David said. "And Ibrahim Mohammed is still with them."

"All very innocent," Ramses said. "Except that it's late in the day to start on a trek like this. And why did they rush off after they learned we were here?"

"Pure panic," David said promptly. "By the time we catch them up they'll have had time to think it over."

Half an hour's ride brought them to the village

of Abu Roash and another group of disappointed merchants. Their faked antiquities and colorful local handicrafts had been rejected. The travelers had headed west across the desert.

Ahead of them a rocky hillock rose against the sky. The sun was halfway down the west; the light shone straight into their eyes. Ramses shaded his with his hand.

"There they are," he said. "Near the foot of the hill. They've stopped. I think they've seen us."

"Ibrahim Mohammed won't let them take the horses up that slope," David said.

It was that simple, Ramses thought. The fool tourists could damn well make the ascent on foot and the dragoman would be content to remain with the horses. He urged his horse to a gallop.

The Pethericks were nowhere in sight when they came up to Ibrahim Mohammed, who was squatting on the ground smoking. "They have gone on," he said in answer to Ramses's question. "Up the path to the top. I saw you coming and told them they should wait for you, but they would not. Are they friends of yours?"

"Yes," Ramses said. His heart was hammering.

It was a steep climb to the top of the rise where once the king's pyramid had stood looking out across the fertile valley toward the tombs of his predecessors. Only a few courses of stone remained at the base of a natural mound that had formed the core of the pyramid. The ruins of the mortuary temple and other subsidiary structures littered the ground with obstacles ranging from pebbles to fallen blocks several feet high.

"Slow down," David panted, vaulting one of the blocks and catching Ramses by the arm. "The fellow has a gun. God damn it, Ramses, wait. Nefret warned you not to go charging at him."

"Right." Ramses stood still, trying to catch his breath. In the silence he heard voices. They came from the north side of the pyramid mound, where the entrance was located. Harriet's voice, sharpened from contralto to soprano by strong emotion, rose over that of her brother.

"Give it to me, Adrian. Please."

The sound of scuffling feet and a sharp cry from Harriet propelled Ramses forward. He didn't need David's grasp on his arm to proceed slowly. The wrong move now could precipitate the very thing he feared.

Brother and sister were standing on a cleared space in front of the great pit that dropped at a steep angle toward the burial chamber. It gaped wide behind them, more than sixty feet deep. Harriet leaned against a fallen stone, her hand raised to her cheek. Her magnificent hair had been cut short and was now a dreadful shade of mahogany streaked with orange—henna, hastily and inexpertly applied. It altered her appearance dramatically. Adrian was several feet away, square in front of the shaft. He held a rifle, which was pointed at Ramses.

"Don't come any closer," he said coolly.

"Whatever you say." Ramses stopped. "Why don't you put that down and we'll talk."

"There's nothing to talk about. This is the end."

"It needn't be," Ramses said quietly. He could feel David beside and a little behind him, taut as a coiled spring. "We want to help you, Adrian, that's why we're here. Come with us."

"To what, a madhouse? Or to the gallows? I killed her. I deserve to be punished, but I'll choose my death, thank you. I wanted Harriet to come with me, but she wouldn't, and then I got to thinking . . . Is she in love with you?"

The pathetic, childlike curiosity in his voice raised the hairs on Ramses's neck. Harriet was crying. The tears ran down her face, over the marks of her brother's fingers that reddened her cheek.

"She loves you," Ramses said, praying he had found the right answer. "You can't do this to her, Adrian. Not after all she's done for you."

"She means well," Adrian conceded. "But she

won't leave me alone. That can get on a fellow's nerves, you know."

Adrian swung round toward Harriet, and the rifle swung with him. She held out her hands in appeal. "Forgive me, Adrian. From now on we'll do everything your way. I promise."

"Why are you crying?" Adrian asked curiously. "I wouldn't hurt you, Harriet, you know that."

Ramses never knew what pushed Adrian over the line—his own loud catch of breath, the movement of David's arm hard against him, ready to push him aside, or Harriet's step forward. The gun went off. Harriet dropped to the ground, her arms covering her head. She hadn't been hit; the bullet had gone high. Adrian let the rifle fall to his side, his eyes wild, and Ramses jumped. He was in no mood to take chances. He hit Adrian hard and low, caught him by the collar, and dropped him onto the ground a safe distance from the open shaft. Harriet flung herself down beside the limp body and lifted her brother's head onto her lap.

She raised wet eyes to meet those of Ramses. "He didn't kill her. I did."

"Not another mysterious disappearance!" Emerson raised eyes, fists, and voice to heaven. "Not another visit from the damned black afrit!"

Bertie had obviously dressed in some haste. He wore no hat, his shirt was only half buttoned, and his boots were laced askew.

"No," he gasped, breathless with agitation. "She's gone to the West Valley. She left a letter."

He fished the crumpled paper from his trouser pocket and handed it to me. Jumana's neat formal script set out her reasons for taking action, and I had to admit they made perfect sense. She had concluded that the West Valley was the most likely place for Lidman to have holed up. He knew the area and he had had plenty of opportunity to squirrel away supplies from the overflowing baskets Cyrus's chef always provided. Her reason for going alone—that she would be better able to creep up on him than a crew of clumsy-footed men—also made sense—to someone who was indifferent to her safety.

"Cyrus sent me to bring you," Bertie went on. "He's gone on ahead."

"Alone?" Emerson shouted. "Good Gad, he's as defenseless as Jumana. We must go after them at once."

"Now, now, Emerson, be calm," I implored. "In my opinion—"

"Excuse me, Mrs. E.," Bertie said, "but opinions don't enter into this. Most likely Lidman is not there, but we can't take the chance."

He scarcely ever interrupted me, or anyone else, for that matter. Recognizing this as a sign of extreme perturbation, I nodded and said graciously, "You are correct, Bertie. I did not mean to suggest that we should refrain from taking action, only that—"

Emerson was already out the door, with Bertie treading on his heels.

"I had better go with them," I said to Sethos, who was reading Jumana's note. "And you?"

"Back to the confounded railroad station." Sethos handed me the note. "We can't risk missing him there, but I think the girl has made a convincing argument. She's a clever little creature, isn't she?"

"Too clever. I only hope it will not be the death of her one day."

I paused only long enough to collect my accoutrements, waving aside Fatima's attempts to make me wait while she packed a basket. When I reached the stable Jamad had finished saddling a horse for Emerson and another of our Arabians for Bertie. I had known it would take Jamad a while, he was not a hasty man. It took a while longer to put saddle and bridle onto my horse. I made them wait for me.

"They are at least an hour ahead of us," I pointed out. "Haste will accomplish nothing."

Despite this reasonable remark Emerson and Bertie soon forged ahead of me. I went on as fast as I dared, but I did not catch them up until I got to the West Valley. There, near the tomb of Amenhotep III, I found my husband and Bertie talking with Cyrus.

"Not a sign of her," Cyrus reported. "I've been up and down the Valley, calling her name."

"Not even her horse," I said, for there were only four of the animals, including mine.

"She came on foot." Cyrus tugged agitatedly at his goatee. "By one of the paths over the hills, maybe. She could have fallen and hurt herself badly. Wouldn't she have answered me if she could?"

"She is as nimble as a goat, and knows every foot of the cliffs," I said, trying to reassure myself as well as Cyrus. Accidents can happen even to the most expert. "Let us go about this in logical fashion. We will proceed slowly along the Valley to the tomb of Ay, where you have been working."

The sun had risen, bathing the barren ground in light except for the shadows below the eastern cliffs. No sign of life rewarded our anxious eyes; no voice responded to Emerson's stentorian calls. When we reached the tomb of Ay we dismounted and left the horses; they had all been trained to stand.

"Either she is out of earshot or she has chosen not to answer," said Emerson. He was in command, of himself and of us, as Emerson always is in cases of emergency. His next order admitted another possibility, one none of us wished to face. "Bertie, you and Cyrus go that way, Peabody and I will work along the west face. Stay within hailing distance."

It was a slow, painful search. Painful in every sense of the word, for anxiety increased the discomfort of heat and rough terrain. We looked into every crevice and down into every gully and hole, fearing to find a crumpled body. "She may have given up and returned to the Castle," I said.

Emerson grunted.

There had been four possibilities, not three; and the fourth possibility was, after all, the correct one. A shout from Bertie stopped us in our tracks and sent us hastening back. Though they were not far distant we did not see them until we were almost upon them, owing to the unevenness of the cliff face. They had reached the unfinished tomb we had briefly investigated—number 25. Cyrus had both arms round his stepson, trying to hold him back. In the mouth of the tomb were two forms. Lidman's pale, unshaven face showed the effects of two days of privation, but he had strength enough to hold Jumana tightly against him. Her hands and feet were tied; over the folds of the gag her eyes blazed with frustrated fury. The point of the knife in Lidman's right hand rested against her breast.

"Stop!" he shrieked. "Don't come any closer."

"You heard him, Bertie," said Emerson. "Stand still and be quiet."

That deep, powerful voice never failed in its effect. Bertie stopped struggling and Cyrus relaxed his grip. "I'm sorry," the boy gasped. "I lost my head."

"Perfectly understandable," said Emerson, in the same calm voice. "But not sensible. Let me do the talking. I presume, Mr. Lidman, that you are prepared to negotiate."

Lidman nodded. He was breathing hard and the hand holding the knife trembled.

"Just take your time, Mr. Lidman," I said soothingly. "You don't look at all well."

My sympathetic tone calmed him. "I ran out of food and water," he muttered. "Tired . . . thirsty . . ."

"Oh dear," I said. "Would you care for a drink?" I held up my canteen invitingly. The gurgle of water drew Lidman's eyes. He swallowed, and said hoarsely, "No, Mrs. Emerson, you won't catch me so easily."

"All right so far, Peabody," said Emerson out of the corner of his mouth. "May I get a word in now?"

"By all means, my dear. I only meant to assure Mr. Lidman that we mean him no harm."

Bertie's murderous expression contradicted that statement, but he remained motionless.

"I don't want to hurt anyone either," Lidman faltered.

"Excellent," Emerson said. "We see eye to eye on that. What is it you want?"

Lidman drew a deep breath and burst into speech. "The statue. It is mine by rights. I have hidden it where you will never find it. Let me take it away with me, give me free passage out of Luxor, and I will release the girl unharmed."

"Agreed," said Emerson. "Now let her go."

Lidman's sunken, shadowed eyes hardened. "I am not so far gone as that, Professor. You are a man of your word, but you would lie to save a life. We need to work out the details of our agreement, is it not so? One of you must accompany me to the railroad station and go with me to Cairo."

"Hmmm." Emerson rubbed his chin. "I see several difficulties in that scheme, Lidman. I could get you past the police at the railroad station and onto the train, but you aren't fool enough to suppose you can keep me under control during the entire journey, even with a knife in my ribs. I'd have you flat on your back before we reached Qena."

"Good Lord, Professor," Bertie cried. "Why are you arguing on his side? Look here, I'll go with him."

Emerson shot him a look that silenced him. I knew, of course, what Emerson was doing. Lidman's offer had not been serious. We were in the first stage of negotiations. But they could not go on long, not with two impulsive young persons involved. Jumana's eyes were closed and she leaned against her captor. She was going to do something foolish, I knew it, and if she didn't, Bertie would.

"Mrs. Emerson will accompany me," Lidman said.

"No, she won't," said Emerson. "Not," he added, with a nod at me, "that she isn't perfectly capable of laying you by the heels as effectively as I, but I would never live it down if I allowed my wife to take on such a job. Come, come, Lidman, you can do better than that."

"All right," Lidman said. "All right. The statue. It is mine by rights, but I will give it up in exchange for freedom. When Mrs. Emerson has escorted me to Cairo I will tell her the hiding place. You will never find it otherwise. Even if you captured me and tortured me I would not speak. Wild horses could not tear the truth from my lips!"

"We haven't any horses of that sort," Emerson said absently.

Like the sensible man he was, Cyrus had not spoken, though he had tugged at his goatee so persistently that it hung limp and twisted. Now he said, "See here, Lidman, what about if I go with you? I'm a harmless old fellow, not nearly so dangerous as Mrs. Emerson. What's more, I'll pay you for the statue. We'll go straight to my bank in Cairo and I'll hand over fifty thousand pounds. I'll trust you to keep your part of the bargain."

"I must think," Lidman muttered. "You have me confused."

"Go ahead," Cyrus said.

I wondered what trick Lidman had up his sleeve. He must know his proposed plan and all its variants were doomed to failure. There were too many of us; he couldn't herd the lot of us onto the train or control the activities of those left behind. Unless he had a confederate? I looked up at the cliffs towering toward the sky and saw only a pair of vultures swinging on the blue air. And what had he meant by that claim, repeated a second time— that the statuette was his by rights? As I pursued these thoughts I also kept a close eye on the less predictable members of the group—Lidman, Bertie, and Jumana. Bertie was poised on the balls of his feet, his hands clenched into fists, his face distorted. Jumana was quiet—too quiet.

Even as the thought entered my mind, the reckless girl acted. Stiffening, she pulled away from Lidman's grasp and threw herself sideward against his right arm. At the same instant, almost as if they had been in mental communication, Bertie made such a leap as I have never seen, even from Emerson. He caught Lidman's knife hand and dragged it away from Jumana. As the two struggled for possession of the knife, Jumana fell and rolled, a helpless bundle, down the stairs into the tomb. Cyrus rushed after her; Emerson pulled Bertie away from his adversary and clamped a hard hand over the boy's wrist, which was spurting blood like a fountain; Lidman looked wildly around and began to climb up the cliff.

Emerson reached in his pocket, and, to my astonishment, produced a handkerchief. He hardly ever has one. Knotting it tightly around Bertie's arm, he shoved the boy at me. "Here," he said, and began to climb after Lidman.

The makeshift tourniquet had stopped the worst of the bleeding. Single-minded and staggering, Bertie made for the opening of the tomb. I considered my choices, selected the most imperative, and took my little pistol from my pocket. Lidman was a good twenty feet above, slipping and stumbling, and dislodging stones that bounced off Emerson's bare head.

"Get back, Emerson," I shouted. "I am about to shoot."

Emerson looked down. "Peabody, don't do that," he exclaimed loudly. "Oh, good Gad . . ."

He ducked, trying to force his body into a crack less than a foot wide. I pulled the trigger.

I had aimed at Lidman's leg. Somewhat to my surprise, for the angle was difficult, my aim was true. Lidman screamed and lost his balance. He fell quite heavily, hitting the cliff face at least twice and missing Emerson by a narrow margin before his body came to rest at my feet.

"So much for the statuette," said Emerson, lowering himself to the ground. "Peabody, I told you—"

"He isn't dead," I said. "But he might have got away, Emerson, if I hadn't fired. I hit him, you see!"

"Very nice, my dear," said Emerson. He turned the crumpled body over with his foot. Lidman's face was smeared with blood and his shirt was torn to bloody rags, but he was still breathing. "Your bullet didn't do as much damage as the fall. He's had a rough few days, hasn't he?"

Leaving Emerson to guard Lidman until we

could send a litter, we got the other wounded back to the house. Nefret put several stitches into Bertie's arm while her assistant Nasrin and I tended to Jumana.

"This family is certainly hard on clothing," I remarked. "I fear your shirt and trousers are beyond repair, Jumana."

I tossed them into a corner and, since she was now attired only in her undergarments, pulled the curtain that separated that part of the examining room from the outer half, where Nefret was working on Bertie. Perched on the edge of the table, with her feet dangling, Jumana pressed her lips tightly together while I applied antiseptic, and Nasrin smeared Khadija's green ointment lavishly over face and limbs and body. Jumana had a number of nasty bruises, not only from her tumble down the stairs of the tomb but from her initial encounter with Lidman. Not until we had finished did she speak.

"I did wrong. If you will not punish me for my stupidity, at least scold me!"

"I think you have been punished enough," I replied. "You will be stiff and sore for days. Thank God it was no worse."

Her wide eyes were fixed on the curtain. There hadn't been a sound from Bertie.

"It might have been worse, much worse. I only

meant to find him, if I could. There were foot-prints, not yours or Bertie's or the Professor's, at the entrance to Tomb 25. I was going to go back to tell Mr. Vandergelt when he jumped out at me and knocked me down, and—and he was strong, stronger than I thought. I didn't think he would do that."

He had seen the advantage of taking a hostage and he had handled the poor girl ruthlessly. She was wiry and strong, but so small, and Lidman's strength had been that of a desperate man.

Bertie had overheard. "You behaved like a bloody little fool," he shouted. "If you suspected Lidman was there, why didn't you tell me and Cyrus? Oh, no, you had to prove your superiority. It would serve you right if you had broken every bone in your body."

Jumana stiffened. "You didn't think of it, did you? We caught him, didn't we?"

"No thanks to you. The only thing that saved you was the fact that Lidman hadn't the least idea how to use a knife. If he'd had it at your throat—"

"Well, he didn't," Jumana yelled.

The curtain was yanked aside. Bertie's shirt had been another casualty; Nefret had strapped his arm to his chest and every muscle was rigid with rage. Jumana gasped. "Are you . . ."

"All right? No! I might have bled to death.

Damn it, Jumana, if you ever pull another stunt like this . . ." His eyes moved from her swollen, green-streaked face, over bare brown shoulders and arms, down to her little bare feet. "Good God. Are you . . ."

"She'll be fine and so will you," I interrupted, before his naturally kindly nature could destroy the effect of that admirable shouting match. "Now go and rest. We need to clear the examining room for Mr. Lidman."

Lidman was still unconscious when they carried him in. After a quick examination Nefret's face lengthened. "It doesn't look good, Aunt Amelia. There are internal injuries. I daren't operate under these conditions. His blood pressure is dangerously low."

"Will he recover consciousness?"

"One never knows. But it isn't likely."

Emerson had refused our medical assistance. He had no more bumps and cuts than was usual after a day at work, and for a wonder his shirt was relatively intact. I expected he would declare his intention of returning to work—somewhere—but instead he hung around getting in Nefret's way and asking after Lidman every few minutes.

"Leave the man alone, Emerson," I scolded. "We'll find the statue, he can't have taken it far."

"It isn't only that." Emerson fingered the cleft

in his chin. "He's guilty of something, no question about it, but of what? If he is a murderer as well as a thief, who shoved him in the river?"

I countered with another question. "Are you ready to commit yourself as to the identity of the killer?"

"Hmph," said Emerson, and took his departure.

I had sent one of our fellows across to Luxor to tell Sethos and Inspector Ayyid that they could abandon their stakeout, as I believe it is called, at the railroad station. Both of them arrived shortly thereafter, and I brought them up-to-date.

"He cannot be questioned," I informed Ayyid, who had expressed his intention of doing so. "Nefret and I are of the opinion that he will probably pass on without ever regaining consciousness."

"Can she do nothing to rouse him?" Ayyid demanded.

I wondered what he had in mind—smelling salts or a touch of torture? I said firmly, "You may rest assured that she will do whatever her physician's oath permits. She is with him now, and I will sit by him tonight. You can count on me, I believe, to conduct a proper interrogation should that be possible."

"Believe me," said Sethos, "you can count on her. And," he added, with a secretive little smile, "on Nefret."

Ayyid had to accept that. I promised to inform him at once if there was any change in Lidman's condition.

When I relieved Nefret after dinner, a single glance was enough to assure me that Lidman's condition had worsened. His breathing was shallow and his face bloodless. Nefret looked exhausted, her blue eyes sunken. It was mental distress, not physical weariness that affected her; a doctor hates to lose a patient, even one as despicable and beyond help as Lidman. I sent her off to bed, promising to call her if there was a change.

My vigil was twice disturbed, once by Emerson, who took one look at Lidman, swore, and went away, and again by Sethos. The latter was disposed to linger. He selected the most comfortable of the armchairs in the guest chamber whither Lidman had been moved, and sat down.

"I received several telegrams this afternoon," he said. "Would you like me to tell you about them?"

"That depends on what they contain."

"One was in answer to my inquiries about Heinrich Lidman. He did work for the Germans at Amarna. When war broke out he joined up, like a loyal lad, and was declared missing in action in 1917."

"Then his story was true."

"In the confusion following the cessation of

hostilities many men were lost sight of," Sethos said. "And some records were never corrected."

"It is irrelevant now."

"Is it?" Before I could answer, he went on, "The second telegram was from one of my associates in London. Aslanian purchased the statue two years ago in Cairo, from Zahi Gabra."

"Well done," I said. "Another step along the trail."

"The trail ends there, I am afraid. Gabra is dead. If he kept records, which is unlikely under the circumstances, they have been lost."

"And the third telegram? You said there were several."

"Margaret. She arrived in Cairo this morning and will be coming on to Luxor shortly."

"How nice."

"Yes, isn't it?" He rose lightly to his feet. "I would offer to take your place, but you wouldn't let me, so I will say good night."

The night wore on. Sitting by the bed, notebook and pencil in hand, I beguiled the time by thinking over what Sethos had told me and making one of my little lists. It clarified my thoughts wonderfully and kept me from drowsiness. (So did the chair, a hard wooden object that did not permit slumping.) In the small hours after midnight the change I had hoped for occurred. It is at that time, according to old folk legendry, that the soul of the dying takes wing. Lidman's eyes opened. He knew me.

"Are you in pain?" I asked softly, for the duty of a Christian woman demanded that I ask that question first.

"No." The word was so faint I had to bend close to hear it.

"In that case, perhaps you have something you would like to tell me."

"Am I dying?"

"Yes. By the mercy of Providence you have been given an opportunity to cleanse your conscience before you face His judgment."

"I never meant you harm," Lidman whispered. "I never meant harm to anyone. I only wanted what was mine."

"Tell me," I urged. "If you make a clean breast of it you will have my forgiveness to carry with you into—er—whatever hereafter awaits you. Where have you hidden the statue?"

If he heard me he did not answer. Slowly and with difficulty, his broken speech interrupted by long pauses, he began to speak, not so much to me as to himself, and I knew he was reliving parts of the past.

At daybreak the last breath rattled out of Lidman's laboring lungs. I said a little prayer, folded his hands over his breast, and closed his staring eyes.

• • •

You missed Mr. Lidman's funeral," I announced. "But the case is solved. I have his confession."

"That makes three confessions," David said.

He and Ramses had arrived shortly after midnight, unannounced and unexpected. Jamad's shout of welcome roused the household; we all tumbled out of bed and, attired in a variety of hastily assumed garments, rushed to the veranda. I had ordered them to sit down and Fatima hurried off to make tea. Ramses's eyes were shadowed with dark stains of exhaustion. I knew what had caused them; neither he nor David had suffered physical injury, but mental distress affects my son almost as painfully. Nefret sat next to him on the settee, holding his hand in hers.

"Both the Pethericks confessed?" I exclaimed. "Nonsense. Tell me what happened."

After one glance at Ramses, Emerson had gone back into the house. He came out with a glass in his hand.

"Here," he said gruffly. "This may prove more therapeutic than tea."

Ramses took the whiskey but did not speak.

"It is quickly told," David said, watching his friend. "We had some difficulty finding them, since they registered under Mrs. Petherick's nom de plume. Unluckily the desk clerk at the Mena House informed them we were there, and they set off into the desert before we could speak to them. We followed; they rode to Abu Roash, and when we came up with them Adrian was holding a rifle. He was in a state of considerable agitation, and actually fired the rifle before Ramses tackled him. No one was hurt."

It was a bald and boring narrative, but I did not insist on elaboration at that time. "What did you do with him?" I asked.

"We escorted them back to Cairo, and late last night managed to get Adrian admitted to the Presbyterian Hospital. He had relapsed into a state of stupor and did not resist. Harriet stayed with him, of course."

"Of course," I murmured. "And you say he confessed to murdering Mrs. Petherick?"

Nefret had managed to get Ramses to drink some of the whiskey. He looked up and spoke for the first time. "His confession doesn't count. Neither does hers; she was trying to take the blame for him, as she has always done."

"It must have been distressing," I said, for my sympathetic imagination had filled in some of the gaps in the narrative. "Thank you, Fatima, but I don't believe either of them is hungry, or in a proper state of mind for prolonged discussion.

Sleep is what they need. We will have a little council of war tomorrow, after we have all rested. Cyrus will wish to be present, I am sure. Now off to bed with you, boys."

In fact I was not sorry to postpone my account. It may come as a surprise to my Readers to learn that I myself have, on occasion, a weakness for the theatrical. I had deliberately held back from Emerson some of the information I had learned from Lidman, and certain of the conclusions I had drawn from it, and I was looking forward to addressing a larger and more appreciative audience.

After a late breakfast Fatima assisted me in arranging chairs and tables in the sitting room. As our friends arrived, I directed them to their seats.

"Is this to be a lecture?" Emerson inquired, taking in the rows of chairs and the desk behind which I had seated myself.

"A discussion, my dear," I corrected. "Will you take this chair at my right? Thank you. Katherine, you there—and Jumana—Daoud and Selim—"

It took a while to get everyone settled, since Ramses exclaimed over Jumana's spectacular bruises and David asked about Bertie's arm. I was forced to exert my authority and make everyone sit down and be quiet. I took my place behind the desk and arranged my papers. First I invited David and Ramses to give their account, since some of the others had not heard it. Ramses, who was looking better, gave a more detailed version of their adventures. It inspired quite a variety of reactions.

"He is mad," Daoud said. "A madman is not responsible for what he does."

"You're right there, Daoud," said Bertie.

"Ha," said Selim, scowling. He had not his cousin's kind heart and was as skeptical about psychology as Emerson.

"Did he describe how he killed her and why?" I asked.

Ramses shook his head. "He said very little after he recovered consciousness. There's no real motive, Mother. You can talk about ambivalence all you like, but postulated emotions aren't evidence."

"He didn't do it," Emerson said, fidgeting. "We know who did. Peabody, why don't you get to Lidman's confession?"

"First," I began.

"Second, you mean. Or third?"

"If I am boring you, Emerson, you may be excused. Go play with the children."

Emerson grinned. "I beg your pardon, Peabody. Proceed."

"First," said Ramses, "if you will allow me, Mother, I would like to know how you caught Lidman. It seems to have been a rather physical encounter."

"That is precisely what I intended to do, dear boy. It all began when we learned that Lidman had broken into the drawer in Emerson's desk and taken the statuette."

By raising my voice at intervals I was able to keep comments and questions to a minimum. "And now," I said, "we come to the heart of the matter. The identity of Mrs. Petherick's murderer. First"—I quelled Emerson with a stern look—"first I want to read you the biographical notice her publishers put out."

Having done so, I went on without pausing. "And now, my friends, I will read you the true story of her life.

"Magda Ormond—no 'von'—was born in Leipzig to a respectable merchant family. From an early age she displayed considerable intelligence and her father, having no son, hired tutors for her. One of them was a young teacher of English, Morritz X. Daffinger. He too recognized the girl's abilities. She had a taste for tales of the supernatural and made up stories which she told her indulgent tutor.

"He had fallen in love with her. She was at that

time approximately sixteen years of age, and quite striking in appearance. She returned his love, and when her parents got wind of the situation they dismissed young Mr. Daffinger and arranged a marriage for her with the son of a prosperous butcher. The lovers eloped to Berlin, where they were married. To augment his paltry salary as a teacher, Daffinger got the idea of writing novels. At first it was a collaboration; she wrote the books, basing the plots on the tales of werewolves and vampires in which she reveled, and he rewrote them in proper English. The books were an immediate success. Realizing that they might appeal more strongly to a female audience if they were written by a woman, the lovers invented a romantic background for Magda. The publishers never questioned it because they too realized it would sell more books. To do them justice, they had no reason to question her biography, but I fear the mercantile instinct is strong in the industry.

"Then war broke out. Daffinger shouldered arms and went off to battle. Magda never heard from him again. I am forced to believe that she didn't try very hard to find out what had become of him; she had begun to yearn for a more exciting life and here was her chance to achieve it. In the last months, when the German lines were crumbling and the populace was suffering from despair and privation, she made her way to England. Success, popularity, and a good marriage followed."

I turned over a page. "Daffinger had suffered greatly during the War. He had served on the Russian front and been taken prisoner. Ill and impoverished, he made his way back to Berlin and searched for his loving wife. The search took months. No one knew what had become of her. He was forced to dubious expedients, including theft and assault, to stay alive. Not until two years ago did he come across a story in an English newspaper about her most recent book—and her forthcoming marriage to Pringle Petherick."

I could tell by the looks of dawning comprehension on the faces of my listeners that they had anticipated my denouement, so I hastened on.

"You can imagine her consternation when her husband—her legal husband—came back from the grave and confronted her. I am sorry to say that his was not a forgiving nature, and he certainly had grounds for bitterness. She was now rich and successful, in part because of his help; he was poor and unknown. To make a long story short, he demanded payment in return for his silence. She sold many of her jewels to satisfy him; when her resources began to run out, Petherick conveniently passed away."

Emerson had maintained his silence; now he

could control himself no longer. "She killed Petherick?"

"We will never know for certain," I replied. "What we do know is that Daffinger increased his demands. One of the men who had served in his unit during the War was a young archaeologist named Lidman. They became friends and talked about their various interests. In the final bloody weeks, Lidman was killed—blown to bits, as Daffinger put it.

"Daffinger had learned a great deal from Lidman, including the value of antiquities. He wanted half of Petherick's estate. Magda fled, taking with her the most valuable object in the collection. Furious at what he considered her betrayal, he pursued her."

I turned over another page. "By the time he tracked her down, Mrs. Petherick had got her nerve back. She pointed out that if he spoke she stood to lose her inheritance, but he stood to lose everything, and might have to face a charge of blackmail. They entered into negotiations; fearing he might attempt to steal the statuette from her room, she presented it to us. She had already concocted her story about the curse and taken another room in the name of Mrs. Johnson, in order to set up her scheme."

Emerson had heard most of this before, and was

waxing restless. "She took us in completely," he growled. He does not like to be taken in. "With all that talk of curses and black afrits."

"I didn't believe it, and neither did you," I retorted. "But I admit we might have been more skeptical about her motives. At any rate, Daffinger was furious when he found out what she had done. He made several attempts to break into the house; being unsuccessful, he tried another trick, representing himself as his deceased friend in order to be hired by Cyrus, which would, he hoped, gain him entry to this house. He was an intelligent man with an excellent memory, and he had spent hours listening to Lidman expound on Amarna. I suppose there wasn't much else to talk about in the trenches."

"It was he who killed her, then?" David asked. "Why? It's usually the blackmailer who is murdered, not the victim."

"She tried to kill him," I said. "That night when they went walking along the river. She had offered to meet him to discuss his demands. She was a large, strong woman, and he wasn't expecting danger. It was pure bad luck for her that he survived. Naturally that angered him even more, and when they met next, in the Winter Palace garden, he was in no mood for trifling. Seeing her sumptuously attired, bewigged and bejeweled, with no sign of remorse, was bad enough; then she made the fatal mistake of offering him a trumpery pair of diamond earrings and told him this was her last payment. She had learned that he had a criminal record in Germany; now he was the one who stood to lose most. In a fit of rage he attacked her, and in the process of stifling her cries for help, caused her heart to stop. He claimed he didn't intend to kill her. Perhaps he didn't; but once the deed was done he had no choice, as he explained, but to conceal the body. He took the earrings, though, and stripped her of her jewels, in order to give the impression that robbery had been the motive. The strangest thing of all was what he did after he had placed her under the coral vine. Daoud's informant was right; there were white petals strewn over the body. Ayyid, who is not interested in horticulture, did not observe them; but white roses were her favorites."

Nefret shivered. "Why do I find that horrifying?"

"Ambivalence," I said. "Love and hate intertwined and inseparable. To those of us who never feel such conflict it **is** horrifying."

"What about the wig?" Nefret asked. Her mouth was tight with distaste. "Did he keep that as a—a memento?"

"Nothing so bizarre," I said. "It fell off during their struggle, and he couldn't get it back on. One can imagine how difficult that would have been, with his hands shaking and her head—"

"Quite," said Ramses, glancing at his wife. "So he took it away with him?"

"And discarded it. He didn't say precisely how."

"Well done, Mother," said Ramses. "You got all that from Lidman's—Daffinger's—confession, did you?"

"Most of it." I stacked my papers neatly. "That concludes my lec—— the discussion. And the case."

"Not quite," Ramses said. His eyebrows were tilted and his eyes were intent on me. "We still haven't found the statue."

FROM MANUSCRIPT H

Not that they hadn't tried. No one except his mother and Nefret had bothered to attend Lidman-Daffinger's hastily arranged funeral; the others had spent the day searching the areas in and around the West Valley tomb where he had been hiding.

"It isn't in the tomb," Emerson said flatly. "I'd stake my reputation on that. We couldn't do a complete excavation, not in such a short time, but we shifted everything that could be shifted—"

"And put it back in the original place, of course," Ramses suggested.

"Of course. Took a cursed long time."

They were on their way back to the West Valley. It was early afternoon and the sun was merciless, but Ramses shared his father's desire to get on with the job. There could be no question now about the legal ownership of the statuette; since Magda Ormond's marriage to Petherick had been illegal, Petherick's children would inherit. They could use the money—and they would get it, one way or another. Emerson would see to that. It was not only the prospect of losing a great sum of money that bothered him, though. His reputation was at stake, and he would spend the next ten years looking if he had to.

Emerson spoke forcibly to his horse and forged ahead to join Sethos, who had taken his place at the head of the procession. The whole family had come, including Selim and Daoud and a full crew of workmen. Those magnificent, soaring cliffs were full of hundreds of crevices large enough to conceal something the size of the small golden statue.

Ramses waited for his mother and Nefret and fell in beside them. He hadn't had a chance to talk to his mother in private since her performance that morning.

"All right, are you, Mother?" he asked.

"Certainly." She wiped her wet face with a neat white handkerchief.

"Cyrus has had the men bring plenty of water," Ramses said. "Enough for the horses too."

"I appreciate your concern, my dear, but it is unnecessary. You have something else on your mind, don't you?"

"That was an impressive summary you gave us this morning," Ramses said. "Are you completely satisfied about the solution to the case?"

A little murmur of amusement escaped her lips. "You noticed a few unexplained items? The others will, eventually, but I threw so much information at them they haven't had time to absorb it."

"Why?" Ramses asked bluntly.

Her smile faded. "For one thing, I hadn't heard your story when I arranged my notes. Obviously it cannot have been Daffinger who was responsible for the attacks on you in Cairo. You don't believe it was Adrian, do you?"

"I don't see how he could have managed them. The man—the person—who shot at us outside Bassam's used a pistol. Adrian had only a rifle. I searched him and his luggage before we went back to Cairo that night."

"He might have disposed of the pistol."

"Possibly. But why would he?"

Emerson, now well ahead, turned and shouted at them to hurry up.

They joined the others, who were gathered in an attentive group around Emerson. "We've been over some of this ground before," said Emerson, his jaw set. "We will do it again, painstakingly and methodically, leaving not a square inch of ground unexplored."

Under his direction they fanned out in three directions, right, left, and up, starting at the mouth of the unfinished Tomb 25, probing into every opening in the rock. It was going to take forever, Ramses thought. He looked at his uncle, who was strolling slowly along, hands clasped behind his back and whistling, in perfect tune and meter, a complicated air Ramses recognized as the opening theme from a Mozart horn concerto. Sethos's ostentatious nonchalance provoked him into speech.

"I didn't know you were fond of the classics," he said.

"There are a number of things you don't know about me," said Sethos blandly. He dusted off a boulder with his handkerchief and sat down. "I am a man of many talents."

"A talent for hard manual labor isn't among them."

"Why should I do that when I can get someone

else to do it for me? For instance," said Sethos, with the slightest sideways movement of his head, "that fellow up there—no, don't turn and stare!—has been watching us for over an hour. Perhaps you would care to wander casually in his direction?"

The direction was straight up, on a ledge that jutted out from the cliff face. There was a path of sorts, winding up from the valley floor. Out of the corner of his eye Ramses caught a flash of light (binoculars?) and what might have been a head looking down.

"Wander and casually don't apply," he said caustically. "He's got a good vantage point. He'll see me start to climb."

"I will provide a distraction," said Sethos. He stood up and dusted off the seat of his trousers. Then he walked back to where Emerson was standing, shouting instructions to the searchers. Ramses didn't hear what Sethos said, but it galvanized Emerson into a furious retort that was clearly audible, not only to his son but to everyone for some distance.

"You dare criticize my relationship with my wife?"

"You don't deserve her." Sethos pointed accusingly at Ramses's mother, who was working her way along the cliff face just above them. She stopped and stared down. "No man worthy of the name would allow her to take such a risk," Sethos shouted.

Ramses didn't see what happened after that; he was too intent on making his way up the cliff with all possible speed. He heard grunts and thumps and several outraged cries from his mother. The outcropping hid him from sight most of the way. When he reached the ledge he hauled himself up and over in a single movement.

The flash of light hadn't been made by binoculars, but by a camera lens. The photographer had his eyes glued to the camera and was snapping photographs of the melee below. He was too absorbed to notice Ramses until the latter caught hold of the camera with one hand and the man's collar with the other.

"Don't drop the camera," he shrieked, squirming.

Ramses got him down by way of the path, which was negotiable for a man in reasonably fit condition. The others were waiting for them at the bottom. Sethos was dabbing delicately at his nose with a bloody handkerchief. There wasn't a mark on Emerson, who was crimson with rage.

"A damned journalist!" he shouted, extending a long arm.

"Don't damage the camera!" the photographer gasped.

Emerson snatched it from him and threw it onto the hard ground. The photographer screamed.

"It's Mr. Anderson, isn't it?" Nefret looked more closely at the man's face. "You fell into the tomb the other day."

"And tried to get information out of my daughter," Ramses said.

"Anderson, my eye," Cyrus exclaimed. "That's the artist I told you about, the one who came asking for a job and never turned up again. Maillet."

TEN

I wondered briefly if Mr. Anderson was a relation of Kevin O'Connell's, a cousin or younger brother. But no, I thought. Kevin's hair was fiery red and this man's was brown; instead of the cerulean blue of Kevin's, his eyes were a muddy green. The resemblance was not physical but one of expression and manner.

"He is a journalist," I said. "Is he also, I wonder, a thief and a murderer?"

The question got Mr. Anderson's mind off the camera, whose broken pieces he was collecting with little moans of anguish. He jumped to his feet.

"Now see here, Mrs. Emerson, don't go round accusing people like that! All I wanted was an exclusive story. Mr. O'Connell is my mentor, my idol; he taught me everything I know and challenged me to equal his success in—um—"

"Worming his way into our confidence," I said grimly. "You represented yourself as an archaeological artist in order to get a position with Mr. Vandergelt. A scheme worthy of Kevin himself."

"Not so clever," Anderson admitted. "I can sketch a bit, and thought I could carry out the deception for a few days, but when Mr. Vandergelt refused to hire me without seeing my portfolio, I knew I'd have to try some other method."

"Ha," Emerson exclaimed. "I was right, you see. I said those bastards would stop at nothing, even blowing up the guardhouse."

Anderson's eyes widened in alarm. "No, sir, I never did that! Look here, let's call it square. You've smashed my camera and ruined some first-rate pictures, so I'll just be on my way."

"How did you get here?" I asked.

Anderson grimaced. "Walked. All the way from the East Valley. Me and a dozen Egyptians. They said you were here yesterday, looking for something, so they figured they would have a look too."

"Damnation," said Emerson. "Did they find anything?"

"I don't think so, but they're sneaky rascals. They ran off when you came along."

"Hell and damnation," said Emerson. "I have a few questions to ask you, Mr. Anderson, and this is not the time or the place for an interrogation. Hassan, escort this person back to our house and keep him there until we return."

Anderson had perked up as the discussion became more civilized. His face fell. "But, sir, I haven't any transport. Not even a confounded donkey."

"You got here on foot, you can return the same way." Emerson bared his large white teeth. "Off you go. And don't try to bribe Hassan, he is incorruptible."

Hassan glanced at his father, Daoud, who stood with arms folded. "He is," said Daoud. "Whatever it means."

We watched them walk off together. Anderson was limping.

Sethos removed the handkerchief from his nose. "Thank you, Nefret. It's stopped bleeding."

"I'm an expert at nosebleeds," said Nefret.

"Er," said Emerson.

"Apology accepted," said Sethos with a grin. "Accept mine as well. I didn't mean what I said."

"It was well done," Ramses conceded. "Anderson was so fascinated he didn't spot me until I was on top of him."

Emerson, who had gone as far as he was capable of going in the way of apology, uttered the familiar litany. "Back to work. We have to find the statuette today or risk one of those energetic rascals stealing a march on us."

"It's over there," said Sethos. "About eight feet to the left of the entrance, buried in the scree."

No one so much as questioned that arrogant

assertion. In an unruly scamper the whole lot us of went pelting back toward the spot he had described. It took a few minutes to retrieve the wrapped bundle, since we had to proceed with care, but the disturbance of the scree was so obvious I could only wonder why none of us had observed it. Because it was too obvious! We had assumed Daffinger would take greater pains to conceal his prize.

Emerson unwrapped enough of the bundle to make certain we had found what we sought. Cradling it as tenderly as if it were an infant, he hurried back to where his brother had seated himself nonchalantly on a rock. "How did you know?"

Sethos ruefully examined his stained handkerchief. "I asked myself where I would have hidden it. Like Daffinger, I am averse to strenuous exercise."

Cyrus burst out laughing. "Like the old saw about where to look for the lost horse, eh?"

"As Amelia would say, there is often profound truth in such aphorisms."

I had been just about to say that.

We passed Mr. Anderson and Hassan on our way back to the East Valley. Anderson raised a face of piteous appeal; he looked so miserable, hobbling and dripping with perspiration, that Nefret pleaded with Emerson to let him ride for a while. Emerson, who could have walked the whole distance without breaking into a glow, shook his head and gave Mr. Anderson an evil smile. He hates journalists even more than he hates tourists.

However, he is not a cruel or vindictive man, and Nefret's good opinion means a great deal to him. When we reached the donkey park he sent one of the men back with a mount.

Again I found myself side by side with Ramses. "Another suspect," he remarked.

"I hardly think so," I replied.

"Daffinger's confession doesn't explain everything, Mother."

I gave him an affectionate smile, thinking with some complacency how well he had turned out. Except for his father, there was not a finer-looking man in Egypt—or anywhere else. He sat his horse with the ease of an athlete, and his features were as finely shaped as those of a Greek statue (except for his nose, which was a trifle large, and in my opinion all the better for it). I did not doubt that Harriet Petherick had been motivated by more than concern for her brother when she made that clumsy attempt to win Ramses over.

"Well?" Ramses demanded. My intent regard had made him self-conscious.

"My, but you are persistent. We will discuss it later."

"Vandergelt has asked us to stop at the Castle for a spot of luncheon." Emerson turned to address me. "I presume that is agreeable to you, Peabody."

"Yes, Katherine will be anxious to know that we have found the statue."

Emerson's smile was particularly smug.

"You agreed to the delay because you want to keep Mr. Anderson sweating awhile longer," I said accusingly.

"How can you think that of me, Peabody? We need to discuss our future plans. Our work has come to a complete standstill these past days."

"Murder takes precedence over excavation," I said. "You needn't pretend, Emerson, I know you too well. Your strong sense of duty demanded that you avenge Mrs. Petherick and now you have done so."

"Hmph," said Emerson, and urged his horse ahead.

When we unwrapped the statuette we found that a few more bits of the inlaid collar had fallen out. Thanks to our care, they had been preserved and could be replaced.

"It's a pity about the uraeus serpent," Cyrus said.

Daoud rumbled in agreement. "We should try to find it," he declared.

"I'm afraid that's a lost cause, Daoud," Ramses said. "We can't sift every tomb in Egypt."

With the statuette as a centerpiece, we sat down to a sumptuous meal, served by Cyrus's aging but devoted majordomo, Albert. At Cyrus's direction he opened several bottles of champagne, and we toasted our success and, as Cyrus put it, the triumphant conclusion of another investigation.

"I don't know how you do it, Amelia," he declared.

"She had Daffinger's confession," said Emerson.

"It sounds to me," said Ramses, toying with his glass, "as if he confessed to everything except sinking the **Titanic.** Mother, are you sure you didn't—I don't quite know how to say this—"

"Put words in the mouth of a dying man?" I finished the sentence with perfect good humor.

"Unconsciously, of course," Ramses said quickly.

Emerson twitched. He had become somewhat sensitive to any mention of the unconscious.

"He was not as coherent as my account suggested," I admitted. "Especially toward the end. However, I already had reason to suspect him."

I took a folded paper from my pocket. Emerson groaned, Cyrus chuckled, Sethos grinned broadly, and Daoud put his fork down, prepared to give me his full attention.

"Another of your little lists?" Sethos inquired.

"Clues," I said. "There are three of them. The Clue of the White Petals, the Clue of Generosity, and the Clue of Excessive Erudition."

"I get the first one," Cyrus said eagerly. "The flower petals meant that she was killed by someone who knew her well—who cared for her, even."

I nodded approvingly.

"Generosity," Ramses said thoughtfully. "I presume that refers to Mrs. Petherick's handing the statue over to us."

"Precisely," I said. "We assumed her motive was to involve us in the publicity she was courting, but she could accomplish that without actually giving it into our hands. I asked myself whether her real motive was fear. A potential thief would transfer his attentions to us and leave her alone."

"I say," Bertie exclaimed. "This is as good as a Sherlock Holmes story. But so far all you've proved is that she was afraid of someone. What about the third clue?"

"That one pointed directly to Lidman-Daffinger," I said. "Aside from the coincidence of his turning up when he did, his familiarity with Egyptology was of a highly suspect nature. He knew a great deal about matters that could have been learned from others—in person or from books—but he always found an excuse to avoid actual field excavation."

"Whenever anyone asked him a question he couldn't answer, he started lecturing," Ramses said in some chagrin. "I ought to have spotted that."

"It was far from conclusive," I said. "There were other suspicious circumstances, though. His illness was feigned; Nefret was unable to find anything seriously wrong with him. It accomplished two purposes: getting him out of a job he couldn't do, and admitting him to this house. He was in a perfect position to feed the dog a sleeping potion and make another attempt at searching for the statue."

"It seems so obvious now," Bertie said ingenuously.

It always does, afterward. I caught Ramses's skeptical eye and smiled pleasantly at him. "We had better be getting home. Poor Mr. Anderson must be in quite a state by now."

"Poor Mr. Anderson, bah," said Emerson.

Hassan had taken his instructions seriously. Mr. Anderson was seated on a very hard chair, his eyes fixed on Hassan, who stood over him fingering his knife.

"Please," Anderson gurgled. "Tell this man to back off. He threatened me!"

"Well done, Hassan," said Emerson. "You can go now."

Hassan did so, and Anderson let out a long breath of relief. He took off his hat, not so much as a token of courtesy but in order to push his damp hair back from his face. "That was intimidation," he declared. "I could sue."

"O'Connell would be proud of you," Emerson said, taking a comfortable chair. "You are as resilient as he. But he ought to have mentioned that threats get you nowhere with us. You're damned lucky to get away without a sound thrashing."

"All I wanted—"

"Yes, yes. An exclusive story. Well, you've got it. I'm sure you can make a lurid tale of this morning's events even without photographs."

"Would you care for something to drink, Mr. Anderson?" I asked. "You look very warm."

Anderson's wary eyes moved from Emerson to me and back to Emerson. "What do I have to do?"

"Say 'please,' Mr. Anderson."

Fatima was peeping out the door. At my gesture, she came out with a pitcher of lemonade and we each had a glass. Mr. Anderson had two.

"Now," I said, taking a paper from my pocket, "a few questions before you go."

This time my little list consisted of what I had labeled "Untoward Events." "We have accounted for all but a few," I explained. "I want to know which you are responsible for. The first attempt to break into the house?"

"I did that," Anderson admitted. "But I only wanted—"

"Blowing up the guardhouse?"

"No! No, I never did that."

"Luring Ramses out into the hills and attacking him?"

"What?" His consternation appeared to be genuine. "I never attacked anybody, Mrs. Emerson. That's the God's truth!"

"He's too much of a coward," Emerson declared. "Like his mentor."

I went through the list, item by item, and then I said, "Very well, Mr. Anderson, I am satisfied. For the moment."

"Then I can go?" He put down his empty glass and jumped up.

"One little reminder," said Emerson, grinning broadly. "You have confessed, before witnesses, to breaking and entering." Anderson's lips parted, and Emerson amended his accusation. "Entering, then. I could have you arrested for that, and I will if you cause us any more trouble."

Anderson was so glad to get away he didn't even

ask for the loan of a horse. As he ran down the road toward the landing I called, "Give my regards to Kevin, Mr. Anderson."

"That takes care of that," Emerson declared, rubbing his hands together. "Now we can get back to work."

"I like the way you coolly dismiss murder, theft, and violent assaults," Nefret said, perching on the arm of his chair and patting his hand. "Where do we go first, Father?"

"I have it all worked out," Emerson said. "Deir el Medina tomorrow. I want to see what Selim has been up to."

"Then we finish with KV55?" David asked.

"Er—hmm." Emerson looked shifty. "Not yet. No, not yet. We will put in a few days at Deir el Medina. I think it's time we closed down the dig there, as soon as I've made certain everything is in order for the French. Isn't tea ready? Where are the children?"

I had been going through the post basket. I looked up from the letter I was reading. "Dear me, M. Lacau sounds somewhat put out with you, Ramses. Did you break an appointment with him while you were in Cairo?"

"There was no appointment, only a somewhat brusque summons," Ramses said. "I had more urgent matters on my mind."

"I will just drop him a little note explaining the situation," I offered.

"The devil with Lacau," Emerson said. "Who does he think he is, ordering us about?"

"The director of the Antiquities Service, that is who," I reminded my husband. "There are a few other loose ends to be tied up as well. We have the statue back and we know who the legal owner is, but we must inform the authorities about what we have discovered. I doubt they are aware of Mrs.—of Magda's first marriage. I must also get off a telegram to Harriet, giving her the good news. She will be glad of the money; the small inheritance she received from her mother was expended on her trip to Egypt, and Adrian's care will probably be expensive. And Inspector Ayyid must be told that we know the identity of the murderer."

"I thought you did that this morning," Emerson said.

"I dropped a few little hints, but we must make an official report, and give Ayyid a copy of Daffinger's confession. I promised we would do that today or tomorrow. I had hoped we would be able to report that the statue had been recovered, and as you see, my optimism was justified."

Sethos's silence was as provocative as speech. "Thanks to you," I said, nodding at him.

"We'd have found it sooner or later," Emerson said.

"Don't be a dog in the manger, Emerson. Say thank you."

"Not at all." Sethos waved a languid hand. "I trust that now you are willing to concede that my reformation is sincere, though I wouldn't mind an apology for your suspicions. You did suspect me, didn't you?"

I said, "I fear your past conduct could not help but inspire a certain doubt—not about the murder of Mrs. Petherick but about several of the attempts to steal the statue. Lidman-Daffinger's suspicious behavior on the occasion of the dog that did not bark in the nighttime rested solely on your word and you had as much opportunity as he to drug Amira."

"I wasn't even here when the first attempt at robbery occurred," Sethos protested. "Or the second."

"I don't doubt that we had more than one would-be thief at work," I said. "However, for what it is worth, I apologize."

"I too." Emerson sounded as if the words had been wrenched out of him.

"Good heavens." Sethos clapped a hand to his heart. "I hope the shock won't be too much for me."

Emerson declared we might as well go to Luxor and get the official part of the business over with. Sethos offered to accompany us. I declined the offer.

Our business was expeditiously concluded, as was our interview with Ayyid. I had taken the liberty of adding a few remarks to Daffinger's confession, praising the work of the police and the dedication of the inspector.

Ayyid read the final sentence aloud. " 'Had he not immediately acted to prevent the suspect's escape, the man might have been able to leave Luxor and lose himself, with his ill-gotten gains, in the teeming slums of Cairo.' Very—er—eloquently put, Mrs. Emerson. Thank you."

"You didn't tell him about that bastard Anderson," said Emerson, as we strolled arm in arm toward the riverbank and our waiting boat.

"I am holding it over Anderson's head," I replied. "That method is more effective with journalists."

Emerson helped me into the boat and took his place beside me. "We're in no hurry," he informed Sabir. "Take your time, eh?"

Moonlight made a shimmering path across the dark water. Emerson glanced at Sabir, who had tactfully turned his back, and put an arm round me. "Good to be alone at last," he declared. "That bas—— that—er—Hissinhurst was always on our heels."

"Bissinghurst," I corrected. "You mustn't let him get on your nerves, Emerson, 'he only does it to annoy because he knows it teases.' "

I had expected the romantic ambience would keep Emerson occupied, but he had something on his mind.

"Why were you and Ramses exchanging those meaningful glances?"

"When did we do that?"

"Off and on all day. Don't equivocate, Peabody."

"Never, my dear." I moved a little closer to him. "Ramses isn't satisfied that Daffinger's confession solved all the unexplained incidents."

"You said yourself that there were dozens of people after the statuette."

"A slight exaggeration, my dear. To be honest, I would love to find Sir Malcolm guilty of something, but I fear he is too cautious to break, or even bend, the law. However, the points that bother Ramses are the incidents directed at him, here and in Cairo. Daffinger couldn't have been responsible for the latter, since he never left Luxor."

"It was the Petherick boy," Emerson said flatly.

"So I assume. Ramses doesn't want to believe it."

"He's too damned softhearted," Emerson said in a fond grumble. "I pity young Petherick—he's another casualty of that filthy, unnecessary War—but he can't be held blameless because of his misfortune. I wonder what will become of the girl."

"Harriet? You rather liked her, didn't you?"

"I admire her spunk. And her loyalty."

"I fear she is another casualty of the War. She will spend the rest of her life taking care of Adrian, with no chance for her own happiness. I wonder if I ought not make a quick trip to Cairo—"

"Now there I draw the line, Peabody." Emerson gathered me into a close embrace. "You cannot take all the troubles of the world on your shoulders. I need you here. Tomorrow—"

"We go to Deir el Medina. And Ramses gets back to work on his papyri."

"Oh," said Emerson. "Hmmm. It will help distract him, I suppose."

"I do wish you would take more interest in his work, Emerson. He seems to be quite excited about some of the fragments we found this year."

"I don't mean to denigrate his work," Emerson said guiltily. "It is of first-rate importance. You think I haven't been complimentary enough? Very well, my dear, I will try to make it up to him."

He meant it most sincerely, as he proceeded to demonstrate at dinner. His unexpected interest so astonished Ramses that at first he replied only in monosyllables.

"Tell us more, my boy," Emerson urged, leaning forward with his elbows on the table. "Consciousness of personal sin, you say?"

Ramses hadn't said that; I had, when I explained his theory to Emerson. He couldn't avoid the question, though, and as he went on, enthusiasm overcame his modesty.

"I think the concept appears much earlier than Professor Breasted believed," he explained. "There is one fragment in particular—quite a large one—that from the handwriting would seem to be Eighteenth Dynasty. I haven't had a chance to translate it as yet, but the words 'crime' and 'forgiveness' appear several times."

"Then it's time you did," Emerson declared. "Get your friend Katchevsky back, why don't you?"

"Katchenovsky," Ramses said patiently. "I'm sure he is waiting to hear from me. Thank you, Father."

"Not at all, not at all." Emerson looked at me

for approval. I nodded and Emerson beamed. "Tell me more, my boy."

Our morning's work at Deir el Medina went smoothly. We had borrowed Bertie, who began a final plan, and Emerson's praise made Selim glow with pride. The only one of our crew who appeared somewhat sulky was Daoud.

"We did nothing to help," he said. "All by yourselves you found the evil man and what he had stolen. We did nothing."

"You protected the house and brought us the dog," Ramses offered.

Daoud's large face wrinkled. "The dog did nothing."

"There was no need," I said, realizing that his distress was genuine. "It was the magic of the Father of Curses that prevailed—er—eventually."

"Ah," said Daoud. "Eventually means—"

"That the magic took a little longer than usual to work," Ramses explained.

"Ah." Daoud thought it over. "Yes. The black afrit was very strong."

"The black afrit has gone for good," I said. "It will not return."

"Inshallah," said Daoud.

Fatima was preparing the tea tray when we got

back to the house. "You are early," she said accusingly.

"We are in no hurry," I said. "Where is Ramses?"

"With his friend. They have been working."

"I will tell them tea will be ready soon."

When I approached the workroom I heard their voices. I stood still and listened, my heart pounding.

FROM MANUSCRIPT H

Katchenovsky had been slow to respond to Ramses's message. Ramses had been working on the papyri for some time before he arrived, full of apologies and questions. Ramses answered the latter somewhat abstractedly. The suspicion that had entered his mind seemed absurd. The Russian looked and behaved as he always had, eager and humble. He took the text Ramses handed him and began transcribing it. Ramses watched him for a while. Then he selected another piece of papyrus.

"You translated this, didn't you?"

Katchenovsky looked up. When he saw what Ramses was holding, he got quickly to his feet and backed off a few steps. Ramses's heart sank. He had been almost certain, but he had hoped he was wrong.

"I know you did," Ramses said. "It wasn't in quite the same position where I put it originally."

Katchenovsky raised both hands, as if in protest, and then shoved them into his pockets. "Why deny it? Your memory is faultless. I read it, yes."

"A remarkable document," Ramses said, scanning the crabbed lines. "It would make your reputation if it were published."

"It's worth more than that, and you know it," the Russian said. "One might look at it as a treasure map. There are some people who would give a great deal to have the information it contains."

Ramses straightened and turned to face the other man. Katchenovsky had taken a pistol from his pocket. Ramses recognized it as the one that had belonged to Adrian Petherick. He had hidden it at the back of a shelf in the workroom, high above the reach of small hands. He'd meant to dispose of it eventually and had never got round to doing so. Serves me right, he thought, noting that Katchenovsky held the gun like a man who had had experience with such weapons.

"Why, Mikhail?" he asked.

"I don't want to." Katchenovsky's eyes were haunted. "But I must. If I take it you would know, you remember every wretched scrap. You are the only one who would know it came from here. I can say I bought it from a dealer."

"That's why you tried to kill me in Cairo?"

"And in Luxor, when you replied to my message that night." Katchenovsky's bowed shoulders straightened. His hands were steady. "I had to. If you were dead no one else would know."

That takes care of the unexplained items on Mother's list, Ramses thought. He was faintly surprised at his own coolness, at his relief that he had been right about Adrian Petherick. He simply couldn't take this threat seriously, not from the mild, amiable Russian.

"You can't kill me now," he argued. "The house is full of people. They'll hear the shot. You'll be caught red-handed."

Katchenovsky glanced at the open window. "I'll tell them someone burst in. Two shots—one for you, one minor wound for me. He dropped the gun and fled."

Sethos had been right. When Katchenovsky was standing straight, his head lifted, he was taller than anyone else had noticed, and his thin frame had a wiry strength. His will was as strong. Ramses didn't doubt the man had struggled with his conscience, but now he had made up his mind and there wasn't much chance he could be persuaded to change it. There was a slim chance, though, and he was prepared to go on talking as long as he could.

Then he heard a sound outside the door—a too-familiar sound—and knew the time for talk had passed. Katchenovsky turned toward the door and his finger tightened on the trigger.

She burst into the room and ran straight at the Russian, firing her little pistol. As usual, she missed. Katchenovsky didn't.

Ramses didn't feel the bullet that tore through his sleeve. He didn't hear the cries of alarm and the sound of running feet. He was only conscious of his fists ramming into yielding flesh, and the collapse of the Russian. Falling on his knees beside his mother, he pressed his hands against the bloodstain spreading across her blouse.

Her eyes opened. A smile of triumph curved her white lips.

"I suspected him . . . from the first!" she whispered.

She would consider that a fitting epitaph," Emerson said hoarsely.

Ramses sat with his elbows on his knees and his face hidden in his hands. He couldn't stop shaking.

They were waiting on the bench outside Nefret's clinic, all in a row like worshipers in a church pew—Ramses and his father, David, Sethos, and Selim. There wasn't room on the bench for Daoud; he stood next to them, monolithically calm. Overhead the feathery fronds of a tamarisk rustled lightly. Sunlight filtered through the leaves like a rain of gold.

A hand clasped his shoulder. "She'll be all right," Emerson repeated, for the fourth or fifth time. "Nefret said so."

"I thought she was dying," Ramses said, through his fingers. "There was so much blood."

"Some of it was yours," said his wife, standing in the open door of the clinic. "Come in and let me have a look at you."

"It's nothing." He didn't want to move.

"Go on, my boy." Emerson's hand tightened. "She's all right now. Isn't she, Nefret?"

"Inshallah," Daoud intoned.

"Inshallah," Nefret echoed. She looked like a weary angel, Ramses thought, with sunlight stroking her hair and her blue eyes warm. "She'll be waking soon. I think she will want to see you and Father."

I had never beheld Abdullah in such a rage. He shook his fist at me. "What did I tell you? Why did you not heed me?"

There was no pain here. I took a deep breath of the fresh morning air. "Did I die?" I asked.

"No," Abdullah said grudgingly. "Not this time. You have as many lives as a cat, Sitt, but you have used most of them."

"What was I supposed to do?" I demanded. "Stand by and let him kill my son?"

Abdullah's scowl softened. "You love him best, next to Emerson."

"Love cannot be measured, Abdullah. 'The more I give, the more I have to give.'" I couldn't remember the rest of it, so I paraphrased. "For love is infinite as the sea."

"Poetry?" Abdullah asked suspiciously.

I laughed and threw my arms wide, embracing the day. All in all, I was glad to hear that my life was not over. I had a good many things left to do.

"Stop scolding and tell me you are happy to see me," I coaxed.

"Hmph," said Abdullah. He stroked his black beard and covered his smile with his hand.

"I have remembered the clue you gave me."

"Is it so?"

"Will I still remember it when I wake up?"

"Only the god knows," said Abdullah, no longer hiding his smile.

Waking was not a pleasant process. Hot air smelling of antiseptic replaced the morning breeze and I had a feeling that deep down under the cottony comfort of morphine, something was hurting. There was a lump on my feet, heavy and warm. And there was Emerson's face, hovering over me and his strong hand holding mine. Anxiety had carved deep lines in his face, which was set in a scowl.

"Don't yell at her," said Nefret's voice, distant yet distinct.

"I don't mind if he does," I murmured. "Ramses. Is he—"

"I'm all right, Mother. Thanks to you."

"Excellent. What is that weight on my feet?"

"The cat," Emerson said. "I'll take him—ouch!"

"That's all right, Emerson, leave him," I whispered. "We have a great deal to talk about."

"Not now," Nefret said.

"Tomorrow," I said. "I have remembered."

It was late the following afternoon before I awoke from a refreshing sleep, feeling almost myself again. I was in my own bed and the Great Cat of Re was curled up at my feet. Sunset light gilded the air and there was the scent of flowers. Emerson sat beside me. When I stirred he pounced, his big gentle hands on my shoulders.

"Don't move, Peabody. Fatima, run and tell Nefret she's conscious."

Cautiously I turned my head. On the table

beside the bed was an enormous bunch of flowers, jammed helter-skelter into a vase—roses, zinnias, marigolds, hollyhocks, bougainvillea, sticking out in all directions in a horrible confusion of color. Tears came to my eyes.

"Oh, Emerson! Did you pick them for me?"

The hand that brushed my cheek was covered with scratches.

Everyone has been round to ask about you," Nefret said. "Daoud and Selim, and Mr. Winlock and Mr. Barton, and half the village of Gurneh, including a curious goat, and Marjorie Fisher and Miss Buchanan, and a dozen others. The Vandergelts are here now."

"How nice," I said. "Ask them to come in, will you?"

"Mother, you mustn't overdo. Too many visitors—"

"Will enliven me," I declared. "And I want to see Ramses, and David, of course. And—"

"All right," Nefret said reluctantly. "For a few minutes. Promise me you will remain quiet and not talk."

"I must talk, I have a great deal to say."

Nefret's grave face broke into a smile. "Ten minutes, Mother, and not a minute longer."

They crowded into the room, and the sight of those beloved faces would have lifted anyone's spirits. "All right, are you, my boy?" I asked Ramses.

He nodded speechlessly. "Excellent," I said. "I overheard much of what you said to Katchenovsky. What have you done with him?"

"He's in hospital," Emerson said. "Ramses damaged him rather extensively, but he'll live—to face a charge of attempted murder."

"I am sorry about him," I said. "He is a talented scholar and was, I believe, a good man before temptation got the better of him. His confession clears up the remaining items on my list. Adrian Petherick is guilty of nothing except bullying his sister."

"You mustn't talk too much," Nefret said, feeling my brow.

"Then let Ramses talk. What the devil—what was in that papyrus?"

"I've made a preliminary translation," Ramses said. He took a paper from his pocket. "Parts of it were damaged or missing, so I have filled in the gaps as best I can. It is the confession of the original thief, describing where and how he found the golden statue.

" 'I took the image of this god from his tomb in the Great Place. Bakenamen son of Ptahmose took the other image and Sebekhotep the draftsman took rings of gold and a jeweled collar. The guards of the necropolis came upon us and seized Sebekhotep and Bakenamen, but I ran away without them seeing me. Now a sickness has seized my limbs and the gods are punishing me for my crime, and I cannot put the image of this god back. So I offer it to you, Lady of Turquoise, Lady of Mercy, that I may not profit from my crime and that I will win forgiveness in the Hereafter.' "

"Lady of Turquoise," Nefret said. "The goddess Hathor."

Ramses smiled at his wife. "The Golden One. He buried it near her temple, and that is where it was found, a few years ago, by a modern thief. In the last place one would expect—Deir el Medina, where the thief lived over three thousand years ago."

"Amazing," Bertie exclaimed. "It must be absolutely unique."

"There are other papyri dealing with tomb robberies and the confessions of the thieves," Ramses said. "They are Twentieth Dynasty in date. This is much earlier—Eighteenth Dynasty, if my analysis of the grammar and handwriting is correct. However, this is the only case where we have not only the confession of the thief but the actual object he stole."

"I still don't see why that is so important. Except, of course, from a scholarly point of view," Bertie added, with a glance at Jumana.

"Be quiet, Mother." Ramses placed his fingers lightly on my parted lips.

My voice somewhat muffled by Ramses's fingers, I said, "There are two unknown royal tombs in the Valley of the Kings. Abdullah told me so."

"She's delirious," Katherine said anxiously.

Nefret shook a thermometer under my nose. "She won't be quiet while you are all here. Out, everyone."

FROM MANUSCRIPT H

"How is she this morning?" Ramses asked. He was too familiar with his wife's features to miss the faint signs of worry—the two light lines between her curved brows.

"A little feverish. That's only to be expected. But I think I'd better stay with her today."

Emerson pushed the food around his plate. "Of course. If someone doesn't sit on her she'll be up and doing. I won't go either."

"There's no need for you to stay, Father," Nefret said. "She needs to rest."

Ramses didn't want to go either, but he understood what Nefret had not said: that his mother stood a better chance of resting if everyone was out of the house. He was fully prepared to argue with his uncle if he had to, but Sethos went without demur. He pitched in more energetically than he had ever done, even offering to sift the debris and brushing aside Emerson's doubts that he could do it properly.

"If I can't spot a shaped object among the rubble I've wasted a good many years in the wrong profession."

He was working in order to keep his mind off what might be happening back at the house. So were they all. Movements were slower and clumsier, voices louder. Fear was like a small, distant cloud, no matter how Ramses reassured himself. "Only to be expected," Nefret had said. "A little feverish." And those two faint lines on her forehead . . .

The only one who was unaffected was Daoud. He had absolute confidence in Nefret, and he had prayed for long hours. When they sat down to lunch he talked of nothing but the golden statue and the thief's confession. "To think it was here all the time," he said, waving a chicken leg in the general direction of the temple.

Emerson, enveloped in frowning silence, did not reply. "Not at this temple, Daoud, it is much later than the Eighteenth Dynasty," David said. "There were older temples to Hathor. We worked at one of them last year, d'you remember?"

"Yes," said Daoud, who never forgot any site where he had excavated. "And still we did not find it!"

"We may have missed it by only a few feet," Ramses said. "But it doesn't matter now, Daoud. There's nothing else there. The thief mentioned only the statue."

"Back to work," said Emerson mechanically.

He called a halt much earlier than was his habit. Daoud and Selim went back to the house with them, the former carrying a silver charm in the shape of a hand of Fatima.

The lines on Nefret's forehead were deeper but she welcomed them with a smile. "We'll have tea early," she said with forced cheerfulness. "Oh, Daoud, how thoughtful of you! It's beautiful; I'm sure she'll love it."

"I will give it to her," Daoud said.

"I'd rather you didn't disturb her," Nefret said. "She's slept most of the day."

Sethos sat down. "She's worse," he said heavily.

"No! Her temperature is up, but that doesn't mean—Father, wait."

"I want to see her," Emerson said. "Only see her. Only for a second."

Nefret's face twisted as if she was trying not to cry. "All right," she said gently. "Just for a second. Look in and don't speak."

Daoud rose ponderously to his feet. "I will look too. I will not speak."

He followed Emerson into the house. "Daoud is a restful person, for all his size," Nefret said with that painful smile. "Soft-spoken and slow moving."

Her need of comfort was so transparent that for once Ramses didn't give a damn about his audience, not even his supercilious uncle. He took his wife in his arms and held her close.

"It's just that the responsibility is so enormous," she whispered.

"It's not your fault, you're doing everything you can and more. If I had moved a little quicker—"

"Stop it, both of you," Sethos said roughly. "Nefret, she couldn't have a more competent physician or one who cared more for her. As for you, Ramses—do you suppose she would rather it were you lying there? She knew what she was doing, she always does."

"He's right," David said. "This is no time to give way, Nefret, you said yourself that the wound wasn't mortal."

It might have been his gentle reassurance, or Sethos's blunter variety of comfort, that made

Nefret laugh even as she brushed the tears from her eyes. "Do you know what saved her life? That blessed belt of tools! The bullet was deflected by her canteen and went at an angle through that leather belt, so that it penetrated her side instead of going straight into her intestines."

Emerson and Daoud came back to find Sethos pouring the whiskey. "She's asleep," Emerson reported. "Fatima is with her."

Daoud did not speak at all. After a few minutes of profound cogitation he left.

Carla and David John knew Grandmama was sick and that they must be particularly quiet and well behaved, but thanks to the strenuous effort of the adults they remained unaware of how ill she really was. Sethos was magnificent. He lost again and again at knife, paper, rock, and got the cat's cradle into a hopeless tangle. But it was a relief when the children went off to bed. No one ate much at dinner. Ramses let his father take the place at his wife's bedside, as was his right. The rest of them stood outside her door until Nefret ordered them off to their rooms.

"You'll call me if there's any change?" Ramses couldn't help asking.

"She's tough as a lion," Sethos muttered. "She'll fight it off."

Ramses went back to his house, to be near the

children. He flung himself fully clothed onto the bed, but he didn't sleep. Staring open eyed at the shadowy ceiling, he knew Sethos and David—and Fatima and the other servants—were doing the same. The night seemed to last an entire year. There was no summons from Nefret. When the first pallor of dawn entered the room he got up.

Anxiety and cowardice pulled him in opposite directions. He wanted to hear good news and he was afraid to face a bad report. He walked slowly along the paved pathway, under the trees, while the light strengthened and the night-blooming datura lifted great white trumpets toward the sky. It was going to be a beautiful morning.

The house was silent. From the back he heard the clatter of pots and pans. Fatima was preparing breakfast. His stomach turned over at the thought of food.

As he stood outside the door of the veranda, with his cowardly hand unable to turn the handle, he saw someone coming around the house. That giant form was unmistakable.

"Salaam aleikhum," Daoud said. "I have found it." He held out his hand.

Gleaming against his broad brown palm was a small object, less than an inch long. The cobra raised its hooded head, defying enemies. Its eyes glittered an impossible green.

As Ramses stared, struck dumb, Daoud said, "We will give it to her now. Come."

To my extreme vexation, it was several days before Nefret would allow me to sit up and talk as much as I wanted. On the Friday, Emerson carried me to the veranda and it was like a kind of rebirth to be back in those familiar surroundings, with all those I loved around me. The Great Cat of Re stood by the outer door glowering at Amira; he had abandoned his vigil on my bed as soon as I was out of danger.

"It is the nature of cats," Emerson had said, "to seek out a warm, comfortable nest. So don't wax sentimental about the creature, Peabody."

He had been sneaking treats to the cat ever since.

Foremost on my mind was the uraeus serpent I had found tightly clasped in my hand when I broke free of fever. Insignificant this might seem to others; but to me the image of Daoud's large patient form squatting by the holes he had dug, sifting by lamplight, was a supreme token of friendship.

"Your fever was already going down," Nefret said. "But I wouldn't for the world disabuse him of his belief that the uraeus saved you. He worked so hard!"

"How does he reconcile that heathen image with his religion?" Sethos asked, eyebrows lifted.

"It was an answer to his prayers," Ramses said. "A somewhat indirect answer, granted, but God, whatever his name may be, works in mysterious ways. And you must admit it was something of a miracle that Daoud located that small object."

"Except for the eyes, which had fallen out of their settings," I said, laughing. "Even Daoud couldn't find objects that tiny."

"So he chipped off bits of green glass from one of Khadija's ornaments and rammed them into the empty holes." Nefret shook her head in wonderment. "He said that without eyes the great serpent could not be effective."

"Let's drink to him." Emerson handed round the whiskey. It was the first I had been allowed and after I had lifted my glass I drank, reveling in even that small pleasure. I doubted that spirit were available in the afterlife.

"More important," said Emerson, "Daoud discovery proves beyond the shadow of a doubt had there been a doubt, that the statuette was found at Deir el Medina. You will be glad to hear, Peabody, that we've closed down there. No more sifting rubble for you."

"Even sifting rubble will be a pleasant change from my recent inaction," I declared. "I am ready

THE SERPENT ON THE CROWN 🜁 *533*

to take up the reins again. We must finish with KV55, if only for the sake of thoroughness."

"There's no 'we' about it," Emerson declared. "You won't be dashing round the Valley for a while yet, Peabody. I have been waiting with breathless anticipation for your analysis of the problem that was our first concern, before we became distracted by other events. Where, specifically, did the ancient thief find the statuette?"

"Where in the Valley of the Kings, you mean?" Emerson nodded, smiling, and I said, "You have a theory, do you not?"

"I always have a theory," said Emerson. "You, my dear, have your little lists. Don't tell me you haven't made another."

"Well," I said modestly, "since you ask . . ."

A little ripple of amusement accompanied the removal of the paper from my pocket. I did not mind, since I knew it was prompted by affection. I returned Sethos's smile and unfolded the paper.

"I have set it out in the form of a syllogism," I explained. "The statue is from the Amarna time. The thief took it from a tomb in the Valley of the Kings—the Great Place. There are no tombs of that period known in the Valley. So—"

"There must be another tomb, an unknown tomb," David exclaimed.

"I see one flaw in your syllogism," said Emerson, taking out his pipe. "There is an Amarna period tomb in the Valley—KV55."

"That has always seemed to me an unlikely possibility," I declared. "The tomb was stripped of its valuables by people who ripped off the gold face of the coffin and tried to remove the shrine. They also erased the cartouches of Akhenaton, which indicates that they were not random thieves, but officials of the government that had assumed power after his death and wished to obliterate his heresy. They would have reused or melted down any gold they found."

"Well done, Peabody," said Emerson, his sapphirine eyes shining with the familiar pleasure of debate. "I agree. While we are on the subject of syllogisms and lists, would you care to explain why you suspected Katchenovsky 'from the first,' as you claimed?"

"Did I say that?"

"Yes," Ramses said. He reached for my hand. "But you weren't—you weren't entirely yourself, Mother."

"Oh, yes, I remember now." I gave his hand a little squeeze. "I did suspect him, though perhaps not from the very first. Shall I tell you why?"

"Please," said Emerson, grinning broadly.

"It was after the first attack on Ramses that I began to wonder about Katchenovsky," I explained.

"What, I asked myself, was the one factor that distinguished Ramses from the rest of us? Nothing to do with Mrs. Petherick—er—with Magda. It was his work with the papyri from Deir el Medina, was it not? I concluded that there might be something in those texts that inspired the murderous interest of the only other person here who could translate them. Though I will not claim I anticipated anything as remarkable as a confession," I added modestly.

A round of applause broke out, led by Emerson. "Peabody," he declared, "you really are the most . . ."

"Thank you, my dear."

"You really are, Aunt Amelia," David said. "But to return to KV55—if you believed nothing was to be found there, why did we spend all that time reclearing the confounded tomb?"

"Yes," Nefret said. "Why, Father?"

"For the sake of thoroughness," Emerson replied. "We found nothing. And now we know"—he gave his son a respectful nod—"that the theft of the statuette dates from the Eighteenth Dynasty, some years before the traditionalists began destroying Akhenaton's monuments and memory."

Ramses cleared his throat.

"Now, Emerson," I said sternly, "you see how

important Ramses's little scraps of papyrus, which you scorned—"

"How many times must I apologize, Peabody?"

"Father," Ramses began. "You need not—"

"You are too generous, my boy," Emerson said grandly. "I do apologize. And while I am in a forgiving mood, I would like to apologize formally to my—er—to Sethos, for suspecting him. I will never do so again."

"The more fool you," said Sethos, grinning. "But I appreciate your sentiments, all the same. Perhaps if I repeat them to Margaret she will look more kindly upon me. I'm off to Cairo tomorrow to meet her and, as the saying goes, press my suit."

"You must bring her here for the wedding," I said. "I will make the arrangements."

"Don't let Fatima start on the wedding cake yet," said my brother-in-law amiably. "Margaret may turn me down again."

"You can tell her I have apologized too," Ramses said. "And that if she does accept you she has my heartfelt sympathy."

Sethos burst out laughing. "Spoken like the true son of your father. And the true nephew of your uncle."

Emerson said, with seeming irrelevance, "Carter is in town. He wanted to pay his respects to you, Peabody, but I put him off."

"I would be glad to see Howard. Ask him for tea tomorrow."

"He and I have an appointment tomorrow in the Valley of the Kings. No, Peabody, you cannot come along, so don't badger me."

I put my glass down. "Emerson, you have been playing games with me for weeks. I know why you have been so slow to finish in KV55, and I think I know what you are up to. It is time you confessed."

"Hmph," said Emerson. His eyes moved warily from one face to the next—David's open and candid, Nefret's curious, Sethos's wearing a knowing smile, and Ramses's even more enigmatic than usual.

"You can trust all of us," I said.

"Hmph," said Emerson again. He picked up the statuette, which occupied a place of honor on the tea table, the uraeus restored by Ramses's careful hands. "This is not Akhenaton, and it did not come from any tomb of his. It came from the burial of the only Eighteenth Dynasty pharaoh whose tomb is still missing—namely and to wit—"

"Tutankhamon," said Ramses.

Emerson turned a reproachful look on his son. "I beg your pardon for interrupting you, Father," Ramses went on. "But although Mother's analysis was brilliant, as usual, it does not entirely eliminate the possibility that ordinary thieves entered

KV55 before the official government party did so. I can now prove that was not the case."

"What?" Emerson cried. "How the devil?"

Ramses leaned back and folded his hands. I had the distinct impression that he was enjoying himself. "As I told you, the papyrus was fragmentary and partially indecipherable. I have been working on it for the past few days. The scrap I located yesterday has an additional sentence. It includes one of the names of the king whose tomb was robbed: Nebkheperure."

"Tutankhamon!" I exclaimed.

"Hmph," said Emerson, obviously crestfallen.

Ramses is a kindly soul, and he adores his father. Having enjoyed his moment of triumph, he at once made amends. "But you knew that, Father. When you spoke some time ago about your far-fetched theory, as you put it—"

"Ha, yes," said Emerson, cheering up. "I thought at once of the missing tomb of Tutankhamon, but it seemed impossible that any modern thief could have found the place without anyone knowing of it. In fact, the idea was so preposterous I felt it necessary to examine the other tombs of the period, in case the excavators had overlooked something."

"Well done, Father," said Ramses. "That idea never occurred to me."

"Or to me," I said. "Brilliant, my dear Emerson!"

"Would you care for another whiskey, my dear Peabody?" Emerson asked, smiling broadly.

More cursed tourists than ever this year," said Emerson. He shook his head sadly. "Very difficult working in that part of the Valley."

He had brought Howard back with him for tea, after their visit to the Valley. I had been touched by Howard's concern for me, though the sight of the statuette had distracted him somewhat.

"When will you start work?" I asked. "It is getting to be late in the season."

Howard accepted a second glass of whiskey. "His lordship is due in a few days. I had hoped to find a few good pieces in the Luxor antiquities shops, but no one has come up with anything worthy of Carnarvon's interest."

As if drawn by a magnet, his eyes went back to the statuette.

"Well, well," said Emerson. "One never knows what may happen, does one?"

Emerson does not lie, but this was unquestionably a misleading statement, since Harriet Petherick had accepted Cyrus's offer for the statuette.

"So where are you going to excavate this year?" Emerson inquired politely.

"I was thinking," Howard said, "of finishing up that small section near Ramses the Sixth, under the workmen's huts. We left it, you know, because there were so many visitors that year."

"Same problem this year," Emerson said. "It took us longer than I had expected to finish in KV55 because of the cursed tourists."

Mellowed by Emerson's affability and the whiskey, Howard became confidential. "It doesn't seem fair, does it?" he demanded. "I mean to say, look at Theodore Davis—one royal tomb after another for that old reprobate, and not a confounded thing for his lordship. I mean to say, it almost makes a fellow believe in—in curses, and luck, and that. Why should Davis have that kind of success?" He took another sip.

"Carnarvon deserves better," said Emerson.

Howard shook his head and leaned forward. "He's showing signs of losing interest," he said in a hoarse whisper. "This could be my last season here, Emerson, old chap."

"Then I hope it will be successful," Emerson said. "I have a few ideas."

Carter brushed his hand across his eyes. "You're a fine chap, Emerson, old chap. I knew I could count on you. What would be your advice?"

Emerson leaned toward him. Their foreheads almost touched. "I told you the ibn Simsahs had been digging in that debris near Siptah's tomb. One of them went so far as to fire a pistol at me while I was investigating the area."

"That's right, you did! Significant, isn't it?"

"Quite," said Emerson. "You never finished there, did you?"

"No. No, we didn't. Time ran out . . . So you think we ought to go back to that area?"

"Why not?" Emerson inquired.

Emerson," I said, while we prepared for bed, "that tomb is not where you told Howard to look."

"I didn't tell him to look there," said Emerson virtuously.

"No," I admitted. "But you think it's some-where else, don't you?"

"My dear Peabody, I do not know where Tutankhamon's tomb is located. Anyhow, it's probably been looted, like all the others."

I seated myself at my dressing table and began brushing my hair. "Very well, Emerson, keep your own counsel."

"It's only a guess, Peabody." He came up

behind me and gathered my loosened hair into his hands. "And a distant possibility."

"That Lord Carnarvon will abandon the concession, you mean."

"I left it in the hand of Fate," said Emerson. "You see, I promised—that is—"

I twisted round to face him. "You promised? Who?"

"Er," said Emerson.

"You are pulling my hair, Emerson."

"Oh. Sorry. Turn round again, why don't you?"

"Emerson, did you pray? You?"

Color stained his cheeks, but he met my eyes squarely. "I don't know to whom or what, Peabody. It may have been more along the lines of a threat than a request . . ."

"Knowing you, I expect it did sound like a threat," I agreed. "What did you promise?"

He knelt beside my chair and put his arms round me. Face hidden against my breast, he said in a muffled voice, "That I would give up every bloody damned tomb in Egypt if you were spared to me."

"Oh, my dear," I said softly.

"I couldn't get on without you, you know."

"Yes, I know."

Emerson raised his head. His lashes were a little damp, but he was smiling. "You might return the compliment."

"I couldn't get on without you either, my love."

"That's all right, then." Emerson sat back on his heels. "Er—I meant it. Every word."

"All the same," I said, stroking his tumbled hair, "it is not always necessary to complete the sacrifice. You recall the case of Abraham and Isaac. The willingness is all."

"We will see what Fate has to say about it, Peabody."

"Next season should be interesting," I mused.

"Next season be damned," said Emerson, seizing me in a firm grip.

"Just as you say, my dear."

ALSO AVAILABLE IN LARGE PRINT BY ELIZABETH PETERS

CHILDREN OF THE STORM
ISBN 0-06-053333-1

The theft of valuable antiquities is followed by a series of "accidents." It is up to Amelia to put things right . . . but this time she's facing an adversary of a sort she has never before encountered, and innocent young lives are at stake.

"Filled with romance and fraught with peril."

—*New York Times*

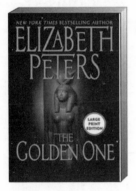

THE GOLDEN ONE
ISBN 0-06-009386-2

Another dead body, only too fresh, is found in a looted tomb, leading the clan on a search for the man who has threatened them with death if they pursue their excavations. And that's just the beginning . . .

"Nail-biting suspense." —*Washington Post*

GUARDIAN OF THE HORIZON
ISBN 0-06-058980-9

Rich with suspense, surprises, unforgettable characters, and the intoxicating atmosphere that has earned its author the coveted title of Grand Master two times over. The remarkable Elizabeth Peters proves once again that, in the world of historical adventure fiction, she is truly without peer.